BLOOD MAGIC

"An intense and suspenseful tale. For anyone who enjoys were-wolves and romance, *Blood Magic* is a must read . . . Eileen Wilks is truly a gifted writer. Her newest novel is truly a work of art as her words paint a picture of a modern-day Romeo and Juliet."
—*Romance Junkies*

"A tantalizing glimpse into the past of one of the series' most enigmatic characters, Lily's shape-shifting grandmother. Wilks's storytelling style is so densely layered with plot complexities and well-defined characters that it quickly immerses readers in this fascinating world. There is no better way to escape reality than with a Wilks adventure!"
—*Romantic Times*

"Another great addition to the Lupi series, Eileen Wilks's *Blood Magic* is an engaging paranormal tale full of action and adventure that should not be missed!"
—*Romance Reviews Today*

"Terrific."
—*Midwest Book Review*

MORTAL SINS

"Filled with drama and action . . . This story is number five in the World of the Lupi series and is just as good as the first."
—*Fresh Fiction*

"Held me enthralled and kept me glued to my seat . . . The characters and world are intriguing, and the solution to the murders is unusual and thought provoking . . . Ms. Wilks has a skill with description and narrative that truly brings a world and its characters alive."
—*Errant Dreams Reviews*

"Fabulous . . . The plot just sucked me in and didn't let me go until the end . . . Another great addition to the World of Lupi series."
—*Literary Escapism*

continued . . .

"Terrific . . . The cat-and-mouse story line is action packed . . . A thrilling tale of combat on mystical realms." —*The Best Reviews*

"Gripping paranormal romance." —*Fresh Fiction*

FURTHER PRAISE FOR EILEEN WILKS AND HER NOVELS

"If you enjoy beautifully written, character-rich paranormals set in a satisfyingly intricate and imaginative world, then add your name to Eileen Wilks's growing fan list." —*BookLoons*

"Exciting, fascinating paranormal suspense that will have you on the edge of your seat. With a mesmerizing tale of an imaginative world and characters that will keep you spellbound as you read each page, Ms. Wilks proves once again what a wonderful writer she is with one great imagination for her characters and the world they live in." —*The Romance Readers Connection*

"Destined to become a big, big name in romance fiction." —*Romantic Times*

"Fantastic . . . Fabulous pairing . . . Ms. Wilks takes a chance and readers are the winners." —*The Best Reviews*

"Fun [and] very entertaining!" —*The Romance Reader*

"Should appeal to fans of Nora Roberts." —*Booklist*

"Fast paced." —*All About Romance*

"Eileen Wilks [has] remarkable skill. With a deft touch she combines romance and danger." —*Midwest Book Review*

Books by Eileen Wilks

TEMPTING DANGER
MORTAL DANGER
BLOOD LINES
NIGHT SEASON
MORTAL SINS
BLOOD MAGIC
BLOOD CHALLENGE

Anthologies

CHARMED
*(with Jayne Ann Krentz writing as Jayne Castle,
Julie Beard, and Lori Foster)*

LOVER BEWARE
(with Christine Feehan, Katherine Sutcliffe, and Fiona Brand)

CRAVINGS
*(with Laurell K. Hamilton, MaryJanice Davidson,
and Rebecca York)*

ON THE PROWL
(with Patricia Briggs, Karen Chance, and Sunny)

INKED
(with Karen Chance, Marjorie M. Liu, and Yasmine Galenorn)

BLOOD CHALLENGE

EILEEN WILKS

BERKLEY SENSATION, NEW YORK

THE BERKLEY PUBLISHING GROUP
Published by the Penguin Group
Penguin Group (USA) Inc.
375 Hudson Street, New York, New York 10014, USA
Penguin Group (Canada), 90 Eglinton Avenue East, Suite 700, Toronto, Ontario M4P 2Y3, Canada
(a division of Pearson Penguin Canada Inc.)
Penguin Books Ltd., 80 Strand, London WC2R 0RL, England
Penguin Group Ireland, 25 St. Stephen's Green, Dublin 2, Ireland (a division of Penguin Books Ltd.)
Penguin Group (Australia), 250 Camberwell Road, Camberwell, Victoria 3124, Australia
(a division of Pearson Australia Group Pty. Ltd.)
Penguin Books India Pvt. Ltd., 11 Community Centre, Panchsheel Park, New Delhi—110 017, India
Penguin Group (NZ), 67 Apollo Drive, Rosedale, North Shore 0632, New Zealand
(a division of Pearson New Zealand Ltd.)
Penguin Books (South Africa) (Pty.) Ltd., 24 Sturdee Avenue, Rosebank, Johannesburg 2196,
South Africa

Penguin Books Ltd., Registered Offices: 80 Strand, London WC2R 0RL, England

This is a work of fiction. Names, characters, places, and incidents either are the product of the author's imagination or are used fictitiously, and any resemblance to actual persons, living or dead, business establishments, events, or locales is entirely coincidental. The publisher does not have any control over and does not assume any responsibility for author or third-party websites or their content.

BLOOD CHALLENGE

A Berkley Sensation Book / published by arrangement with the author

PRINTING HISTORY
Berkley Sensation mass-market edition / January 2011

Copyright © 2011 by Eileen Wilks.
Excerpt from *Death Magic* by Eileen Wilks copyright © by Eileen Wilks.
Cover art by Tony Mauro.
Cover design by George Long.
Interior text design by Kristin del Rosario.

ISBN: 978-0-425-23919-3

BERKLEY® SENSATION
Berkley Sensation Books are published by The Berkley Publishing Group,
a division of Penguin Group (USA) Inc.,
375 Hudson Street, New York, New York 10014.
BERKLEY® SENSATION and the "B" design are trademarks of Penguin Group (USA) Inc.

PRINTED IN THE UNITED STATES OF AMERICA

10 9 8 7 6 5 4 3 2 1

ACKNOWLEDGMENTS

As always, I had help. Thanks to Lisa for putting me in touch with her sister, Shannan Jones Naiser, a crackerjack trauma nurse who answered my gushing fountain of questions. I'd also like to thank Anna Brewer from J-R's Water Well Service for her expertise.

PROLOGUE

Two months ago...

"KNEEL."

The two young men did as they were bid. One was fair and lean, with hair the color of wheat and eyes the sunny blue of the sky that ripens it. The other was ruddy, with dark hair and a mouth that seemed permanently bent up, as if he smiled so often his face was trained to it. Both wore cutoffs, nothing else.

Isen sat in his favorite armchair and studied them. It was an interesting moment. David Auckley and Jeffrey Lane were the first Leidolf to set foot inside his home since it was built.

Unless, of course, he counted his son.

Isen glanced at Rule standing several feet behind the two youngsters. Somehow, at the *gens compleo* that brought these two into their clan—into Leidolf—as full adults, Rule had also brought them into Nokolai. Isen had felt it when it happened. The imprint new clan members made on the clan's mantle was subtle but unmistakable.

This shouldn't have been possible. But then, Isen's second-born son was the first lupus in roughly three thousand years to hold more than one mantle. The impossible was becoming commonplace these days.

The next wrinkle was more implausible than impossible. After accidentally bringing David and Jeff into two clans instead of one, Rule had been unable to remove them from Nokolai. Rule held only the heir's portion of that mantle, but it should have been enough. Neither he nor Isen understood why it hadn't worked.

Today they amended that. Isen held the full Nokolai mantle, and had for a very long time. In a sense he held even the portion carried by his son and heir, for the full mantle was his to command, regardless of where it lay. It would do his will. He no more doubted that than he doubted his ability to direct his foot or his hand.

They would do this without ceremony. No one was calling *seco*, though the procedure was the same as when a lupus was made clanless. But there was no shame to these young men in what must be done. They would no longer be Nokolai, but they wouldn't be left without a clan.

"David," Isen said, keeping his voice low and matter-of-fact. "Jeffrey." He placed a hand on each man's shoulder. The mantle stirred, recognizing them. He held that recognition in his awareness . . . and denied it, with words and with intent, calling back the tiny portions of mantle swimming in each of them. "You are not Nokolai."

Nothing happened. For a very long moment, nothing at all happened.

Isen leaned back in his chair and laughed loud and long.

"Isen," Rule said. Just that, and his tone gave away as little as his words, but Isen knew he was worried. No doubt he meant to hide that from the two pups who were staring at Isen now, the blond one alarmed, the darker one sufficiently astonished to have lost that small, perpetual smile.

That, too, amused Isen. "Ah," he said, wiping his eyes, which had watered from mirth. "The joke's on me, isn't it?"

"I'm not finding the humor," Rule said dryly.

Isen looked at his son with great love and almost as much patience. He had two living sons, and both were a trifle too serious. Still, he understood Rule's anxiety. Thus far, he and Rule had managed to conceal the condition of these young Leidolf–Nokolai hybrids by bringing them here to train as guards for their Rho. Supposedly this was to honor Rule's first *gens compleo* as Leidolf Rho, and to signal the newly friendly ties between Nokolai and Leidolf.

It did those things, but more importantly, it provided an explanation for the way they smelled. They trained with Nokolai, lived with Nokolai. People would assume the whiff of Nokolai scent they carried was acquired, not innate.

Their little sleight-of-smell wouldn't work forever. And then, as the saying went, the shit would hit the fan.

Isen met his son's eyes as one last chuckle escaped. "Ah, well. You and I don't always laugh at the same things. The mantle didn't answer me."

"I noticed that."

"Rule." Fond but slightly exasperated, Isen shook his head. "A Rho commands his clan's mantle entirely . . . with one exception."

Rule's eyes widened. His gaze slid to the men still obediently kneeling. He said nothing, then looked at his father again, a question suspended in his dark eyes.

Isen nodded. *Yes, you understand correctly.*

Ah, hubris. Isen smiled wryly at himself. He'd forgotten that exception, hadn't he? Though there was some justification. The Lady hadn't acted directly on the mantles in over three thousand years. Not since the Great War, in fact. But they, like the lupi she'd created, remained hers to command.

Why did she want these two to remain in two clans? Who knew? Clearly, though, she did. Just as clearly, many in other clans would not believe this.

Interesting times, Isen thought. That was the Chinese curse, wasn't it? *May you live in interesting times.*

ONE

FEAR comes in many flavors. Tonight's dish was sour apples with a soupcon of bile. Arjenie swallowed and swallowed again.

The moon was high and nearly full. A few tatters of high-flying cirrus clouds marred the sky's dome like scuff marks left by skidding giants. Arjenie held herself still so as not to send any crackles or crunches out into the moon-flooded night.

She was glad of the moonlight. There wasn't much ambient light this far from the city, just the landscape lighting around Robert Friar's big, expensive house. That sprouted up everywhere like electronic fungi—path lighting, spots trained on trees and shrubs, the diamond glow of underwater lights in the pool.

Everywhere except at the guesthouse, that is. About fifty feet past the sparkling pool was a log cabin the size of a two-car garage. Here it was dark, especially behind the thorny bush where Arjenie crouched. Neither moonlight nor landscape lighting reached inside the window two feet to her left. The window was open an inch. Behind the glass lay darkness. A whisper floated out to her from that darkness. "You'd better go."

"Yes."

"And yet you aren't moving."

"I hate to leave you here."

"I can't go with you. You know that. Go now. They'll bring the tears soon."

Arjenie said nothing. There was nothing to say. Dya had to have the tears, but Arjenie hated them and everything they stood for.

"*Tch.* I shouldn't have called you. You're not—"

"You're not about to insult me, are you?"

"You're frightened."

"You can hear my knees knocking from in there?"

"Is that what that noise was?" Dya huffed softly. "Don't worry, little fox. I will be well. Not happy, but well. He doesn't dare hurt me too much."

"He doesn't dare kill you," Arjenie corrected. "That's what you said. Because your family would find out—"

"They are your family, too. *Jidar* relations are still family."

Family she'd never met and never would. "My point is, if you miss your scheduled contact, they'll raise a stink and then Friar has to produce you alive and well or they'll have a grievance. That's a big deal where you come from, so he'll be disinclined to kill you."

"I am also very important to his plans. He does not want me dead."

"There can be a world of pain between well and dead."

A single cluck of the tongue. "Then leave before you grow weary and make a mistake and are found with those vials in your pockets. He would punish me severely for them."

"Good idea." Especially since no one would hold Friar accountable if she disappeared. Arjenie had a dreadful suspicion that making her go away permanently would be at the top of Friar's list of options if he caught her here. "You've got the prepaid phone I brought. You remember how to use it? Mobile phones are a little different—"

"I can use it, but I won't. Do not be thinking things are bad if I don't call you. I don't want you in danger."

Big sisters never stop thinking of their little sisters as little, Arjenie supposed. At least Dya had called when she really needed to. "I'll be back. Love you, Dya."

"Not unless I call. Love you, Arjenie-hennie."

The pet name made Arjenie smile. If the smile wobbled, well, she was the only one who knew. She twisted so she could start easing out from behind the bush and . . . "Ow!"

"What is it?"

"Stupid, vicious bush," she muttered. "It stabbed me."

"Is there blood? Arjenie, if there's blood—"

"Can you fix it?" There was certainly blood on her hand, so there was probably some on the bush.

"Pass me the part that wounded you."

Arjenie felt for the branch, being more careful this time. She snapped off the offending portion and froze at the *crack*, instinctively pulling on her Gift—and winced at the stab of pain in her temple. She was too close to the window's glass to push that much power through her Gift.

No one came to investigate, thank the Light, the Lord, and the Lady. Arjenie leaned forward awkwardly so she could push the thorny twig through that open inch of window.

For a long moment she waited, breathing as quietly as she could. Then: "Done," Dya whispered. "No one will track you from it now." The branch slid back outside the window and rustled faintly as it fell to the ground.

"Dya—"

"Go! And don't bleed on anything else."

Arjenie made it out from behind the bush with no further injuries, then paused, still crouching, to suck on the side of her hand so she wouldn't drip blood anywhere. Cursed thorny whatever-it-was. No wonder Friar thought no one could get near his guesthouse. He'd stationed attack plants around it.

Of course, he had the guards, too. And the wards.

The guards wouldn't be a problem, she told herself firmly. She wasn't depleted—not too depleted, anyway. They'd never notice her. As for the wards . . . she'd made it here without tripping any, hadn't she? She just had to make it out again.

Slowly she stood. There was nothing but fifty feet of path and some low-lying plants between her and the pool—and beyond it, the house. She felt horribly exposed. Her heart pounded. Her mouth was dry.

Stupid, she told herself. No one would notice her, so there was no point in being a scared little bunny. But all the glass in the house worried her.

Her heart kept up its double-time beat as she walked slowly down the stone path that led to the back of the little log cabin, so out of place in southern California. But Friar went for the rustic look. The version of it he'd employed on the main house was far more sophisticated—lots of wood, lots of glass, a gabled roof pitched to repel snow that never fell.

Stupid glass. It buzzed at the edge of her awareness, a low-level but irritating static. Glass disagreed with her Gift. It was too far away to be a real problem, though, she assured herself.

However inappropriate for its setting, Friar's house was beautiful. She wished it wasn't. She knew evil didn't go around fingering its mustache and twirling its cape, but it just seemed wrong that someone like Robert Friar could recognize and appreciate beauty.

The house's setting was lovely, too, in a rough and wild way. She'd driven past in the daytime . . . not all the way to the house, which sat well off the highway on a private road. But close enough to appreciate the peculiar beauty of these scrubby mountains . . . or was she still in the foothills? Where did one end and the next begin?

Never mind, she told herself sternly, aware of her tendency to lose herself in the pursuit of interesting facts. Whatever she called it, the land around Friar's home was all ups and downs. Not too steeply pitched, thank goodness, since she'd had to make her way over one of those ups to get here. She might be able to hide herself, but her ability didn't extend to her rental car, which was parked on a dirt road that wasn't on most maps of the area.

Arjenie was good at finding information that wasn't readily available.

The cabin didn't have a backyard. There was a little deck and then trees—pines, mostly, and they were spindly things. She supposed this was what passed for woods on this side of the country, where things were so dry. It wasn't much like the woods she was used to, back in Virginia.

Over the river and through the woods, to grandmother's house we go . . . no river here, and no grandmother, but she did have to go through the trees and over the hill. Or mountain. Whatever.

She'd just left the path for dirt crunchy with pine needles when she heard voices. She froze, her heart doing its frightened rabbit thing. With an effort, she managed not to pull harder on her Gift. The voices were on the far side of the cabin, and she'd been using her Gift continuously for two hours. She wasn't that powerful. She couldn't afford to run out of juice.

The voices were male, the words indistinct . . . something about having a beer later. A moment later she heard the cabin's front door thud closed, and the voices were cut off.

Her breath shuddered out. She wished she'd stop panicking. This was no different from hundreds of other times she'd used her Gift for fun or practice . . . except, of course, for those militia guys. Guys with guns. Multiple guns. Handguns holstered at their hips and rifles slung over their shoulders.

Assault rifles, she thought, and she moved cautiously into the trees. Arjenie had never actually seen an assault rifle, but she'd researched them, and she had an excellent memory. Assault rifles were capable of selective fire, which meant they could be set to fire automatically. The M-16, for example, could fire up to 950 rounds per minute, depending on the model. Of course, those were intermediate-power cartridges, not as powerful as the load in a regular rifle. But 950 rounds per minutes of anything did a fine job of turning a person into bloody hamburger.

How long were those rifles the militia guys carried? She frowned as she began heading upslope, trying to remember. Assault rifles had shorter barrels. But she hadn't been close to the guns—thank goodness—and she'd been scared spitless. And she was used to seeing stuff like that on a screen or on paper, not in person.

Maybe they'd been battle rifles, such as the M-14. Arjenie didn't know as much about them as she did assault rifles, never having researched them specifically, but she knew they were longer in the barrel and fired high-power cartridges.

Military units used them to hit targets at ranges up to 1000 meters—which was roughly 1100 yards—but she didn't think—

A ward—a ward right *there*, and she was about to step on it. She stumbled back, away from the line she *knew* but couldn't see.

Her left foot turned under her. Her arms flailed. She landed on her butt in the dirt with a prickly pain shooting up the side of her ankle.

Her breath came fast. She patted her pockets. Both glass vials seemed intact. She checked the stoppers—still snug—exhaled in relief, and rubbed her ankle, scowling as her eyes teared up.

When would she learn? She couldn't just *walk*. She had to pay attention. She really had to pay attention while clambering around on a big hill or small mountain in the darkness—a hill with wards and men with guns who'd come running if she set off one.

"Fudge," she whispered. Her ankle started to throb in a hot, red way, pulses of pain that kept her eyes wet. "Holy Dalmatian fudge and—and rats."

At least she hadn't tripped the ward. Maybe she wouldn't have set it off even if she had walked over it—her Gift would fool most wards—but this one had a fair amount of juice, and she didn't. She'd used a lot of power staying hidden so long.

The ability to sense wards was a side effect of her Gift. She didn't see them. She didn't feel them. She just knew. She had to be actively using her Gift, but when she was, she could look around and know if any wards were close. It was as if her Gift did the seeing, not her, so the information didn't get processed by her visual cortex. It arrived directly. Usually she got a rough idea of how strong a ward was, how complex, and sometimes, what type.

The one she hadn't quite stepped on was a summoning ward—she knew that much—and a strong one, probably designed to notify Friar if something large and living crossed it. And she'd *known* to watch out for it. She'd found it on the way in, so she'd known where it was. The plan was to follow it to the place where Earth disliked it.

Many practitioners would pooh-pooh the idea that Earth had likes and dislikes, but Arjenie's mother had been an Earth witch, and a strong one, and that's what she'd taught her daughter. Arjenie thought that might be why she could sense Earth a bit herself, even though her own Gift was tied to Air.

Earth was not uniform. It was granite here, sand there, clay somewhere else. Some parts liked to grow plants, some didn't. The part of Earth that didn't like the ward wasn't cooperating with it, so the ward was weak there. Her Gift would let her cross unnoticed.

Now she was genuinely crippled, not just inconvenienced. If only she'd been paying attention, she could have . . . Arjenie made a face at herself. "If only" never got anything done. Better stand up and see how much damage she'd done herself. No, wait. First see if she could spot a branch to use as a walking stick. That ankle was going to need some kind of help.

Her cheeks were wet, so she wiped them. Pain always made her cry. She used to be embarrassed about that—it seemed so childish—but embarrassment was a waste of worry. Tears were one of many things that were standard for the Arjenie model: trips easily, great memory, cries when she hurts.

Arjenie had excellent night vision and the moon was right overhead. It wasn't hard to spot a nice, long stick that looked strong enough to do the job. Or the big, furry beast sitting next to it, watching her.

Her heartbeat took one bounce and shot straight into the stratosphere.

He was big. Much too big. And he could see her. She was sure of it. She hadn't heard him approach, but there he was, huge and dark . . . was his fur black, or did it only seem so in the moonlight? His head was up and alert, ears pricked, not laid back—that was good, wasn't it? No snarling, no show-ing teeth . . . "N-nice doggie," she stammered, knowing even as she said it that this was no dog.

He cocked his head. Their eyes met as if he were about to reply. Met and held.

She fell. Sitting on her butt in the dirt, she still fell—for an instant, for some immeasurable flash of time, the world upended itself around her, or she fell through the world and ended up . . .

He surged to all four feet. Took a step back—a clumsy step, almost staggering. Then another.

"No—not that way. Watch out for—"

Too late. His back foot strayed over the ward. Light erupted up from that spot, bright as a flashlight.

"Oh, no." A *visual* summoning ward. Those were rare. It hadn't occurred to her Friar might have one, but it made sense. The militia guys would see it and come running. "Go." She shooed him with both hands. "Go on, get away."

Instead, he used his mouth to pick up the stick she'd spotted at the same time she saw him. He walked right up to her and set it on the ground beside her.

Oh, he was huge. She swallowed.

But he was not just a wolf. That was good, she told herself firmly. She hadn't ever met a werewolf, but a couple times she'd *almost* met Rule Turner—the one they called the werewolf prince, though that wasn't what he called himself. But then, his people didn't call themselves werewolves, either. They were lupi. Lupi were not ravening, bloodthirsty beasts, and they didn't go around killing people.

At least, not without a really good reason. FBI agents didn't kill people without a really good reason, either, and she worked with them all the time, didn't she? So her heart really shouldn't be pounding this hard.

"Uh—thanks." She took the stick and used it to wobble to her feet. Her eyes filled again. The ankle was definitely not going to let her run, but she could walk. Carefully. Slowly. Maybe she could get away from the glowing ward before the guys with guns arrived. She started hobbling, following the line of the ward toward its weak spot.

The wolf stayed with her, but on the far side of the ward. Could he see or sense it? His head came to her rib cage. The top of her rib cage. "Go on," she whispered. "They won't see me, but they'll sure see you."

He shook his head.

"I don't want to go with you," she explained. "I'm safe enough, but if you're with me—"

He bumped her. Just once, but intentionally, using the side of his body to jostle her. She wobbled, but didn't fall.

What did that mean? Was he . . . oh. He was staring back the way she'd come. Listening, maybe. Lupi had very keen hearing. Maybe he'd wanted her to shut up so he could hear better. The militia guys might be coming. What did he—

Faster than she could blink, he went from statue-still to a full run, grace and speed merging in a blur of motion.

He was beautiful.

Also noisy, crashing through brush as if he couldn't be bothered to go around. He ran straight back toward the house. Where the armed men were. He ran right at them.

Her free hand lifted as if she could summon him back— but he was already out of sight.

The first shot was impossibly loud. The second was just as loud, but the third seemed a little farther away. Arjenie's eyes filled and overflowed as if they could drain the new fear, vast and formless, that swamped her.

She swallowed hard. Her hand still stretched out, still trying to call him back. She let it fall to her side.

Arjenie turned. Blinking at the tears that just kept coming, she began to make her slow, painful way along the hill, following the ward to its weak spot. She'd go back to her car. She was sure now she'd make it. She had to. He'd thrown himself at the guys with guns on purpose, hadn't he? Diverting them from her.

She couldn't help him. Couldn't do a thing except take herself away. She had no weapons, no skill with weapons, no way to stop whatever was happening. But she wished, fiercely and futilely, that she could remember for sure about the guards' rifles, how long the barrels were. So she'd know if they could fire those 950 rounds per minute.

Arjenie had crossed the ward and was near the top of the hill when that question was answered. The burst of gunfire was distant, heavy, and prolonged. Clearly, at least one of them had a rifle with fully automatic fire.

TWO

YEP. All four tires, slashed and flat.

Sweat trickled beneath Lily Yu's athletic bra, ran a clammy finger down her spine, and threatened to sting her eyes. Not that it was terribly hot. The heat wave had finally broken, and San Diego was enjoying its customary late-September balminess. But the city liked to make up for a lack of rain this time of year by brewing up high humidity, especially in the mornings. The sweat her body had pumped out during her run had nowhere to go.

She dragged her forearm across her face, smearing the wet around rather than getting rid of it, and scowled.

Werewolfs Whore.

That was spray painted in black across the hood of her government-issue Ford. The perp had forgotten the apostrophe, but he'd added a PS of sorts on the trunk: *Fucking Bitch Traitor.*

One of her neighbors? She considered that as her heartbeat settled. They had easy access, but otherwise they weren't a good fit.

The rabid haters—the ones most likely to escalate from words to actions—fell in a predictable demographic. There were exceptions, such as the guy who'd killed a guard at the Holocaust Museum. He'd been nearly ninety. But chances were that the asshole who'd defaced her ride was a white, heterosexual male between the ages of twenty and sixty, and either unemployed or working a dead-end job. He probably also hated gays and immigrants, blacks and Jews—everyone he could blame for having upset "the natural order." The natural order would have him on top. Since he was miles and miles away from that spot, someone was clearly at fault.

Lily had plenty of neighbors who fit the age and sex demographic. Some might hate their jobs, too, but they weren't bottom-of-the-heap workers. The high-rise she lived in these days had correspondingly high rents.

But not all haters were financially challenged. Robert Friar proved that.

Lily shook her head. Hell of a way to end a good run, finding this shit. Really messed with all those endorphins she'd produced. If the perp had still been around, she might have gotten back some of that high by kicking his sorry ass, but she was alone in the parking garage . . . except for a few of her neighbors.

The Prius pulling out of its spot now belonged to a single mom on the second floor. Wendy Something. Wendy left about this time every weekday with the kids so she could drop them at day care. She was white, brown and brown, under forty, and worked at some bank—Lily couldn't remember which one—and looked tired all the time. Highly unlikely that she'd spray bad words on a car with her kids watching.

The man crossing the cement to his Lexus left around seven every weekday, too. He was in management at some alphabet-soup company. He was overweight, well-groomed, around forty, and Hispanic. Black and brown, with some gray mixed with the black. Fifth floor, she thought. He was possible, but only just.

Then there was the motorcycle she'd seen tearing out of the garage as she approached it. Jack was a nice guy in a resoundingly unsuccessful band. He got the occasional modeling job, too, but could never have afforded the rent if not for his boyfriend, who had some kind of trust fund. Said boyfriend was, in Lily's opinion, an asshole, but not the sort of asshole who got up before seven A.M. to spray-paint insults on an FBI agent's car.

It was unlikely the perp was still present. She kept her senses tuned anyway as she took her phone from the armband she used on a run. She used it to take a few pictures of the damage, then checked out the surveillance cameras.

Didn't seem to be damaged, so maybe they'd get a look at the asshole who'd defaced her ride. It would be nice to know for sure it wasn't anyone she shared the elevator with.

Of course, to see the images from the cameras, she'd have to tell Rule. He owned the building. Or rather, his father did, but it really belonged to the clan. Nokolai clan, that is. Rule had two clans now, and that was another source of trouble.

Lily got in the elevator and punched the button for the tenth floor. She did not want to tell Rule. She'd have to, but she didn't want to. She hadn't realized how overly protective he'd gotten until the heat wave broke and she could abandon the treadmill to run outside again. He didn't want her running alone. At first he'd found reasons to join her, but when he couldn't he'd tried sending one or two of his guards along.

She'd put a stop to that. Sure, there'd been a situation last month when the guards had been useful. But that case, that situation, was over. His caution was excessive and annoying, and that was half the reason she didn't want to tell him about her car.

The other half was the guilt. Rule was all too grimly certain to blame himself for the vandalism, and that was harder for her to deal with because she couldn't get mad about it. She even understood. She'd handled similar feelings herself, worrying about how their upcoming marriage would affect him.

When Rule asked her to marry him, he'd broken a centuries-old taboo for his people. When she accepted, she'd given the haters of the world a new target. Her.

The elevator dinged. Lily got off and turned left. Rule had a corner unit. No, *they* had a corner unit. It had been four months now since she let her old apartment go; longer than that since they basically started living together . . . and nearly a year since she first saw him, sitting in the cacophony and bad lighting that was Club Hell.

Nearly a year since her life changed, and changed, and changed again. Time to stop thinking of it as his place.

Maybe if she bought some new pillows or a rug . . .

Two of Rule's bodyguards stood in front of the apartment door, this set being from Leidolf clan. She'd decided to think of them as nosy but well-intentioned neighbors—like a lot of really buff Mrs. Kravitzes from *Bewitched*—only with guns and a disconcerting willingness to lay down their lives, if necessary.

They both looked young. One of them really was. Jeffrey Lane was twenty-four, barely an adult in lupi eyes, one of the two Leidolf Rule had brought to San Diego to be trained as guards.

"Jeff," she said as she approached. "What were you thinking?"

The shorter of the two touched his hair self-consciously. "Hey, it's California, right?"

"It's pink."

He grinned. "I already got in trouble for it. José says I don't blend in. But, you know, I thought out here—"

"You see a lot of guys with pink hair in this building?" the taller man said. "In some of those clubs where you like to hang out, maybe, but not here where Rule lives. You don't blend in here." LeBron shook his head, which he'd recently begun shaving. Combined with his height and build, it gave him the look of a café au lait Mr. Clean, only without the earring.

Jeff tried to look abashed. He wasn't good at it.

"Have a good run?" LeBron asked Lily.

"Pretty good." She didn't mention her car. That was FBI business, not a matter for either clan. Besides, she wouldn't have told her nosy neighbor about it, would she? "We're supposed to get some rain today. Think it'll happen?"

"You mean it really does rain in San Diego?" LeBron said. "I thought that was, like, a myth. Something you tell newcomers to see if they'll swallow it."

The Leidolf guards were from North Carolina—green,

wet North Carolina. She shook her head. "Damn. You're on to me. Have you heard from Samuel? He get that job?"

LeBron had two sons, both grown. Samuel was the younger one. LeBron looked maybe a decade older than Jeff, but he was closer to sixty than thirty. Of course, that *was* young—for a lupus. They didn't hit middle age until eighty or so.

"No word yet, but he thought the interview went well."

"Let me know when you hear." Lily used her own key on the door. Either of the men could have opened it for her, but she preferred to do that herself. She liked to think that was good sense—it left their hands and their attention free for any sudden threats—but deep down she knew there was a healthy dollop of denial involved, too.

If she opened the door herself, she could pretend they didn't have keys.

It was a gorgeous apartment. That was part of the problem. Nothing she could afford fit the place. Rule had furnished it in man-modern, with low-slung leather couches and beautiful old wood. The crystal dish where she tossed her key rested on a two-hundred-year-old console table in the small entry. Her water bottle didn't exactly go with the décor, but it was a handy spot to leave it when she went for a run. She grabbed it, twisted, and started chugging as she walked.

The great room was the star of the show. A huge window-wall framed the combined living and dining areas. Freshly minted morning sun poured in through the glass, striking mahogany sparks from the hair of the man seated at the big, dark wood dining table at one end of the room.

In other lighting, Rule's hair was nearly black. In any light, it was shaggy. She used to think that was part of his persona, the look he cultivated as the public face of the lupi. In fact, Rule just didn't like getting his hair cut. He could get away with that, being so outrageously sexy. But she liked knowing the shaggy hair wasn't part of the persona, but part of the man.

Rule spoke without looking up from the laptop that anchored the sprawl of papers covering half the table. "Your mother found a cheaper printer for the invitations. She wants you to call her about it. You'll have time for that, as I've already called about the damage to your car."

Her feet stopped. "Ah . . . oh. Who did you call?"

"Your current comrades-in-arms. The local FBI office." Now he looked up. "You did plan to tell me, didn't you?"

"I was considering it. How did you find out?"

"José saw it when he was leaving on an errand."

José was Nokolai and the head bodyguard. "So you called the office, but you didn't call and warn me."

Now he looked at her. "I did. You didn't answer."

Lily opened her mouth to argue—and shut it again. She stripped off the armband, took out her phone, and checked. And grimaced. "The ringer's turned off. Sorry. Who did you talk to?"

"Agent Gray. He assured me he'd send someone out right away. He wanted me to tell you that the handwriting expert confirmed that the letter you received last week was written by the, ah, perp you suspected. The one with a habit of writing sexually explicit letters."

"It's nice to be right." The letter had been yucky, not scary. The guy who wrote it was a known quantity—not known by name, maybe, but by habit. He got off on writing dirty "love letters" to people in the news, and was sadly promiscuous in his attentions. He'd written everyone from Britney Spears to the First Lady. "I told you about that letter."

His eyebrows—he had wicked eyebrows—lifted. "Yes, you did. Unlike the other letters you've received. The ones serious enough that the FBI is investigating them. Those, you haven't mentioned."

Busted. Damn that Gray for tattling. "Because you'd jump to conclusions. The FBI has a policy of tracking any threats its agents receive. Standard practice, not anything to worry about."

"When someone threatens you, I worry." He rose. "You will not, in some misguided effort to protect me, keep such things from me."

Rule was one of those rare men who look elegant in anything. Maybe it was the shoulders, or the runner's legs, or the sheer grace of the man. Today's choices were black, as usual—black slacks with a black dress shirt with the sleeves pushed up. His feet were bare.

It was inappropriate to find those bare feet sexy when he

was clearly angry. And with reason, she admitted. If their situations were reversed, she'd have been pissed. "Okay."

His eyebrows shot up. "Okay? Just like that?"

"On one condition. We are not having the bodyguard argument again."

He considered that a moment. "I'll table it for now. I reserve the right to bring it up later if conditions warrant."

"Rule, I can't go everywhere trailing lupus bodyguards! Aside from the fun Friar would have with that story once he found out—and he would, eventually—there's the matter of confidentiality. I can't have civilians privy to an investigation."

"I thought we were tabling the argument."

She huffed out a breath. "Why, when I got what I asked for, do I feel like you won?"

His smile came quick and easy. "Because you're a deeply suspicious woman. About those threatening letters—"

A herd of elephants galloped down the hall from the bedrooms. A second later, the herd came into view, transformed into a nine-year-old boy with dark hair and his father's eyebrows. He was wearing his tighty whiteys—and nothing else.

Toby skidded to a stop in front of them, grinning. "I'm hungry! What's for breakfast?"

"Hamburgers," Rule said. "But you don't seem to be ready to eat."

"It's my new strategy," Toby explained. "Hi, Lily. You're all sweaty."

"I am," she agreed, baffled by the feeling that rose inside her. How could she feel this way about a boy she'd known such a short time? "I need a shower."

"I had mine last night. That's part of my strategy. See, when Dad tells me to get up I lay out all my clothes, but I don't put them on until after I eat. This way I don't have to worry about spilling stuff on them. Well, except for my underwear, but if I spill something on them it won't show."

Rule nodded thoughtfully. "I believe that would be called a tactic, not a strategy. A tactic is the immediate means used to achieve a goal. Strategy is the overarching vision of how to employ tactics and other assets to achieve a goal."

"Yeah?" Toby considered that. "So my strategy is keeping my clothes clean, and my tactic is not wearing them when I eat."

"Precisely. Unfortunately, that tactic only works at home."

"Well, yeah! The kids at school would think I was pretty weird if I stripped in the cafeteria at lunchtime."

"Which makes this tactic ineffective. The overall goal is for you to learn to keep food from decorating you."

Toby's face fell. "You mean I gotta get dressed."

"I'm afraid so."

"I don't gotta get dressed before breakfast when I stay with Grandpa."

Grandpa was Rule's father, Isen Turner—the Nokolai Rho. Toby had stayed with him at Clanhome until school started.

"That was summer vacation," Rule said firmly. "The rules are different once school starts."

That was a telling argument. The boy had been raised by his maternal grandmother, Louise Asteglio, until two months ago, when Rule was finally able to gain custody. Lily knew Louise had insisted on dressing before breakfast during the school year.

Toby's face fell. "But—"

"Toby."

Toby heaved a sigh, then brightened. "Hamburgers?"

Rule nodded.

"Are you gonna make one for Lily, too?"

She answered that one. "I ate before I went for my run. It's not a good idea to exercise on empty."

"Yeah, but . . . *hamburgers*. For *breakfast*."

That hadn't happened back in North Carolina at his grandmother's house. It hadn't happened at Lily's home when she was growing up in San Diego, either. Rule was keeping some of Mrs. Asteglio's rules, both because they worked and because he thought the continuity would help Toby adapt. But he saw no objection to burgers for breakfast. Even a fully human boy needs protein in the morning, he'd said.

And Toby wasn't fully human. He was lupus, though he wouldn't turn wolf until he hit puberty. Lupi needed extra protein even before the Change.

"I don't think I have time," Lily said. "I've got to take my shower and get dressed, or I won't get you to school before the bell rings." Dropping Toby off at school in the mornings was her idea. Rule could have done it. Any of the guards would have been happy to do it—and might need to sometimes, when her job got crazy. But Lily wanted those minutes with Toby in the car when it was just the two of them.

Toby nodded. "Dad can make you one to take with you. Hey, Dad!" Excitement overtook him. "Did you tell her about—"

"Not yet," Rule said, "and it's my surprise, so go get dressed before you ruin it."

Toby giggled, shot Lily a mischievous look, and raced off.

Lily shook her head in wonder. "He's sure riding a high of some sort this morning. Rule, about this surprise—"

At the same time he said, "About those letters—"

They looked at each other. Smiled. "Okay," she said, "the letters came up first, so we'll hit that, but fast. I do need to shower."

THREE

"TALK while I cook," Rule said, and headed for the kitchen.

That was next to the entry. It was small compared to her parents' kitchen, but huge compared to what she'd had in her old apartment. Of course, until recently the only use she had for a kitchen was as a place to park a coffeemaker and a refrigerator, but she was learning to cook. Slowly. "I'm not hungry. I ate before I ran."

"A yogurt smoothie is not a meal."

"Not for you, maybe. I had a banana, too."

He took out the hamburger meat. "I'll cook it. You don't have to eat it. How many threats have you received?"

"None I consider serious."

"That's not an answer." He began shaping a patty.

Lily bent to pull out the big grill pan and gave in. "Seven altogether. Six were addressed to the local FBI office. One was sent to Quantico. Two of those nuts signed their names," she added dryly. "They've been checked out and given a stern warning. The rest contain either explicit or implicit threats."

"You'll tell me exactly what it is they do threaten."

She shrugged. "One was very traditional: 'Thou shalt not

suffer a witch to live.' They got a couple good partials and a full thumbprint from that one, but no match so far. The rest . . . Rule, they're ugly, but there's no reason to think the writers will go from words to actions. The vast majority of the time, the letter-writer is satisfied with venting and doesn't escalate."

"Someone did. He vandalized your car."

"Which means we ought to have his picture, right?" She set the pan on the burner. "Medium heat?"

"A little higher. I want to see those letters."

"There's no point in it. You'd just—"

"Lily." He slapped patties onto the griddle—one, two, three, four, five. At least two were for him, maybe three. She didn't think Toby could eat two of the thick patties. "I am not going to panic. Do you really think I haven't received my share of threatening letters?"

She felt foolish. Of course he had. "You think you have a handle on when it's a real threat, when it's a caution light, and when you can set it aside."

"They're all at least a caution light."

"Okay. And how many letters have you received since Friar started appearing on all those talk shows?"

He stilled. Then his mouth twitched. "Ah . . . I'll show you mine if you show me yours?"

She kept her mouth firm. "How many, Rule?"

"Four. But they're—"

"Not anything I need to worry about? Nothing to be taken too seriously?"

He ran a hand through his hair. "Dammit, Lily, no matter how many people enjoy mouthing off, the number who will actually take on a big, bad werewolf is vanishingly small. You're—"

"A big, bad federal agent," she finished, before he could say "small" or "a woman" or anything else that would get him in trouble. "Believe it or not, very few people want to take us on, either. We're not as scary as you, but we've got that whole power-of-the-law thing going."

For a long moment he just looked at her. She could see thoughts moving behind his dark eyes, but had no sense of where he was headed with them. So it should have been no surprise that he surprised her. "Then it wasn't the threats you've received that gave you nightmares last night?"

She considered several replies, but settled on "No."

He crossed to her and brushed her hair back, his face softening. He settled his hands on her shoulders. "Did you think I wouldn't notice that you woke smelling of fear?"

"Sometimes your ability to smell what's going on with me is a comfort. Sometimes it's a pain in the ass."

That made him smile, but briefly. "You had a session with Sam yesterday."

She didn't say anything. They'd already talked about this. Okay, not much—she wasn't a talk-it-out person—but they'd talked.

Last month, Lily had learned her Gift came with bonus abilities. The first one made her uneasy. It would be too easy to abuse, even with the best motives. No one should be able to suck out another person's magic . . . except in extraordinarily rare situations. Like when the other person was a millennia-old out-realm being who was trying to kill you so she could drive millions of people into madness and feed on their fear.

Lily was okay with what she'd done then, but that situation wasn't likely to arise a second time. She figured she could retire that particular trick. The other one was freaky in its own way, but nowhere near as disturbing.

Mindspeech was a dragon thing, but Sam said she had the potential to learn it. She'd actually done it once with Rule, but that had been an accident she hadn't been able to repeat. But she'd been offered the chance to learn. After thinking it over, she'd accepted.

Her teacher was Sam, also known as Sun Mzao, the black dragon, who was sort of her grandfather-in-magic, if not DNA. A couple times a week she went to his lair and sat with him. It was hard to describe what happened. On a thinking level, not much did. She'd sit. After awhile he'd light the wick of a candle—easy for a dragon to do, no matches needed—and tell her, *Watch*. The first time he lit the candle, he had given her one additional instruction: *Find me here*.

So far, all she'd found were the nightmares.

Rule was every bit as good at saying nothing as she was. He waited, his thumbs making soothing circles along her collarbone.

"It was Helen again," she admitted. "I don't have to be a psych major to see why she stars in the nightmare. I'm trying to learn mindspeech, which Sam insists is not telepathy, but the two are next-door neighbors. I killed the only telepath I've ever met."

"You killed a crazy woman who was trying to kill you and open a hellgate."

"True, but somehow not pertinent." She shook her head, disliking her own vagueness but unable to dispel it.

His thumbs circled back, pressing more firmly, finding the tension at her nape and easing it. "Are you committed to learning mindspeech? At first you weren't sure it was worth it. If it opens you to such fears—"

She snorted. "This from the man who moved into a high-rise on purpose so he'd be forced to ride in the elevator every day."

He smiled faintly. "Damn those torpedoes, hmm?"

"Pretty much. I get a week off, though. Sam will be gone for at least that long for one of their sing-alongs. Um . . . I'm not to speak of it, except to you, and you're not to tell anyone." Dragons were mostly solitary, but at unpredictable intervals they gathered to sing together—though Lily thought she and Rule were the only two in their realm who knew this. Except for Grandmother, of course. "That reminds me. While Sam's gone, Grandmother and Li Qin are heading for Disneyland."

He grinned. "That I'd like to see."

"She loves Disneyland. She used to take me and my sisters every year. Are the burgers burning?"

"Shit." He let her go and spun to the stove.

Feet thudded in the hall. "I'm ready!" Toby called. "Are the burgers done? It took me a little longer 'cause I had to pet Harry. He was lonely."

Harry was Dirty Harry, Lily's cat. Though he and Rule had achieved détente—based mainly on Rule's willingness to give him ham at regular intervals—Harry had never gotten beyond a sort of disdainful tolerance.

He adored Toby.

That made no sense. According to Rule, Toby didn't smell of wolf yet, but scent wasn't the only reason Harry didn't like Rule, probably not even the main reason. Harry was not a friendly beast. He had to be sedated to go to the vet. He attacked the bodyguards whenever he got a chance. He couldn't stand Lily's family—well, except for Li Qin, but no one could dislike Li Qin.

Lily had worried about how the cat and the boy would adapt to each other. Toby was a normal nine-year-old boy . . . which meant he did everything a suspicious and territorial cat hated. He ran. He jumped. He grabbed. He yelled. She'd been sure Toby would be scratched, clawed, disdained.

Yet from the moment Harry had sniffed Toby's outstretched hand, he'd become a Toby acolyte. He purred when he saw Toby. He slept with Toby. He even condescended to play with the cat toys Toby insisted they buy.

And Toby had decided not to get a dog right now, though he'd talked of little else for ages. It wouldn't be right, he said. It would make Harry awfully sad.

It would make Harry homicidal, Lily thought. Some puppy out there was going to live a long, unscarred life because Toby had abandoned his dog dreams for now.

Lily took down a couple of plates and put them on the counter next to Rule, then went to the refrigerator. Toby didn't sully his hamburgers with vegetables, but he was big on condiments.

"The patties are done," Rule said. "Would you get out the buns, please, Toby?"

"Sure!" Toby bounced over to the pantry—they had an actual pantry, a luxury new to Lily—and pulled out a package of buns. "Did you tell her?" he demanded, looking between Lily and Rule. "She doesn't look excited."

"I was waiting for you." Rule accepted the buns. "It seems we'll have to allow Toby to stay up late next Wednesday. Late enough to catch *The Daily Show*."

She looked from Toby's grin to Rule's more restrained smugness. "You're going to be on Jon Stewart?"

"Isn't that cooler than catsup?" Toby burst out. "He's gonna be talking to Jon Stewart!"

"Definitely cool," she agreed. "But is it . . . I mean, Stewart's not vicious the way some of them are, but he goes for the laughs. Is that going to . . ." Her voice trailed off. "Right. You'll do fine."

Rule smiled, amused, as he slid meat patties onto their buns. He didn't say a word.

He didn't have to. It would take more than Jon Stewart to make Rule put a foot wrong in front of cameras. It helped that he was so photogenic. Mostly, though, he was just good at it. He'd become the public face for his people almost the instant the Supreme Court made it safe for him to declare himself. His public persona was sort of a werewolf James Bond—mysterious and sophisticated with a whiff of danger. Only a whiff, though. Enough to intrigue, not frighten.

It helped that he really was mysterious and sophisticated. "Doesn't he film in New York?" She ran through her current cases in her head, trying to figure a way to fly to New York City. The mate bond had its good points, and she was a lot more aware of them these days. But the downside was that it put geographical limits on how far apart they could be. If Rule flew across the country, she had to go, too.

"The show is filming in L.A. next week. Stewart is emceeing the Emmys again, so they decided to move the show there for the week preceding the awards."

"What about St. Paul? The circle?" Rule was meeting with the Lu Nuncios of the other North American clans. It was a big deal. She was supposed to be there to prove to the others that Nokolai intended no violence. To the clans, a Chosen was sacrosanct. Not the most paranoid among them would suspect Nokolai of putting its Chosen at risk. Plus Lily's officialness was a deterrent to naughty behavior, period. She was known to take the law seriously.

"That's Monday."

"I know." She'd had to clear her schedule to go with him. The others wanted it held in neutral territory, which had turned out to be St. Paul. "But if it doesn't go well—if you bleed or something—"

"We're going to talk, not cry Challenge at each other. Even if it goes badly, I'll be able to fly to L.A. by Wednesday.

The question is, will you? We can fly up and back the same night, if necessary."

He could probably go to L.A. on his own. The mate bond had been giving them plenty of slack lately, but they couldn't take the chance because the physical limit it imposed changed. Without warning. Without reason, from what Lily could see. That bugged her a lot more than it did Rule.

At least it had never contracted as much as it had right after it hit and they made love the first time. They'd been all but glued to each others' sides then. "Okay," she said at last. "I can make it work. None of my cases are hot and all the task force does is talk, so a couple hours on a plane shouldn't be a problem. This is about Friar, isn't it? Him and Humans First."

Toby made a face. "He's a turd."

"Are you allowed to say that?" Lily asked, then glanced at her watch. "Damn. I've got to go shower."

"Tell her the rest, Dad," Toby said. "Quick, so we aren't late."

The rest? Lily looked at Rule, eyebrows raised. "Letterman?"

"He does film in New York, so I had to turn him down."

He'd been asked, though. Sometimes it was deeply weird, living with someone who got asked onto Letterman. It wouldn't have been his first time, either. "Who, then?"

His bland smile made her instantly suspicious. "You'll have to agree to this one, since the invitation includes you. It's for two weeks from today, and we'd have to go to Chicago."

Toby couldn't stand it anymore. "*Oprah*! You get to be on *Oprah* with Dad! She particularly asked for you."

She stared at Rule in horror. "You haven't accepted yet, though. You can turn them down."

"Lily!" Toby was shocked.

"I don't want to be on *Oprah*. She makes people say stuff. Personal stuff that no one . . . I don't want to say stuff."

"And you don't have to," Rule said soothingly. "Not much, anyway. You can talk mostly to me and to Oprah's other guest."

She could feel that other shoe about to hit the floor. "Who will be—?"

"Robert Friar."

Oh, shit. "You've trapped me. If he's going to be there, I can't . . . You made it so I can't say no."

"Actually, I believe the credit for that goes to Oprah herself, or to those who handle bookings for her show. I had nothing to do with it."

"I can't guarantee anything. If something big comes up, or if the task force stops talking and actually does something—"

"Oprah will understand, I'm sure, if you have an urgent investigation and can't travel. But it does have to be urgent."

Oh, yeah. She was trapped.

ROBERT Friar, founder of Humans First, was going to be on *Oprah*.

Lily adjusted the shower temperature to cool and stepped in, brooding on that. It wasn't as if Rule needed her to pin Friar's ears back. He could do that just fine. He knew how to handle himself on TV. She . . . well, she could handle a press conference, but Oprah was a whole 'nother kettle of fish. You were supposed to confide in Oprah. Get intimate. Reveal stuff.

Lily so did not want to reveal stuff. But Friar would be there, so she had to go.

Robert Friar had started the rounds of the talk shows the day after she and Rule announced their upcoming marriage at a press conference. At first he'd hit the hard-right radio shows, then FOX, and now a couple mainstream news pundits had had him on. Any controversy was good controversy when you had twenty-four hours to fill with something vaguely news-related.

Friar called Lily's relationship with Rule bestiality. He wanted the California government to rule that a lupus couldn't marry a human. On his last appearance, he'd gone even further. He wanted to make it a crime for a human woman to conjoin with a lupus. That was his word—*conjoin*, as in "this unnatural conjoining of the races."

Lily ground her teeth as she scrubbed her scalp.

Friar knew—everyone knew—that lupi were always male. If he could eliminate all that conjoining, after awhile there wouldn't be any more lupi. That would suit him. Oh, he didn't come out and say he wanted an end to lupi and brownies and witches, to anyone of the Blood, anyone with a Gift, anyone who carried the taint of magic. He was too slick to say that outright, talking instead about legal remedies.

So she had to go to Chicago. She had to try to get him to show his true colors.

And it was sick to be wishing for a triple murder by some whacked-out witch to keep her here. She shut off the water and grabbed a towel.

Lily worked for the FBI's Unit Twelve, which on paper looked like part of its Magical Crimes Division. MCD usually handled the more routine cases, while the Unit got the weird ones. And Lily, because of her background as a homicide cop, often got the ones involving dead bodies.

Not always, though. At the moment she had four open cases and nary a murder in sight. One case was all but closed. A pissed-off girlfriend had cursed her cheating partner—who, as it happened, was also female—and had left plenty of non-magical tracks for Lily to follow, which was fortunate. A good curse was hard to track magically.

Not that Lily could do that, anyway. She was a touch sensitive, able to experience magic tactilely, but she could neither work magic nor be affected by it. Mostly she liked it that way.

The curse Sheila Bickner had plucked from the Internet wasn't all that good. It had made the victim seriously ill, but that was more a matter of the practitioner's power than the curse's efficacy. At least that's what Lily had been told by the experts—the Wiccan coven who would be doing their thing today, tracing the curse to its caster to tie up the last bit of evidence.

The courts accepted very little magically produced evidence, and then only from Wiccan practitioners. That was being challenged in court as a religiously biased criteria—which, of course, it was. Lily expected the criteria would change. She just hoped the congressional committee work-

ing on a new bill came up with something reasonable before
the courts struck down the old law.

Two of the other cases were both felony theft involving
magic. So far, she was ringing up a big zero on both of them.
The warehouse theft shouldn't even be hers, she thought as
she slathered on lotion with sunscreen. Magic had been used
to gain access, sure, but otherwise it was a straightforward
burglary. It would be solved by regular police work, which
was best carried out by regular cops.

She'd talk to Ruben about handing that one back to the
locals, she decided as she gave her hair a quick blast with the
blow-dryer. No time to dry it completely, but she could keep
it from dripping.

The other case was relatively minor, but she wasn't letting it go. It involved theft by magical means of a controlled
substance—gadolinium.

Gadolinium was a rare earth metal with a handful of le-
gitimate applications, but it was best known as the key ingredient in gado. Gado was the drug the government had used to
control lupi—any they could identify, that is, and register—
until the Supreme Court put a stop to it.

Gado stopped the Change. It also tended to drive lupi
insane.

The amount of gadolinium that had been stolen from a
medical lab was quite small, but Lily meant to find out who
had it before he or she used it to make some lupus miserable.
Or dead.

Then there was the task force. Lily shook her head and
pulled on underwear, bra, black slacks, and a black tank. She
wore a lot of black, too, she admitted. But only because it
was easy, not because she was working on a certain look.
Black slacks, black tee—add a colorful jacket to hide her
weapon, and she was good to go.

It wasn't that the task force wasn't important. It was.
There was a new drug on the streets in California, one with
a magical component, and several agencies—federal, state,
and local—were working together to stop its spread. Lily
had personally confirmed that magic was involved by touching one of the very few samples the DEA had. The street
name for the drug was Do Me, which pretty much said it all.

Best date rape drug ever, from all accounts. It only affected women; it was impossible to detect within a couple hours of ingestion; and there were no known side effects. Just lust, and lots of it. The only upside was that there didn't seem to be a plentiful supply.

So it wasn't the task force itself that bugged her. It was her role on that task force. She was liaison for MCD. Being liaison meant she went to meetings, reported to Ruben on those meetings, and now and then passed on a request from some other agency for information.

It did not mean investigating.

Lily stepped into her flats, slipped on her watch, then her shoulder holster, and grabbed a jacket at random. It turned out to be one of her favorites, a pale turquoise with over-size buttons. She glanced at the time. Looked like she'd go makeup-free today. She took one more second to grab a scrunchy and stick it in her pocket. It had been way too long since she had her hair cut, and it was long enough now to get in the way if she didn't do something with it.

She called out as she slipped on the jacket, "Toby, we should be able to make it. Got your books?"

No answer. Frowning, she hurried to the living area.

Rule stood near the dining table, his expression wiped clean. "Toby's gone. I asked Jeff to take him this morning."

Lily stopped. "Something's wrong. Something's happened."

"While you were in the shower, I heard from Alex about a Leidolf clan member, Raymond Cobb. At one thirty this morning East Coast time, Cobb was at some sort of party. A human party, not clan. He killed three people and injured ten others before the party's host retrieved his rifle and shot him."

FOUR

THE overhead fan clicked with every revolution. *Need to get that fixed*, Benedict thought. Could come a time that small sound masked another small sound, one Isen needed to hear.

It was easier to think about the fan, about security issues, than about why he was here, in his father's big, comfortable den. Benedict had been in charge of security at Clanhome for thirty-one years. He was good at it. Some might say he was obsessive, but his obsessiveness had paid off more than once.

Aside from the fan, the room was silent. The silence, the waiting, was hard. He'd given his report. His Rho needed to know what took place on Robert Friar's property last night.

Everything that took place.

"You're sure you don't need Nettie to take a look at that arm?"

"It's been eighteen hours. It's almost healed." Fire enough bullets and even a slow, sense-dead human could hit something, but Benedict was still annoyed that he'd been clumsy enough to pick up a wound from a ricochet.

"Eighteen hours. Yes."

Benedict neither tensed nor looked up. He sat on a large

hassock with his back to the fireplace, leaning forward with his hands clasped between his knees. His palms were damp.

"I won't tell you were derelict in your duty, waiting so long to report," Isen said. "You already know that, and I understand why you delayed. Have you spoken to anyone else about this?"

He shook his head. "I won't. Not yet. Not until . . ." He didn't know how to end that sentence. What conditions could he place on this? It was out of his control. Entirely out of his control. "Not yet."

"The Rhej has to know."

"I hoped that you would tell her."

Another pulse of silence. "I can do that. She's sequestered with Cynna now, but I can go up there and wait. Sooner or later, she'll be free to step outside and see what I want. You want this kept quiet."

"I need time." Benedict's fists clenched. "I'll tell Nettie. She deserves . . . I have to be the one to tell her. But no one else. It can't be kept secret long, but a day, two days . . . I need time."

"Where are you now?"

The simple question sent the past shuddering through him. It had been forty-two years since Isen had needed to ask him that: *Where are you now?* Back then, he'd answered many different ways: *the abyss, her grave, the desert, I don't know but it's dark and the darkness has teeth . . .*

Today he said, "A swamp. Quicksand, gators, mud, mosquitoes. I need . . ." He squeezed his closed fists tighter. "I need dry land, but I don't know where it is."

"Are you fit?"

The blunt question steadied him. "I'm functional, but not stable. I want to go to my cabin. A week, maybe two."

"No."

That brought Benedict's head up, anger blazing through him.

Benedict's father—who was also his Rho, leader of his clan—sat in his favorite wingback chair. Isen Turner was burly, bearded, and nine inches shorter than his oldest son. He looked to be in his fifties, though unusually fit for that age. He was ninety-one. His eyes were sad, but there was no give in his expression, none at all.

There never was when he gave an order. "Is my Rho speaking, then?"

"Yes, although your father and your Rho agree on this. As Rho, I need you here, even if you don't have your head straight. Too much hinges on the heirs' circle Rule has called."

Benedict stared blankly. He'd forgotten the meeting of Lu Nuncios. How could he have forgotten something so critical?

"You've done all the setup for security already, but I can't have you holed up in your cabin now. Given the current tension—"

"Because my brother decided to get married." He kept his voice level. He wanted to spit.

Isen's voice sharpened. "You know better. Some are upset about that, yes, but it's the union—or what they fear is a union—of Leidolf and Nokolai that worries the other clans."

Benedict took a deep breath and let it out, forcing his body to relax. Isen was right. Nokolai's relationship with a couple of the clans had been troubled ever since the Leidolf mantle was forced on Rule. It could grow worse at any moment—especially if anyone realized the truth about those two blasted Leidolf Rule was having trained as guards. "My apologies. My reaction . . . that's why I'm not fit. I'm not thinking clearly."

"Clearly, you aren't," Isen said with a thread of humor that quickly evaporated. "What you don't know because you've been hiding it is that a Leidolf lupus went crazy last night. He killed three people and injured several others before someone put a couple bullets in him."

Benedict's head jerked up. "Beast-lost?"

"No. He stayed two-footed."

"That's bad. You have a name?"

"Raymond Cobb."

The small jolt of surprise landed him a few steps closer to normal. "Ray Cobb?"

"You know him?"

Benedict frowned. "Not really. He took second in the pole vaulting at the last All-Clan, though. Fifth in shot put. Competed in wrestling, too, but didn't place. He's got the strength, lacks the speed. Good control, though. I'd have sworn his control was good. He was attacked?"

"Apparently not, but Rule had very few details when he called. He's headed to Tennessee now."

"The circle—"

"Will proceed as planned on Monday, unless Rule finds the situation to be more than it appears right now."

Benedict nodded slowly. Whatever had gone wrong with Cobb, the meeting was too important to delay. "Rule took guards with him?"

"Two of the Leidolf guards, yes. Lily's with him, of course. She'll be handling the investigation, such as it is. It sounds open and shut, from a legal standpoint. Plenty of witnesses, Rule said."

"Is Cobb still alive, then?"

"He's hurt, but not dead."

Benedict considered consequences. "Is Rule going to announce himself to the press as Leidolf Rho?"

Leidolf clan had vehemently opposed the mainstreaming Isen promoted. The previous Leidolf Rho had forbidden any of his clan to live openly as lupi. Rule had lifted that ban, but hadn't yet announced the existence of the clan to the press, or his position as Rho.

Isen chuckled. "I asked. He told me it was my son and heir who'd called me, not the Leidolf Rho, but if I wished to speak to the Rho he'd see if he could arrange it."

Benedict's eyebrows shot up. "And did you?"

"He gave me to understand that he hasn't told Leidolf his plans yet, so he couldn't tell me."

Benedict supposed it didn't matter greatly. Humans wouldn't care that it was a Leidolf lupus, rather than a No-kolai, who'd killed. Their fear would encompass all lupi, and their fear was dangerous. Dealing with the human world was Rule's job, and Isen's, but threats from that world were his business. Keeping Clanhome and his Rho safe were his business. He couldn't retreat to his cabin.

Isen said simply, "Ben."

His father was the only one who called him Ben. No one else did, including his Rho. It was his father he'd hear from now. Benedict swallowed. "Yes."

"That swamp you're in—that's the past. No one could blame you for bogging down in it now. How could you not? But you won't find dry land holed up in your cabin away from everyone. Just more swamp."

"I don't understand how the Lady could do this," Benedict burst out. "I don't understand at all."

"I don't, either," Isen said gently.

"It's never happened twice to one lupus. Once is rare. Twice is . . ." Benedict shuddered. His father was right, as usual. He couldn't run away from this. He had no choice but to stay and face it. His voice dropped to a whisper. "I haven't been scared like this in so long. So long."

"You don't know anything about her other than her appearance?"

Benedict had given her physical description to Isen in his report: late twenties or early thirties. Five-seven, skinny, pale skin, glasses, wildly curly hair tied back in a ponytail. He didn't know what color all that frantic hair might be, save that it was neither especially dark nor especially light. Wolf eyes saw well in the dark, but they didn't pick up colors at night.

He knew how she smelled. He hadn't tried to describe that, or its effect on him. He knew she'd been afraid the whole time—before she saw him, the moment she saw him, and while he walked beside her. She hadn't let the fear interfere. "She knew what I was."

"Did she?"

"From the moment she saw me." Never mind what she'd said. The ghost of a smile touched Benedict's lips. *Nice doggie.* "She didn't freak about me staying with her. She tried to persuade me to go, but she didn't freak."

Isen nodded. "That's encouraging. And, as the proverb says, 'The enemy of my enemy is my friend.' She enjoys sneaking around Friar's property at night, which isn't the act of one friendly to the man."

Dryly, Benedict said, "I don't think she was enjoying herself. Aside from the danger, which she seemed well aware of, she has a physical impediment of some sort. Hip, maybe knee, on her left side. I couldn't tell."

"You said she twisted her ankle."

"There was something off in her gait before that. It's slight, nothing obvious, but it's there. I'd guess it's something she's used to. She wasn't paying attention to that leg the way she would have if it were a recent problem." She hadn't been paying attention at all, which was why she'd ended up on her ass.

And then he hadn't paid attention. He'd stumbled across the ward, attracting the guards, and had been forced to leave her to draw them away. "She's got a Gift," he said suddenly. "I don't know what kind, but she knew about the ward. She knew exactly where it was."

"Your brain's starting to work again."

Benedict grimaced. He should have thought of that earlier. He should have thought of it last night, at least by the time he circled back to follow her scent and make sure she'd gotten away.

But he hadn't been thinking. Just feeling, feeling way too damned much. "A Gift's not the only possibility. Could be she has something like that fairy dust Seabourne made for me." The magical powder Seabourne had rubbed on Benedict's pads made them tingle when he drew near a ward. That's why he'd been at Friar's last night—marking the wards the wolf way, with a few drops of urine, so his people could keep an eye on the man without tripping the wards.

"Could be. You'll have to ask Cullen how likely it is someone other than him could stir up something like that."

Cullen Seabourne was Nokolai . . . now. He'd been born Etorri, but had been kicked out of his clan years ago because he was also a sorcerer, which went against the way things were supposed to work. Lupi didn't work magic. They *were* magic. They for damn sure weren't sorcerers, able to see magic.

Cullen Seabourne was and did. He broke rules. That had been survival for him during his years as a lone wolf. If he'd accepted the usual way of things, he'd have killed himself— either in a straight-up suicide or by losing control in some devastating way that led to him being put down.

Lupi weren't meant to live clanless.

Benedict respected the man, even liked him. But he didn't want to see Seabourne now. He was too raw. One smart-ass remark and Benedict might go for his throat. "I will," he said, rising. "But later. If I'm not going to go to my cabin, I need a workout."

"I'm feeling some sympathy for Pete," Isen said dryly as he stood. "Don't bleed him too much."

"I won't damage my second."

"I know that. You're in control when you fight. That's one reason you need to spar now—to reclaim control."

Of course his father understood that. "I'll bring Tommy in, too, I think. Or Sean. Sean's coming along." Two opponents of their skill would push him. He needed to be pushed, forced to shut off all this damn thinking.

"Ben." Isen came to him and hugged him hard, then stepped back, still gripping Benedict's arms. "You're not coming unwound. I don't know if you see that, but I do. You're scared, you're pissed, you're shook up. For a bit you weren't thinking straight. But you aren't coming apart."

Yet. Benedict swallowed the word, holding tight to the rope his father tossed him. Isen didn't always speak the truth, but on this he would. And he knew what Benedict looked like when he came unwound.

"I won't pretend I understand what you're feeling. I don't think anyone can who hasn't been given what you were, or suffered the loss of that gift. But there's one who might understand, and I have to tell him anyway. You might talk to your brother."

Rule was Lu Nuncio to the clan, and so had to be informed. As intimate and personal as this felt, it was also a clan matter. "To Rule."

Isen nodded.

"No." His response was immediate and visceral. He took a moment to examine that response and found a solid wall of aversion . . . and behind that wall, feeling. A bloody tsunami of it. That tsunami would hit if he looked behind the wall.

Eventually, he would have to. He wasn't ready. Would it be better or worse if, when the time came—when it could no longer be avoided—he talked to his brother? Benedict shook his head. "Not now. Maybe not at all, but I'll consider it when I'm steadier."

"Good enough. I won't speak to Lily about this, and I'll

ask Rule not to, if that's your wish. I don't know if he'll agree, but I'll ask it on your behalf. You can't keep this private for long."

"No." But he could claw free a day or two. A day or two when he didn't have to deal with everyone bloody *reacting* to the news.

"Might be a good idea if Lily knew. She could probably find her for you."

"I don't want her found." Benedict pulled away.

"Ben, you have to. You can't leave her to—"

"No." That had been his father talking, not his Rho, so he headed for the door. He didn't slow down or look back, and he did not give a damn if that was unreasonable. His Rho told him to stay close instead of retreating to his cabin, so he would. His father wanted him to believe he'd be okay. He'd try.

But damned if he'd be *reasonable*.

Last night, for the second time in his life, he'd felt a mate bond snap into place. The Lady had chosen for him. Again.

As far as he was concerned, the Lady could damned well deliver her precious Chosen to him, if she was so bent on giving him one. If the only thing in his control was whether or not he hunted her down, he voted for *not*.

FIVE

AIRPLANE air stinks.

Even humans were aware of the problem, Rule thought, shifting to stretch his legs out better. They complained about staleness rather than stink, but they knew there was something wrong with the air. He'd read an article which identified one culprit: TCP, an organophosphate found in jet oil. When that oil leaked, TCP fumes entered the cabin because of the way cabin air was drawn off the engines. Airlines used top-notch filters, but air filters don't stop fumes.

The overwhelmingly floral cologne of the woman two rows up was a worse irritant. Rule liked the scents of roses, gardenias, and lilies, but they did not play well together, especially when used at saturation level on a woman whose body chemistry turned them acrid. Rule wouldn't mind the human fondness for perfumes so much if they'd been better at selecting fragrances that complemented their natural scent.

On the upside, the overwhelming fragrance did distract him somewhat from the fact that he was confined in a hollow metal cigar hurtling through the air under someone else's control.

And that, Rule admitted as he resisted the urge to shift his legs again, was not the real problem. The real problem was that *he could not get off.*

His heartbeat picked up. He took a slow breath, focusing on the inhale for a count of five . . . hold briefly . . . and exhale for five. Two more rounds of controlled breathing and he was okay. Not great, but okay.

The important thing was to keep from giving off any silent cues that LeBron might pick up. It was easy not to look frightened. He was good at that. Keeping his emotions from telegraphing themselves in his scent and heartbeat was trickier, but possible. He didn't want to contribute to his bodyguards' unease on the four hour-plus flight.

LeBron, one row up and on the other side of the aisle, seemed to be coping well with their airborne imprisonment. Rule couldn't tell about Jeff, who was back in economy. But Jeff claimed to be less affected than most by the claustrophobia common to lupi.

Rule wished he could say the same for himself. Jeff was in the economy section because there had only been four seats available in first class—one for LeBron, who was senior; one for Lily; and two for Rule. On long flights, he needed one of the seats next to him empty. It kept him from pacing the aisle. Much. Fortunately, they'd been able to get three of those seats together, so he had Lily on one side and an empty seat on the other.

Flying didn't bother Lily. Not at all. She worked or she talked or she napped, entirely at ease. The last time they flew across the country—which was, unfortunately, quite recent—he'd asked why the loss of control didn't trouble her.

"I don't have control over all the drivers I encounter when I'm driving," she'd said, "but that doesn't keep me off the road. And statistics show I'm a lot safer on a plane than surrounded by the idiots on I-5."

Wonderfully logical, and no help to him. It wasn't the dangers of flying that got to him. It was being locked up.

He hadn't asked how she dealt with that. Intellectually he accepted that humans didn't respond to entrapment the way he did. Deep down, though, he worried that if he drew her attention to the fact that they *could not leave*, she'd start noticing it, too, and lose her easy acceptance. She was . . .

Studying him, he found when he glanced at her.

His eyebrows lifted. "Do I have mayonnaise on my chin?"

"I was just wondering what it would be like to miss you."

He kept his face straight. "I didn't realize you were angry with me."

"That's not what I mean. I'm pretty sure you know it isn't what I mean. I'm not upset by the m—"

He cleared his throat before she could use the words, jerking his chin at the seats in front of them. Mate bonds were exceedingly rare. They were also a tightly kept secret, not to be spoken of where out-clan might hear.

"Right," she said. "Anyway, I'm not upset about that anymore. Frustrated sometimes, but not upset. But most couples know what it feels like when the other one's away on a trip or something."

"Hmm." Crossing the country hadn't been on Lily's to-do list today. She'd had to tie a few quick knots in some of the loose ends on her open cases, which was a frustration for her. "I don't think I'd like missing you."

"I don't think I'd like it, either. It's just weird to not know how it feels." She slid her hand into his. Immediately some of his tension eased. The mate bond's gifts, like its drawbacks, trended toward the sudden, the unstoppable, and the physical. "Of course, we were separated when you were in hell—at least part of my memories are about separation. But that wasn't a normal absence."

His lips twitched. "True. I suppose *most* couples experience absence because one of them is in Detroit or Dallas, not the demon realm."

"You're laughing at me."

"Only a little." The plane jittered as they hit a spot of turbulence. He didn't flinch, and was proud of himself for it. "You're getting good at that."

Her eyebrows lifted.

"Distracting me." He lifted her hand to his lips and kissed it. "Thank you. Although there's one means of distraction you haven't tried." He tickled her palm with his tongue and her fingers curled in, cupping her scent there. His *nadia* didn't wear perfume. Nor did she object to his selecting lotions and shampoo for her, so the subtle blend of almond from her skin and apple from her hair pleased him almost as much as the underlying scent that was Lily. He inhaled deeply, dreaming on that scent, his eyelids drifting down.

She cleared her throat. "It's kind of crowded here for that sort of thing."

He smiled agreeably. "It takes ingenuity, but I could ask for one of those skimpy blankets they have. If you put it in your lap—"

"Now who's being distracting?"

"It's working, then?"

She smiled and pulled her hand away, bending to take out the small spiral notebook that went everywhere with her. "I have some questions."

"Naturally." So far, they'd spoken very little of the killings. There had been a great deal to do, and do quickly, so they could leave. Rule had spoken with his father and his guards, and he'd a second, brief conversation with Alex. He'd also had to call the Lu Nuncios of the five other clans involved to assure them he still planned to hold the circle he'd called. Meanwhile, Lily had been busy with calls to the local FBI office, someone in the coven she'd been working with, her Grandmother, her mother, and her boss, Ruben Brooks.

Brooks was one of very few humans who knew about the mate bond. When he recruited Lily for the Unit ten months ago, he'd understood and accepted the limitations the bond imposed on her. So far, he hadn't complained about the way it sometimes affected her job.

Once they boarded the plane, they'd quietly discussed how Rule planned to handle the press. Then they'd worked on their laptops. Rule was playing some risky financial games, trying to get Leidolf on a sounder footing, and had to stay on top of currency fluctuations. Lily had worked on a report—one of those loose ends.

"The killer has been ID'ed as Raymond Cobb," she said. "I have precious damn little on him. You've met him, right?"

"When he came for the *gens subicio*, yes." Every Leidolf lupus had attended that. Exceptions were made only for the dying. Each clan member presented himself to his new Rho and ritually submitted, allowing the mantle to recognize him.

Normally, the submission was the important part; the Rho would have grown up knowing every clan member. Rule had grown up knowing Leidolf as his enemy. He'd needed both the submission and the mantle's recognition.

"Do you remember anything about him?"

"A tall man, grizzled, looks about fifty. Angry, but it seemed an old anger, not directed at me. A bitter man, perhaps."

Her eyebrows shot up. "There were over six hundred lupi at the ceremony. He must have made an impression for you to recall that much about him."

Rule shrugged. "Not really. Ah . . ." Lupi kept many secrets, but only one was the Lady's secret. The mantles. They were not named where out-clan might hear. "You might say that my gut recognized him and helped me remember all those I met that day. I could name each Leidolf clan member now."

"You didn't mention that before."

She was right. He hadn't noticed the omission, but now that she mentioned it . . . "What I carry encourages silence about it. Them. They don't enforce or even suggest secrecy, but they . . ." He fell into vagueness, as he so often did when trying to describe the mantles. "It's more as if silence is the default setting, easily overridden, but I have to notice to override it."

"Hmm."

Two-mantled, some were calling him now. Rule wasn't comfortable with the phrase, which struck him as both pretentious and portentous. Portentous because of a prophecy Etorri spoke of about a two-mantled leader—a prophecy they hadn't shared with the other clans, but that was Etorri for you. Their vague mutterings lent "two-mantled" its portentous aura.

It was also pretentious. Rule didn't carry two full mantles. He held all of Leidolf's mantle, yes, now that the old Rho was dead, but only the heir's portion of Nokolai's. But "one-and-a-portion-mantled" didn't have the same ring, did it?

"You know anything else about Cobb?" Lily asked, tapping her pen on her pad. "Gossip, hearsay, whatever. Anything that might give a clue why he went homicidal at three A.M. this morning."

"I asked Alex about him, of course." Alex Thibideux was Rule's Lu Nuncio in Leidolf, just as he was his father's Lu Nuncio. Their positions weren't identical, however. Normally a Lu Nuncio was both heir and deputy to his Rho, but Alex was not heir. There was no Leidolf heir now, and wouldn't be until Rule's son was old enough to invest with the heir's portion of the mantle.

Not that either Nokolai or Leidolf—or Toby, for that matter—were aware that would happen. "Cobb wasn't his original surname. He changed his name and place of residence about thirty years ago. Ah—he's close to eighty, Alex thinks."

"He's got a sheet under the other name?"

"Not unless you consider being registered by the government and given gado a criminal record."

"Thirty years ago . . . he must have been among the early catches. Was he kept under gado for long?"

"A handful of months. The gado affected him. It may be why he struck me as angry. It didn't drive him insane thirty years later."

"Hmm." Tap, tap, tap. "So what was his original name?"

His legs wanted to move. He didn't let them. He didn't answer, either.

"Rule, I need the name. I need everything about him, including what he did, who he was, before he became Raymond Cobb."

"I don't know it. I didn't ask."

She frowned. "You knew I would."

Yes, he had. That's why he didn't get the name from Alex. "I'm . . ." He spread his hands. "This is difficult. I'm his Rho, but I don't know him. I hold his life, but I don't know him, not the way I know every member of Nokolai. Within the constraints of what is best for the clan, I owe him support—but it's a different clan. It's not Nokolai. I don't have a *feeling* for Leidolf," he said, his voice tightening. "I'm doing my duty, but it's all being worked out in my head. I have no feeling for the clan."

Rule's restlessness mounted. He wanted to move, to pace, to . . . *I'll check on Jeff back in economy in a moment*, he promised himself. Not right away, but soon.

Lily tilted her head, considering. "Not having a feeling for Leidolf is several steps up from hating their guts. That's progress."

His breath gusted out in something less than a laugh. "I suppose it is. It's not enough, but it's progress."

"The, uh . . . what you carry doesn't help with the way you feel about Leidolf?"

"It creates a tie, but . . . this is almost impossible to discuss here."

She unfastened her seat belt, pushed up the armrest, and snuggled up against him.

Automatically he put an arm around her, but he frowned. Lily was seldom willing to cuddle in public. "If you're trying to relax me—"

"I'm trying to get you to talk. Whisper in my ear."

"Hmm." He nuzzled her hair, breathing in the apple scent of her shampoo . . . and beneath that, Lily. Just Lily. The lingering sense of being trapped eased. "You're a smart woman," he murmured.

"True." Her voice was barely above a breath—easy for him to hear when she was this close, impossible for anyone else. "Also a curious one. Tell me why the mantle doesn't help you feel loyal to Leidolf."

"It's not a matter of loyalty, but of a bond, one based on experience. I lack that experience." He knew she worried about the effect the Leidolf mantle had on him. He tried again to reassure her. "My thoughts and feelings are my own. My decisions are my own."

"So you've told me. I guess your Lady wouldn't have infected you with—"

"Infected?" Rule's eyebrows rose.

"Maybe *injected* is a better word. She wouldn't inject her Rhos with something that wanted to take over. That could make more problems than it solved. But it does affect you, even if not in a takeover way."

"*Affect* isn't the word I'd choose." He lowered his voice even more, to a whisper no human other than Lily could hear. "You know that each clan's mantle is different from the others."

She nodded, her head moving against his shoulder in a

pleasant way. "Because they've been carried by different people, right? The mantles are affected by the Rhos who carry them. You said that, though you couldn't tell me how, exactly."

"You might think of it as an imprint. The mantle doesn't change its essence, but it accepts the imprints of all adult clan."

"Is that what happens at the *gens compleo*? The mantle accepts the imprint of the newly adult clan member?"

"More or less. But the imprints of most clan are, ah . . . important, yet insubstantial. The Rho's imprint is more significant." He frowned, hunting words. "In the months since Frey died, there's been a change in some elements of—no, that's the wrong word. *Scent* comes closer. It suggests a subtle and complex mix that may vary with the situation, yet has an underlying integrity."

"That's not clearing things up for me."

He smiled. "You always smell like Lily, even when you change shampoos. Leidolf still smells like Leidolf, regardless of who's Rho."

"But you're the new shampoo."

He grinned. "Yes. Herbal scented, perhaps. The thing is, there remains that which is Leidolf, unaffected by me or any other Rho. My own suspicion—this isn't in the stories, so it's just a guess—is that the differences exist because each mantle was ineradicably stamped by its first holder."

"The first Rho of each clan."

"Yes. And according to the stories, the first Leidolf Rho was high dominant."

She heaved a frustrated sigh. "How come there's still so much stuff I don't know? Okay, I'll bite. What's a high dominant?"

"All Rhos are dominants, of course, but high dominants are different—and rare, fortunately. In my lifetime, I've only known two. A high dominant is incapable of submitting. Circumstances don't matter. He will die rather than submit to another's authority." Even with a mantle enforcing that authority.

"Victor Frey," Lily said flatly.

His eyebrows lifted. "Good guess. Yes, he was a high

dominant, but he's an extreme example of an extreme condition. The other one I knew—Finnen Ap Corwyn—was a friend. Not close, because he was Cynyr and lived in Ireland, but I liked and respected him."

"Past tense?"

As usual, she'd plucked the significant detail from the pile. "Yes. He was killed in Challenge several years ago. I don't know the circumstances; it was a Cynyr matter. But I assume he challenged because he could not submit. His death grieved me, but it didn't surprise me. Or him, I suspect."

"So high dominants aren't always evil bastards, but they are über dominant, right? And that tendency is part of Leidolf's mantle."

"Über dominant sounds like über bully. The inability to submit to others is not the same as requiring everyone to submit to you. But yes, there is a certain approval of dominance built in." In fact, Leidolf had a rep for throwing high dominants more often than other clans. It had been a Leidolf high dominant who founded the youngest clan—Ybirra—back in the 1800s, after leaving his birth clan. Tomás Ybirra had gathered enough strays to begin his own clan, though no one outside Ybirra knew how he'd acquired a mantle to unite them.

"So what you carry inclines you toward dominance, not conciliation."

"Those who become Rho are not by nature conciliatory," he said dryly. "What is it you're trying to ask?"

She waved one hand vaguely. "It's more trying to grasp than ask. I get the feeling dominance means something different to you than it does to me. Never mind. We started this discussion with me asking if what you carry helps you want what's best for Leidolf. If you answered that, I missed it."

"I'm trying to answer. It . . . the more clearly I feel a decision aligns with Leidolf's best interests, the more what I carry aligns with that decision. If I'm unsure, or if I reach a decision more through my head than my heart, then it . . . withholds itself. My decisions for Leidolf are all coming from my head," he said, his throat tight with frustration. "I want to do the right thing more than I want what's best for Leidolf."

"Wanting to do the right thing doesn't count?"

"Not exactly." He shook his head again, unable to put into words what he knew.

"I guess that explains how a scum like Victor Frey was able to use his power as Rho to do commit such major ass-holery. He didn't give a shit about doing the right thing, and he was sure that whatever worked for him had to be best for everyone."

That made his lip twitch. "I suppose it does, yes."

"If the—" Her phone chimed softly from her purse. She straightened. "I'd better get that."

Rule's hearing made it easy to eavesdrop. The caller spoke in a deep bass—and deeply familiar—voice. "Lily, I apologize for disturbing you, but I need to speak with my Lu Nuncio."

She frowned. "Isen, I don't use my in-flight phone privilege for family conversation."

"It's a clan matter."

"Unless it's urgent—"

"I have spoken as your Rho only once before, Lily. I am speaking as your Rho now."

Her frown lingered. Rule didn't literally hold his breath, but it took an effort. Lily had been formally adopted into No-kolai soon after they were joined by the mate bond. Female clan had different rights and responsibilities than male clan, of course; they couldn't Change and couldn't be included in the mantle. But male and female alike had to obey their Rho.

Lily was not good at obeying. "All right," she said at last. "But first, tell me what you know about Raymond Cobb."

"Nothing personally. Benedict says he's strong, but not fast. Competitive. He took second in pole vaulting and placed in shot-put at the last All-Clan."

"Did Benedict say anything about Cobb's control?"

"He considered it good. Please pass the phone to Rule, Lily."

She grimaced, but did so.

Rule took it. "Yes?"

"The Lady has Chosen for your brother a second time."

SIX

~~~~~

THE thunder was all in Rule's head. It was still loud, a crescendo of thought and feeling that held him silent for a long, stunned moment. "But that's . . ." He leaned his head into his hand, rubbing his temples with one spread hand. "No. Clearly it isn't impossible. *Unheard of* doesn't mean impossible. He wouldn't consider this good news, would he?"

"No. He's asked that you not tell Lily."

Automatically he glanced at her. She was making no pretense of not listening, but her human ears would give her only his side of the conversation. "That's difficult for me, but understandable. Tell him I'll delay a day or two, no more. How is he taking it?"

"Hard."

"What about her? Who is she? Does she know yet?"

"We don't know who she is. She doesn't know about the bond. He was in wolf form, marking the boundaries of the wards Friar has set around his property, when he noticed her. He followed without her being aware of him, and confirmed that she was aware of the guards, and avoiding them. She was also aware of the wards."

Rule frowned. "Gifted, then. A reporter?"

"Possibly, but very few of them do that sort of covert investigative work. I'm thinking she's either a personal enemy of Friar's, or she's with a coven or other organization that's threatened by Friar. If such a group exists, I want to know about it—but that's a question for another time. What we know is that she's young, Gifted, about five-seven, rather thin, with a limp. She wears glasses. Her hair is long, curly, of some medium shade."

"He didn't Change and talk to her?"

"In the shock of the moment when the bond hit, Benedict accidentally tripped the ward. It flashed, attracting the guards. To protect her, he drew them away. He circled back once he'd shaken them off and followed her trail to where her car must have been parked. No blood spoor, no sign of a struggle, no scent of the guards, so he believes she left safely."

"He didn't see her car, then." Which meant they had no make, model, or license tag.

"No. But since he refuses to find out who she is," Isen said dryly, "that doesn't bother him."

"Shit. He has to. He can't let . . ." Rule stopped before he gave too much away. The distance restrictions imposed by the bond were unpredictable. Benedict and his new mate might be able to function normally. Or they might pass out at any moment. "That's foolish in the extreme."

"He's not himself. He wanted to go to his cabin. I refused him."

Rule contemplated that for a moment in silence. "You've told the Rhej?"

"I'll hike up to her place when I get off the phone. If she has anything useful to say, I'll let you know."

"It must mean something." He couldn't remember there ever being two Chosens in a single clan, but he supposed it could have happened. But for the same man to be given a Chosen twice . . . Rule couldn't make sense of it. There couldn't be another Lily. It wasn't possible. "When the unheard of happens, it's good to know why."

"We'll need to talk about that, but maybe not on Lily's dime." A thread of humor lightened Isen's voice. "She's glaring at you right now, isn't she?"

Rule looked at her. And smiled in spite of her narrowed eyes. "Not glaring, no. Vexed, though, and wishing for my ears."

"If you're going to talk about me on my phone," Lily said, "put it on speaker."

"I'd better go," Rule said.

"I expect you had. *T'eius ven.*"

"*T'eius ven.*" Rule repeated the blessing automatically, bemused. *Go in her grace*, it meant—the Lady's grace—or *travel in her hunt*. It was a common enough phrase, but Isen seldom closed a conversation with it. Perhaps this second Choosing had him thinking of the Lady. She was certainly one of many thoughts coursing through Rule's mind.

He handed the phone to Lily. "Well?" she said.

"I'm asked—not ordered, but asked—not to speak to you about this matter yet. I agreed to wait a day or two."

Her eyebrows drew down. "Was it urgent?"

"Perhaps not urgent, but important."

"And I'm not allowed to know. Do I get to ask questions?"

"Only if you want to make me extremely uncomfortable."

She considered in silence for a moment, then said, "Okay, back to Cobb. Tell me what else Alex said about him."

"Hmm. Well, he never attended college. Leidolf lacks a fund for higher education—"

"Something you plan to change."

He gave her a quick smile. "I do. Even had such a fund been available, though, Cobb might not have taken advantage of it. He seems to be a highly physical man. He competed in the last three All-Clans, and he tends to choose physical work. Carpentry and logging, in the past. Currently he's a certified personal trainer and owns a small gym in Nashville."

"That's unusual, isn't it? Mostly you guys stay away from human athletics. You're too good, and it's hard to rein yourselves in enough to pass. Unless his customers are all lupi?"

Rule thought of a certain Olympic swimmer and smiled, but said, "Generally that's true, yes. I gather Cobb's clientele is mostly human, but two nights a week he closes the gym to the public. Those are clan-only nights. There are a fair number of Leidolf in Nashville," he added, "who need a physical outlet. He offers that at no charge, and in return the clan exempts him from the *drei*." Rule hadn't known of that arrangement until this morning, but that wasn't Alex's fault. Alex had never been privy to Leidolf's financial matters—which were an unholy mess—and hadn't known about the waived *drei* until he began asking about Cobb. "Also, Cobb had a child, a daughter, but she died about ten years ago. No sons, but he has a *pernato* grandson—"

"Hold on. *Drei* is your head tax. I know that one. But what's *pernato*?"

"One without a lupus father."

"Without . . . oh, you mean like the ones you call throwbacks or lost ones? Only these *pernato* are known to the clan."

"Exactly. A *pernato* is lupus because of recessives in both parents' genes. In this case, Cobb's daughter proved fertile with a young man who is essentially human, but whose maternal grandfather was lupus."

"A *pernato* grandson wouldn't be considered full-blood."

"It's a distinction without a difference. *Pernato* are lupi. Sometimes they're below average in one of our abilities, but there's variance among the full-blood, too."

"Why haven't I heard about *pernato*?"

"*Pernato* clan are rare in Nokolai. Leidolf is known for throwing them more often than most. It's one reason they're the largest clan."

"Plus they have a habit of absorbing smaller clans, though I don't see how the—no, I'll ask that later. This gym Cobb owns. Do you know its name and address?"

"I don't have the address. It's called Cobb's Gym."

"Not an imaginative guy," she said, making another note. "You say his clientele is human except for those two nights a week. That suggests he's comfortable being around a lot of humans a lot of the time, even training them."

"It does."

"It doesn't suggest someone balanced on an unholy edge, teetering toward multiple homicide."

Rule considered what to say. How much to say. He snuggled her close so he could speak very softly. "You read about the fury in that history of the clans the Rhej gave you. You asked me about it."

"You're talking about the berserker thing. One of the clans—I don't remember the name—had a bad rep with the others because its members fell 'into the fury' too often. This was a long time ago, well before the Purge, and there wasn't a lot of communication between the clans, so the Nokolai guy who wrote the history didn't know the details, but— wait, stop, I'm sidetracking. Basically, you said, the fury is when a lupus goes berserker in battle."

"That's the short version. You need a longer one to understand what may have happened."

"I'm listening."

"Pack wolves and lone wolves fall into the fury easily— that's one reason they're so dangerous." Pack wolves were clanless wolves who'd gathered in a small pack—something almost unheard of these days, since the clans allowed very few lone wolves. Lacking a mantle, they were susceptible to the fury. "Clan wolves are more protected, but in battle we can succumb, too, if we're fighting two-footed and aren't trained to avoid it."

Her eyebrows lifted. "Not when you're wolf?"

"No. The fury is . . ." He spread his hands. "The fury is of the wolf, but the wolf doesn't experience the fury. You might call it an unhappy blending of the two states arising from the way the man experiences the wolf during battle. It's born of rage, but it isn't rage. Just as anger may be born of fear, but isn't fear."

Her brow pleated in concentration. "You think it's a truly separate experience. Not some composite of other emotions, but an emotional state humans don't have."

He shrugged. "The closest analogue in humans seems to be the berserker state, which is why I explained it that way before. The fury is raw and red and dangerous. In its grip, pain has no meaning. We lose all intentions but one: to kill our enemies. And everyone within sight or scent of us is the enemy."

She tipped her head. "You've experienced it."

"As part of my training, yes. I was fourteen." He smiled ruefully. "The fury is uncommon in adults, but not in adolescents—who are, as the saying goes, all balls and no brain. We have to experience it to learn how to avoid it, so it's triggered in us intentionally, in a controlled situation."

"What happened?"

"I thought I was in a normal practice bout, but Benedict had arranged for two opponents to attack me from behind quite . . . unexpectedly." At fourteen, he hadn't yet attained *certa*, the optimal battle state, which rendered the fury impossible. Back then, no one knew if he would. Many lupi didn't, so they had to learn other ways to avoid the fury. By Changing, for example. You couldn't fall into fury if you were wolf.

"Is an unexpected attack a trigger?"

"Triggers vary, but Benedict knew me well enough to have a good idea of what would work with me. Ah . . . let's just say he was right. My opponents were well-trained adults, of course," he added. "Not other youngsters. They knew what to expect, so the moment they smelled it on me, they got out of the way and Benedict pinned me until it passed. Then he, ah, spoke firmly to me."

"Firmly. I'll bet. Does it pass quickly, then?"

"It depends on the situation. Benedict pinned me so I couldn't fight. Fighting feeds it."

"You think that's what happened to Cobb. He fell into the fury."

"If the information we have about what happened is correct, I have no other explanation. He didn't Change, so he wasn't beast-lost. He seems to have had no reason to kill, much less to do it so publicly."

"Lupi don't just go nuts sometimes?"

"Define 'go nuts.' We aren't subject to psychoses, hallucinations, or other physically based forms of insanity."

"But you are—sometimes, in some situations, for some individuals—subject to the fury. Something triggered it in Cobb. A threat?"

"I don't know. Adults don't react like adolescents, except . . ." He shifted his legs restlessly. "Some lupi, like some humans, have what you might call anger issues. Those who carry habitual anger, if they also have trouble with control, might slip into *furo* without being engaged in actual battle. Such clan are usually brought to live at or near Clanhome."

"Nokolai does this, too? They bring the angry ones to Clanhome?"

He smiled. "If you're worrying that the lupi you meet at Clanhome are dangerous, don't. When such clan have more contact with—I will say with their Rho"—because he couldn't mention the mantle—"they're calmer, more able to control themselves."

She looked down at her notebook, but obviously was consulting her thoughts, not the few things she'd written there. When she looked up at him again, her expression was carefully neutral. "You aren't living at Leidolf Clanhome."

"No." And it gnawed at him. That he was doing the best he could didn't mean it was enough. A Rho should live among his clan. They needed the sight and smell of him. They didn't have to like him—which was just as well, because many Leidolf couldn't stand him. They still needed him.

"But what you carry doesn't depend on proximity. The clan still feels it, even when you're on the other side of the country."

"In the most important sense, yes. But I can't use it directly from a distance, plus there's a psychological need, especially for those whose control isn't great. They need to know someone can control them, if necessary."

Her eyebrows lifted. "They find that calming?"

"I understand that you wouldn't. But yes, they do."

Rule and Lily had been flying to North Carolina, where Leidolf Clanhome was located, about once a month. It was all he could do . . . and it wasn't enough. "Alex has been keeping an eye on those within Leidolf who have trouble with control. Cobb wasn't among them. He's an angry man, but his control has been excellent."

"Until now, and according to Alex."

"Yes." And Alex was shaken by what he considered his failure.

"Will you be able to tell if Cobb was in fury when he attacked? Will you smell it on him the way Benedict smelled it on you?"

"Not so many hours after the fact, no. But he'll tell me

what happened. If he fell into the fury, he'll know, and he'll tell me."

Three people dead, ten injured . . . and it wouldn't have happened if Cobb's Rho had known him, understood him, and been watching for the signs of an unstable anger. The clan experienced the mantle whether Rule was among them or not, but some needed that experience reinforced in a way only frequent contact could provide.

If Raymond Cobb had indeed fallen into the fury, it was as much Rule's fault as Cobb's.

Restlessness poured through him like a tide of ants. His legs twitched with the need to *move*. But this time he recognized what he was trying to run from.

You have to turn and face it. You always have to turn and face it, no matter how keen the claws or how bloody the teeth. And sooner works better than later. He spoke very low. "Tell me about them. The victims. The ones he killed and the ones he hurt."

"I don't know much." Lily studied him. She knew something was moving inside him, even if she couldn't sense the shape of it. "The Nashville PD is playing coy, not cooperating worth a damn. But the two men killed were both white, one middle-aged, the other a lot younger. The woman—"

"Woman?" Rule's head jerked. "He killed a woman?"

"Four of the victims were female. One was killed outright. The other three were among the injured. I don't have details on them specifically, but three of the ten people injured are in critical condition."

"He attacked three women?" Disbelief sharpened his voice. Carefully he brought it back down. The people around them didn't need to hear this. "You didn't tell me that. Alex didn't, either. He didn't say there were female victims." Alex must not know. He wouldn't have left that out.

The pleat was back in Lily's brow. "I know that's hard for you to accept. Your people are big on not harming women."

"It's deeper than that. Women are to be protected, just like—"

"If you say 'children,' I'll have to hit you."

His grin flickered. "I was going to say, like you automatically protect civilians."

"Good save."

"It's not training and custom, Lily. Or not just that. In the fury, we lose track of who's friend, who's foe. Instinct itself goes awry, but it's not revoked. For that rage to focus on women does not make *sense*."

"Men turn their rage on women all too often."

"Not lupi. And especially not in the fury. The fury is a battle state. I could see Cobb falling into it if he saw a woman being threatened or harmed. He shouldn't, but it's possible. But if he were so twisted he could see women as *enemy*, Alex would have noticed. He would have been watching the man and he would have warned me about him."

"Alex is Leidolf. He might not see what you would."

He shook his head. "I despise the way Leidolf tries to subjugate their women, but they don't beat them. It's . . . it's like the difference between intentionally frightening a child to correct him and eating one. The first is misguided. The second is insane. A lupus who is so distorted he could see women—not just one particular woman, but women in general—as his enemy . . . Alex would have noticed. Everyone would have noticed."

She didn't respond.

He grimaced. "You don't accept that."

"People miss the craziness in their neighbors and co-workers all the time."

Frustration balled up his gut. How could she have lived with him for so long and not understand? "We don't hurt women."

"What about clanless wolves? They, ah—they don't have the same stability."

This was hard to explain without referring to the mantle. "A clanless wolf can see humans of either sex as prey when he's four-footed. On four feet or two, he'd probably see human males as rival predators to be chased off, killed, or avoided. Pack wolves are more likely to chase or kill; lone wolves prefer to avoid. But neither a pack wolf nor a lone wolf would see women as competing predators. And none of that applies to Cobb. He wasn't beast-lost or clanless."

"What if a woman was attacking him, trying to stop him? Wouldn't that put her in the enemy category?"

"Even if that's what happened, it wouldn't generalize. He wouldn't go on to attack other women."

"You know what a fight is like. People get hurt even if they aren't the target."

"If Cobb accidentally hurt a woman because he didn't see her, perhaps . . . but three women? No. That's not accident. And it isn't possible."

"Yet he did it."

"Not because of the fury."

"What, then?" she demanded. "What else could it be?"

"I have no idea."

SEVEN

~

NASHVILLE had a different take on September than San Diego: hotter and wetter. At six ten local time, their plane was bumping its way through heavy cloud cover as it approached the airport. The pilot informed them it was eighty-two degrees and raining in Nashville.

Lily put up her laptop. She'd spent the last hour scanning online news sources for information about the shooting without learning much, except that the talking heads were having a great time speculating in shocked tones. She still didn't have an official report, but she'd sicced Ida, Ruben's secretary, on the local cops, so she expected to get one soon.

Rule was pacing. He'd found an excellent excuse for it, one Lily estimated to be about five months old. And teething.

Rule loved babies. They usually loved him right back. This one, a little baldy with chocolate-kiss eyes and dusky skin, had been screaming his head off back in economy. Rule—who'd been getting seriously restless—had decided to ask his mother if he could try to settle the boy.

Lily had been sure the woman wouldn't hand her baby over to some strange man. She'd been wrong. The baby was sound asleep now, crumpled into a terrycloth lump on Rule's chest, drooling happily onto the fine Egyptian cotton of his shirt. Rule cradled him there in two spread hands, humming quietly as he headed back down the aisle.

It made Lily's chest ache. Some of that ache was for Rule, who would love to have a baby of his own again. He'd missed out on so much with Toby. But some of the ache was about her.

She didn't know what to think about that. She didn't want a baby . . . did she? Not now, certainly. How could she do her job if she had a tiny little human depending on her? Besides, she'd never been one to dream over babies the way some women did. Although she'd always assumed that one day . . .

One day might never come. Lupi weren't very fertile.

Cullen thought that might change now that the level of ambient magic was increasing, but even if he was right, the increase was gradual. Even if he was right, there was no guarantee things would change enough, soon enough.

One of the flight attendants stopped Rule. Lily didn't hear what the woman said, but it was probably a request that he take his seat. The seat belt lights had flashed on.

Rule answered with a smile. The woman—who was in her late forties, at a guess—smiled back shyly. That was better than slipping him her phone number, Lily supposed. Babies weren't the only ones who adored Rule.

Her phone chimed the opening bars to "The Star Spangled Banner" as Rule passed their seats, no doubt returning the sleeping charmer to his mom. Lily answered. It turned out to be Ida, rather than Ruben himself, letting her know that a preliminary police report was in her e-mail in-box; they were booked into the Doubletree Hotel downtown; and they'd be met at the airport by an Agent Sjorensen from the local office.

Lily disconnected, ignoring the scowl of the pudgy man across the aisle. The FAA gave Unit agents a pass on the no-cell-phones rule. That was part politics, part practicality, because almost all Unit agents were Gifted.

Post-Turning, airlines used routes that didn't directly overfly nodes, but ambient magic levels were rising even away from nodes, and magic was not good for tech. They'd discovered that having one or more Gifted aboard a plane meant a significant drop in the number of instrument malfunctions. The theory was that the Gifted unconsciously soaked up enough juice to make a difference.

The theory was true in her case. Lily had found out the hard way that she not only sopped up stray magic the way dragons did—though on a much lesser scale—but she could do it intentionally. One-on-one.

Twice now, she'd drained another's magic.

The first time had been an accident. A killer had used her Earth Gift to trigger an earthquake. Lily had stopped her without realizing what she'd done, much less how. Afterward, the woman's Gift had been gone, but Lily had assumed she'd burnt out.

The second time Lily had done it very much on purpose. If she hadn't acted, she'd have died, along with most of the people she loved. And at the very least, Southern California would have descended into unremitting nightmare so that an out-realm being could feast on human fear.

No regrets there. Nightmares sometimes—hello, Helen, back again?—but no regrets. Still, Lily wasn't reconciled to everything she'd learned about herself recently. Turned out her Gift wasn't a human ability. Like the mindspeech she was so far flunking, it came from another aspect of her heritage, one she hadn't known about until last month.

The dragon aspect.

Sam did not want her calling him Grandfather—and thank God for that—but in terms of magical ancestry rather than DNA, that's what he was.

Lily drummed her fingers. Why did things have to keep changing? There'd been so much of that this past year. Things she'd always known about herself had turned slippery. Not quite false, but not quite true, either.

Did she want a baby? Yes, she admitted, looking out the small, thick window obscured by cloud. Or no, not really, at least not now. Or maybe that was a yes, however heavily qualified. But it wasn't really up to her, was it?

Rule slid into the seat beside hers. "Seems to be raining in Nashville," he observed, pulling his seat belt around him.

"Seems to be. You're relaxed. Jiggling a screaming baby calms you?"

"Cute little bugger, isn't he?"

"Were you ever a tender?" That's what lupi called those of the clan, male and female, who tended children at Clanhome. There were a few permanent tenders, but most only worked for a year or two to give everyone a chance at it. Tending was a sought-after position.

"For a while in my late twenties, yes." He smiled reminiscently. "I had four months with the babies and three with preteens. Later I had a brief stint tending the toddlers—that's real work." But his face said the memory was pleasant.

"You weren't Lu Nuncio yet?"

He shook his head. "Once I was named, I had other duties."

She hesitated. "Rule, back when we met, you told me that a Lu Nuncio had to prove himself through blood, combat, and fertility. I wasn't clan then, so you couldn't mention the—uh, the thing I can't mention here." The mantle, that is. Only those connected by blood to the Rho could carry it, so that was the "blood" component. Combat meant exactly what it sounded like, but fertility . . . "You were named Lu Nuncio well before Toby was born."

His expression faltered, flattened. After a moment he said, "A lady I was with when I was thirty became pregnant. The child was mine. She miscarried, but technically, my fertility had been proven."

Lily took his hand. She said nothing, asked none of the questions that pushed at her. The miscarriage had happened over twenty years ago, but his pain was still palpable.

His grip tightened on hers, then relaxed. "Her name was Sarah. She miscarried in the fourth month."

Cautiously Lily ventured a question. "No one doubted your word about it? I mean, you knew it was your baby, but there was no proof."

His eyebrows lifted. "It wouldn't occur to anyone to doubt me. It's . . . all but inconceivable that any of us might lie about siring a child. Even if I had, however, I couldn't lie successfully to my Rho." He stroked the side of her hand with his thumb. "I should have told you about this earlier."

Probably. When he told her Toby was his only child and would probably always be his only child—that would have been a good time. But . . . "You didn't keep it from me on purpose."

He slid her a glance. "I only learned last month about a man you once loved."

She smiled. "I didn't keep it from you on purpose."

He squeezed her hand.

The captain came on the intercom to tell them they'd be landing shortly, then a stewardess began announcing gates for those who had a connecting flight.

"Rule . . ."

"Yes?"

"Does it ever get easier? I mean . . ." She groped for words. Rule might look thirty, but he'd turn fifty-five in a couple of months. He ought to know stuff she didn't. "Do you ever get your feet planted solidly enough that you don't lose your balance when something new turns up? Something you didn't know about yourself until—pow! There it is, right in your face."

He looked at her a moment, his eyes dark and serious. Then he smiled, raised her hand to his lips, and kissed it. "No."

AGENT Sjorensen met them inside the security perimeter. She had icy blond hair, red-framed glasses, and creamy skin; looked about twenty, but had to be older. Good jacket. Her skirt was too long for her height—which was short, about the same as Lily's—and she wouldn't be able to run in those heels.

But they were great heels. Red patent leather peep-toes.

Her mouth was a pink cupid's bow. Her eyes were big and blue. She compensated for these professional drawbacks with a short, no-nonsense hairstyle and a ban on smiling. "Special Agent Yu." She nodded briskly, but didn't offer to shake hands. "And you're Rule Turner."

"I am, yes." Rule seemed to be trying to hide amusement.

"And these are—?" She gestured at LeBron and Jeff, who were standing behind Rule.

"LeBron Hastings and Jeffrey Lane," Lily said. "They're

Rule's bodyguards. It's a clan thing." She held out a hand. "You're Agent Sjorensen, I take it. First name Anna?"

The woman's pale cheeks flushed. "Yes, of course. I should have . . ." She noticed Lily's hand and belatedly took it.

Oh, my. Lily had only touched that sort of magic once, but that once had been memorable. Lily released Sjorensen's hand.

"You pronounced my name correctly. People mostly don't, since my grandfather didn't Anglicize the spelling."

Lily made a mental note to discuss what she'd learned from that handshake when she and Sjorensen were alone. The woman deserved privacy for that discussion. "I had a Swedish roommate one semester. It drove her nuts when people put a hard *j* in her name instead of *y*. Jeff and LeBron won't be going with us—I just wanted you to be aware of them." As she spoke Rule nodded to the guards, and they moved off. The two of them would pick up the luggage and meet them at the hotel.

"I see." Clearly, she didn't. "I've been told to put myself at your disposal while you're here, Special Agent."

"I appreciate it. We'll head to the hospital first. I understand Cobb is at Vanderbilt?"

"Yes, it's the one medical facility with a containment room considered sufficient for a lupus prisoner." She darted a glance at Rule. "Not that he's in any shape to fight his way out, but I understand your people heal quickly."

"We do. Do you know what his injuries are?"

"He took a bullet in the chest. That's all I know." She switched back to Lily quickly. "Do you need to stop for your luggage?"

"No, the guards will get it." Was Sjorensen uncomfortable talking to Rule because he was a civilian, or because he was a lupus?

Sjorensen's lip curled, but whatever it was she disapproved, she kept her commentary silent. "My car's this way." She turned, her heels clicking as she set off down the concourse.

Lily and Rule exchanged a glance. Neither of them cared

to trail after the young woman. Lily caught up with her on her left side; Rule bracketed her on the right. She didn't look at either of them.

Lily wondered what she smelled like to Rule—angry? Frightened? "I scanned the police report while we were landing. Cobb took two bullets from a hunting rifle. One passed through, puncturing his lung on the way. The other bullet lodged somewhere unspecified. There's nothing about what treatment he received, which is a concern." Lupi couldn't be put under anesthetic, so operating on them was almost impossible without a healer who could hold them in sleep.

The Leidolf Rhej was such a healer. Rule had sent for her, but she hadn't been able to leave right away. She had a baby to deliver.

Agent Sjorensen frowned. "You got the Nashville PD to cough up a report already?"

"It's been about fifteen hours since the incident occurred. That isn't exactly speedy, and I had to pull out the big guns to get it."

"You won't find local law enforcement eager to cooperate. There's some history between our office and them which, uh . . . to put it bluntly, they don't like us. And you don't exactly have clear jurisdiction." She darted a glance at Lily. "Frankly, I'm not sure why you're here."

"In part, to determine jurisdiction. Like you said, it's a muddle. If Cobb had Changed, he could be charged with using magic to commit felony murder. Since he didn't . . ." She shrugged. "A muddle. Legally, though, I get to poke my nose anywhere I want, if I think it might be a case for the Unit. According to the report, the police don't have a confession."

Sjorensen's carefully darkened eyebrows climbed. "They don't need one. They've got plenty of witnesses."

"A confession always helps. That's another reason I'm here."

"What could—oh, crap." She stopped. Just beyond the security checkpoint—right beside a small stage, unpopulated at the moment, in front of the Ernest Tubb Record Shop—people with cameras and people with mikes peered down the concourse. "You think they're waiting for us?"

"Bet on it," Lily said grimly. "How did they know my arrival time? They shouldn't even know I was coming, much less when I'd get here."

Sjorensen glared at the reporters. "I don't know. I'm guessing Chief Grissim arranged a leak, but I don't actually know that."

Lily looked past Sjorensen to find catch Rule's eye. "What do you think?"

"Now's as good as later for me. I can get a cab to the hospital. That's where you're going?"

"Yeah. Hang on a minute." She dug into the oversize yellow shoulder bag she'd started carrying when they traveled. It held enough to double as an overnight case. "Here." She handed him three strips of beef jerky.

He smiled ruefully and tucked them in his jacket's inside pocket, then studied the small mob of news critters, who'd seen them and were jostling for position. "The blonde with the excellent elbow work is with CNN, but I can't remember her name."

"Emily Hanks," Sjorensen said. "The one with the crew cut is Kyle Rogers with the NBC affiliate here. The other—the black guy—he's with FOX. Armand something-or-other."

"Here's the deal," Lily told Sjorensen. "You and I bull on through—strictly 'no comment.' Rule will distract them."

Sjorensen shot Rule a suspicious look. "He can't speak for the FBI, so why would they talk to him?"

Rule smiled blandly. "I think I can retain their interest. I'll be speaking for Leidolf."

EIGHT

"So what's Leidolf?" Anna Sjorensen asked as they approached the exit.

The reporters had mobbed them for about ten seconds. Rule was clearly willing to give them sound bites, and Lily clearly wasn't. Print reporters might have stuck to her anyway, but the TV folks needed good visuals and they needed them fast.

"A lupus clan. Rule's their new Rho. He'll be telling the piranhas of the press about that." Lily refused to worry on that score. Rule had decided he would have to out Leidolf to the press. How else could he explain his presence? He'd warned Alex, who was spreading the word to as many of the clan as he could reach quickly.

There would be repercussions. Some in Leidolf were bitterly opposed to their clan's going public. Even those who were okay with it were likely to be unhappy. This wasn't exactly an ideal way to make the big reveal. People were going to associate Leidolf with a crazy killer, and even someone as good at spin as Rule would have trouble separating—

"He's what?" Sjorensen said.

Lily dragged her mind away from what she was *not* worrying about. "Their Rho. The leader of the clan."

"I thought his father was the . . . oh, no. You mean his father—"

"No, no. Isen's fine and is still the Nokolai Rho. Leidolf is a different clan." She glanced at Sjorensen. "You know that lupi are divided into clans, right?"

"Of course." She was chilly, affronted. "They're like tribes."

"Close enough. The Navajo aren't the same as the Apache or the Cherokee, and they don't share a chief. Lupi clans differ, too, and each has its own Rho."

"Does that mean Mr. Turner changed clans?"

The prim phrasing made Lily smile. "No, he's both Nokolai and Leidolf. It's complicated." Beyond the glass lay a lot of wet cement, wet cars, and wet air. Lily was ready, though. She'd spent enough time on the dawn side of the continent to know that water fell from the sky here a lot.

The doors opened automatically, bathing them in warm, damp air and exhaust fumes. The traffic lanes they needed to cross were roofed by a wide overpass of some sort, but Lily went ahead and dug her umbrella out of her purse.

Sjorensen raised one eyebrow. "Prepared for anything, aren't you?"

Lily was getting tired of all the attitude. "If I'd wanted to be prepared for anything, I'd have brought something more than my SIG. It takes a lot more firepower to put down a demon. An AK-47, at a minimum."

"But you're not—we aren't—this case isn't connected to demons."

"Not as far as we know," Lily agreed, "which is why I only brought a 9mm." Maybe that was a mistake. Demons didn't call ahead to see if it was a good time. The last time she fought one, Rule had been sliced by poisoned claws and a young man had bled out on the pavement.

But . . . no. She shook her head at herself. Barring another power wind to help one cross, demons could only arrive if summoned, and true summonings were thank-God rare. "My SIG should be enough for this trip. What do you carry?"

Sjorensen stepped out into the traffic lanes. "A 9mm Baby Eagle. I like the grip, and it's under two pounds."

"It's a subcompact, right? How many rounds?"

"Ten. And it may be small, but it's got stopping power."

It probably lacked accuracy, though. The barrel on a sub-compact was short. "I'm happy with my SIG, but your Baby Eagle sounds like a good clutch piece. I've got a little .22 for that, but it lacks punch."

"If you're here long enough, I'd be glad to let you try it at the range." A tentative smile. "Not that many weapons fit my hand. I'm guessing you have the same problem?"

"Too true. And shoulder holsters—it's hard to find one that fits both me and my weapon. I gave up and had one custom-made."

As they left the protection of the overpass, rain fell in a weepy, genteel sort of shower that made Lily feel as if she should offer the sky a handkerchief. She opened her umbrella without eliciting any snide comments. Gun talk carried them all the way to Sjorensen's car, a white sedan that looked a whole lot like the one Lily drove.

The woman was pleasant enough now. Maybe she'd been nervous earlier. She must be pretty brand-spanking new, after all. Probably not long out of Quantico.

Lily decided to try some straight female bonding. "Couldn't help noticing your shoes," she said as she buckled up. "They're gorgeous. I hope all the wet didn't hurt them."

"Thanks." She flashed Lily a second smile and started the car. "They were a major indulgence, so I keep them treated with water repellent."

"They're worth the effort. You couldn't run in them, though."

Sjorensen grimaced as she backed out of the space. "I'm not likely to need to chase down a perp, not with what they've got me doing. I made the mistake of minoring in accounting, so—" The trill came from her purse, not Lily's. "Um. That's this guy I'm seeing. I left him a message canceling our date. Would you mind if I take it?"

And that, Lily thought, accounted for the rest of the young woman's initial attitude. Canceling a date to play chauffeur could spoil anyone's day. "No problem."

Lily took her notebook out of her purse and began glancing through her notes while Sjorensen spoke in a low voice on her phone, steering with one hand as she eased into the line of cars exiting the parking area.

Cobb had been at a postgame party, a cookout, with the game being college football. There'd been nearly a hundred people present. The police report she'd read was skimpy, but it included preliminary statements from a few witnesses. Seems there'd been an argument about one of the plays, or maybe about the coach. Witnesses said it was the usual sort of armchair quarterbacking, with opinions flying, but no fists—until Cobb suddenly exploded. Two of the witnesses used the same phrase to describe it: "He just blew up."

Rule was convinced Cobb couldn't have been in the fury. Lily had to admit it was hard to see why a man who'd managed to keep his control for seventy-odd years turned homicidal when someone disagreed with his postgame analysis. But if not the fury, then what?

Sjorensen put her phone up and apologized again for the personal intrusion.

"It can be a real stretch, fitting in a personal life around the job," Lily said agreeably. It occurred to her that she and Sjorensen were alone. She'd probably better bring up what she'd learned when they shook hands. Might not get another chance. "I need to ask you something. Have you had training for your Gift?"

"What? What are you talking about?"

"You've got a minor patterning Gift. Have you had training?"

Sjorensen turned icicle. "I don't know what kind of game you're playing. I'm not Gifted."

"I'm afraid you're wrong about that. Patterning is a rare Gift, so you might not have heard of it."

"I haven't."

"And it doesn't always manifest in an obvious way. Do you sometimes have runs of extremely good luck? Or extremely bad? Bizarre coincidences?"

"I don't—" Her breath hitched, quick and telling. "I don't believe you came to Nashville to discuss my luck, or lack of it."

"No, but you don't know anything about the case, so we might as well get this covered. Patterning can be a dangerous Gift if you don't learn how to use it—and how to avoid tapping into it. Otherwise, a bad mood can turn into anything from a flat tire to a five-car pileup." The young woman's face was a mix of confusion and suspicion. "Maybe I shouldn't have said anything. I usually don't, but patterning's potentially a—"

"I was tested," Sjorensen blurted out. "Before I left Quantico, I was tested. I know you're a sensitive, but you're wrong about me."

Lily's eyebrows rose. Testing for Gifts was not standard practice at Quantico. It probably should be, but there weren't enough qualified testers. "You know why you were picked to be tested?"

She shrugged. "They never told me. They don't test everyone, so I thought maybe . . . but they didn't find anything. No magic at all."

"That was before the Turning."

"Well—yeah. It was just before I graduated, so that would be about six months before the Turning hit."

"You do know that some people had a Gift wake up then, right? The theory is that they had a nascent or potential Gift, but until then lacked the magic to kick-start it. The power storms changed that."

"I thought . . . I thought that was urban legend. They—this show I watched—they debunked it. And I haven't been starting fires or anything else weird." She frowned. "Everyone gets flat tires sometimes."

"I don't know what show you watched, but 'they' were wrong. As for doing anything weird . . ." Lily tipped her head, considering the way Sjorensen had been singled out for testing. "Did you ever consider joining the Unit?"

Big blue eyes blinked several times. "I did. I do," she corrected herself firmly. "I know there are a few in the Unit who aren't Gifted, so it's possible. Though now you say I am Gifted, so I . . ." Confusion overtook her.

"Uh-huh. And you just happened to be assigned to babysit someone who could tell you that yes, you do have a Gift. Someone who works in the Unit. You don't call that weird?"

Sjorensen's jaw dropped. Alarm widened her eyes. "But I got the assignment because Matt came down with a stomach bug. He was supposed to pick you up, not me, but he . . . are you saying I made him get sick?"

"In a roundabout way, yes, that's likely." Lily was brisk. Sjorensen had to understand the possible consequences of her Gift. "As I understand it, there had to be a chance he'd get sick anyway. You're not very powerful, so there was probably a good chance of it. Your Gift bumped it up from 'a good chance' to actually happening. That's why you have to be trained. I'll call Ruben."

"What? What? You mean Ruben Brooks? You're going to call him about me?"

"He'll want to know." The glow on the young woman's face made Lily realize she'd raised hopes. "This isn't a recruitment or anything. I can't recommend you—I don't know you. But you need that Gift trained."

Sjorensen nodded briskly. She wasn't smiling—but she was still glowing, dammit. Better follow through. Lily dug out her phone and called her boss. She used the office number, not his personal line. He'd probably gone home by now, but she could leave a message . . .

"Ida Rheinhart," a familiar, polished-steel voice said.

"Ida, this is Lily Yu. I—"

"Lily. You were on my list to call. I have some unfortunate news. Ruben had a heart attack approximately two hours ago. He's in intensive care."

NINE

RULE wondered which of his many sins in this life or any other caused him to have to spend so damned much time in hospitals. They were not a comfortable place for a lupus, stinking as they did of sickness and injury.

"This your first time in Nashville?" the cabbie asked.

"No, but it's been a few years." He was no stripling to lose control, he reminded himself. Nor did his wolf see humans as prey, but the smell of blood was . . . stimulating. And he hadn't eaten.

"Guess you're not here for fun, seeing as how you're headed straight for Vandy," the driver announced cheerfully.

"Not really, no." Rule retrieved one of the strips of jerky and smiled faintly. Lily had planned ahead better than he had. Jerky wouldn't fill him, but it would help.

"Even if you can't make it to the Opry, maybe you can check out the General Jackson's Showboat. Man's got to eat, after all, and it's—hey, would you look at that!" the driver exclaimed as he turned onto Medical Center Drive. "Somebody's picketing the damned hospital. Whatcha think that's about?"

"Have you heard of Humans First?" Thanks to the questions at his impromptu press conference, Rule already knew about the protesters ranged outside the oldest part of the medical complex. They were a wet, lonely little group at the moment. The TV cameras had already been and gone, getting a clip for the late news, and no one else seemed to be paying attention. But that clip would air, and probably nationally.

"They those folks that want to lock up all the weers?"

"Something like that," Rule said dryly.

"Well, that's kinda extreme, ain't it? Though I can't see why the government stopped registering them. Seems to me that worked pretty well. They couldn't turn furry, so they didn't cause any trouble."

"Aside from the legal issues, there was a problem with the drug they used. It drove lupi insane."

"No kidding? I thought it was supposed to stop them from going nuts."

"Government doesn't always get it right, does it?"

"You got that for damned sure right. Say, have you heard the one about the werewolf, the rabbi, and the priest?"

Rule listened and laughed at the punch line as they passed the protesters. The man finished just as they pulled up at awning over the entrance to the tower that held Cobb's room. Rule checked the cabby's license, making a note of his name, as he took out his wallet. "Do you mind if I steal that joke, Jake?"

"Hey, spread it around. Everyone needs a laugh, right?"

"Right. You might want to catch Jon Stewart's show next Wednesday." Rule passed the man a twenty for a ten-dollar fare. "If I get a chance, I'm going to use your joke. If so, I'll mention you."

"You're what? You mean you're gonna be on Stewart's show?"

Rule smiled as he stepped out into the heavy drizzle. "Watch it and see." He closed the door.

It was a small thing, maybe, but Rule was betting Jake would tell that story often to friends, family, and future fares—about how he'd had "that weer prince" in his cab and didn't know it—and that Rule was a good sport and used *his* joke on Stewart's show. He'd probably tell them the joke, too. And a few of those people would begin to think lupi were more like them than unlike. That was Rule's job: making his people seem less alien and scary.

Cobb's killing spree was going to make that job a lot harder.

So would Humans First. At least, they were damn sure trying.

Rule had gotten a good look at the protesters as they drove by. A small but determined group, clearly, to be out in this weather—four men and two women, all white, mostly middle-aged. One of the women was clearly younger. She was pregnant. Between them they carried four signs. One read, HOSPITALS R 4 HUMANS; two others said, SUPPORT PEOPLE. PUT HUMANITY FIRST; and the pregnant woman held a sign with a single capitalized word in ragged red paint: UNCLEAN.

Good staging, Rule thought as he entered the hospital's incongruously modern tower. Visually coupling that word with fertility tugged at sexual, racial, and religious fears. And Friar's movement was all about fear.

That hadn't been his first thought. In the first instant of seeing her with that sign, he'd wanted to take it away, to carry it for her or get someone else carry it. No doubt she'd have spit on him if he'd tried, and he supposed she considered herself his enemy. But she was a life-bearer. She shouldn't carry heavy things.

Lily knew his people were protective of women, yet she didn't, not really. She didn't understand how deep it went.

Cobb had attacked *women*.

Rule was surprised to see the pretty young agent waiting for him near the information desk. Her heels clicked on the linoleum as she approached. "Special Agent Yu asked me to wait for you," she said crisply. "This place is a bit of a warren. I'll escort you to Cobb's room."

"Thank you," he said gravely. Anna Sjorensen was earnest as only the young can be, and trying so hard to be tough. Her attraction to him embarrassed her, especially since she wanted badly to impress Lily. Wanted, he suspected, to be just like Lily.

He doubted that Lily was aware of this. She could be

oblivious to her effect on others. As they set off down a short hall he asked, "Is Lily already with Cobb?"

"She wanted to wait for you. Ah . . . he's awake and uncooperative, I'm told, and is refusing medical treatment. Special Agent Yu was discussing that with his doctor when I came down here to wait for you. She believes you can persuade him to cooperate. You would be able to restrain him, I take it?"

"If necessary, yes." They'd reached a stairwell. He'd expected either this or an elevator; his sense of Lily's location told him she was belowground. "Though I trust he'll respond to my presence and not need to be restrained."

Ann headed down the stairs in front of him. "She said you're the, uh, Rho of Cobb's clan."

"That's right. Did you find out more about his condition?"

"They dug out the lodged bullet while he was unconscious. He had a collapsed lung, but apparently he healed that. They're more concerned about the other bullet's path, which includes damage to his colon."

"Are the local police cooperating now?"

"They don't have much choice. The Special Agent is Unit Twelve. Though the lieutenant—that's Lieutenant Matthews—and Agent Yu argued about something. It was very polite, but they were clearly not agreeing. Then he left."

"You don't know the nature of their disagreement?"

"I couldn't hear." That was regret, surely, in her voice. "He took her aside for the discussion. Agent Yu wanted me to tell you something else."

"Oh?"

"I guess you know who Ruben Brooks is? He had a heart attack earlier today."

"What?" Automatically he gripped her shoulder, halting her. "Pardon me," he said when she scowled up at him over that shoulder. He released her. "Is Ruben alive? Do you know if he's alive?"

"He was when Special Agent Yu called." Her voice was stiff. Since he could smell her reaction to his touch, he understood the cause of her discomfort. It was instinct for him to touch, but he'd need to restrain that instinct with her.

"She said that Martin Croft will be handling the Unit while Brooks is incapacitated."

He nodded absently. Croft was a good man and a good administrator, but he wasn't Ruben Brooks. He tended to play things safe. To be fair, he had reason. Brooks could afford to gamble on a hunch, both because he had a good deal of political clout and because his gambles almost always paid off, thanks to his precognitive Gift.

Rule pried more information from her as they proceeded to the foot of the stairs and down two more hallways. And *pry* was the right word. He couldn't tell if she disapproved of him because he was lupus, because he was a civilian, or if the disapproval she radiated was more about herself and the sexual buzz she did not want to feel. Still, Lily had told her to fill him in about Ruben, so she answered his questions.

It had been a major heart attack. No word yet on how much damage had been done to the muscle. Brooks had been in his office when it happened. Ida had responded with her customary efficiency, summoning an ambulance, summoning Croft, and putting an aspirin under Ruben's tongue . . . *possibly all at the same time*, Rule thought. He'd met Ruben's secretary a time or two.

Rule had never and would never experience a heart attack, but he knew pain. He knew how it felt for your body to turn into a hostile zone, as likely to kill as to sustain you. He knew how alien and terrible the tubes and beeping machines of ICU felt. And he knew what it was like to wait while someone you loved was tied to those tubes and machines. He ached for Ruben's wife, Deborah. And as they turned down yet another hall, he began to tense up.

This was clearly not a patient section. Labs and storage, from what he saw and smelled. "Cobb is supposed to be a patient," he said sharply. "Where are we going?"

"Um . . . the room he's in . . . it was used for your people back when the government registered you."

"Gado," he said, disgusted. "They put him in the room where lupi were held so they could be injected with gado." It might even be the same room where Cobb had been confined years ago when he was given the drug. "No wonder he's refusing treatment."

"No, no, he knows he isn't here for that. They explained, so he knows."

"I doubt very much he believes them."

One more turn in the hall, and he saw Lily. She was at the end of the corridor, standing in front of a steel door with a small, barred window. She was talking with a uniformed officer. The instant he saw her, she turned her head—met his eyes—and started toward him.

Rule stepped up his pace and met her several feet from the door. He touched her arm. "I heard about Ruben. Are you all right?"

She waved that aside. "I called Nettie. She said it would take her too long to get to D.C. and the timing's critical for this kind of thing. Most healers can't do much about damage unless they get to the patient within an hour of the attack, but she knows someone, this healer who's kind of a recluse. He's good, he's powerful, he's not far from D.C., and he owes her a favor. She's going to get him to go to Ruben. Ida's making the arrangements. She has to make sure this guy isn't seen by the press—he's fanatic about his privacy. I don't know his name. Nettie wouldn't tell me his name. But she thinks he'll do it."

She was shaken. It was clear to him, maybe not to others. He wanted to wrap his arms around her, but she'd call that unprofessional—which he translated as *don't look weak*. He understood the need to conceal weakness in public, but the urge to hold and comfort was strong. He settled for squeezing her arm. "You've done all you can."

She nodded, but the pleat remained between her brows. She glanced at Sjorensen. "Thank you for escorting Rule. Excuse us a moment." She jerked her head at Rule—*come on*—and went through the nearest open door.

The room appeared to be used for storage of old office furniture. Lily stopped a few paces inside and looked at him. "You know what that room is where they've got him?"

His mouth tightened. "Yes."

"It's a bad place for him, but I see why they did it. They've got a violent lupus, a killer, but he's wounded. The law says he gets medical treatment. Where else can they put him? But that's a really small room."

"You've looked in on him?"

"It's small," she repeated. "Eight by ten, maybe. No furniture, nothing he could break up to use as a weapon, so he's lying on the floor. I don't think he's dealing with confinement well. That's why I told Lieutenant Matthews he couldn't go in with us. Too many people, too small a space."

Ah. That's what she'd argued about with the lieutenant earlier. "Is Cobb mobile? Agitated?"

She shook her head. "He's just lying on his back, staring at the ceiling. According to the guard, that's all he's done since he came around. He's not responsive. The only time he did speak was to tell the doctor not to touch him and to get out." Her frown deepened. "I'm thinking you'd better go in first."

That was both sensible and atypical. "You're worried about something you haven't mentioned."

She lowered her voice. "They'll have to shut us up in there with him. It's a small room, Rule."

Oh. He felt foolish. He admitted—to himself, not out loud—he was already a bit uncomfortable simply because he was underground. That was a relic of Dis, when he'd done a good deal of crawling around in small, underground spaces. He didn't think Lily was aware of that mild, lingering discomfort, and didn't intend to tell her. "I'll be all right."

"You'll hold my hand."

Appreciation and amusement bloomed into a smile. "I am always happy to hold your hand, *nadia.*"

Lily spoke briefly with Sjorensen, letting her know what they intended to do—some of what they intended, at least. The police officer guarding the door had the key. He gave that to Lily, but insisted on keeping his weapon out and ready. Lily didn't roll her eyes, but her voice suggested she wanted to. "Just don't shoot Rule."

Rule turned his attention to the mantle coiled in his gut, preparing himself to use it, if necessary, to subdue Cobb.

Lily used the key. The lock clicked audibly. She opened the door and let Rule in.

TEN

❦

LILY was right; the room was small. Painfully so. And it stank of terror, blood, and despair.

Fear is an acrid and distinct smell. Even humans were aware of it sometimes. Despair is a subtler scent, an amalgamation of flattened fear, guilt, and abject submission. The second he inhaled, Rule knew Raymond Cobb wouldn't erupt in violence. He was already beaten.

Cobb lay on the floor, as Lily had said, a beefy man with bandages wrapped around his chest and abdomen, with a thin blanket covering him from the waist down. His hair was short and dark, graying at the temples. He had a square block of a head, his features crowded together beneath a high forehead.

He turned his head, met Rule's eyes briefly, then closed his own. "Thank God. Thank God you came."

"Our Rhej is coming, also. She'll be able to help you." Rule didn't speak directly of Cobb's pain, which must be great. Others could have, but not the man's Rho, not without giving insult.

Cobb made a soft sound, too breathy for a proper snort. "Waste of her time."

"You can come in, Lily," Rule said, and took two steps

inside before sitting cross-legged on the floor. He put a hand on Cobb's shoulder. The mantle recognized the man in a way he knew Cobb would feel, too, and take some comfort in.

Rule heard and felt Lily enter behind him. He heard—distinctly—the door shut and the lock click. The muscles across his shoulders cinched.

Lily moved up quietly and sat beside him, sliding her purse from her shoulder to the floor. She'd placed herself near Cobb's feet, while Rule was near the man's midsection. Even if Cobb confounded reality by attacking, Rule would be able to stop him.

She placed a hand on Rule's thigh. The touch helped. He glanced at her. She nodded once: *You take it for now.*

Rule did his best to ignore the locked door behind him. "I can't remember if you met my *nadia* at the *gens subicio.* You know who she is, though."

"Cop," Cobb said without opening his eyes. His voice was hoarse and soft. He would be trying to inhale as shallowly as possible with that wound in his chest. "FBI cop."

"That's right. I require you to answer her questions fully and honestly." He put a whisper of the mantle behind that order, just enough to make it clear he meant exactly what he said.

Cobb nodded fractionally. "I have a request to make of my Rho."

Rule's throat tightened. He feared he knew what that request was. "You may make it after you have answered Lily's questions."

Lily took a recorder out of her purse, set it on the floor, and turned it on. "Special Agent Lily Yu of Unit Twelve, MCD, Federal Bureau of Investigation, interviewing suspect Raymond Cobb." She gave the date and time and recited the Miranda warning. "Mr. Cobb, this is an official interview. It is being taped. Do you understand your right to counsel?"

"My Rho's here. He's my counsel. Get on with it."

"You're wounded. Your doctor is unsure of your ability to withstand questioning, due to your nature and your refusal to allow him to examine you. If at any time you feel unable to continue, or if you require medical help, let me know and we will end the interview." She paused. "For the record, Rule

Turner is present at this interview, acting as counsel for Raymond Cobb. I am delegating the initial questioning to him, due to his position as Rho of Raymond Cobb's clan."

Cobb's eyes popped open in the same startlement Rule felt. He glanced at her. She gave another small nod.

Rule looked down at the man who'd killed so suddenly and wantonly. He kept it simple. "Ray, what happened?"

"I don't know." Cobb's eyes were a muddy brown. He fixed his gaze on Rule's chest, emphasizing his submission. "It was . . . I was fine. Annoyed with that jerk Reynolds, but that's nothing new. He's a . . ." Cobb stopped. Swallowed. "He was a prick. Maybe he still is, if there's an afterlife. So I was kinda pissed, but not paying that much attention. All of a sudden my stomach cramped—a real monster of a cramp, like someone squeezed my guts. I thought, what the hell?"

"Was it like bane sickness?"

"I dunno. No nausea, and there was just that one huge cramp, but I guess it was kinda like it. Then . . ." His voice flattened. "Then I picked up Reynolds and broke his neck. Then Sonja . . . Sonja . . ." Tears gathered in his eyes. "I killed Sonja. I don't—I can't—there were more. I don't remember it all, but there were more. I didn't . . . after Sonja, I almost came back. I knew I'd killed her and I—I tried, but it was too much. I couldn't stop, but I threw people instead. I didn't break their necks, but I threw them hard." His voice sank. "I guess I killed more than Reynolds and Sonja."

"One more, with ten injured," Rule said. "What was too much?"

"The rage. The rage." His faded to a whisper. "I've never felt anything like it."

Lily spoke. "Was it the fury, Ray?"

Cobb's gaze flicked to Rule. Rule nodded, telling him it was okay to speak of it on the record.

"It must have been. It was different than I remember, but it's been a long time, so maybe I don't remember right. The fury, yeah . . . only it wasn't about enemies or winning. It was just . . . rage."

Lily took up the questioning now, asking more specific questions: Who was nearby when the rage hit? What had he eaten, what had he drunk? Had he felt threatened? Had he specifically wanted to kill Reynolds?

He'd eaten three hamburgers and a handful of fries. He'd drunk two or three Cokes . . . no, not out of a can, but from one of those red plastic cups. Someone had put booze in the last one . . . sure, his human friends did that sometimes. They didn't know he was lupus, so they teased him about being a teetotaler. He hadn't finished it. He didn't like the taste of bourbon.

He didn't remember who all was nearby, other than Sonja and Reynolds. He'd just killed whoever was closest. There'd been nothing to him at that time but rage—no memories, no thoughts, no fears.

Lily said, "Yet you almost came back after you killed Sonja."

"Almost." His eyes were haunted. "Wasn't horseshoes, was it? Almost doesn't count."

Rule spoke quietly. "What about your wolf, Ray? The moon's three quarters full. Your wolf was close, but you didn't Change. Was your wolf enraged, too?"

Ray blinked in dull surprise. "I dunno. There wasn't enough of me present to notice if my wolf was in on the rage, and I didn't think of it. Changing, I mean."

He was clearly tiring, his pain mastering him. Rule glanced at Lily. "He's spent. He'll keep answering as long as you keep asking because I told him to, but I think he needs to rest."

"All right." The vee between her brows told him she was as little satisfied with what she'd learned as he was. "Mr. Cobb, we'll prepare a statement—a confession—from the transcription of this interview. I'll bring it to you to sign in the morning."

Cobb nodded weakly. But his grip wasn't weak when he reached for Rule. "She's through. You said I could make my request when she was through."

"Yes." Rule glanced at the recorder, lifting his eyebrows to ask silently if it could be turned off.

Lily considered the request briefly, then clicked the recorder off.

"I've shamed the clan." Cobb was hoarser than ever, but

his eyes had lost their film of despair. They burned. "I have to be put down. I understand that. Whatever went wrong with me, I have to be put down. But I can't live in a cage. They'll turn me off, shoot me full of that goddamned drug, and lock me away. I can't do that. I can't live in a cage, not hearing the moon. Maybe I deserve to, for killing Sonja, but I . . . something broke in me. I didn't—I wouldn't—" He stopped. Swallowed. "I ask for final mercy from my Rho."

It was what Rule had expected. He nodded slowly. "Your Rho grants—"

"Wait a minute," Lily said sharply. "Wait. Is he asking you to kill him?"

"He isn't asking for anything illegal."

"Because he'll Change first. That's what you mean, isn't it? *No.*"

Cobb's gaze flicked to her, then away, dismissing her. He was over seventy and Leidolf. It didn't occur to him that a female could have any say in this.

Rule knew better, but this time Lily couldn't have her way. Pity, regret, fury, fear—all crowded up in his gut, in his throat. They burned the way ice does, a cold sear. "I don't tell you how to do your duty. You won't tell me how to do mine."

"You are not offing my witness. I don't care whether he's furry or not."

"I am honor-bound to grant his request unless I believe he deserves to suffer. I don't believe that."

"Forget it." She pushed to her feet. "I'll stop you. If you try, I'll stop you, and if I can't, I'll charge you with interfering with a witness."

Rule's eyebrows lifted. "You would put me in a cage?"

"I can't—hell." Her phone was chiming the opening bars of "The Star Spangled Banner." That ought to mean it was Ruben, but with him hospitalized it must be Ida or Croft. She bent and dug the phone out of her purse. Lousy timing, but if there was news about Ruben, she'd want to hear it. "Yu here."

"Lily, I have news. You aren't going to like it."

It was Croft. Rule spoke quickly and subvocally to his clansman: *Wait. I need to hear this.*

"How is he?" Lily demanded, as if she could force Croft to make it good news after all. "How's Ruben?"

"It isn't about Ruben. I'm sorry. I should have made that clear. Ruben's pretty much the same—still in ICU. Ida says you've got some high-powered healer coming in to see what he can do, but he isn't there yet. No, this is about the Cobb case. I have to pull you off it."

"What?"

"The director's taking too much heat. Political heat. He's told me to pull you."

"The Unit isn't under the—"

"*Ruben* isn't. I'm not Ruben. I can't call up the president and tell him his appointee is making trouble and to please back him off—not when you don't have clear jurisdiction. Unless you've found something to change the picture?"

"No." She grudged it, but she gave him the truth. "But I do have a confession. One the police weren't going to get because he wouldn't talk to them."

"That's good. That's going to help. It will make the director's concerns about a conflict of interest less—"

"What the hell does that mean?"

"That's his reason for pulling you. 'The inherent conflict of interest,' he said. And you have to see his point. You took Rule with you. I understand why, but I can't explain, and Rule is—"

"Lupus, yes." She bit off each word. "So is the suspect. And if Rule were black, would it be considered a conflict of interest if I investigated a case involving a black suspect?"

"Dammit, don't twist things around! Rule isn't just any lupus—he's the Nokolai prince, their spokesman, the big muckety-muck as far as the press and public are concerned. And in this instance, we can't assume his interests are the same as the Bureau's—and you're engaged to him, for God's sake."

"If I were engaged to the head of the NAACP, would I be barred from pursuing cases involving African Americans? Or maybe I shouldn't investigate any crimes involving Asian Americans. I don't know if you've noticed this or not, but I'm Asian, so there's an inherent conflict of interest with—"

"Enough." Croft was angry. "You're off the case. Book a flight home." He disconnected.

Lily scowled at the phone in her hand. "Son of a bitch."

She was off the case. Lily was off the case, which meant this might be Rule's only chance to grant Cobb's request. She'd be flying back to San Diego. Willy-nilly, he would have to go, too. For the first time he was pissed, royally pissed, about the mate bond's restrictions.

Blood pounded in Rule's temples. He was abruptly aware of the tiny room, the locked door. That unease had been present all along, but it exploded in him now, his wolf howling, *Out, out, out!*

He could signal Cobb to Change right this second, then kill him. It was the honorable action, the decent action. Cobb had killed, but he'd killed due to some terrible defect, not from evil intent. The man wouldn't survive in any meaningful way, locked up for days and weeks and years, shot full of gado so he couldn't escape. Death, quick and as near painless as Rule could make it, was his choice—one he had a right to make.

Out, out, out!

But if Rule killed Cobb, it would reverberate on Lily. She'd brought him here. She didn't have Ruben standing behind her now, and Friar's people would create a huge stink. She could lose her job. Being a cop—that's what Lily was. It was a matter of identity, not income or status or achievement.

Honor demanded the one thing he *could not do.*

Rule shoved to his feet and looked down at Cobb. "I am sorry. I do not refuse your request, but I must delay granting it." He looked at Lily. "I need out. Now."

Conflict rode across her face like a crosswind ruffling the water. But she didn't hesitate. She went to the door, thudded on it with her fist, and called out to the cop on the other side.

The door opened. Rule's chest was a bony kettledrum for the mallet of his heart. He spoke without looking at her. "I'll find my own transportation." He didn't let himself run, but he walked very quickly—out the door, and down the hall. And kept on walking.

ELEVEN

BACK when she was a homicide cop, Lily had slept in her own bed every night—or as close to it as made no difference, given her stunted social life at the time. As a special agent in the Unit, she slept in lots of beds. The one at the Doubletree was better than most—plenty big, and the mattress didn't resemble a rock. The room itself was pleasant enough, with honey beige walls and a comfy armchair. But there wasn't much space for pacing.

Lily did her best. She reached the window, turned, and headed back along the aisle between the bed and the armoire that held the TV. The demon's-eye-red numerals on the clock watched her from the bedside table.

Ten-oh-seven.

Rule had stalked out of the hospital around seven twenty. She hadn't seen him since. Or heard from him. She knew roughly where he was—about ten miles southwest of the hotel. He was alive. That was all she knew. She'd tried calling. No answer.

She expected this sort of thing from Cullen. If he got too angry, he took off until he could cool down. That had been necessity for a lone wolf; it was habit now, she supposed.

Rule was not a lone wolf. He'd never done this before, taking off without a word. Was he that angry at losing the chance to kill Cobb? Was something else going on?

Lily was pretty sure she could check the "something else" box. But what?

Eight steps to the door. Turn. Head back.

She'd eaten. She couldn't remember what, but she'd eaten something, assuring herself that Rule wasn't an idiot. No matter how upset he was, he'd have made sure his wolf was fed.

He was not himself, though, was he? He'd been cooped up too much today—first in an airplane, then in that tiny room at the hospital. That had to part of this. Whatever the hell "this" was. It involved him needing to run. She knew that much because he'd told his guards.

Not her. He hadn't called her.

Lily stopped just short of the curtain, turned, and paced back toward the door.

When Sjorensen dropped her off at the hotel, Lily had thought Rule might already be in their room. Instead she'd opened the door on LeBron. Jeff had not been in the adjoining room, as she'd immediately assumed. LeBron explained that he'd gone running with Rule.

A quick flash of anger had stiffened her. It hadn't lasted, but she was glad she'd been angry at first. Better for LeBron to see her angry than worried. There was a lot Lily didn't understand about lupi dynamics, but she knew it was best if LeBron wasn't frightened for his Rho.

She'd asked LeBron to guard her from the adjoining room and she'd ordered dinner and she'd Googled Warner Park, because that's where Rule had gone to run, according to LeBron. It was in an area that ought to have cell service. She'd tried calling again.

Nothing. While waiting for room service, she'd very sensibly started writing her report. The Cobb case might not be hers anymore, but the paperwork was. Dinner arrived and she ate, then called Ida to check on Rubin. Ida said the secretive healer had arrived at the hospital. No word yet on whether he'd be able to help.

That's when she made the mistake of turning on the

news. First she watched a pasty-faced guy ranting about how America was being destroyed by nonhumans who wanted to eat people. His pale eyes brimmed with tears at the idea. That hadn't done much for her digestion. She'd switched to a channel where another talking head was interviewing Friar.

That's when she started pacing.

For the first time in nearly a year, Lily felt the loneliness of a hotel room. The emptiness. And if—

Her phone beeped, signaling a text message. She stopped, scowling at the phone sitting beside the demon-eyed clock, and hated the way hope made her heart lift. And hurried to check the message.

Gone running, the little bubble read. *Wolf needs it. Back late. Eat without me.* The last sentence pricked her into looking above it at the date/time stamp: SEP 23 7:44 P.M.

She sagged onto the bed. He'd sent the text hours ago, just after he left the hospital. For whatever reason, it had taken its sweet time arriving. Could be a problem with AT&T; could be the kind of glitch common to cell service in areas that lacked a resident dragon to soak up excess magic. Either way, it could explain why she hadn't been able to reach him.

Lily looked at the phone in her hand. She knew what she needed to do. She didn't want to. Some weird twist of pride and guilt made it hard to admit she had no idea what had really happened this afternoon. Just how big a deal was it for a Rho to refuse a "kill me" request from one of his clan?

When you don't have enough information, you go looking for it. She knew who to ask.

"It's about time you called," Cullen Seabourne snapped.

Lily looked at her phone, bewildered. "What?"

"About Ruben. That is why you called, isn't it?"

More guilt. Cullen had gotten to know Ruben fairly well when he, Cynna, and Ruben had been transported to Edge. "It probably should be, but it isn't. I didn't realize you'd heard."

"It's on the damn news. 'Ruben Brooks, head of the secretive Unit Twelve of the FBI, was taken to Walter Reed today—' and blah, blah, blah. Nothing about what happened or how he's doing, and when I called, no one would talk to me."

Briefly she told him about the heart attack and Nettie's intervention. "This healer is at the hospital now," she finished, "but I don't have any word on whether he's been able to help."

"If Nettie says he's good, he's good." The snap had left Cullen's voice, replaced by curiosity. "Why did you call?"

"I need advice."

"You know my rates."

Cullen had recently increased his consultation fee. As a soon-to-be-dad, he'd decided he needed more income. As the only known sorcerer in the country, he could get away with charging sky-high fees. Fortunately, he was married to an FBI agent, who'd insisted he keep his fees reasonable when he worked for the Bureau.

"This is personal, not professional."

Dead silence, followed by a wicked chuckle. "Well, my personal best is nine times, but that was a special situation, and I'd just as soon you didn't mention it to Cynna. She wasn't one of the participants, and I hate to set up expectations I might not be able to—"

"Okay, okay, you've made your obligatory sexual comment." But Lily smiled as she said it. It was perverse, but the sheer predictability of Cullen's response unwound some of the tightness. She rolled her shoulders, trying to dispel more of it. "I don't know if it's really advice I need, or just information. It has to do with clan expectations and a Rho's obligations."

"I'm not sure I'm the one to talk to." Cullen was uncharacteristically cautious. "You might do better to ask Isen."

"I think Rule wouldn't be happy if I did that. It's, ah, I guess it's Leidolf business, so maybe I shouldn't talk to the Nokolai Rho about it."

"Maybe not." Cullen paused. "I'm Nokolai."

"So am I. This isn't a deep, dark clan secret. I just think Rule would rather I asked you than pretty much anyone else, but I need your promise not to repeat what I tell you."

"Too general. I can promise I won't speak of it to anyone unless my Rho asks me directly, or I consider the need to reveal it both pressing and urgent. If it's pressing but not urgent, I'll let you know before I speak."

Lily grimaced. She'd forgotten how meticulous lupi were with promises . . . which meant there was a difference between "I can promise" and "I do promise." "That should work. So do you promise?"

He chuckled low in his throat. "You've a devious mind, don't you?"

"I've been around Sam more lately."

"That would do it. Yes. I promise, as stipulated. There's a reason you can't talk to Rule about this?"

"He isn't here. That's the problem, or maybe it's a symptom of the problem, and I need your help to understand the real problem."

"Since you aren't making sense, I'd better hear the rest of it."

She told him. Pretending she was making a report helped; she gave him the conversation with Cobb as close to verbatim as possible. She'd gotten to the part when Rule abruptly stood up when Cullen let out a low whistle. "Rule turned down Cobb's request?"

Her heart sank. "Not exactly. He said he wasn't refusing, but he had to delay granting the request. This is a big deal, then?"

"Lily." Her name sounded heavy, weighted with frustration and something else. Worry, maybe. "Given any choice at all, we do not surrender clan to imprisonment."

"No, mostly you just kill the perp yourselves, if you're sure he's guilty." That bugged the hell out of her. "The last time a lupus was clearly guilty of killing a human—I'm not counting that self-defense case in Louisiana—his clan delivered his body to the courthouse." Her voice soured. "He was in wolf form, so killing him was legal."

"You don't understand. If the human world requires that one of us be punished for a real or imagined crime, the Rho may choose to requite the offense with the death of the transgressor. But it's more likely that the transgressor will ask that of his Rho—a quick death rather than the long insanity of living in a cage. The Rho always grants that request. Always."

"It's a big fucking deal, then."

"Yeah. It is."

"But Rule delayed granting Cobb's request. He didn't refuse outright."

He was silent a moment. "I don't know what that means. If he believed Cobb didn't deserve an honorable death, he'd grant the request but have someone else handle the kill. He wouldn't delay granting the request, though. That's not what we do. The whole situation is peculiar, though. Rhos don't visit a jailed clansman—mostly because until recently they haven't been public about who they are. That's changing, but . . ." His voice trailed off.

Lily could almost hear Cullen scowling in the silence that followed. She remembered how grateful, how glad, Cobb had been to see Rule. He hadn't expected his Rho to come to him. He hadn't thought he'd have the chance to ask for the one mercy his Rho was obligated to grant. "Does the clansman have to make his request in person? He can't pass it along through someone else?"

"Normally he does, but the granting of the request . . . this gets complicated. Like I said, the request is always granted, but the Rho may not carry it out himself. If he does, it's an honorable death. If he has someone else handle the kill, it's a dishonorable death. Sometimes, though, a Rho can't grant final mercy personally. Maybe he'd have to travel to do so, and that isn't safe. Or maybe he's wounded, or the clansman is already in jail. There are plenty of reasons he might have to delegate the act. There's a ritual, a way he can pass that duty to another of the clan, so that the death remains honorable even though the Rho didn't grant it personally."

An honorable death. Lily knew that was important to lupi, even if she couldn't see the honor in having your leader kill you. "So even if Rule intended to have someone else kill Cobb, he wouldn't have delayed granting the request."

"I don't understand what he did, but I know why. You do, too, don't you?"

And here came the guilt. "Because of me." She'd just been pulled from the case. Had he acted, the repercussions to her could have been huge. She sighed.

"You understand enough now?"

"No, but that's probably all you can help me with. Rule had the right idea. I'm going for a run."

LILY left Rule a text plus a written note on the pillow in case the text didn't reach him. Then she told LeBron she'd be downstairs in the hotel gym. Much as she preferred to run outside, it was after ten and she could be sensible when she had to. Muggers were so damned distracting.

Telling LeBron didn't work out like she'd intended. He went with her. He apologized, but Rule had told him to guard her, not their room, so that's what he had to do. The hotel gym didn't work out, either. There was only one treadmill, and it had an OUT OF ORDER sign.

She looked at LeBron when she saw that. "I tried. You're witness to that. I tried to do this the cautious way."

LeBron grinned. "We're still going to run, then." Clearly he liked the idea.

She grimaced at the "we," but didn't argue. He'd go with her whether she agreed to it or not. On the upside—she could be a glass-half-full person if she tried, dammit—LeBron was six-five and bodybuilder buff. Having him along ought to cut down on the risk of an unpleasant inter-ruption. "I'll check with the concierge to map out a route, but yeah, I still need a run. You could probably use one, too, after being cooped up so much." She considered a moment. "I'm going to head back upstairs first and get my weapon. I've got a tidy little pancake holster that lets my clutch piece ride at the small of my back. You aren't carrying, are you?" He was wearing cutoffs with a tank. Not many options for concealed carry.

He looked sheepish. "I didn't think of it."

LeBron shared the usual lupi distaste for guns. He was receiving weapons training, but she suspected guns still seemed foreign to him. "You probably don't have a permit for it here, anyway. You can follow a little behind me, okay? I need to think about some stuff."

"I hate to argue, but a black man running after a woman? In the South?" He shook his head. "I'd just as soon not get the local boys in blue all excited."

She should have thought of that. "I'm not used to this."

"After a while, you'll forget I'm there," he assured her.

DOWNTOWN Nashville was downright pretty. Streets and sidewalks gleamed wetly in the glow of streetlights, taillights, and headlights. It was almost too clean for an urban center and far from deserted, with enough nightlife to bring people downtown even on weeknights.

The air was muggy with the brassy taste of pollution. By the time she and LeBron reached a spot called Victory Park, Lily's skin was already filmed with a light sweat.

Lily did not forget that a ridiculously tall hunk was running beside her. At first she made conversation—they weren't running fast, so she had enough breath, and naturally LeBron wasn't winded. That was the downside of running with a lupus. You couldn't measure yourself against them at all. He had pointed out it would be harder to forget his presence if he was talking to her.

True. But now that she had what she wanted, she didn't want it anymore. Her thoughts made for uncomfortable company.

Victory Park wasn't what Lily would call a real park. It was more like an oversized, paved veranda for some sort of public building to the north. Trees sprouted from their designated strips of dirt, and a large water feature sprouted a tall spray. She and LeBron ran up some steps—good for the quads—and veered right, their feet slapping wet pavers as they headed toward the Tennessee Capitol Building on the other side of Charlotte Avenue.

That was a thoroughly Greek structure with a plethora of columns and a single round tower giving the sky the finger. Lights trained on the building burnished the stone to soft gold. The grounds surrounding it were broad and dark and higher than street level, so it seemed to loom over them as they ran alongside it on Charlotte. No foot traffic here, except for them. Not many cars.

Rule must have known Cobb might ask for final mercy. All this time, he must have known it could happen. And he hadn't told her.

Lily's muscles had warmed up by now. She ran easily, her body loose. She tried to focus on that, on the sensations in her calves and thighs, on keeping her elbows in and her shoulders back. For a little while, she didn't think.

The route the concierge had suggested took them past the Capitol building, past the state library, then turned onto James Robertson Parkway, which curved in a large half circle around the buildings. They'd follow it to Fifth Avenue, take a right, and run along past the Nashville Auditorium and on back to Deadrick, which would return them to the hotel.

They swung onto the sidewalk flanking the Parkway, and LeBron dropped back a couple of paces. He didn't need to—the sidewalk broadened here. Maybe there were lots of pedestrians in the day, when the government offices were open. Not now. They had it to themselves. On the left, headlights flashed and passed, flashed and passed. On the right was a grassy embankment studded by trees that ended in a parking lot. A sparse sprinkling of cars suggested that a few government employees were working really late.

LeBron stayed behind her, but on her left, closer to the highway. If she'd thought there was a real threat, she'd have placed him on her right. With his night vision, he could pick out any lurkers in the deep shadows beneath the trees a lot better than she could.

Was his choice of highway-side instinct? Did cars and the people in them seem more of a danger to a part-time wolf than the darker, unpopulated stretch of grass and trees?

Lupi were human-like or human-plus, but they were not plain old human. Their default settings were different. They doted on babies. They never let themselves get too hungry. They were subject to the Change, the fury, and a nasty form of late-life cancer. They were promiscuous and beautiful and deeply, irrationally protective of women.

They kept secrets.

Rule's tendency to keep things to himself had tripped them up more than once. He tried, but sometimes he simply didn't notice he was keeping things from her, no more than she'd notice she hadn't commented on her menses lately. Was his silence this time merely habit? Had it just not occurred to him to tell her he might be asked to kill his clansman?

How could it not? When you got down to it, Rule had used her to gain access to Cobb, knowing what Cobb was likely to ask of his Rho. Knowing—he had to know!—she could not allow him to kill the man. Maybe she'd used him, too, but he could have said, *No, I'm not going to use my position as Rho to get my clansman to confess.* She might not have liked it, but she would have understood. He had the right to refuse to help in that way.

He hadn't given her a chance to refuse. And that was not like him.

Rule insisted the Leidolf mantle didn't affect him. Lily was growing more and more sure that it did . . . because if she was wrong, he'd knowingly withheld information so he could use her.

Somewhere to the north and east he was running, too, seeking the surcease of the physical. She knew he'd been pulled by opposing needs—his duty and hers. In the end, he'd backed away from his duty for her sake, and maybe that should make everything okay.

It didn't. It mattered. It meant a lot, but it wasn't enough. Not when she felt separated from him by more than eight or nine miles of city.

He needed to see that the mantle was affecting him. She didn't know how to make that happen, but somehow she had to.

Lily picked up the pace. LeBron kept up easily. She pushed herself, craving the burn, knowing he'd have no trouble with any pace she could set. A less confident person could get a complex, going running with—

With the first sharp *crack!* something tugged hard at her arm. She didn't have time to drop. Two hundred and forty pounds of LeBron hit her from behind even as a second and third shot split the air—and he wrapped himself around her, so that she hit the ground helpless but cushioned.

They rolled—another shot, another—and she ended up on top, her arms free, but when she reached for her weapon her right arm barely twitched. Pain rocketed straight to her brain in a hot blur.

Tires screeching, a horn blaring—

She started to roll off LeBron, flatten herself better. And saw his face.

One eye open and staring. The other gone, just gone, vanished in the bloody, jellied wreck the bullet had made on its way out of his skull.

TWELVE

FLASHING lights. Cop lights, strobing their red emergencies into the street, onto the bloody grass. Lily sat on the wet grass, her arm pulsing out of sync with those lights, driven by a frantic heartbeat, each pulse a hot beat of pain too large to think through or around.

"What?" she said. "I didn't hear . . . you need to send someone to talk to the concierge."

"Later," the officer kneeling beside her said soothingly. He was young, dark-skinned, with a teensy little mustache. "You said you're FBI. Do you have ID on you?"

"In my holster." She'd already surrendered her weapon, knowing the officers had to have it. Lily started to reach behind her—and hissed at the fresh blow from her injured arm.

"I'll get it. Stay still. You aren't bleeding out, but—"

"I'm okay. Didn't get the plates, though. First we were tumbling, then I saw . . . they were gone by the time I looked. Shot us from behind, hit the gas."

He'd managed to extract her ID. As he shown his flashlight on it, a siren's mounting wail grew closer. Ambulance, she saw when she glanced at the street. It pulled to a stop, adding its flashing light to the two patrol units.

But they were too late. LeBron was dead. "Could be an opportunistic hit, could be planned. If the concierge talked to someone . . ." The world did a slow loop. She closed her eyes to see if that made the dizziness go away.

When she opened them, she was flat on her back and someone else was bending over her. A woman, thirty-something, brown and brown, square chin. Not a cop. "Take it easy, ma'am," the woman said. "We're going to get you loaded in just a minute. I need to know where you hurt."

Paramedic. Brown-and-brown was a paramedic. "My arm. That's it. I need to call people. My phone's in my armband. Get it for me, okay? Can't reach it." She'd tried, but the armband was on her left biceps and she couldn't contort her left arm enough to reach it.

"You need to be still. You've lost some blood."

Blood loss? Was that why . . . she'd thought the mate bond had yanked on her, making her pass out. That's how it felt when she and Rule were too far apart—dizzy as hell, followed by unconsciousness if they didn't close the distance quickly. But blood loss made sense. "Talking won't make me lose more blood. I need to call Rule and . . ." Not Ruben. He'd had a heart attack. God, her brain wasn't working right. "Croft. I need to tell him. And Rule."

"We can make a call for you, but first we have to get you loaded. Hold on a minute now, we're going to—"

Someone did something to her arm that seared her brain to white. When it came back online, someone was saying *dammit, dammit, dammit* . . . oh, that was her. Apparently she could curse even without a brain. "Call now."

"We'll call soon. We're going to move you now."

"O-NEGATIVE." Lily lay on a gurney in the back of the ambulance. The motor was idling, the siren silent. Up front, a door slammed as the driver got in. "And that's all you get until you call."

"Special Agent," Brown-and-brown said, "no doubt you are used to being in charge. You aren't in charge now. I said I'd call, and I will—after we reach the hospital. Now you need to answer some questions. Any allergies?"

Lily set her jaw and stared at the ceiling. It was way too close. Everything was too close and cramped in the back of an ambulance. Rule would hate it.

"I need to know if you're allergic to any drugs."

They pulled away from the curb. Just as Lily thought maybe they'd spare her the siren, it came on. She winced. It probably wasn't as loud in here as outside, but that urgent blare made her heartbeat jump back into double time.

They'd bound her arm. The pressure was necessary to stop the bleeding, but God, it hurt. No more dizziness, though, thanks to the IV now dripping fluid into her vein, so she tried to get her brain working.

It was not, she thought, a professional hit. A pro would have used a rifle or an automatic. It clearly hadn't been an automatic—she was too alive for that—and it had sounded like a pistol, not a rifle.

Brown-and-brown sighed and surrendered. "All right, I'll call. What did you say his name was?"

"Rule. Rule Turner."

VANDERBILT had the closest ER, barely five minutes away. That was irony, not a coincidence; Ida had booked them into the Doubletree precisely because it was close to the hospital.

Brown-and-brown hadn't been able to reach Rule, but she'd left a message. She'd called Croft, too, just as the ambulance pulled into the emergency bay. She hadn't let Lily speak to him, but at least she'd called. Lily made sure she told Croft about LeBron.

Not Rule, though. He shouldn't learn that from voice mail.

Many painful minutes had since passed. Lily's time sense was too skewed to guess how many. Time enough to cut away her top, though it was obvious her only damage was to her arm. Time enough to steal more of the blood they said she was low on. Time enough to get X-rays, during which she'd passed out again, but not, she thought, for very long. They'd followed that up with a CT scan.

Now she lay flat on a hard treatment table, enveloped in pain. Her own fault, she supposed, for refusing pain meds.

But she couldn't turn loose yet, couldn't . . . only she was tired. So tired.

Still, she tried to pay attention to the doctor who was telling her a great many important things involving her tibia. Or was it her fibula?

No, neither of those were right. Her arm, anyway. Her arm was screwed up. Hollow-point bullet, most likely. They really tore things up on their way out. Like LeBron's eye socket, exploded into obscene red jelly . . .

". . . very fortunate there is no significant vascular damage, so we won't need a vascular surgeon. The surgery may take awhile, given the shattering of your humerus—bone fragments, you know. Got to chase down as many of them as we can, but we have an excellent orthopedic surgeon. He'll be here very soon, and he'll take good care of you," he told her, hearty in his reassurance. "Do you have any questions?"

"Not going into surgery yet."

The ER physician was a portly man with twin patches of sandy hair in parentheses around his ears. He had a mole just under his chin and a shiny head. He frowned at her in disapproval. "You need surgery, young lady."

Lily gritted her teeth at the "young lady." "I'm not refusing treatment. Just not yet. He's almost . . ." No, wait, she wasn't supposed to say that. "I need to see him first."

"He? Who do you mean?"

There was no door to her treatment cubby, so she heard the commotion in the hall clearly. First a woman's voice: "Sir! Sir, you can't go—"

Then a wonderful voice. "No, now, you'll have to get out of my way. My *nadia* is in there."

"Visitors are not allowed for that patient—sir! Security! Stop him!"

Relief rolled over Lily in a huge wave. "That's him, and you'll let him in here or I swear I'll get up off this goddamned table and go out there to him."

"The officers left word that you—"

"I am a goddamned officer, and I say . . . oh. Oh, there you are."

Rule appeared in the doorway, his hair disheveled, his eyes frantic. "Lily."

From behind him another man spoke. "All right, you! Hands up and step back. Step away from the door."

Rule didn't move, and he didn't look away from her. "I suggest you put that gun up before you hurt someone."

"Harvey," the doctor said, turning, "don't be waving that gun around. It's all right. My patient knows this man— whoever he is—and she is not going to cooperate until she sees him."

Harvey started arguing. The doctor started for the hall. Rule stepped aside for him politely—and came in. Came to her.

"Lily." He swallowed and touched her cheek so carefully, as if he feared even that might hurt.

She seized his shirt with her good hand and pulled him to her. He let her, and at last, at last she could bury her face in his shoulder, his shirt wrinkled and soft, his scent filling her. At last she could let go. Rule was here.

A shudder hit like a small quake. "LeBron is dead."

"I know." He stroked her hair. "I was still four-footed when the mate bond yanked at me—"

It did?

"—so I raced back to the car, Changed, and got that message from the paramedic."

"But she didn't say—"

"I called Croft. He told me."

Her hand clenched in his shirt. "He died for me. He wrapped himself around me and took the bullet. For me." The first sob shook her, shocked her, sent a white bolt of pain shooting from her damaged arm . . . but that didn't stop her.

She wept.

THIRTEEN

THE moon's lumpy face beamed down on the land in its remote, silvery way, making Arjenie think of that "from a distance" song. Maybe things on Earth looked just fine from 238,857 miles away.

Actually, it was closer to 233,814, though that figure might be imprecise. She'd done the calculation herself a couple years ago because the other figure was the center-to-center distance between Earth and its satellite, and she'd been curious about the surface-to-surface distance. She'd used the equatorial dimensions of both bodies to keep things simple, so . . .

So she was distracting herself with trivia again. Not that the distance between Earth and the moon was trivial, but it was not relevant.

Arjenie took a deep breath and opened her car door. The dome light did not come on, and she congratulated herself for remembering to remove the bulb. Lights could be seen much farther away than her Gift could operate, which was why she'd driven the last few miles without headlights.

Tonight's mission would not be nearly as scary as visiting Dya had been, she assured herself. This time the worst-case scenario didn't involve anyone killing her.

Though it might involve someone *seeing* her. She hoped—no, she believed, as firmly as she could manage— that last night's big, beautiful wolf had gotten away unscathed. Which meant he might be around to see her tonight. Which would be bad, but much better than him not being around at all anymore.

All that determined believing contributed to her thudding heart as she grabbed the tool belt she'd bought that afternoon and got out.

The tool belt went around her waist—or her hips, really, since even the smallest size was a bit large for her. She wiggled her hips, making sure nothing clinked or rattled. Then she reached into her left pocket and withdrew the smaller vial.

It held a tablespoon of clear liquid. Arjenie tugged off the stopper and downed that tablespoonful in one gulp. No taste, no scent—it was like thick water.

She didn't experience a thing. Dya had told her she wouldn't. Still, she lifted an arm and sniffed her hand, then under her arm. No change that she could tell. She'd just have to trust that the potion did what Dya said it would. Her Gift would let her go unnoticed, but she needed the potion to keep from leaving her scent on things.

Then she reached into the car for one last tool: a cane.

Arjenie hated the cane. She had one at home, but it spent almost all the time in the back of her closet. She'd long since resigned herself to the clunky orthopedic shoes, but the cane felt like an accusation, an exclamation point at the end of *Oh, no, I did it to myself again!* But her ankle hadn't stopped aching since she took that tumble last night. She'd kept it elevated, she'd used a healing cantrip, she'd alternated hot and cold packs. Still it complained, even when wrapped snugly in an elastic bandage.

Unfortunately, she couldn't wait for it to quit fussing. Her life might not be on the line, but other lives were. That's what Dya said, and Arjenie trusted her. Not that she thought Dya had been utterly and completely honest. Arjenie suspected Dya's life was more at risk than she admitted, and there was so much Dya hadn't told her. But Dya wouldn't trick her.

Sometimes the best outcome was no noticeable outcome

at all. She'd go in, do what she came here for, and nothing would happen.

With that goal firmly in mind, Arjenie and her cane and her complaining ankle set off down the road to Nokolai Clanhome.

The road hadn't been resurfaced recently, and that was a blessing. The gravel was mostly packed into the ground. She still made some noise as she walked, but hopefully anyone close enough to hear would be within range of her Gift. But lupi hearing was terribly acute. She didn't know precisely how acute because they'd never let anyone study them that way—and she couldn't really blame them, given the history between lupi and humans. But it would be interesting to find out.

Only not tonight. Tonight she'd settle for ignorance on her own part as long as it meant ignorance on their part, too.

The air was crisp, the sky cloudless, and her ankle hurt.

Two miles. That's not so far, she told herself. She might be clumsy, but she was fit. Two miles to the entrance, then another mile or so to her target. If she hadn't turned her ankle last night, that would be a breeze. It was still doable. Pain was a familiar sparring partner. It might make her cry, but it didn't stop her.

She was a little worried about the walk back, though.

Nokolai Clanhome covered three hundred forty-nine acres of rough terrain. Fortunately, she didn't have to hike up and down all that terrain. The road ran right up to her target. Unfortunately, she couldn't just drive up. Even if her Gift were strong enough to make an entire car impossible to notice, the glass in the windows would blow that plan. Glass impeded magic—Arjenie's magic, anyway.

Focus Fire, stop Air, seal Water, open Earth. Her feet kept time with the little ditty she'd learned when she was five years old.

Like many mnemonics, it wasn't strictly accurate. Useful when one was first learning the Craft, she supposed, but not accurate. Glass did magnify some aspects of Fire magic, like precognition, which was sometimes linked to Fire. Some practitioners with that Gift found crystal balls helpful in clarifying the information they received. But others didn't, and some types of Fire magic were unaffected by glass. Uncle Hershey said glass had no impact either way on his ability to call fire.

Then there was Air. Arjenie's Gift was tied to Air, and glass didn't *stop* her magic. It interfered. The closer the glass, the greater the interference. If she used her Gift while standing right next to a window, for example, she'd get a dreadful headache and lousy results. If she were foolish enough to use her Gift while actually touching a big plate glass window, she'd black out.

So would anyone within twenty feet of her. She knew that because she was foolish sometimes . . . but she'd wanted to *know*. And she'd only tried it that once.

The mnemonic was right about Earth and Water, though. Glass was open to Earth magic—it had no effect at all. And glass did seal Water. That's why most potions were kept in glass bottles. Potions drew on lots of different energies, but they used Water magic to hold their action in potential.

Arjenie's fingers brushed the lump in the pocket of her jacket. The reminder of Dya made her heart ache and started her mind down another worry-path.

Arjenie did not understand Binai ethics, but she knew contracts were their high holy writ. Violations of contractual obligations were far more serious than, say, killing someone you didn't know. Killing a relative was murder, but otherwise, the morality of murder depended on the context—and the contract.

Dya was risking a contract violation by sending Arjenie here. She said Friar was violating Queens' Law. Normally Queens' Law only applied to the sidhe realms, not to Earth—but Dya said it applied to her even here because it was in her contract. She could not be tasked with or coerced or tricked into violating Queens' Law.

Robert Friar had tricked her. Maybe. Probably.

Dya had overheard something. That's all Arjenie knew, but whatever Dya had heard, it had shaken her badly enough to risk breaking contract. Of course, if she was right, Friar had already broken contract and she was off the hook on that score. Breaking Queens' Law invalidated any contract.

Queens' Law. The words sent cold tingles along Arjenie's

spine. Dya had reason to be shaken, and Arjenie had reason to be hobbling down a dark road well after midnight, doing who knew how much damage to her ankle.

Arjenie was leaning on the cane a lot more by the time she neared the gate. It was the kind made from pipes, and it was closed. Beside it stood a young man in cutoffs with a rifle slung over one bare shoulder.

Arjenie took a deep breath, pulled harder on her Gift, and kept going. The young man didn't notice her, not even when she climbed up awkwardly on the gate, careful not to let the tools in her tool belt clang against it. Her Gift would probably keep him from noticing sounds, but *probably* wasn't good enough.

She swung a leg over and clambered back down. Success. She grinned at herself, at the young man who didn't know she was there, and limped forward.

A wolf stepped out of the scrub beside the road. He looked right at her.

Arjenie froze. He was much more silvery than last night's wolf. And he wasn't looking at her, she realized with a rush of relief. In her direction, yes, but his gaze was focused a little to one side. Maybe at the guard?

Still, she didn't move as he trotted up the road toward her . . . and on past. Her heart pounded so hard she was almost sick from it. But he did pass.

She looked over her shoulder, curiosity temporarily defeating fear. Sure enough, the wolf went right up to the young man, who made some kind of sign with his hands. The wolf shook his head. The man made another sign. The wolf nodded and set off along the fence.

Whew. Dya's potion must have worked. Obviously she hadn't left any scent on the gate.

Arjenie's hands were shaking as she started moving again. Maybe not just her hands. Excess adrenaline was a lot like sheer terror in that way.

The rest of her mission was anticlimactic. She didn't see anyone as she trudged down the road, and the only wolves she heard were yodeling at each other up in the mountains. The cluster of houses and a few commercial buildings that she thought of as Nokolai Village lay about three miles beyond the gate, but her target was quite a bit closer. There was one largish dwelling she'd have to pass, however.

The largish building was dark when she reached it, as it should be at this hour. Her heart beat a little faster as she walked by, but no one stirred. About forty feet beyond it she spotted the twin ruts of the trail she needed.

In the end, she didn't need any of the tools she'd brought, not even the penlight. She had unusually good night vision, and with the moon so near to full she had no trouble finding the wellhead.

Nokolai had multiple wells—probably three, according to the expert she'd consulted. She'd only had time to locate the most recent well, drilled after the state began requiring permits. But Nokolai had a large water tank, easily spotted on the aerial photos. That tank supplied the forty-two houses and six other buildings in its central village. It, in turn, was supplied by all the wells.

In other words, she didn't have to find and dose all the wells. Whatever she put in one would mingle with water from the others before reaching the houses.

Had the man Friar sent here emptied his vials into a single well, or had he poured them into the water tank? It probably didn't matter, but she'd never been good at not thinking about something once it caught her interest. Friar's agent had had a potion like hers to nullify his scent, but he couldn't have gone unseen the way Arjenie did. There was no such thing as an invisibility potion. How had Friar's agent snuck around without being spotted?

Very likely he'd put the potion in one of the other wells, she decided. This one would have been hard for him to reach without being seen, and the tank was way too exposed. But he'd had a lot more time than she had to do his research. He'd probably found a well he could approach more secretively.

She lowered herself to the ground beside the wellhead. Her ankle throbbed once, hard, as if surprised by the sudden lack of weight grinding down on it. Then the pain gentled. She smiled in relief.

The cap was right where she'd been told it would be,

sticking out of the seal. "People have to chlorinate the water, yaknowwhatImean?" the driller she'd spoken with had told her. That's how he said it, with the words melted into a single blob. "Got to keep it simple for folks, yaknowwhatImean? Unscrew the cap, pour in the chlorine. That's it."

Sure enough, that's all Arjenie had to do. Unscrew the cap, pour in the potion.

This potion was in a larger vial. There was roughly a cup of highly viscous fluid, more like a murky gel. Arjenie's human nose picked up a faint scent when she removed the stopper. Something similar to cloves, yet not cloves.

It smelled like Dya. Arjenie leaned forward carefully. Dya had warned her not to get any of the potion on her skin. Though it worked best if taken internally, it was extremely potent. Getting even the teeniest bit on her skin would undo the potion she'd taken earlier.

That's what tonight was for—undoing. Making sure things *didn't* happen.

"But, Dya," Arjenie had said when she heard what Dya wanted her to do, "won't Friar blame you when nothing happens?"

"I do not wish to insult your world, but people here are very ignorant. After I became suspicious, I chastised Friar about chlorine."

Arjenie had blinked. "Chlorine?"

Dya had chuckled. "You are not so ignorant as he, little fox. I wished him to believe this chlorine might interfere with my potions. He had not told me that you people put it in your water here, you understand, and so I suggested that if the potions did not work, it was his fault for not informing me of the chlorine. He will be angry when nothing happens, for that is his nature. He will not think I have acted against him."

"Couldn't you just . . . well, instead of going through all this with the antidote—"

"It is not an antidote, Arjenie. It is an undoer."

"Okay, but wouldn't it have been simpler to just make the potions a little bit wrong, so they didn't work?"

Dya had been silent for a long moment, then said softly, "I did not like Friar's purpose, but it is not for me to approve or disapprove of the use to which my work is put. I did as I was bid. When I heard . . . when I began to suspect . . ." Her voice sank to a whisper. "Queens' Law, Arjenie. If Friar violates it, then so must my lord be doing, also. He loaned me to Friar. He must know, but it—it is a very large thing to suspect one's lord of such evil."

"You haven't told me which Queens' Law Friar is messing with."

"Do not ask."

And that's all Dya would say about it. Don't ask.

Sidhe had many realms and many rulers, but only two queens: Winter and Summer. The Two Queens didn't bother with many laws, but those few covered some terrible ground. Eledan had told her about Queens' Law. He was supposed to have come back and explained those Laws more fully once she was adult, but he never had. Very likely he'd forgotten. His notions of fatherhood were extremely casual.

What Queens' Law was she upholding tonight? Arjenie wanted to know and she didn't, and on a personal level that sucked. But given the overall potential for ghastliness, it didn't really matter. What mattered was stopping Friar. She poured the undoer into the opening, holding it tipped and steady as it slowly *glug-glugged* out and down.

She sighed, reinserted the stopper, and screwed the cap back in place. Done.

Now she just had to get herself out of here.

Arjenie knew how much her ankle hurt. She didn't realize until she struggled to her feet how tired she was. Now that she'd accomplished her mission, exhaustion seemed to radiate out from her bones.

She hadn't had much sleep last night, but she'd never needed as much sleep as most people did. Losing an hour or two didn't affect her much. No, this kind of blood-and-bone tired had little to do with sleep, and everything to do with her Gift.

Like most Gifted, Arjenie could use outside sources to power a spell or a charm, but she couldn't power her Gift itself that way. Unlike the other Gifted she knew, however, she could draw power directly from another source if she had to: her own body.

There was, of course, a price for that.

Arjenie dug into one of the pouches on her tool belt, but instead of a screwdriver she pulled out a candy bar. She wasn't hungry, but experience had taught her that her body's signals could not be trusted when she'd pushed herself too far. She needed fuel. Sugar first, then some jerky for the protein, then more sugar. By then, hopefully, she'd be back at her car and could drink the Coke she'd left there. That ought to get her back to her hotel, where she could crash safely.

Judging by how tired she was now, with roughly three miles still to walk and all of that spent drawing strongly on her Gift, the crash was going to be bad this time.

Couldn't be helped. She peeled back the paper, bit, and chewed as she started back down the ruts that led to the main road.

Would it last two days? Three? She took another bite of chocolate. Could well be the latter. That wouldn't be a problem as far as work went—she'd taken a full week off, and had warned her boss that she wouldn't be checking e-mail or voice mail very often. Aunt Robin, though . . . if her aunt called and couldn't reach Arjenie, she'd worry. And she'd probably call. Aunt Robin's trouble radar was uncanny.

Best to call her on the way to the hotel, Arjenie concluded glumly, and warn her that a crash was imminent. She'd get a lecture, but that was better than upsetting her aunt. Not that she could tell Aunt Robin—or Uncle Clay, or Uncle Ambrose, or Uncle Nate, or Uncle Stephen, or any of her cousins—why she'd abused her Gift tonight.

Are most adventures like this? she wondered as she reached the road. Lots of preparation and worry, a distracting level of pain, not much happening for long stretches of time, and a whole litter of complications to deal with afterward.

Still, she'd been lucky. Also clever, and she gave herself credit for that, but luck had surely played a big part. And now that it was over, she could admit that she'd liked parts of her adventure. She did enjoy sneaking around. That was no news flash. How could someone with her Gift not develop a love for . . .

Uh-oh.

FOURTEEN

THE largish building Arjenie had passed on her way to the well was nothing fancy— just a long, stucco rectangle roofed with the red tiles you saw everywhere in California. A wooden deck ran the length of the building's front. The thirty feet that separated it from the road couldn't be called a yard—it was mostly dirt with some stubborn tufts of native grass.

The windows were unexpected. They were unusually tall, running nearly from floor to ceiling, and she hadn't seen any on the sides or back, just in the front along the deck.

Those windows spilled light into the darkness now. And voices. Men's voices.

Arjenie's feet stopped entirely. From this far back she couldn't hear what the voices said. She could, however, see inside. Men moved swiftly and purposefully in what seemed to be one huge bedroom—she glimpsed several beds, anyway. No, wait, the beds were on either end; the middle part looked more like a living room. Several of the men were naked. And not everyone was a man.

Arjenie's heartbeat leaped for the stratosphere. *Move*, she told her feet, and they obeyed for two whole steps when something happened that made her forget everything else.

A tall, dark-haired man with a wiry build and no clothes stood near one of the windows. She watched, transfixed, as he splintered himself. That wasn't the right word, but there were no words for what she saw—reality shorting out in a fizz of impossibilities, fractal glimpses of flesh and fur and *change*.

"Go," said a man's voice, deep and commanding. And the wolf who'd been a man a second ago did, spinning to leap out the window—as did four more wolves, launching themselves through four more windows.

They all but flew, those wolves. As if they'd choreographed this, they sailed out the windows and over the porch, landing on the hard ground. And kept going, streaks of shadow cutting across the night like wind made visible.

One of them ran right past her. Not quite close enough for her to reach out and touch, but nearly. Arjenie swallowed and pulled hard on her Gift and remembered her feet, which agreed that it was time to move. Even her poor ankle was on board with that plan.

What had alerted them? Had they found some trace of her? Could the potion have worn off? No, that was stupid— that wolf had raced right past her, which he surely wouldn't have done if she were leaving a scent trail.

She hobbled forward slowly. Much as she wanted to hurry, that would end badly. Her ankle wouldn't tolerate any rushing.

Men were coming out now. A couple stepped through the windows like the wolves had, only not in such a rush. Others exited more prosaically through the door. They were all armed, and mostly dressed—at least, all but two wore cut-offs. Arjenie's gaze flickered over the men, counting compulsively as she walked, leaning on the stupid cane . . . two, three, five, seven, nine . . .

The tenth man was in charge. Arjenie knew that the second she saw him. It was clear in the way the others watched him. His voice was a low rumble, too low for her to make out the words—something about the road, or maybe the Rho—and he was big. Big like Arnold Schwarzenegger in his bodybuilder days. Big like a pro football player or the

G.I. Joe doll her cousin Jack used to play with. Big as in all muscle.

His hair was black and straight, pulled back in a stubby tail. He had coppery skin. Lots of coppery skin. He wasn't quite naked. He had on cutoffs. And a sword. She was pretty sure that was a sword strapped across his back, plus there was a rifle in his hand and some kind of gun holstered on his hips.

She wanted him.

The rush of hunger astounded her. It was so misplaced she had nowhere to *put* it, no context by which such an absurd upwelling of desire could be understood. She stood and gaped at him.

He finished speaking to the men with him. Two of them peeled off, racing toward the gate, and he—he looked at her. Right at her.

"It's you," she whispered.

Did he hear her? She couldn't tell. His face gave nothing away. He started toward her, moving slowly, like a big cat stalking its prey . . . would a part-time wolf be insulted if you called him a cat? His gaze never left her.

He made a gesture with one hand, some kind of signal. Two of the other men fell into step with him. "Lights," he said. A second later Arjenie was blinking against the sudden flood of light—all of it directed out at the yard and the road. The porch itself remained unlit. The men remaining on that porch looked watchful and wary, but she could tell they didn't see her.

He did.

His eyes never left hers as he stepped off the deck and kept coming. He looked about forty, with crow's-feet tucked in the corners of his dark eyes. His face had no expression at all. He didn't so much as blink. Maybe he was a robot? A robotic lupus, because she somehow knew he was last night's wolf. A Native American robotic lupus, because that copper skin was stretched taut over broad cheekbones bisected by a high-bridged blade of a nose.

Apache? Navajo? She wanted to ask him which tribe, and why he could see her, and why his men weren't asking him what he was doing, stalking something they couldn't see. She wanted to stretch out a hand and touch him . . . and that was stupid, because he was a lot scarier in this shape than when he was a wolf. She tried to swallow, but her mouth was too dry.

He stopped about five feet away. He'd been a big wolf. He made a very big man. "I am so scared," she whispered.

"You don't smell scared." His voice was so low, rumbling out of him like a big cat's purr. "You don't smell like anything."

"You *can* hear me!"

"Hear you, see you, but I can't smell you."

She blinked. That was interesting. Apparently her Gift didn't work on him, but Dya's potion did. "That's because of the potion," she whispered. She could not bring herself to speak out loud while using her Gift. Or maybe her voice was strangled by fear.

"You'll tell me about that shortly." He gestured at the cane she was leaning on. "You fell last night. Are you injured?"

She nodded. "Are you? I heard shots. So many shots."

"Nothing significant."

"Benedict?" one of the men with him said—a redhead with freckles everywhere. Truly everywhere. He hadn't bothered with cutoffs. "Who are you talking to?"

"You don't see her," the robotic lupus Native American said. The redhead shook his head. "Do you not hear her, either?"

"No."

There was no point in exhausting herself further. She was well and truly caught. With a sigh, Arjenie released the draw on her Gift.

"What the—"

"Where did she—"

"Ohmygod, she—"

Arjenie squeaked. It wasn't good to startle armed men. A gun had practically jumped into the hand of a blond man on the porch. He aimed it right at her.

The large robotic lupus in front of her never looked away from her face. "Who drew?"

"I did," said the man who was pointing his gun at her.

"Put it up. You and Saul go to the Rho's. Wake him and report." He used another of those hand signals, this one sort of like a beauty queen's wave. The two men took off at a run in the general direction indicated by that wave.

For a moment she watched them. She couldn't help it. They were so lovely and so swift.

The one they'd called Benedict shook his head. "Damned if she didn't deliver you to me. You might as well tell me your name."

FIFTEEN

"I'D rather not," Benedict's Chosen said apologetically.

Her hair was red. Somehow he hadn't expected that. It was also insane. She'd pulled it back, as she had last night, but it was so frenetically curly he half expected to see it wiggle out of its bonds right before his eyes.

There were many details he'd missed last night. Part of him noted them, appraising an intruder who'd violated Clanhome's boundaries for an unknown purpose, using unknown abilities, on the same night that Lily had been attacked and injured.

Worry beat in him like a second heart. Lily had needed surgery. She'd made it through that, and Nettie was consulting and would fly out if she was needed. Benedict could do nothing right now to make Lily safer or speed her recovery, so he focused that worry where he could make a difference—on Clanhome's security.

Even as he did, part of him drank in other details.

His prisoner wore jeans, a jacket, a T-shirt, and ugly brown shoes. The shoes looked orthopedic, suggesting he'd been right about a physical impediment. No visible weapons aside from the cane. She wore a silver pinkie ring on her left hand. A Wiccan star.

Her skin was porcelain, with a few freckles sprinkled across a small, crooked nose, as if someone had salted her. Her eyes were the color of sea glass.

Her glasses were framed in thin black metal. The lenses weren't Coke-bottle-thick, but were substantial enough to suggest she saw poorly without them.

Her jacket was too large for her. It hid her breasts.

It could also hide a weapon. He didn't smell one, but he didn't smell her, either. That disturbed him. Both that lack and his response to it made it hard to assess her properly.

Her legs were long. Though she was only slightly above average height for a woman, she looked taller because so much of that height was provided by those long, thin legs. He wanted to know what those legs felt like wrapped around his waist.

She presented no physical challenge, but her abilities and motives remained unknown. He had to treat her as a possible danger.

"You're staring at me."

Yes, he was. The breath Benedict drew was ragged. He wanted to sink his hands into that crazy hair. To sniff and taste that smooth, pale skin. He was supposed to do those things, and more. She was his mate, though she didn't know it. This fragile woman with huge, frightened eyes was his mate.

Was the Lady *insane*? "What are you doing here? Were you looking for me?"

"No, I—oh, I should have said yes. You might have believed that." Her face fell. "I can't tell you why I'm here, but it's a *good* reason. I'd like to leave now."

"No." Benedict refused to feel sorry for her, no matter how fragile and frightened she seemed. "Matt, call Seabourne. Tell him to meet us at the Rho's house. Be sure he knows we're on yellow alert."

"Cullen Seabourne?" She had pretty eyebrows, perfect half circles she lifted now over the frames of her glasses.

"You know him?"

"No, but I . . . I talk too much. I should shut up now, but I need to call my aunt."

"Your aunt."

She nodded vigorously. An escaped curl bobbed into her face and she brushed it back. "I'm going to pass out soon. I don't want her to worry, so I need to let her know ahead of time."

"How soon?"

She gave that a moment's thought. "It's hard to say. Within the hour, probably."

Matt called out, "Cullen's not answering."

"Then go get him." Matt leaped off the porch, hitting the ground at a run. Benedict spoke to his captive. "Give Shannon your cane and your tool belt and remove your jacket."

"What?"

"I need to check you for weapons before I take you to the Rho."

She considered that with a small frown, then hooked the cane in her jacket pocket, freeing both hands so she could unfasten the tool belt. That, she handed to Shannon without complaint, but she held on to the cane. "I assure you, there's no sword concealed in this hunk of wood."

"A cane makes an excellent weapon on its own. It doesn't need a concealed blade."

She looked at the cane in her hand, amazed. "I had no idea. How cool. I don't suppose . . . well, no, you probably wouldn't," she answered herself. "But maybe I can find out more later. Not that I have many adventures, but you never know, do you?"

"Your jacket," he repeated. "And your cane."

"I really can't walk far without it."

"You won't have to."

She bit her lip, then handed the cane to Shannon and shrugged out of her jacket. She gave that to Shannon, too.

Her T-shirt was snug. Her breasts were small, but beautifully shaped. He wanted to . . . but he wouldn't. Not now. Maybe not ever. He didn't know what he was going to do, what he could do—or do without. He didn't know, and the lack of plan or purpose, of any sense of what was needed, was as disturbing as her lack of scent. "Hold your arms out."

Her cheeks colored. "You are not going to search me."

"I am. Only a cursory search, however." He didn't wait

for her cooperation. If she'd spoken the truth about passing out, he needed to get her to the Rho quickly. One long step forward, and he knelt in front of her. He placed his hands on her hips—nothing in her pockets—and ran them down the outside of her legs.

Fragile she looked, and skinny she might be, but there was muscle beneath the denim. Approval hummed in him. Whatever her limits, she worked her body, respected it . . . and pushed those limits at times, as the elastic bandage wrapped around her left ankle indicated.

If this were a proper search, he'd unwrap the bandage and make sure there was nothing concealed within. He settled for probing it thoroughly. "A sprain?"

"Yes."

Her voice was breathy. He looked up and found those gray-green-blue eyes looking down on him. And the look in those eyes . . .

Thick and sweet, desire rose in him. He couldn't smell her, but he heard the hurry of her breath, saw the slight peaks of her nipples beneath the T-shirt. She enjoyed having his hands on her. She wanted more.

Neither of them could afford that. "Lift your arms," he said again, and if the huskiness in his voice gave him away, it couldn't be helped. "I'll inspect the rest of you visually."

The color in her cheek rose higher. "No more touching?"

"Not unless I see something I need to check out." And that came out full of meanings he hadn't intended.

She lifted her arms. Her breasts lifted, too.

"Benedict," Shannon said. He held a pair of vials, one larger than the other. Both empty. "They were in her pocket."

"Potions," Benedict said flatly.

"Well, yes." She smiled hopefully. "One of them cancelled my scent, like I said."

"The other?"

"Cancelled something else."

Did she think she could get away with such an insufficient answer? It was for the Rho to question her, however. Benedict rose and circled her. The T-shirt was snug enough for him to be sure she carried no large weapons. There could be a garrote or a needle concealed in her bra, but he'd chance it.

"All right," he said. "I'll take you to the Rho now. Whatever you do to make yourself invisible, it doesn't work on me."

"It's not invisibility, it's—*eep!*"

He'd scooped her up in his arms. The pleasure of holding her was a distraction he couldn't wholly ignore. He'd have to allow for that distraction. "Pete," he said to his second, "maintain yellow alert. Todd, Shannon, with me." He started forward at quick jog.

His Chosen was glaring at him. "You're not supposed to just pick people up."

"This way, if you pass out, you won't injure yourself further. Also, the Rho's house is 4.2 miles from the barracks. That would be slow and difficult for you even with your cane. Did a doctor look at your ankle?"

She shook her head. Her lips were thin with temper. Her body was stiff, too, and she gripped his arm too tightly.

"Relax. I'm not going to drop you. You have some other physical problem. Your hip?"

"I don't see what business that is of . . . oh, oh, I'm sorry!" Her clutching hand had squeezed last night's wound, and in spite of himself he'd winced. Her hand hovered over his arm like a nervous hummingbird. "You did get hurt!"

"Nothing significant, like I said. It's not quite healed yet."

"Then you really shouldn't be carrying me."

For some reason that made his mouth crook up. "I caught you. I get to carry you if I want to. You might as well tell me your name. It's probably on your car registration."

"You found my car? I guess that's how—but it's not—" She stopped abruptly and clamped her lips shut.

"Not your car? We'll still be able to learn who it belongs to. Or the police will."

Distress flashed over her face. "You don't need to call the police."

"I've caught a trespasser. Why wouldn't I call the police?"

"Please," she whispered. "Please don't. I—I can't tell you why, but someone's life would be in danger."

He very much doubted Isen would involve the human authorities, but there was no point in telling her that. No point other than easing the fear in those big eyes. "The Rho will make that decision, not me. My name is Benedict, by the way."

"Yes, I gathered that. You sent people to my car."

He nodded.

"They'll find my purse, then, so there's no point, I guess. I'm Arjenie. Arjenie Fox. Who's the 'she' you mentioned? The one you think sent me—no, you said *delivered* me—to you."

"No one you know." She felt good in his arms. Too good. He picked up his pace. Carrying her himself made sense. Her mind tricks didn't work on him. But it complicated things. "Why were you at Friar's last night?"

"I can't tell you. You can't possibly know who I know and who I don't."

It took him a second to backtrack mentally to her earlier question. "The Lady."

"The . . . oh! You mean the demi-deity your people serve?"

His eyebrows lifted. "Demi-deity?"

"Is that the wrong term? I don't mean to be insulting. How did you find out I was here? Not me, specifically, but you were alerted somehow."

Not only had she heard of the Lady, she even phrased it correctly. Lupi didn't worship the Lady. They served her. "Who are you?" he asked abruptly.

"I told you."

"Your name tells me very little. Last night you said Friar's men wouldn't see you. I understand that assertion now. How do you go unseen?"

She regarded him with a little vee between her brows. "Maybe I should trade answers with you. I'll tell you how I go unseen. You tell me . . . let me think. If I ask what you're going to do with me, you'll just say it's up to your Rho."

"It is."

"Uh-huh." She was skeptical. "You didn't tell me your last name."

"I seldom use it."

"Why not?"

"Is that the question you want answered in exchange for

telling me how you go unseen when you're prowling around
where you don't belong?"

"Prowling." She sighed. "That sounds much more interesting than hobbling. No, that's not the question I want answered. I want to know what alerted you and why you could
see me."

"I can't answer your second question now." He wasn't
ready to tell her about the mate bond. He would have to, but
this was a poor time for such a revelation. "In answer to your
first question—footprints."

She was chagrined. "The ground's so dry I didn't think
I'd leave any."

"They weren't very noticeable, but your cane leaves a
distinctive imprint, even in dry ground. The marks it left
made Kendrick curious enough to look more closely. When
he found footprints that had no scent, he alerted me."

She shook her head. "I didn't think about the cane leaving
a mark. I guess it's my turn to answer. Have you heard of a
spell that lets someone make something hard to spot?"

"Yes. It's supposed to be almost impossible to apply such
a spell to a moving object, like a person."

"It would be hard, but I don't use a spell. Going unnoticed is my Gift."

An impressive Gift, and one he'd never heard of. Perhaps
Seabourne would know something about it. "You said you
were going to pass out. I've heard of Gifted doing that when
they were at risk of burnout, but I thought the effect was
immediate."

"Um . . . I've heard that, too. It doesn't work that way
with me."

Evasive . . . but why? She'd announced her impending
unconsciousness easily enough. He made a mental note to
return to the subject later. "How long do you expect to be
out?"

"A couple days, though it might be longer. It helps if I eat
first. I've got some jerky and a Snickers bar in my tool belt."

"We'll feed you."

They'd nearly reached his father's house. The windows
were dark, of course; that was part of the protocol for a yellow alert. Also part of that protocol were the two sharp yips

he gave to announce himself so the guards would know he wasn't acting under constraint. Had he called out verbally or remained silent, they would have shot him.

"That's weird, you making that sound when you aren't being a wolf. Were you telling them something? Your men?"

She was bright and observant and—"You aren't afraid anymore," he said abruptly.

"You look scary, but you touch carefully. Like with my ankle. And when you picked me up . . . which you should not do without my permission! But you were careful when you did that. I don't think you're going to hurt me."

Feelings stirred in him, dark and ugly. "Not physically."

"Good. I'm a real baby about pain."

COULD you develop Stockholm Syndrome in a matter of moments?

Arjenie considered that question as her two-legged steed slowed down, and the two men who'd escorted them peeled away, heading for who-knew-where.

She was pretty sure you couldn't, not this fast, though she'd never actually researched the subject. But being carried by this man felt impossibly good, and not just because she was really tired and her ankle was really glad she wasn't walking on it anymore. He was so large and warm and male.

Her whole body approved. She didn't understand. It hadn't been *that* long since she'd shared sex.

Benedict. It was probably from the Latin *benedictus*, which meant *blessed*. Why didn't he want to tell her his last name? For that matter, why didn't she already know it? He was mentioned in the Bureau's files on Nokolai clan—at least, she was assuming he was the Benedict who was the Nokolai Rho's oldest son. But she couldn't remember his surname.

Maybe it was Turner, like his father's. Though since lupi didn't marry, that didn't seem likely. And she couldn't remember. How odd. Maybe the FBI didn't know it.

They'd nearly reached their destination. Though the house remained dark, she knew by its location that it must be the Rho's house. It had been marked on the aerial photo.

Benedict loped up a flagstone path curving its way through terraced beds filled with artful tumbles of stones and what she thought was a mix of native plants and drought-tolerant imports, though she was no horticulturalist to be sure. But the yucca was unmistakable, and those shrubby plants were probably some kind of sage, and she smelled rosemary.

The house itself was larger than the others she'd seen, but not by any means a mansion. A pale, rambling stucco, it snuggled into the slope at the end of the narrow valley that held the little village. Were there guards inside the house? She didn't see any outside—not even the two men who'd run here with them.

Benedict Last-Name-Unknown came to a stop at the big front door, which looked like it belonged on an old mission. His chest rose and fell against her. He was breathing deeply, but not hard. Apparently it took more than a four-mile run carrying an extra hundred and twenty pounds to leave him winded.

He didn't knock or ring a bell. The door just opened.

It was too much darker inside than out for her to make out much, but a shadowy form loomed a few steps inside that doorway. "Benedict," that shadow rumbled. His voice was even deeper than her steed's, but a lot friendlier. In fact, he sounded delighted, as if he'd been hoping his son would lope up to his door carrying a woman in the middle of the night. "I trust you can introduce me to our guest."

"I had been thinking of her more as a prisoner. Her name is Arjenie Fox."

"Benedict disapproves of my answering the door when you might have confederates lurking about somewhere," the bulky shadow explained. "You haven't come here to kill me, I hope?"

"Oh, no," she assured him. "That is, I didn't come here to kill anyone. I think you're Isen Turner?"

"I am. And I am pleased to meet you, Ms. Fox. Do come in. Or rather, Benedict, put her down so she can come in."

"She injured her ankle last night," his son said. "She needs to stay off it as much as possible. I don't know what her other physical liability is. She's been unwilling to tell me."

"Because it isn't any of your business," she said, exasperated. Really, she wished he'd stop harping on that.

"Hmm. Well, bring her to my study, then," Isen Turner said. "I regret the lack of light, Ms. Fox, but the study is an interior room, so we'll be able to turn on a light there."

The darkened house was a security measure, then. Arjenie was relieved to learn that, because it meant they weren't doing it just to intimidate her. "I'd appreciate that," she told him politely. "But I could walk on my own if that guard—Shannon?—if he hadn't gone off somewhere with my cane."

"I'll see that it's returned to you. Now—"

"She needs food," Benedict said. "I'll explain in a moment, but she needs food."

"Ah. Carl," the shadow said without raising his voice, "put together a sandwich or two for our guest, please." With that, he moved away from the door, and Benedict moved forward.

Her eyes adjusted quickly once Benedict crossed the threshold, but she didn't see Carl. She did see Isen Turner's broad back heading down a wide entry hall. She also saw an ornate console table with a cello propped up against the wall beside it, and two doors, one open and one closed, both on the right. There was another door on the left. After about twenty feet, the entry hall opened into a room at the back of the house. Moonlight flooded in from that end, admitted by a large picture window.

Isen Turner opened the door on the left. Benedict followed, and as soon as they were both inside, his father shut the door and turned on a light. She blinked at the sudden brightness.

Isen Turner's study was square and windowless and covered with books. Shelves stretched from floor to ceiling along every wall, and every shelf was full of books—paperbacks, hardcovers, oversize tomes.

"What a wonderful room!"

"Thank you." Isen Turner stood beside one of the four comfy leather chairs arranged in a circle in the center of the room. He was a comfortable-looking man, she thought—burly and strong like her Uncle Clay, who was a blacksmith. He had a craggy face, a very short beard, and shrewd eyes. Unlike his son, he was fully dressed in jeans and a button-down shirt. "Please have a seat."

"He doesn't have reins, so I can't steer—oh, thank you," she said as Benedict placed her in one of the chairs. He didn't sit down himself, but remained standing behind her chair. "Could you stand somewhere else instead of hovering over me?"

"No."

"He's guarding me from you," Isen Turner explained, seating himself across from her. "Benedict? Why are we feeding her?"

"She believes she's going to pass out due to overuse of her Gift, which is a type of mind-magic that allows her to hide in plain sight. She claims that eating delays or mitigates the effects of this overuse."

"Ah. I'd rather you didn't pass out," he said to Arjenie.

"Well, I'm going to, but food will help. He wouldn't let me have my candy bar."

"We can do better than a candy bar, I think. If you—ah, yes, Carl, come in."

Carl wasn't invisible after all. He was tall and lanky, with gray hair and creases in his leathery skin. He was silent, though, handing Arjenie a plate with two fat sandwiches, then leaving without saying a word.

Arjenie peeked under the bread. Roast beef with thick slices of tomato. She loved roast beef. "Thank you," she said, and dug in.

"Report," Isen Turner said.

Clearly and concisely, Benedict described what had alerted him to an intruder, how he'd found her, what she'd said, what he'd observed. Arjenie listened as she ate, fascinated. He finished about the same time she did, and she twisted around to look up at him. "That was well done. I've an excellent memory, but I'm not good at summarizing. I tend to include too many details."

"Thank you," he said gravely. "Would you care to add anything?"

"I don't think so," she said, turning back to face his father. "No, wait, I think there's one thing you should know. Robert Friar is clairaudient. Can I call my aunt now?"

Isen Turner's eyebrows lifted. "Friar's a Listener? And how do you know this?"

"I can't tell you, but he's exceptionally strong, only for some reason he can't Listen in here at your clanhome. I really need to call my aunt."

"And yet I have to insist that you do add a few of those details you tend to include in your summaries. I need to know what was in those vials and what you did with it."

"Nothing that can possibly hurt you or anyone here."

He shook his head sadly. "That's not good enough. What if you're wrong? What if you're lying or misled or simply mistaken?"

She nodded. "We do have a problem. I can see why you can't take me at my word, but I can't tell you any more than I already have."

"There's a difference between *can't* and *won't*." He leaned forward, his elbows on his knees—and everything about him changed. "I'm going to have to help you find that difference."

Arjenie flinched back in the chair, eyes wide. It wasn't the words, it was the way he looked—implacable, unreachable. As if he would do anything necessary to make her answer his questions. Anything. "I can't," she whispered. "I know the difference, and I *can't*."

"You were at our enemy's house last night," he said in that cast-iron voice. "You show up here tonight, playing mind tricks on my people and armed with some sort of potions. You will tell me why."

Oh, this was not going to be pleasant. She pressed her lips together.

"You realize I have complete control of what happens to you, don't you? It's not hard to make a body disappear in the mountains."

"B-Benedict?" she whispered—then wondered why she'd done that. He would be on his father's side. On his clan's side, and he had no reason to think she'd come here to save them, not harm them, and she couldn't explain.

"I'm here," he said from behind her. And then, even more tersely: "Isen."

Isen Turner's gaze flicked up to meet his son's eyes—then locked on as if magnetized. One heartbeat, two, three . . .

A knock on the door interrupted their staring contest.

"Come in," the Rho said.

The door on Arjenie's left opened. Automatically she looked to see who was here—and did some staring of her own.

She'd seen a lot of bare male chests tonight, a lot of hunky men wearing not much, and a few wearing nothing at all. But this man . . . oh, my. His spicy brown hair was shaggy and disheveled. He needed a shave. He was scowling. He was oh-my-God beautiful.

"Sorry it took me so long," the beautiful man said, not sounding apologetic at all. "I wasn't home, so I didn't get word right away. What do you need?"

"What do you see?" Isen Turner said, and gestured at Arjenie.

Blue eyes locked on her like twin lasers.

This had to be Cullen Seabourne—who was a lupus and also a sorcerer. Which meant he could see . . .

"I don't recognize the Gift," he said after a moment, "but I recognize the heritage. Elf. Not pureblood, maybe not even half, but she's part-sidhe."

Dizziness swung through Arjenie, not in a slow tide but fast. Oscillating. Picking up speed with each swing.

"Uh-oh," she said. And passed out.

SIXTEEN

THE orthopedic surgeon was a string bean—an inch taller than Rule and at least forty pounds lighter. His brown hair was thinning on top; his eyes were that peculiar pale blue that almost vanishes next to the black of the pupils. His lips were thin and so pale that, like his irises, they nearly disappeared. He reeked of disinfectant soap with a faint undertone of tobacco. His name was Robert Stanton.

Rule disliked the man, but he was a top-flight surgeon in his field, according to Nettie, and that was what mattered.

". . . recovering well from the surgery," Stanton was saying, "but I cannot say precisely when you can be released. Certainly not until after the skin graft, and I have explained why the wound must be left open for a few days. Dr. Cummings will perform that procedure. Has he been by to speak with you?"

The back of Lily's hospital bed was elevated so she could sit up. She looked weary and hurt and pale and pissed. "Yeah. Gold-rimmed glasses, dark skin, deep voice. Talks slow."

The plastic surgeon had made his rounds early, arriving before seven this morning, about the same time that Rule received a call from his father. Rule hadn't passed on the details of that call to Lily yet. First the nurse had come in with her pain medication—which Lily had only taken half of—then her surgeon had arrived.

"Er—yes," Stanton said, "that is Dr. Cummings. You can have every confidence in him. Now, before I go I need to speak with you about your prognosis. I must caution you that it is unlikely you will regain full function of the arm."

Lily's head jerked back. Her eyebrows snapped down. "Why not? You said the surgery went well."

"It did. Barring infection, I expect the bone to knit sufficiently for limited use in six to eight weeks. It doesn't fully harden in that time, you understand. However, you lost muscle, and there was nerve damage. I do not believe the nerve damage was so extensive that you won't see any regeneration, but such regeneration is a slow process and the extent is difficult to predict."

"Give me a ballpark figure. Eighty percent of normal? Sixty? Ninety?"

"There is no 'ballpark' for these sorts of injuries. You should regain the use of the arm. If you are disciplined with your therapy, you may regain much of its function, but it will likely always be weaker than it was. I cannot say how much weaker. The difference may be acute. It may be negligible. Most likely, it will fall somewhere between those extremes."

"Dr. Two Horses is flying in to begin treatment," Rule said. "That will make a difference."

"The healer." His thin lips tightened with distaste. "Her assistance may be beneficial for the soft tissue damage. There is substantial evidence that intervention by a Gifted healer can speed recovery, but I am aware of no studies showing that such intervention results in greater nerve regeneration than would occur naturally. However, it is unlikely that Dr. Two Horses's treatments would cause any harm, so I have no objection."

"What a relief," Lily muttered. "You can go away now."

Stanton frowned. "Have you spoken with someone from Physical Therapy? We have an excellent facility here, with—"

"I live in San Diego, so I'll be disciplined with my therapy there."

The surgeon should have remembered that Lily wasn't local, but he didn't really see her—he saw a medical condition. No doubt he often found the humanity of his patients inconvenient. Primly he said, "I am not acquainted with San Diego's therapeutic facilities."

"Dr. Two Horses is." Rule moved forward to usher the man out. "She'll be in touch with you when she arrives, I'm sure. Thank you for your skill and your time, Doctor." *And now, as Lily said, go away.*

Stanton's head moved about a centimeter in a nod. "Good day, then."

"He doesn't approve of Nettie, does he?" Lily said once Rule closed the door behind the surgeon. "Hard to have much confidence in him when he's an idiot."

"I suspect he doesn't approve of anything outside his own skill set, and he's suspicious of anything not connected to him in some way. Like San Diego." Rule took a moment before he turned to face her, schooling his expression. At least he didn't have to worry about her smelling his fear. "He's not convinced we have any therapists, much less decent facilities for them to use."

Lily's smile was brief and abstracted. Her eyes were shadowed; her gaze distant. Her arm . . . her poor arm. It was supported by a sling, a padded contraption with straps. They couldn't cast it, not with unhealed wounds.

Lily had "an open, comminuted diaphyseal fracture of the humerus." Translated, that meant multiple breaks in the shaft of the bone combined with an open wound—the messy exit the bullet had made as it blew out the front of her biceps. Because bone has a poorer blood supply than the soft tissue around it, infection was a worry. Less blood meant fewer immune cells delivered to the wound site. That's why they wouldn't do the skin graft over the exit wound yet. They wanted to be sure there was no infection before closing things up.

People kept saying she was lucky. There was no significant vascular damage, no joint damage, and the surgeon had been able to use internal fixation—in other words, he'd nailed the bone back together inside her arm instead of using an external rod with pins or screws that impaled skin and bone alike to hold the pieces together. And yes, Rule supposed that was luck of a sort.

But now the surgeon said she wouldn't regain full function. The horror of permanent, unhealed damage . . . Rule couldn't get his mind around that. It was something he'd never face. If a lupus didn't die from a wound, he healed completely.

And there was nothing, not one damned thing, he could do about it. She was human, and he . . . he was useless. "Nettie will help the healing more than the good doctor realizes. The mate bond will make a difference, too."

His words had no impact on her abstracted expression. "You've suggested that before—that the mate bond may be giving a boost to my immune system."

"It helps with healing, period. We don't know how much, but it will help." If only he could will the bond to steal some of his healing and give it to her! "Are you ready for your other pain pill?" She'd taken one; the other was still in its little paper cup.

"Not yet." Her gaze tightened, focusing on him. "You need to go get some rest. Crash at the hotel awhile. You didn't sleep much."

He hadn't slept at all. How could he? "I'm fine. I'm not leaving."

"At least go get some breakfast. The chips you got from a vending machine when I was eating my yummy broth won't carry you."

He smiled. "Soon. Not yet."

Her mouth tipped wryly. She held out her hand. Her left hand.

He moved close and wrapped his hand around hers. For a few moments neither of them spoke.

Rule noticed the sorrow first . . . a deep, gray sorrow, like being wrapped in rain clouds that held no lightning or thunder. Only grief, gray and formless. Grief for Lily's hurt. Grief for a tall man with café au lait skin and a smile that would not be seen again on this earth.

After a moment he also noticed that he was hungry. Too hungry, considering where he was. He gave in. "You're right.

I need to eat. Would you object to having Jeff in your room while I'm gone?"

"Yes." Her gaze sharpened. "Don't tell me he's here."

"Of course he's here. He's guarding your door. Alex is sending more guards, but until they arrive—"

"Wait, wait. I don't want guards."

His hand tightened on hers. "You'll have them whether you want them or not. Someone wants to kill you. They damned near succeeded."

"They killed LeBron. They killed him instead of me. I hate it. I hate it. I won't have guards."

All sorts of things rose up in Rule's mind—orders, reasons, arguments . . . words. All sorts of words that would explain and persuade. The words wanted to burst out, wrap themselves around her, protect her.

His wolf wouldn't let them. *Wait*, the wolf commanded, looking through the man's eyes at the woman he loved beyond words or reasons. He saw such grief in her face, such pain. Saw, too, that she was fighting that pain. His words wouldn't help. They would only give her more to fight against.

He waited.

The breath she drew broke in the middle. "I resented them. LeBron and Jeff and all the rest. Not them personally, but I resented them always being around. I thought I was being so reasonable by bringing him with me on my run. I was following the rules, wasn't I? I didn't want him there, but because I was so damned reasonable I let him tag along. And he died. I didn't have to go running, but I did, and he died. He died saving me."

Ah . . . Rule wanted to gather her close and croon to her. She hadn't grown up, as he had, knowing that others would die to protect him. Or because he sent them to fight the clan's enemies. Or because he simply made a mistake. She didn't know how to accept that, how to honor such choices. She was the one who defended others. How could she allow others to risk themselves for her?

Lily's childhood had broken apart when she and a friend were taken by a twisted man—or a thing that walked and looked like a man. Her friend hadn't survived. Lily had, and she'd knit those broken pieces back together by growing into a warrior, one who fought for others, for justice. Most of all, one who fought the monsters in whatever form they took.

Time, now, for words, but carefully. Carefully. "Le-Bron couldn't stop the monster who wanted you dead. There wasn't time. The best he could do was to deny that monster his target. He succeeded. Will you deny him the honor of his victory?"

"It isn't . . . I don't . . ." She stopped. Swallowed. "I need to do something," she whispered. "I don't know what, but I need to do something."

He nodded. "There will be a ceremony. You've been to our funerals before, but when a warrior falls in defense of his people—"

"I'm not his people. I'm not Leidolf."

"You are a Chosen, touched by the Lady. His Rho's Chosen. In defending you, he defended his Rho and all his people. You don't have to agree, Lily, simply accept that this is how we see it. How LeBron saw it."

She bit her lip and nodded.

"LeBron's death rites will be different from those you've seen. The *firnam* may be physically difficult for you. It may also be hard on you emotionally. We will celebrate him as a warrior who died a warrior's death. But if you are willing, there is a place for you in this ceremony."

Lily was silent for a long moment, then sighed, slow and deep. "Yes. I want to be part of it. They aren't going to let me out of here real soon, though."

"Soon enough." He raised her hand to his lips and kissed it. "I'll let Alex know. He's making the arrangements." He needed to tell her what had happened at Nokolai Clanhome last night. She still didn't know that Benedict had been gifted with a Chosen, much less that the woman had snuck into Clanhome for some unknown purpose involving unknown potions. But not now. She was exhausted, dragged down by grief and more than one kind of pain. "I know you dislike being doped up, but I think you—"

His stomach growled.

Her laugh was weak, a little breathless, but real. "I'll take my drug now. And you'll go eat."

"I believe I will," he said wryly. "I'll ask Jeff to remain on the other side of your door, not inside the room."

She gave him a level look. "I can live with that for now. We're going to talk about this business of guards again."

"I can live with that." He carried her hand to his lips for another kiss. "For now."

RULE left as soon as Lily downed her pain pill. He spoke with Jeff first. The youngster was barely trained, and he wanted to be sure Jeff didn't allow anyone in the room other than medical personnel he'd already seen and smelled. Unless the police came again, of course. Which they undoubtedly would, and probably sooner rather than later. Jeff couldn't ban them, but he could summon Rule, and he could go into the room with them.

Rule also told Jeff that Lily would participate in the *firnam*. Jeff nodded solemnly. "Good. That's good. She'll be the wounded? Though with so few *reliquae*—" He stopped, blinking. "I shouldn't assume."

"True, but you may always assume I honor those who serve. LeBron won't be slighted. I will serve as *reliquae* also, and I'll bring all of my Leidolf guards here for the *firnam*."

Jeff's eyes widened. "You will? The guys will be glad to hear that. I knew the clan's coffers were low, so I didn't think they'd be able to, but—now, don't take this wrong. Me and the guys will be honored to have you serve with us, but some of the older clan . . . well, they're used to doing things a certain way."

Leidolf's style of *firnam* set the Rho apart, rather than having him serve as *reliquae* alongside the other witnesses. "Tradition is important. I'm returning Leidolf to some of the older traditions. It will be at least a week and probably longer before we can hold the ceremony."

"That's not a problem. Uh . . . I talked to Samuel earlier to see how he was holding up. He said you called and told him about his father yourself. I guess you called both of LeBron's sons, and their granddad, too."

"Of course." Such a duty could not be delegated.

"You called them while Lily was in surgery. You told

Samuel that she'd lived to be operated on because of his father's courage."

Rule nodded, unsure of Jeff's point. Did he need reassurance that Rule could be a proper Rho to Leidolf?

Jeff sighed. "I miss LeBron. It was a good death, but I miss him something fierce. I wish I knew who to kill."

"So do I," Rule said. "Though we may not be able to . . . ah." Relief dawned as he saw who was coming down the hall. "The others have arrived."

Alex had sent five guards. Two replaced Jeff at Lily's door; one went with Rule to the Courtyard Café. The other two, along with Jeff, would have the night shift, though one would run an errand first. Rule needed his laptop.

Rule hadn't originally intended to go to the café, which was in another building, but with additional guards around Lily, he decided he could take a little more time. The café offered freshly cooked food and real coffee. Starbucks might not be his first choice, but they brewed real coffee.

Rule ordered three eggs over easy with hash browns, a double side of bacon, and biscuits. His guard—Randy Carlson, a bulky young man with sun-streaked brown hair and a mustache—had already eaten, as per instructions. Rule had made sure that any lupi he brought into the hospital were well fed. Randy took up position at a nearby table where he could sip coffee and watch.

Once Rule finished eating, he slipped on an earbud and made some calls. The first went to Alex, who needed to know Lily's status and that she would participate in the *vitae reliquus*. Next was his father, who also needed to know about Lily. It was very early in San Diego, but Isen slept even less than Rule did. Rule expected him to be up, and he was.

They talked about Lily first and the surgeon's unwelcome expectations. Briefly then they touched on Clanhome's odd late-night visitor. She was still unconscious, just as she'd predicted. That was a curious business, but after asking a few questions he hadn't had time for earlier, Rule left the matter in Isen's and Benedict's hands. There was clan business to deal with.

He spoke with formal courtesy. "The Leidolf Rho wishes to speak with the Nokolai Rho."

"The Nokolai Rho greets the Leidolf Rho, and offers condolences on the loss of your clansman."

"Thank you. I've a request to make. I hope you will grant permission to those Nokolai guards who served with my clansman to attend the *firnam*, if they so wish, that they may act as *reliquae*."

"Ah." Silence for a moment. Rule knew Isen was thinking quickly, considering angles. Having more than one clan serve as *reliquae* was unusual, but not unheard of—save between Nokolai and Leidolf. *Reliquae*—a term also used by the Catholic Church, though in a different context—meant those who were left behind. They were drawn from those who had served in combat with the fallen warrior. Guarding a Rho was considered a combat position; all those who had served as guards with LeBron were eligible to act as *reliquae*.

At one time, every clan had observed the same death rites for its warriors. Some clans still followed the old custom in which a Rho served as simply another *reliquae* for any who fell in his service. That was Nokolai's practice, for in death all who serve the clan and the Lady are equal. Some clans—such as Leidolf—elevated the Rho's role in the *reliquus*. Rule disliked that practice heartily.

Isen spoke formally. "I am pleased by your request and grant it gladly. As a token of Nokolai's appreciation of Leidolf's sacrifice and your clansman's courage, Nokolai will pay the travel expenses of any who accept your invitation. Do you wish to extend the invitation yourself?"

"I do. I thank you. You should know that I've already invited one Nokolai. I apologize for not consulting you first."

"I assume you mean Lily."

"Yes."

"She wouldn't know she needed my permission—or care. You do know, but I choose not to find insult in this omission. There was a need?"

"The manner of LeBron's death affects her strongly."

"I see. Tell her—no, she won't need to hear from her Rho. I would speak with my son."

"I'm here."

"Tell Lily there is a difference between pain and damage. Damage may heal eventually. Or not. Pain simply is."

It was an odd message. Dubious but willing, Rule agreed to pass it on and said goodbye. He needed to get back to Lily. He would take her some coffee, he decided. She'd probably fallen asleep again—he hoped so—but if not, she'd appreciate a cup of real coffee.

He got himself a refill, too, and had them put both cups in a bag so he could keep one hand free. He could have asked Randy to carry it, of course, but what use was a bodyguard with his hands full?

He was glad for the free hand a few moments later when he got a call from Stephen Andros, the Etorri Lu Nuncio. And again as he crossed to the building that held Lily's room, when the Ybirra Lu Nuncio called. He'd just entered the stairwell—he needed to stretch his legs, and a trot up five flights would do that—when Edgar Whitman, Rho of Wythe clan, called.

The calls from the Lu Nuncios hadn't surprised him. They'd heard about the attack on Lily on the morning news—it had excited the talking heads—and those involved in the upcoming circle wanted to assure Rule they would wait until his Chosen was recovered enough for travel. They also wanted to extend their support. The Rhos of their clans would probably contact Isen to say much the same things their Lu Nuncios said to Rule. A Chosen was Lady-touched, like a Rhej. Like a Rhej, she was treasured by all clans.

But Rule hadn't expected to hear from a Rho. He was a Rho now himself, yes, but because Lily was Nokolai, he'd expected the other clans to treat with him in this instance according to his status in Nokolai—as heir. In truth, he'd rather talk to the Wythe Lu Nuncio than its Rho. He liked Brian, who laughed easily and was Rule's closest age-mate among the heirs. Edgar was . . . difficult.

Edgar expressed the usual wish for Lily's healing, asked the usual questions. "I'm glad she's doing well," he said then. "Wythe stands ready to hunt for any who would harm a Chosen. Give us word if we may assist."

"Leidolf thanks you. Nokolai appreciates your concern and your offer."

Edgar snorted. "Not easy, wearing two hats, is it? I won't keep you on the phone now, when your attention must be divided. But I need to know Nokolai won't use this as an excuse to delay the heirs' circle."

A flick of anger turned Rule's voice cold. "I am trying not to find insult in your words. Nokolai has worked with Wythe in good conscience to arrange the circle." In spite of considerable argument and insult, primarily from Wythe and Ybirra.

Less than a year ago, Rule had called another heirs' circle—for all heirs, not just those from North America—to inform the others in person that *she* was active in the world again. They had come from all over without any of this prolonged negotiation. The contrast between then and now was sharp and painful.

Edgar snorted. "If I could trust Nokolai's conscience to prevail over its ambition, we wouldn't need to meet. Wythe has negotiated in good faith, too."

Wythe—in the person of its Rho, Edgar—had been a paranoid ass. At first Edgar had denied Rule's authority to even call an heirs' circle on the grounds that Rule was now a Rho.

True, Rhos were usually not included in an heirs' circle; it created imbalance. But Leidolf lacked an heir. Alex might hold the title of Lu Nuncio, but it was empty of its usual meaning. Alex wasn't of the founder's bloodline, so couldn't receive the heir's portion of the mantle. This was a precarious position for a clan, but hardly unprecedented. And precedent clearly allowed a Rho who lacked an heir to attend an heirs' circle.

The claim was particularly galling, coming from Wythe. They were in almost as precarious a position as Leidolf. Edgar's younger brother, Brian, was his Lu Nuncio because Edgar's only son had been killed in a Challenge three years ago. The only one other than Edgar and his brother who was certain to carry the founder's blood was Brian's son, who was barely out of diapers. If anything happened to Brian, Wythe would be in the position Leidolf was until the boy grew up.

Rule said nothing. Silence was preferable to telling Edgar what he really thought. It also encouraged the other person speak to fill it.

"Doubt me, do you, boy?" Edgar demanded. "You shouldn't.

I want the circle to take place, and am willing to alter our arrangements to avoid delay. Your Chosen shouldn't be dragged to St. Paul now—indeed, she may not be well enough for such a trip for weeks. I am willing to allow the circle to be called in San Diego."

That was a concession. A large one. Rule answered slowly. "Leidolf does not object. As for Nokolai . . . I will have to speak with my Rho, of course, but I see no problem. Ybirra may."

"I'll contact Manuel. I want to get this done. I think he does, too."

"Very well. I'll speak with Etorri and Kyffin." Kyffin clan was a dominant, but was temporarily subordinate to Nokolai, so obtaining their consent was a courtesy. A necessary courtesy, but still, Jasper couldn't withhold his Lu Nuncio. As for Etorri, Rule doubted Stephen or his father would object. Etorri supported the call for the All-Clan. "Will you also call Szøs?"

"I will. I'll be in touch after I've spoken with Manuel and Andor. *T'eius ven*," Edgar said abruptly.

"*T'eius ven*, Edgar."

Rule disconnected, frowning. Edgar was not a subtle man—or didn't seem so to someone who'd been raised by Isen Turner. But he was a Rho, and had been for over four decades. His actions often served more than one purpose.

What benefit was there to Wythe in meeting quickly? Rule couldn't find one, yet Edgar was eager enough for the circle to take place that he suggested a meeting place clearly to Wythe's disadvantage. Was he less suspicious of Nokolai than Rule had thought? Or was that misdirection? What advantage could he be seeking that Rule couldn't spot?

Ten months ago, Isen Turner had called for an All-Clan. After centuries of absence, their most ancient enemy had begun stirring. The clans needed to meet, to exchange information, to make ready for whatever *she* planned.

Discussion for the All-Clan had gone well, if slowly. Szøs and Etorri had agreed immediately; two of the European clans had agreed after some haggling. But when Rule became Leidolf Rho, suspicion dragged planning to a halt.

Rule didn't blame the other clans for wondering what he

was up to. In their place he'd have been wary, too. The balance was upset, and he didn't expect them to react otherwise. Yet the All-Clan had to take place. *She* might not have moved again since dragging him and Lily to Dis, but sooner or later, *she* would.

In order to get the All-Clan, Nokolai had to reassure its fellow dominants in North America. To do this, Rule had called for a circle of heirs—in this case, the Lu Nuncios of the dominant clans of North America. Finding a meeting place that didn't favor one over the others had been difficult. They'd finally agreed on St. Paul. That favored Wythe because it was closest geographically to their territory, but Wythe was the smallest of the U.S. dominants, so was less able to take violent advantage of such proximity.

They were also the most annoying. Wythe and Ybirra were the two clans most opposed to the All-Clan, the two most suspicious of Nokolai. Ybirra had some reason; while on the whole the two clans got along well, Ybirra was Nokolai's nearest neighbor. Territorial skirmishes were inevitable from time to time, and Ybirra had the most to fear if Nokolai were up to something. Wythe's intransigence was based more on habit and personality. Edgar simply did not trust Isen and never had.

Now Edgar had contacted Rule directly. That made no sense. Rhos delegated much of the maneuvering to their heirs for a reason. When a Rho negotiated directly, the stakes were higher, the risk of insult greater. And a Rho almost always negotiated with other Rhos. The power was otherwise too uneven. While a Rho could not use his mantle to directly affect those of other clans, all lupi responded to the presence of a mantle. Not all in the same way, but all responded. Rule had once seen his father break up a fight between Kyffin youngsters with a single shouted command.

Of course, Rule was now Rho as well as Lu Nuncio. Perhaps Edgar had decided that made it acceptable. More likely he used it as an excuse to take Rule by surprise . . . yet he called to propose abandoning St. Paul for San Diego, smack-dab in Nokolai territory. Either Edgar had decided to stop opposing the All-Clan, or Rule was missing something.

And either way, he needed to call his father, but he'd

reached Lily's room. He'd check on her first. She was probably asleep, but if not, she'd want the coffee he'd brought.

Her guards said no one had entered since he left. Rule nodded and pushed the door open. She was still awake, still sitting with the head of her bed elevated, still pallid with pain. Her eyes, when they met his, were dark with trouble.

"I just spoke to Croft," she said. "According to the healer, Ruben's heart attack wasn't natural. It was attempted murder, and for reasons of access and timing, Croft thinks it's one of us. Someone in the FBI used magic to try to kill Ruben."

SEVENTEEN

ARJENIE woke slowly to the sound of flute music. She didn't know the song, but it was piercing and plaintive as only a flute can be. Uncle Ambrose played so beautifully . . .

She ached all over. Arms, legs, back, shoulders—every part of her registered its own complaint, as if she had the flu. She knew what that meant. As for the dull ache in her head, even in her half-conscious state, she recognized that as a by-product of hunger, not Gift-abuse.

For a bit she drifted with the music, wondering dimly what song that was and why Uncle Ambrose was here.

Here? Where was here?

Her eyes popped open. The aches and hunger were familiar. The room she'd woken up in was not.

She lay on her back in a bed that wasn't hers. There was a pillow beneath her head and a light bedspread covering her. The ceiling above her was white, but that wasn't much of a clue.

Arjenie squinted as she turned her head on the pillow. Without her glasses it was hard to be sure, but aside from blurry shapes she took to be furniture—a small table by her bed and a chair on the opposite wall—the room seemed empty. Also small. The walls were white, interrupted by one door and one window. The door was ajar, but not widely enough for her to see what lay beyond it.

It was not her hotel room.

It wouldn't be, of course. Memory was seeping back . . . the water well, her ankle, Benedict Last-Name-Unknown. Isen Turner. Cullen Seabourne, who'd said—

She sat up too fast. And winced at the stab of pain in her head.

The flute music cut off. A moment later, the door swung open and a large shape—khaki-colored on top, denim-colored below—loomed in the doorway.

Her hand shot out, scrambling on the table for what she hoped were her glasses. *Yes!* She shoved them on.

Benedict was wearing jeans still, but he'd added a khaki shirt. He'd buttoned it, too, darn it. He wore an earbud which she guessed must connect to the cell phone clipped to his belt . . . which also held a knife sheath, complete with knife. Not a pocketknife—a big, long thing.

No sword, though. "Do you ever have trouble with doorways?"

He blinked. "Doorways?"

"Not the standard ones. I can see that you fit through them. But I'm not sure your shoulders would fit through a narrower doorway. You might have to turn sideways."

He shook his head. "You can't be as guileless as you seem."

"I'm pretty short on guile. That doesn't mean I'm not a complex person, capable of great subtlety. Just not much guile. Am I a guest or a prisoner? And do you give prisoners or guests ibuprofen if their head hurts? Acetaminophen is okay, too, or even plain aspirin, but naproxen sodium doesn't do much for me."

He turned and left the room.

She blinked. Was that a yes or a no? Before she could decide, he was back, carrying a glass of water. He held it out. Automatically she took it.

"Ibuprofen," he said, extending his other hand, where two small brown pills rested. "Nettie thought you might want some."

"Nettie?"

"Dr. Two Horses. She checked you out after you collapsed. Gave you a bit of a boost. She's a healer."

Oh, yes, she'd seen a mention of Dr. Two Horses in the Nokolai files. Plus she'd heard of her elsewhere . . . something she'd read? No, from Uncle Nate. He wasn't a healer, but he was a doctor and he took a good deal of interest in those few—very few—physicians who'd gone public about their healing Gift. He spoke very highly of Dr. Nettie Two Horses.

Arjenie reached for the pill and noticed something. "My ring's gone."

"It's on the table where your glasses were."

Oh. She hadn't seen it when she grabbed her glasses because she hadn't seen very much then. Arjenie snatched the little ring and put it back where it belonged. "My mother gave it to me. I never take it off."

"My apologies. It had a power signature. Seabourne had to check it."

"It's a perfectly harmless little spell to discourage mosquitoes."

"So he said." Benedict held out the ibuprofen again.

This time she accepted the pills, popped them in her mouth, and washed them down with the water.

"More water?" Benedict asked politely.

"No, thank you. I'm awfully hungry, though."

"Supper will be ready in an hour or so. Do you need a snack to tide you over?"

"That would be lovely. How long was I out?"

"About ten hours."

She smiled, pleased. That was much less than she'd expected. Maybe Aunt Robin hadn't had time to get worried yet. "Dr. Two Horses must have given me a big boost. I'd like to thank her."

"She's not here. She had another patient to tend. She said your ankle should be better in a couple days, and that your unconsciousness is a trance state similar to what she does when she puts a patient in sleep. Your version takes you deeper, which is why we couldn't wake you."

"That's a fair description."

"She didn't understand the delay between the overuse of your Gift and the onset of unconsciousness. Neither did Seabourne."

"I don't, either, but I've speculated. Maybe my body is waiting for me to do something to fix things. Replenish my power, maybe. Only I don't know how to do that quickly enough to help. I've tried several methods, but aside from eating, nothing makes much difference, and it only delays things. Do you think Cullen Seabourne knows a way to absorb or access power quickly?" He was a sorcerer, after all.

"Possibly." His voice was dry. "He's eager to talk to you. You can ask him."

She ducked her head, suddenly uncomfortable. Cullen Seabourne had seen in one glance what she'd spent her life hiding.

A pair of jeans, neatly folded, sat on the foot of the bed. Her jeans. "Someone took off my jeans." Her hand flew to her hair as she realized something else. "And took out my hair band."

"Both of them would be uncomfortable to sleep in. Or to pass out in. Seabourne says you're sidhe."

Arjenie bit her lip. There didn't seem much point in denying it. They wouldn't believe her. "Part-sidhe. It's a long story—at least, the only way I know how to tell it is long. It would be nice to know what you plan to do about me."

He considered her silently. He had such an interesting face—hard, yes, with those bladed cheekbones, and his default expression seemed to be no expression at all, so he ought to look scary. He had at first, but she wasn't frightened anymore. How odd, when so many things scared her! But Benedict didn't. She felt as if she could just sit here and look at him for an hour or two.

Or maybe not, she thought as her stomach gurgled unhappily. Her bladder didn't care for the idea, either. "I need to use the bathroom."

"It's down the hall. I'll have to escort you."

That sounded more like "prisoner" than "guest." "Okaaaay . . . but it's awkward to put on my jeans with you watching."

He nodded, turned, and walked out, closing the door behind him—not quite all the way. The not-quite-closed door had to be intentional. "You do that a lot, don't you?" she said, reaching for her jeans.

He sounded amused. "Watch women dress? Occasionally."

She huffed and threw back the covers. "Answer without using words. You don't use a lot of words. Maybe that's why you're good at summaries. You summarize everything." She looked down and saw her shoes lined up neatly by the bed. And her socks.

She picked up the socks. They were clean, fluffy from the drier. Someone had washed them. She tilted her head, considering that. While she was unconscious she'd been tended by a doctor, put to bed in her underwear and shirt, and her socks had been washed.

Having a doctor check her out, putting her in a comfy bed—those could be an attempt to win her trust so she'd tell them what they wanted to know. But washing her socks? That was nice. Just nice.

She pulled them on and stuck her legs in her jeans. The elastic bandage got in the way; she had to tug the denim over it. "Me, I like to talk, and I don't know how to ignore the details, because they're interesting. You didn't tell me what you plan to do about me."

"The Rho has decided you should stay here, as our guest, until you tell us why you're here, or we find out through other means."

"That's a prisoner, not a guest." She bent and pulled on her shoes.

"We can't hold you against your will." He was bland now. "But if you leave, we will notify the police of your trespass onto our land."

Last night his Rho had said they could do anything they wanted with her, up to and including killing her. Or had it been all implication? She cast her mind back over that part of their conversation. The threat had been mostly implied, she decided. In fact, he'd been careful not to say anything that might get him in trouble if she repeated it to the police.

Not that she would. Unfortunately, they'd figured that out. That hadn't been hard, given how she's reacted when Benedict mentioned calling the cops. Arjenie sighed and stood up. She'd pretty much handed that weapon to them. "That's coercion. Where's my cane?"

The door opened. "Here." He came in again and handed it to her. "Nettie says you should stay off the ankle as much as possible for another day. I could carry you."

"No, thank you." He was standing awfully close. Could she really feel the heat from his body, or was that her imagination? "I'm glad you asked this time, though. Uh—where am I?"

"The Rho's home. We'll be dining with him. You are a guest, but not one we trust, so I'll be keeping track of you."

Her mind arrowed straight at one part of that statement. "*You'll* be keeping track of me? Personally?"

"Since your mind tricks don't work on me, yes. They shouldn't work on Seabourne, either, so he'll take over when I need to sleep or have other duties."

"Why wouldn't my Gift work on him?"

"Shields. You know what he is. Why is that?"

Because she'd read about him in the file. And she knew his wife. She'd sent Cynna a present for her baby shower last month, an adorable little receiving blanket with . . . oh. *Oh, no.* She was so *stupid.*

Arjenie limped for the door. Her ankle was much better than she'd expected—tender, but not really painful. Another reason to thank Dr. Two Horses, no doubt.

"The bathroom's to the left. Seabourne scares you."

"Not exactly." But boy, he did throw a spanner in the works. Or rather, his wife did. If he mentioned Arjenie's name to Cynna, they'd know who she was. Then what?

She needed to think. She paused when she reached the hall, looking around. Next to the door was a wooden chair. There was a flute on its seat. To the right the hall ended in a den—maybe the room she'd seen last night, from a different hall. She could see a couch and part of a window. On her left the hall continued about fifteen feet before ending in a closed door.

She limped off to the left. "That was you playing the flute. I thought it was my uncle at first, though I didn't recognize the song."

"You wouldn't. I've never recorded it."

"You write music? You wrote that song?" She had to pause and smile at him. "It's beautiful. How did you know I'd woken up?"

"I heard you move."

"Really? Even over your music? Do you hear as well when you're like this as you do when you're wolf?"

"I hear better as a wolf."

She tried to imagine what that was like. "Which do you like better, being a wolf or being a human?"

"We don't think of ourselves as human. One of my forms is a man. One is a wolf. I like both forms. Which do you like better, your right arm or your left?"

"I'm right-handed, so my right arm is more useful, but I don't like one best . . . oh. That's what you mean. Both forms are you, and you don't have a favorite. But maybe one is more useful."

"You might say I'm ambidextrous. You ask a lot of questions."

"I'm curious." She'd reached the bathroom, but instead of going in, she turned to face him. "What's your last name?"

He didn't answer. It wasn't hesitation. That implies doubt, uncertainty, and his eyes stayed steady on hers. Such dark eyes, like bittersweet chocolate . . . and wasn't that steadiness central to him? He knew how to wait, this man—on events, on understanding, on whatever might rise from inside. Nor did he seem to be seeking something from her. He just looked into her eyes, and the longer he looked, the faster her heart beat. Finally he spoke. "I've used more than one surname, but at birth I was called Benedict Charles Kayani."

Arjenie didn't know why she was sure he'd offered her a secret, a glimpse of something private. She just knew. A little bud opened inside her, so soft and subtle she barely noticed. "It's a growth plate injury."

Those dark eyes blinked once, overtaken by puzzlement.

It made her grin. "Uncle Clay says I'm a firefly—here, there, here, then off somewhere else. Sometimes I forget the conversational breadcrumbs, so there's no trail for others to follow. You keep asking about my physical impairment. It's from a growth plate injury when I was twelve."

Understanding dawned. "One of your legs is shorter than

the other. The left leg. It's not greatly different, but enough to cause problems."

She nodded. "My left tibia didn't grow as much as my right, and it grew crooked. I had a couple surgeries that corrected most of the crookedness, but it isn't *entirely* straight, so that foot turns under me if I'm careless. I've had a lot of sprained ankles."

"How were you hurt?"

"An auto accident. Drunk driver. My mom was killed." Now why had she added that part? She never did. People felt obliged to say they were sorry, or they became uncomfortable, or—

He touched her cheek. Just that, and just for a moment, then his hand dropped.

That's when she noticed the bud. It was singing, or humming . . . yes, a funny little humming feeling inside her, so new she didn't have a word for it. It was not attraction, though heaven knew she was attracted to this man. But that was a known feeling. This—this newness, what was that? It didn't make sense.

She bit her lip in confusion and escaped into the bathroom.

THE bathroom door closed. Benedict leaned against the wall, his eyes closing. His heart hammered against the wall of his chest.

God. God, she was so lovely and frail and strong all at once—and nothing like Claire. How could the Lady Choose twice for him, and Choose so differently? Claire had been all fire—smart and savvy, her beautifully fit body the instrument she used for combat, for sex, for living every second at its fullest. She'd burned, his Claire, burned so brightly. She'd been a fighter in every sense.

God knew she'd fought the mate bond. Fought it relentlessly. Frantically. Fatally.

Benedict drew a ragged breath. He had to tell Arjenie about the bond. Had to. And couldn't, his throat closed by terror of what could go wrong—and by the sick, certain knowledge of just how wrong it could go.

What was she? Part-sidhe, according to Seabourne. Possibly an enemy, according to the facts. Isen didn't think that was likely. He believed the Lady wouldn't have gifted Benedict with an enemy of the clan.

Benedict couldn't remember his father ever entertaining such a naïve notion before. The Lady's reasons were her own. She might have decided the clan needed Arjenie for some reason. That didn't mean the woman could be trusted now.

The potion that blocked her scent was wearing off. When he'd stood close to her, when he'd touched her, he'd smelled her again—not as clearly as in his other form, but clearly enough. Her scent made him think of running flat out with the sun shining hot on his fur. It made him think of summer afternoons when he was young—young enough that an afternoon was an endless stretch of possibilities. It made him think of messy sheets, entwined bodies, and the musky smell of sex.

It made him think of these things now. Then, it had just made him hard.

What had the other potion she'd brought to Clanhome been designed to do? If she wasn't an enemy, why wouldn't she tell them? Someone's life was at risk, she'd said. Friar was clairaudient, she'd said—a Listener, in other words, capable of magically hearing from afar. But she admitted Friar's Gift didn't work here at Clanhome. Why not?

Maybe that was a lie. Maybe Friar wasn't a Listener—or he was, but Clanhome had no effect on his Gift. If she was telling the truth about that, why couldn't she level with them here, where Friar couldn't Listen in?

He'd touched her. The skin of her cheek was as soft as a flower petal. He needed to touch her again.

He was so afraid.

EIGHTEEN

SHE took a shower. A long shower.

Benedict hadn't expected that. When she said she needed to use the restroom, he'd assumed she meant she wanted to empty her bladder. She did that, but then turned on the shower.

He didn't object. The window in that bathroom was large enough for her to escape through, but he doubted she could do it without him hearing. Not once he'd opened the door a crack, that is. And he could use a few minutes to get himself under control. Fear was partly a physical phenomenon. Exertion would diminish or eliminate the effects, but he couldn't go for a run right now, so he used the breathing exercises he taught young Nokolai.

The fear had receded to a manageable level and the shower was still running when his brother called. "Can you talk?" Rule asked.

"Yes, though we'd best keep it brief. My charge"—he couldn't bring himself to say "my Chosen"—"is awake and showering. Isen told you about her."

"Both her unusual arrival in your life and her equally odd reappearance last night. Also that, according to Cullen, she's part-sidhe. Not just the tiny whiff of Fae blood some people possess, but perhaps as much as a quarter-blood."

"He couldn't quantify it that closely, but yes." Benedict understood the disbelief in his brother's voice. The sidhe had never dallied much in this realm. Conventional wisdom had it that they'd stopped coming entirely after the Purge. Earth had become too dry for them, magically speaking, or too unfriendly.

But conventional wisdom was often right in the general, wrong in the specific. Seabourne claimed to have once met a sidhe lord who'd wandered here—"gone walkabout" was the term he used. "He said the power signature was unmistakable."

"What does she say?"

"Nothing yet," Benedict said dryly. "She passed out when he spoke of it. After she woke she admitted it, but called it a long story and changed the subject. Isen will question her about that once Seabourne finishes the charm he's making. How's Lily? Have you told her about any of this?"

"Not yet, but I will. She's sleeping a lot, which is what she needs. Normal sleep at first, but Nettie's here, so Lily's *in* sleep now. Nettie confirmed what the surgeon said about the muscle damage, but snorted when I repeated his opinion on healers and nerve regeneration. Nettie says there shouldn't be any lasting nerve damage."

Emotion roughened Benedict's voice. "Good. That's good."

"The lost muscle tissue is another story. Nettie can't make human muscle regrow the way ours does. The mate bond may make a difference, but it isn't predictable."

"No, it isn't." Benedict gave himself a moment before he added, "But there's hope. Soon after our bonding, Claire was practicing with her knives and nearly severed her index finger. It was attached only by a bit of skin. The doctors didn't see any point in reattaching it. Back then there was a very poor success rate for that sort of surgery. I persuaded them to try. Her finger healed perfectly. I have always believed the mate bond was responsible."

"I didn't know that." Surprise echoed in his brother's voice, then warmth. "Thank you."

Had he spoken to Rule about Claire at all? Very little, he realized, and Rule's memories of her would be limited. She hadn't stayed at Clanhome much, and she'd died when Rule was eleven. "You didn't call me about this."

"No. First I need to let you know that the heirs' circle will take place in San Diego, not St. Paul. Isen has what few details we've hashed out."

Surprised, Benedict asked, "How did you pull that off?"

"I didn't. Edgar called and suggested it. Lily still means to attend."

"You dislike that."

"Immensely. She's right, however, and she should be as safe within a circle as she could be anywhere but the heart of Clanhome. We await Nettie's opinion on whether she's up to it, physically."

Benedict understood. The other clans had accepted a major tactical deficit when they agreed to allow the circle to take place in Nokolai's territory. Lily's presence was more important than ever, the one solid assurance the others had that Nokolai wouldn't take advantage of the changed venue.

"I also called you because I'm trying to decide if there's a connection between the attack on Lily and your visitor."

Benedict glanced at the door he'd left ajar. The shower still ran. "The connection is Friar. She was on his land, and he's responsible for the attack—either directly by ordering it, or indirectly by inspiring some random nutcase."

"Do you think the attack was carried out by a random nutcase?"

"Could have been. Doesn't mean it was. It would have to be a pair of nutcases, for one thing. One to drive and one to shoot. What do the police say?"

Rule growled in frustration. "Neither they nor the FBI office here will tell me anything. They're too busy marking their territory and trying to keep the other side—which ought to be the same side, dammit—from learning anything."

"The Unit isn't handling the investigation?"

"The killer used bullets, not magic, so the Unit lacks jurisdiction. If Ruben were in charge . . . but he isn't, and that, too, may be intentional. The healer Nettie sent believes that Ruben's heart attack was caused by magic."

Benedict's eyebrows lifted. "That makes the nutcase theory a lot less likely. Sounds more like an organized effort against the Unit."

"To me, also. So far the Unit's coven hasn't been able to confirm the healer's claim about the use of magic. And the person who could find out for sure was nearly killed last night."

Lily, in other words. "I'm not a big believer in coincidence. It happens, but I'd suggest you proceed on the assumption that she's still in danger."

"I am," Rule said grimly. "Have you learned anything more about your visitor?"

"She knows too much about us."

"What do you mean?"

"Little things, mostly. I wondered if she might be clan-descended—the daughter of one of our daughters, maybe, who'd heard stories from her grandmother. Our daughters are taught to be careful about what they reveal, but they do pass on stories. However, I didn't find her in the database. She could be there under another name, but—" The shower water cut off. "I can't talk freely anymore."

"All right. Benedict, I know you're even less likely to want to talk out your feelings than my *nadia*, which means that normally you'd rather take a dip in boiling oil. But this is not a normal time for you. If a talk-it-out fit should overtake you, I'm here. I listen fairly well."

Benedict surprised himself by smiling. "You're a diplomatic son of a bitch. I'll remember your offer."

"*T'eius ven*, brother."

"*T'eius ven*." Benedict ended the call. Talking to Rule had been good. It had helped. Even though they hadn't spoken directly of the source of Benedict's fear, it had hung there between them. Somehow Rule had made that okay.

One more reason his father had chosen wisely when he made Rule his heir. Benedict didn't belittle himself or his abilities, but he was incapable of managing people the way Rule did . . . though maybe *manage* wasn't the right word. That implied manipulation and power, while Rule drew more on empathy and an innate understanding of what to say, when to say it. He didn't shove.

Benedict was good at shoving, not so good at talking.

The bathroom door opened. Arjenie stood in the doorway, frowning and smelling of soap and wet hair and her own, heady scent. She must have washed away the last of the potion. Benedict's nostrils flared as he drank her in.

She frowned as she ran her fingers through the wet, corkscrewy mass she'd pulled over her shoulder. It made a damp spot on her shirt over the swell of her left breast. "I could have sworn I locked this door."

"I popped the lock while you were in the shower. I needed to be sure I'd hear if you decided to go out the window."

The frown remained. "I have a strong sense of privacy. I don't like having that intruded upon."

"Understandable. But I'm responsible for the Rho's safety, and you haven't told us anything to explain your presence here."

She considered that, then nodded. "I suppose that's reasonable, from your point of view. I hope you don't mind my using your shampoo and soap. I didn't see a comb, or I would have borrowed that, too. I was wondering if you got my purse out of the car. There's a pick in it, and picks work better on curly hair than a brush, because they don't frizz it up so much. Do you know what a pick is? It looks like—"

"It's on top of the bureau in your room, along with a few other things from your purse." The ones Seabourne had had time to check out to be sure they had no magical function.

"It is? Oh, good. I didn't notice." She started limping down the hall. She wasn't leaning on the cane as heavily as she had last night. Good.

He followed. "You wanted a snack."

"I really do. I still need to call my aunt, too."

"You have three voice mails on your phone. One is from a woman named Robin. Is that your aunt? She wants you to call her immediately."

She stopped and turned to face him. "You listened to my voice mail?"

She was so indignant he had to smile. Being caught had scared her, but she'd gotten over that fast. Being coerced into remaining here struck her as reasonable. She peppered him with questions, avoided answering his, and apologized for using the shampoo without asking first.

But listening to her voice mail? That riled her. "I also read your e-mail. A Nigerian official has a deal you won't want to pass up. You can call your aunt." He handed her his phone.

"This isn't my phone."

"No, it isn't. I'll need it back. I'll be listening while you speak with your aunt, so you want to be careful with what you say." He'd be able to hear both sides of that conversation, too, which she probably didn't realize.

She gave him a dirty look and touched the screen, then turned around and limped toward her room. "Maybe I'll read your e-mail."

"I'll have to take the phone away if you try."

"It's intensely annoying when someone who's stronger than you uses his strength to get his way."

"I imagine it is. Are you going to call?" He was close enough to watch over her shoulder and see what number she used.

She sniffed and used her thumb to tap in the number of the Robin who'd called earlier.

A man answered. "Hey. You got me. Now what?"

"Hi, Uncle Clay, it's Arjenie. I'm using a friend's phone. Is Aunt Robin there?"

"Are you okay? Robin's been having tingles."

"I'm fine. Well, I sprained my ankle, but there's nothing new about that."

"What happened? Or what is happening, because—okay, okay." The last was fainter, as if he'd spoken to someone else. "Hang on. Your aunt is a grabby, greedy woman. I have to pass her the phone." A second later a woman's voice took over. "Arjenie? What's wrong? And don't tell me 'nothing,' because I know there's something."

"It's complicated, but I'm getting things sorted out. Don't worry."

"That's not much of an answer."

"I can't tell you anything else right now. Oh, but guess what? Part of the sorting out means that I was invited to stay with the Nokolai Rho." At the door of her room she paused to shoot Benedict a glance gleaming with purpose and a hint of humor. The purpose he understood. She'd made sure her people knew where she was, just in case Isen started talking about bodies again. That was smart. The humor?

Maybe she didn't really believe she needed to protect herself that way. Which was not so smart. She had no reason to trust him.

"You're what?" her aunt exclaimed.

"Staying with their Rho for a few days. Reception's spotty—you know that their clanhome is in the mountains, right?—plus my phone's acting up. If you have trouble reaching me, don't worry. I'll check in with you every day."

Another smart move. She'd made sure he knew her aunt would expect a call every day.

"Why are staying there?" Aunt Robin didn't sound panicked, but she wasn't comforted, either. "You don't know this Rho, do you? Does this have anything to do with—"

"I really can't talk about it," Arjenie said firmly. "Did Serri and Sammy make it down for the weekend?"

Serri and Sammy were apparently in college, but came home regularly. Serri had a new boyfriend. Sammy had aced his calculus test, but was considering changing his major. After that, the conversation veered to a piece of equipment her uncle had acquired—a swage block. Benedict had heard the term, but couldn't remember what it was.

While he listened, Benedict noticed Carl crossing the den and motioned to him. Arjenie needed food. She didn't seem to notice Carl coming, leaving, then returning. She sat on the bed running that pick thing through her damp hair and chatting with her aunt for fifteen minutes, sounding as relaxed as if she were on vacation. "I'd better go," she said finally. "Supper's almost ready, I think. Blessed be."

"All right, but don't think I didn't notice how little you've told me. All that silence is not reassuring. Blessed be, sweetie."

Arjenie frowned as she disconnected. "She'll worry. I can't keep her from worrying, but at least she won't get the cops to look for me."

She certainly was keen on keeping the police out of her affairs. "Is your aunt a precog?"

"No, she's a Finder, which shouldn't give her the least hint of second sight, but she always knows when one of us is in trouble. She gets tingles."

"Your uncle's a blacksmith." He'd finally remembered who used swage blocks.

"Uh-huh. He's begun to get a name for his sculpture, too, but the blacksmithing is still his bread-and-butter work."

"And your aunt's a Wiccan." As was she, most likely. She wore the Wiccan star on one hand.

"We all are. The whole family, I mean, going back forever on my uncle's side. Though he isn't my uncle by blood, so I can't claim that heritage, but on my aunt's side we've been Wiccan for at least five generations. It gets murky if you go back farther, because my great-great-great-grandmother was adopted after a flood killed her parents—the Great Flood in Galveston, have you heard of it? She was quite young when it happened and we don't know much about her original parents, but we think they must have been Wiccan because her adoptive parents weren't, yet she was, and that just never happened back then. Converting to Wicca, I mean. Is that a trail bar you're holding?"

He smiled. "Two. Here."

"Oh, good." She ripped one open and devoured it in several neat bites. Then she opened the second one. She ate it more slowly, and she asked questions. Did it hurt to Change? How often did he do it? What colors did he see as a wolf? Was his vision different? Why wasn't he asking her any questions?

He was leaving that to his father, and so he told her. Then, of course, she wanted to know why. He preferred not to lie to her, but he also preferred not to tell her precisely why he wanted to wait, so he alluded vaguely to the fact that they would be joined at supper by Cullen Seabourne.

"And his wife?" she'd asked quickly.

His eyebrows flew up. "You know a great deal about Seabourne."

"Never mind that for now. Will his wife be joining us?"

"I haven't been told." Technically true, but he was sure she wouldn't be. Cynna was staying with the Rhej for a few days. It had something to do with her apprenticeship and the memories, though Benedict knew nothing more than that. No one did, save the Rhej and her apprentice.

Arjenie bit her lip, then nodded once as if agreeing with herself. "I think I will tell you some things, but not yet. You're right. I need to speak with your father. He's the one who decides."

NINETEEN

THE one who decides joined them on the rear deck twenty minutes later. Seabourne hadn't arrived yet. That wasn't due to his usual rudeness; he'd warned them that making the charm was tricky and might delay him. But it was a pain. Benedict needed to talk with his Rho, but couldn't do so privately until Seabourne took over guard duty.

He wanted to discuss the attack on Lily and the news Rule had passed on about Ruben Brooks's heart attack. That was the most important. Less important—probably—was another example of Arjenie's oddly detailed knowledge about them. When she said she needed to speak with the Rho, she'd called him Benedict's father. She shouldn't have known that. Few outside the clans did.

The deck was Benedict's favorite part of the house. There were two levels. The lower level, next to the house, was roofed; the upper level was smaller and open to the sky. Benedict had helped his father build the stone retaining wall that separated the two. They would eat on the lower deck, where there were lights enough for their human guest, but for now they sat on the upper deck. Isen liked the view.

Benedict did, too. The sky was putting on a show. Twilight shimmered in the east while the western sky glowed golden, and Venus hung, sparkling, near the top of the old loblolly that lightning hadn't managed to kill five years ago. The air was dry and calm, perfumed by pine and creosote as well as Carl's lasagna. It was probably around seventy-five degrees, a comfortable temperature for humans.

Not that Arjenie was wholly human. How did she experience temperature? Where did she differ from human? Where was she the same?

Arjenie loved the deck. She loved the landscaping around it, and the way the tended parts blended into the wildness around them. She didn't love the cabernet sauvignon Isen poured for her—an elegant vintage, a real treat for the nose—but she pretended politely.

Pretense turned to curiosity when she learned the wine came from Nokolai's own vineyard. She and Isen chatted away happily about wine-making. She knew more about that than most laymen—certainly more than he'd expect from someone who didn't drink the stuff.

She wasn't afraid of Isen anymore. Benedict knew that was his Rho's intention, just as last night he'd meant to terrify her. Today he wanted her to relax her guard, and Isen could be very charming indeed when he wished. But her comfort seemed innate as well. She was like a wolf in that way, Benedict decided as he sipped his wine and listened to his father charm his Chosen. She was good at taking whatever the moment offered. Once she'd determined there was no immediate threat, fear became irrelevant.

Or else his perceptions were entirely distorted by the mate bond, and she was a supremely confident and powerful actress who hoped to charm Isen into letting *his* guard down.

If so, she was out of luck. No one could charm Isen to that degree.

She smelled so good.

"I would *love* to see it," she said in response to Isen's invitation to tour Nokolai's winery. "Which sort of leads into something else I want to talk about. How long do you plan to keep me here?"

"We aren't keeping you," Isen protested mildly. "We are simply—"

"—planning to call the cops if I leave. Right. I understand why you—no, I take that back. I understand why you're suspicious. I don't understand why you haven't just called the cops. I'm glad you didn't, because that would create problems for me and could endanger someone else, but I don't understand why. It makes me think there's something you know that I don't."

"Hmm." Isen studied the wine in his glass, gave it a swirl to release the aroma, and sipped. "Yes, you could say that. It isn't something I'm prepared to talk about now."

She nodded solemnly. "And I'm unable to talk about the potions. At least, I did tell Benedict about one of them—the one that removed my scent—but I can't discuss the other one. Not in any helpful way." She stopped, tipped her head, and looked at Benedict. "How come you're so quiet? You've hardly said a word since we came outside. Are you deferring to your Rho or just moody?"

Isen gave a sharp crack of a laugh.

His father found that amusing, did he? "I'm not very talkative."

"You note that he doesn't deny being moody," Isen said.

"Quiet doesn't necessarily mean moody . . . but I'm getting off-subject." Yet still she looked at Benedict. In this light, her skin was luminous, so pale it almost glowed. Her eyes were more gray than green or blue, and her expression was pure librarian. A librarian confronted with a book she didn't know how to shelve. Apparently he didn't fit the Dewey Decimal System.

After a moment she gave her head a small shake and spoke to Isen again. "I'd like to make a deal."

Isen smiled like the charming wolf he was. "What kind of deal?"

"You want to know things about me. I want to be free to leave by Monday with no more threats of prosecution or anything like that. "

"Why Monday?"

"I'm expected back at work Tuesday."

"You would trust me to honor our deal?"

"We'd be trusting each other, wouldn't we? That's how deals work. You'd have to trust me to answer honestly. I'd have to trust you to abandon your coercion. Um . . . I'd have to ask for one more stipulation."

"And what is that?"

"You recall that I said Robert Friar is clairaudient? I'd like your promise not to talk about what I tell you except here at Clanhome, where he can't Listen. It's extremely important."

"I'm no fan of Friar, yet I can't promise what you ask. My people consider a promise binding in an absolute sense. There is no wiggle room for changed circumstances, so flexibility must be built into the agreement at the start."

"We can build in some wiggle room. What did you have in mind?"

They haggled. Benedict listened with a certain intellectual interest. His father was very good at this sort of thing, but his Chosen seemed to have a good grasp of it, too. He wondered if her long shower had been a way of buying herself some thinking time. She seemed to have put some thought into this already.

They'd just about hashed out the wording when Benedict heard someone yip twice out front. He recognized the voice, but still listened intently for a moment. There was no challenge, so he relaxed . . . mostly. Absolute safety was an illusion.

"One more thing," Isen added casually. "I don't think you'll have a problem with this. I'd like you to wear a little truth charm while you're here."

"Oh." Her eyebrows drew down. "I don't object, precisely, but . . . no, I might as well tell you. I doubt very much it will work."

"Is that so?" Cullen Seabourne vaulted up onto the deck.

She jerked around. "Oh, my, you startled me!"

Seabourne had unusually vivid blue eyes. When he was on the trail of some magical mystery, they almost glowed. They were afire now. "Burning out truth charms—that's a gnomish trait. You don't look like you have any gnome blood."

"I don't, but I'm pretty sure I'll burn it out. I don't do it on purpose." Arjenie shrugged. "It just happens. I don't know how many of them we've tried, hoping to figure out what was going on, but we never did." Her face lit up. "I know! If your truth charm does work on me, we'll make it part of the deal that you tell me how you made it. That is, assuming you're the maker?"

"I am." Seabourne came closer. "Are you hoping to learn how to block it?"

"No, I'm hoping to learn more about my Gift. If I found a truth charm I didn't burn out, I'd want to know why, wouldn't I? Maybe that would explain why I do burn out the others. It's only natural I'd want to learn more about how my Gift works."

His eyebrows lifted. "You don't know?"

"I know some things, but there are these huge *gaps*. I'm the only one with such a Gift in our realm, you see. I understand it's rare even in the sidhe realms, except for . . . I think I'll stop talking now. We haven't agreed on a deal."

"If you wish to learn how Cullen makes his charms," Isen said, "you'll have to make a separate deal with him. Otherwise, yes, I think we have a deal. While you're our guest, you'll answer our questions fully and honestly, save any that impinge on the subject you say you can't discuss. You won't lie about those, but you are free of the obligation to answer. You'll remain our guest until Monday, and you'll wear the truth charm unless you, ah, burn it out. In return, I and those under my authority won't report or seek retribution or prosecution for your trespass, and we'll only speak of what you tell us here at Clanhome unless we have a clear and compelling reason to disregard that stipulation."

"I'm not entirely happy about the exemption." She considered a moment. "Let's make it unless you learn I lied to or substantially misled you, or there is a clear and compelling danger that might be prevented through disclosure."

Was his Chosen a lawyer? Benedict was beginning to wonder.

"Agreed." Isen held out his hand.

"Agreed," Arjenie said firmly, and took Isen's hand. They shook.

"And here," Seabourne said, pulling something from his pocket, "is your new adornment." A small silver disk attached to a silver chain dangled from his fingers. Benedict didn't know much about charms, but he knew silver was magically active. "Shall I do the honors?"

"No," Benedict said, and stepped up, holding out his hand. "I will."

Seabourne's eyebrows shot up. For once, though, he didn't comment, allowing the necklace to drop into Benedict's palm.

He probably thought Benedict had a good reason to do it himself. He'd be wrong. Sheer insanity wasn't a good reason. Having begun, though, Benedict followed through, moving behind her. He looped it over her neck and paused. "Hair."

Obligingly she gathered her hair in both hands—so much hair, frenetically curling and smelling of almonds from the shampoo—and held it up off her nape. He drew the chain around her neck and bent his head and inhaled slowly. Her scent filled him, settled him, excited him. He thought of moving her shirt aside so he could touch the pale skin of one shoulder. Of running his hands under her shirt and up her back, or just laying them flat on her waist and pulling her close. It was stupid to tease himself like this. Wrong to tease her. But he let the sides of his hands skim the skin at her nape lightly as he fastened the little chain.

She shivered.

"Done." The effort to sound normal flattened his voice. He stepped back.

The chain was short. The silver disk rested against her skin just below the graceful indention at the base of her throat. As far as Benedict could tell, nothing happened.

"Damn." Seabourne shook his head. "Can't say you didn't warn me."

Isen spoke. "Does that mean it burned out, like she said?"

"Whiffed out within a couple seconds of touching her skin. If I'd known she had a habit of burning them out . . ." He frowned. "Do you feel anything when it happens?"

"Warmth. It's still kind of warm, see?" She held out the charm. Seabourne took in between his fingers, rubbing it. "Hmm. Maybe if we try—"

"Try later," Isen said. "Carl has brought out the lasagna. Let's eat."

*　　*　　*

CARL often ate with the Rho, but he didn't join them tonight. Not that he'd go hungry. If Arjenie thought it was odd that a large square of lasagna was missing from the pan, she didn't say so. "That smells desperately delicious," she said as Isen held her chair for her.

Carl was the Rho's houseman. He cooked and cleaned and—once in a long while—he spoke. He'd passed the century mark two decades ago and had been houseman to Isen's father as well, and his lasagna was, indeed, desperately delicious.

"Carl is a gifted man." Isen accepted the bread basket from Benedict, took a slice, and passed it to her. "Please help yourself to some lasagna. I was wondering . . . are you a reporter?"

"Oh, no." Arjenie took two slices of buttery garlic bread.

"Do you by chance belong to some secretive organization that is interested in Robert Friar?"

She laughed. "You mean like Wiccans for Justice or something? No, the organization I belong to isn't secret, and I'm an employee, not a member. I work for the FBI. So you can see," she added as she levered out a large helping of lasagna, "that it would have caused me all kinds of trouble if you'd called the cops."

Benedict had seldom seen his father even momentarily struck dumb, but Arjenie had managed that. He understood that. The FBI had not figured in any of his speculations about his Chosen, either.

"What a coincidence," Cullen said pleasantly as he accepted the bread basket. "My wife also works for the FBI."

"Yes, and I'm really glad you haven't mentioned me to her. Not by name, at least, or you wouldn't be surprised now. Cynna would probably have felt obligated to tell Mr. Brooks I was here, and if she didn't, Lily certainly would. Do you like the handwoven blanket I sent for the baby?"

Cullen stilled. "The blue and green one? It's lovely."

"Isn't it? My cousin Pat is a wonderful weaver."

Benedict spoke. "You don't have anything in your wallet identifying you as an FBI agent."

"I'm not an agent. I work in Research. My specialty is magic-related questions—spells, charms, historical refer-

ences, anything to do with magic. I work with Unit agents
a lot. Mostly it's all handled in e-mail or over the phone, so
I haven't met everyone in person, but I know Cynna. We've
had lunch a few times. She can vouch for me. Well, I suppose
all she can vouch for is that I'm who I say I am, but that's
a start, isn't it?" She took a bite of lasagna and hummed in
pleasure. "This is really good."

"I'm puzzled," Isen said. "Why didn't you tell us this immediately?"

She was politely incredulous. "I was hoping no one in
the Bureau would find out, of course. Once I told you, you'd
check with Cynna and Lily, and there would be repercussions, since I couldn't tell anyone why I snuck onto your
land. Believe me, as little as you like me clamming up about
that, the Bureau would like it less. Then I realized you were
going to find out sooner or later, because Cullen was bound
to mention my name to Cynna at some point, or someone
would tell Rule Turner, who'd tell Lily. Cynna might not tell
Ruben Brooks right away, but I bet Lily would. So I made
the best deal I could before telling you."

Isen picked up the fresh bottle of wine Carl had left for
them, already opened so it could breathe. "Are you ready for
more? No?" He filled his own glass. "It's only natural you'd
be concerned with your career."

She nodded. "I love my job. I don't want to lose it. But
there's more at stake than that. I suspect Friar *Listens* to
Bureau discussions sometimes. I know he Listens in on the
local police. He can't do that all the time, not even most of
the time, but something really bad could happen if he were
Listening at the wrong time and found out about me."

"And how do you know this about Friar?"

She frowned and ducked her head. He could almost see
the effort she put into thinking that one over. "Research," she
said at last. "I had a reason to do some research, and that's
what I put together based on Bureau records and on—on an-
ecdotal evidence that was available to me."

"Have we reached the subject you can't discuss?"

She nodded unhappily.

"It might be best to start with the things you can talk about,
then. But let's enjoy our dinner first. And perhaps I will take

your suggestion. It might be best to have Cynna confirm your identity." He added a subvocal comment she wouldn't be able to hear: *"Once she can be contacted. Benedict?"*

"I'd love to see her," Arjenie said.

That wasn't going to happen tonight. Whatever the process might be for transferring the memories, it couldn't be interrupted. Benedict unclipped his phone, selected the camera function, and said, "Arjenie."

She looked at him. He took three quick pictures—she smiled for the last one, the kind of automatic smile people adopt when they know they're being photographed—and stood. "I'll see that she gets the pictures."

"She's not going to join us?" Arjenie asked as Benedict left the room. "Is she all right? She isn't due until next month, is she?"

He could hear Isen reassuring her that Cynna was fine, simply on partial bed rest, as he headed down the hall. He stepped out the front door. "Shannon."

Shannon stepped out of the shadow of the old cedar near the corner of the house.

"I'm sending three pictures to your phone. Take it and a day's trail rations with you to the Rhej's. When you arrive, don't knock or speak. Wait by the door until the Rhej or Cynna comes to see what you want. If and when Cynna is able to speak to you, show her the photos and ask who is in them. Call me with her answer. If I haven't heard from you in twenty-four hours, I'll send someone to relieve you."

Shannon nodded and took out his phone. Benedict sent the photos, then waited until Shannon confirmed that he had them. He signaled for the guard to go and reentered the house.

When he returned to the rear deck, they were still talking about pregnancy. Arjenie kept quoting statistics. Apparently preeclampsia complicated between five and ten percent of pregnancies in the U.S. and resulted in between seventy thousand and eighty thousand premature births.

Interesting that she was so concerned about Cynna, Benedict thought as he sat down to eat. She hadn't asked about Lily, who she also knew. Maybe she didn't know about the attack?

Seabourne tried to steer the conversation to another subject, which had Arjenie patting his arm and saying of course they would talk about something else, and she was an idiot to keep harping on a subject that had to be difficult for him, and did he know that, of those eighty thousand births, the mortality rate was extremely low in this country? Just over one percent. And even in the worst-case scenario, she assured him, involving full placental separation, why, Cynna was in her third trimester, so they'd be able to deliver the baby right away with very few problems.

She was trying to reassure him. She wasn't very good at it. Her hopeful offerings were undercut by a too-bright smile that announced her anxiety clearly.

Benedict didn't like it. Her worry was misplaced and unnecessary. Isen should have leveled with her. "Cynna isn't having problems with her pregnancy," he told her, helping himself to a second serving.

"No?" Arjenie looked at him, questions flooding her eyes. "But Isen said she's on bed rest, and—"

"She's participating in a rite that can't be interrupted. Isen avoided speaking of it because it's secret."

Relief spread over her face like sunrise. "Oh. Whew." She grinned. "I was babbling like an idiot, wasn't I?"

"You were worried." Benedict realized that Isen and Seabourne were staring at him. "She's Wiccan," he said in explanation. "She understands that some rites aren't spoken of."

Seabourne cocked an eyebrow, his blue eyes bright with amusement, and subvocalized: *"You just contradicted your Rho in front of an out-clan stranger who's keeping some pretty big secrets."*

Benedict's fork froze in midair. Yes. Yes, he had, he agreed silently as he resumed eating. But whatever else Arjenie might be, she was Lady-touched, a Chosen. *His* Chosen, and that gave him certain rights. Maybe he couldn't yet bring himself to tell her about it, or even to say the words aloud when he spoke of her.

But whether she knew it or not, she was his to protect.

TWENTY

LILY'S arm ached and throbbed like a bad tooth. It did not, however, hurt enough for her to take the pills Rule was holding out. "I just woke up. I am not going back to sleep. Or in sleep. Or into a drugged stupor, or anything else resembling unconsciousness."

Rule set the little paper cup with the pills back on the rolling table. "Pain saps the body's strength. You'll mend faster with it muted."

"Mute the pain, mute the brain. I can't think when I'm drugged. I need to think." Ever since she'd learned about the probable traitor in the Bureau, she'd been either asleep or drugged. Mostly asleep. Maybe it had been necessary, but she'd had enough. "Caffeine has analgesic properties."

His eyebrows lifted. "You want coffee at nine o'clock at night?"

"I would love a cup, thanks."

He considered arguing. That was clear from his long, unblinking pause. Finally he stood, went to the door, and asked one of the guards to go to the Starbucks in the other building.

"Regular coffee's fine," she said. "I don't need Starbucks."

"Tough. I do." He slipped the guard a bill. "Pick up soup and a sandwich, too."

"I'm pretty sure I ate." She didn't remember what now, but someone had definitely pestered her to eat.

"You ate six bites—two of the Jell-O, one of the cake, and three of the strange noodle mixture which may have had bits of chicken hiding in it somewhere." He closed the door again.

"You counted my bites."

"It helped me resist the urge to force-feed you."

"I guess I've been a pain." Her memories of the last twenty-four hours were fuzzy, but a few stood out. She was pretty sure she'd cursed someone out at one point. "Do I owe Nettie an apology?"

"Probably, though she understands. You hate having others make decisions for you. I do, too, but I begin to think you inherited your magical grandsire's sense of sovereignty."

"I'm not that bad." But her mouth kicked up as she tried to picture Sam as a patient, obedient to nurses' and doctors' ideas of when he should eat, sleep, get up, lie down, or pee in a cup. The mind boggled. It was just as well dragons healed themselves, she decided. "Nettie and the surgeon don't agree on how long my arm's going to be unusable, but either way, I'm going to be on sick leave awhile."

"From your perspective, that bites." He rejoined her, but didn't sit down.

"From yours, too, since I'll probably be hard to live with. Sjorensen was here earlier."

"Yes, you asked for her. Do you not remember?"

"Not clearly. I was drugged." Did she sound aggrieved, or just whiny? "I don't think I told her anything I shouldn't."

"Ah." He nodded. "I see your concern. You didn't. You asked for her after exchanging civilities with the self-important buffoon the local FBI office put in charge of investigating the shooting."

Now she remembered. Millhouse—that was the guy's name. "Oh, yeah. It was him I cursed out, not Nettie. Good."

For some reason that amused him. "You wished me to remind you to call the man's superior. Perhaps you won't need to, though. I spoke with Abel."

"Abel Karonski?" Maybe her mind wasn't working right yet, because she did not see the connection. Karonski was a Unit agent, not regular FBI. He couldn't do anything about the local branch's senior idiot.

"He called to see how you were doing, and I explained the problem with Millhouse. He's going to speak with Croft about it. He seemed to think the personnel difficulty could be dealt with. He was on his way to D.C. when he called."

"He finished up that hex case he was on?"

"No, he had to hand that off to someone else. He's been put in charge of the investigation into the attempt on Ruben's life."

A tight knot of worry eased. "Good." She thought it over a moment, and said it again. "Good. That's excellent news."

"It was Ruben's suggestion. He had a hunch."

"He must be doing better if he's making suggestions."

"Either that, or he's no better at being a patient than you are." Rule smiled when he said that, though, and stroked her hair. "You're not hurting too much?"

"I'm in desperate agony, but I'm tough." At the look on his face she added quickly, "Joke, Rule. That was a joke. It's just pain. I don't like it, and it ups the grouchy factor, but it's already better than it was at first." She expected to hurt more tomorrow, since she'd be moving around more. A lot more, if she had her way. She wanted out of the damned hospital.

Another memory surfaced. "My father called. So did my mother." Two separate calls, one from each, and she dimly recalled that her father had made her laugh. She didn't remember why, but she'd laughed. And her mother . . . Lily frowned. "She's not coming here, is she?"

"It was a near thing, but I persuaded her you'd be home soon, so there was no need. She wants me to assure you that you are not to worry about the aesthetic effect of the sling."

She looked at him blankly.

His mouth twitched. "Assuming you're still using one at our wedding in March, that is. Julia believes a sling could be fashioned out of the same silk as your dress, if necessary."

"She's worried about matching my sling to my wedding dress."

"No," Rule said, "she wanted to be sure you wouldn't

worry about it. I've also taken calls from your sisters, Madame Yu, Detective James, Deputy Beck, one Rho, three Lu Nuncios, Steve Timms, Cullen, Ida, and a couple others. You know that Cynna's sequestered with the Rhej right now. She may not yet know about the shooting."

"Right." It made Lily feel funny that so many people had called to check on her. Funny, but good. "Grandmother used the phone?"

"She had instructions for me."

Lily grinned. "I'll bet. I hope her instructions agree with Nettie's. I wouldn't want to annoy either one of them."

"They're largely congruent. While Nettie didn't prescribe tea, I don't think she'd object. I'm afraid I had to tell everyone that flowers and other delivered items weren't appropriate, due to security."

She would have done the same thing if she'd been arranging security for a potential target. It was weird being that potential target. "You're assuming the shooter is an ongoing threat rather than a one-off, an opportunistic attack. Did the locals talk to the concierge?"

"The locals aren't talking to me. However, Sjorensen intends to . . ." His phone chimed. He checked the screen and grimaced apologetically. "It's Alex. I'd better take it."

"Sure." Why did that make her memory itch? Oh, yeah. He'd taken a call from Isen while they were on the plane. One he hadn't told her about.

This call was about the memorial. The *firnam*, they called it. She tried to listen, but couldn't. Her mind filled with the image she couldn't get rid of: LeBron's head again, the bloody mess of it. The missing eye.

It hurt. It hurt so much more than her arm, and in a place painkillers couldn't reach. Once Rule disconnected, she distracted herself by asking about the other call she'd been reminded of. "On the flight out here, your father called you on my phone and didn't want me to know what it was about. You said you'd hold off. Have you held off enough yet?"

"Actually, I was planning to tell you tonight if you seemed up to listening to a puzzling tale."

A puzzle sounded like an excellent idea. More distraction. "I'm up for it."

"In a moment. This is not a Leidolf matter, so . . . ah, your coffee is here."

So was his coffee and the food. Lily didn't have much appetite, but the soup was chicken noodle, which was what her mother had always given them when they were sick, so eating it seemed right. Tasted pretty good, too. "Okay," she said, putting her almost-empty bowl aside to sip coffee. "You've eaten, I've eaten. Puzzle me."

First Rule asked the guards to take up positions farther from the door. Clearly he didn't want them overhearing. By the time he returned and took her hand, Lily's curiosity would have kept her awake even without the caffeine.

Even after sending the guards out of earshot, Rule kept his voice low. "I delayed telling you at Benedict's request. This event is intensely personal, but it is also clan business." He paused. "The Lady has Chosen for Benedict."

"Has . . . you mean now? Again?" Lily knew almost nothing about Benedict's Chosen, save that Claire had died many years ago and Benedict had gone half mad with grief.

He nodded. "That itself is a mystery. Never has a lupus been gifted twice with a Chosen. Nor am I aware of a time when a single clan held two Chosens. But the manner of her arrival in his life is a puzzle, also."

There was a time for questions, and a time to let your witness—or your friend and lover and bonded mate—talk. Lily didn't interrupt. She didn't make notes, either. Her fingers twitched a couple times, but it was the fingers on her *right* hand. Which she couldn't use, dammit.

Didn't matter right now, though. You didn't write down anything about the mate bond. Ever.

So she lined her questions up mentally. When he finished, she hit the first one. "She was at Friar's two nights ago, then at Clanhome last night. At Clanhome she had some kind of potions with her, but by the time Benedict spotted her, the vials were empty. She says one of them was designed to conceal her scent. She won't say what the other one did. Cullen's checking the vials, I guess?"

"He will. Isen wanted him to prepare a truth charm first."

"Did she have potions with her at Friar's?"

"I don't know. Benedict didn't search her that night."

"No, but he was wolf at the time, right? What did he smell?"

"I don't know," Rule repeated, and spread his hands. "I didn't ask. I don't think Isen did, either. I begin to think we should have told you earlier."

"Of course you should. Benedict's having a hard time with this?"

"Had she not shown up again, I don't know what would have happened. He was refusing to look for her. He's not himself, not thinking clearly."

"Hmm. Well, if he sniffs the containers the potions were in, maybe he could tell if he'd smelled anything like them the night before, at Friar's. Might be good to know if she was delivering potions there, too. Or if she got them there."

"I suspect he could." Rule shook his head. "Benedict is too distracted to have thought of this, but Isen or I should have."

Lily suspected the lupi were more focused on the Lady aspect of this business than she was. That would be of absorbing importance to them. It probably was important, too, but she had a snowball's chance in hell of figuring out what the Lady had in mind, so she ignored that in favor of what she might be able to figure out. "You've been distracted yourself, and Isen is smart as hell, but he's not a cop." She drummed her fingers on her leg. "They've persuaded her to stay at Clanhome by threatening to tell the cops about her."

"Yes. They hope to learn more about her, of course, but also Isen wants to keep her near Benedict. You know what can happen if the bond is stretched beyond its limits."

She damned sure did, and the bond was at its most restrictive when it was new. "Benedict really isn't thinking straight. She has to be told."

"If anyone can move my stubborn brother off whatever high ground he thinks he's defending, it's our father."

"True." Lily considered the nature of the threat Isen had used to keep the intruder at Clanhome. Even people who weren't bad guys could be wary of involving the police, but this woman's aversion seemed excessive. She was up to something. Of course, sneaking onto both Friar's and Nokolai's property already suggested that. "She claimed that Friar is clairaudient?"

"She was quite definite about it, but wouldn't say how she knew."

"Hmm." Lily had long suspected Friar had a Gift of some sort, but so far she'd been unable to touch him and find out. "That's a rare Gift, and a hard one to train, I'm told. Go over what they know about her again."

"According to Isen, she looks to be around thirty. She wears glasses. She has a physical impediment of some sort. Her hair is red, long, and curly. She seems to know a lot about lupi, or at least about Nokolai. Cullen's convinced she's part-sidhe. Her Gift allows her to hide from others' perceptions. It doesn't affect Benedict, of course—"

"Stop there. I don't get that."

"The mate bond supersedes all other magic." Rule smiled and ran his thumb along the side of her hand. "When we first met, it worried you that you couldn't feel my magic when we touched. You still don't. Your Gift doesn't work on me."

True, though she hadn't thought of it in quite those terms. "So Benedict's immune, and that's why he's guarding her. She can't play mind tricks on him. Overusing her Gift makes her pass out?"

He nodded. "So she said, and she did indeed pass out. Nettie examined her and told them not to try to wake her. She called it a natural recuperative trance similar to being in sleep."

"I take it she and Benedict haven't, ah, completed the bond yet." With sex, she meant. The mate bond was cemented the first time the bonded pair had sex—which they'd be really, deeply, wanting to do. "Not with her passed out."

"I don't think so, but she's awake now. When I spoke to Benedict about an hour ago, she was in the shower. Isen plans to resume questioning her over dinner." Rule glanced at his watch. "Which, on that coast, will be happening soon."

"Okay, let's move to impressions—Cullen's, Benedict's, Isen's."

"I didn't talk to Benedict long, and didn't ask for his impression of her. But he thinks she knows more about us than she should. As for Cullen . . . mostly, he's excited."

About the chance to learn new magical stuff, no doubt. "He would be."

"He's also suspicious of her motives. That's typical, if illogical. Obviously she's not an enemy."

"Obviously, we don't know that yet."

"She's Lady-touched, Lily. She might be misguided or coerced, so they are being careful. But she can't be a true enemy."

"According to you, I'm Lady-touched, too, and I damn near arrested you for murder before I figured things out."

He smiled. "But you didn't. Isen called her oddly innocent. Not naïve or ignorant. Innocent. I'm not sure what he means by that."

Lily wasn't either. But she was curious. Intensely so. For so long she'd been *it*, the only one who knew what a mate bond felt like. The only Chosen.

Not literally true, she corrected herself. There was a Chosen in Africa, a member of Mondoyo clan. Lily had never met or spoken to her. Neither had most of the lupi, because the woman didn't travel or speak English. There'd been a Cynyr Chosen, but that was in Wales, and she'd died at the age of a hundred and three before Lily met Rule.

But other than Lily, there hadn't been a Chosen in North America since Benedict's first Chosen died. Now he had another one.

"Okay, so they don't know her name or where she's from," she said, ticking off the obvious. "But you said they'd found her car, so it shouldn't be hard to—"

"No, we do know her name. Sorry. I thought I told you." Rule shook his head. "Maybe I caught a touch of avoidance from Benedict. He doesn't refer to her by name, only as 'she' or his charge. It's an unusual name. Arjenie Fox."

Lily stared. Could there be two people with that name? "I need my computer. Shit. I need to check . . . Rule, I know her. I've worked with her." And *liked* her, dammit. "Arjenie Fox is with the Bureau. Someone in the Bureau tried to kill Ruben."

Rule's eyebrows drew down. "It wasn't her. The timing doesn't work."

She brushed that aside. "I know that. But maybe we aren't talking about a single player here. Ruben's hit, I'm hit, and Arjenie just happens to show up at both Friar's place and Clanhome?" She shook her head grimly. "Chosen or not, that's too damned suspicious. At best, she knows more than she's telling. At worst, she's part of it."

TWENTY-ONE

THE night air had that silken feel Arjenie associated with late spring evenings back home. No fireflies, though. Did they have fireflies in this part of California? She asked Isen, who said no, then told her about some of the bugs they did have.

Isen Turner was an excellent host now that he wasn't threatening her. He listened as well as he spoke—and he was an entertaining speaker, whether he was talking about wine or bugs—and he had a sly sense of humor. Clearly he wanted his guest to feel special.

Special, and relaxed enough to tell him things. That was okay. It wasn't as if she'd accidentally start blurting out stuff about Dya.

She was having a wonderful time. She was very conscious of Benedict sitting beside her, though he didn't say much. Cullen Seabourne did. He'd gotten over his surliness. When Isen took a phone call and left the table to speak with someone privately, Seabourne amused both of them by flirting with her. He was a bit outrageous, but clearly just playing, so she relaxed and enjoyed herself. How often did a woman have an absurdly sexy man say her scent was as fresh and mysterious as a summer night, or that her hair reminded him of calling fire to dance on his fingers?

When Isen returned he still wore his earbud and he placed his phone nearby. Benedict looked at him with raised brows, which made her think this wasn't Isen's usual behavior. She hoped not. Aunt Robin didn't allow phones at the dinner table, and Arjenie agreed with her.

"A developing situation," Isen said vaguely. "My apologies. I need to stay on top of things, but it's nothing for you to be concerned about."

That made her curious, of course, but it wasn't any of her business, unless they were about to be attacked by another clan or something. But surely he'd be doing more than keeping his earbud in place if that were the case.

By the time the silent Carl took away their empty plates, it was fully dark. Carl replaced the lasagna with cheesecake, and the wine with coffee. "That was excellent," Arjenie said after she swallowed the last bite of her cheesecake.

"Would you like another piece?" Benedict asked.

She eyed him. His expression didn't give much away, but she suspected he was amused. "No, thank you."

"Are you sure?" Cullen Seabourne said. "You only had a pound or so of lasagna, along with a few slices of garlic bread—no more than four or five, surely. Plus the cheesecake, of course."

No doubt about the expression on that gorgeous face. He was laughing at her. "I suppose you're wondering where a skinny thing like me puts it all. I have a high metabolism, especially when I've been using my Gift. That sucks the calories right out of my body."

"That's not how Gifts usually work."

"No." The meal was over. It was time for the question-and-answer portion of the evening. "I believe it's normal for those of the Blood, though admittedly my sample is small—me, a few brownies, a half-blood sidhe, a couple others. Do you need to eat after you've been through a Change?"

Seabourne's eyebrows lifted. "We do, as a matter of fact. You consider yourself of the Blood, then?"

"Genetically, I'm about three-fourths human. Magically,

I'm of the Blood, but I may or may not be sidhe in that respect."

"Ah." He glanced at Isen, who gave a small nod. "Maybe you could explain."

"I can. I'm not used to it, but I can do it. Do you want to ask questions, or should I give you a . . . well, not a summary. I don't abbreviate well. But I could tell you about my heritage."

Isen answered this time. "Please do."

"Okay. I'm asking you to be really careful about what you repeat to anyone else. I'll explain why in a minute." She put a hand on her chest. Funny. Her heartbeat had picked up and her mouth was dry. "This is harder than I thought it would be. It's been such a big secret my whole life. I've never spoken of it to anyone outside of family. Well. The short version is that my mother was human. My father is sidhe. Low sidhe," she added.

"The distinction doesn't mean anything to me," Isen said. "Low sidhe?"

"Sidhe divide themselves into three groups or classes: High, Middle, and low. High Sidhe are the immortals. There aren't many of them. I'm told that most people in the sidhe realms go their whole lives without seeing a High Sidhe. Middle sidhe are the elfin nobility—and the way they determine who's noble is confusing, but never mind that for now. Low sidhe are everyone else. Well, not humans—"

"There are humans in the sidhe realms?" Isen asked.

"Sure. We seem to be everywhere. What I meant was that low sidhe includes a lot of elves, plus a lot of mixed bloods, plus races other than elves who share in the sidhe magical heritage."

"What does that mean?"

"It's complicated, but they determine who's sidhe and who isn't based on bloodlines and on common magical descent. It's possible for magic to be passed on in ways that have nothing to do with the physical DNA. Pixies are a good example. They can't interbreed with elves, so there's no shared DNA, but their magic is descended from sidhe magic—don't ask me how—so they're considered sidhe."

"Interesting," Isen murmured. "I suppose that's why you

consider yourself of the Blood? Your magic isn't human, and I suppose your blood would interfere with lab tests. Yet, if I understand correctly, you aren't sure if it's sidhe magic or not."

"It's more that I don't know if the sidhe would consider me sidhe. That's sort of important. My father is just under half sidhe by bloodlines—fifteen thirty-seconds, to be precise. His mother was a one-woman melting pot. If he were exactly half-sidhe, he'd automatically be considered low sidhe. Since he isn't, he had to be tested. His magic tests as sidhe, so he's sidhe."

Isen nodded thoughtfully. "You haven't been tested?"

"No." She sighed. "Like I said, it's complicated. My father did register my birth, which means I'm entitled to be tested, and he thinks I would test as sidhe. Not because I'm powerful, but my Gift is a sidhe ability. Kind of a rare one, too," she added. "Or so he said the last time I saw him, but that was years and years ago. He isn't exactly attentive. But I'd have to go to one of the sidhe realms to be tested, and that isn't possible, which means I'm sort of at risk."

Benedict spoke for the first time in quite awhile. "What risk?"

"There are, um, some people in some of the realms who might want to breed me or use my blood."

He growled.

She blinked. "Wow. That sounds exactly like a wolf. I didn't know you could do that when you were being a man."

He took a slow breath and looked at the lovely man sitting across from her. "Seabourne, do you know what she's talking about?"

Cullen Seabourne took his time answering, his expression abstracted, as if he were thinking hard. Or maybe *seeing* hard. He was watching Arjenie the way a mongoose watches a cobra. "Some blood is more magically potent than others. I assume that's what she refers to."

Arjenie nodded. "Yes, and there are some spells you can only *do* with sidhe blood. I've made some guesses about what they might be, but Eledan wouldn't tell me, and I suppose that isn't important right now. I'm considered Sha'almuireli kin now, but if I tested as sidhe I'd *be* Sha'almuireli—or possibly Divina'hueli, since my father does have some of that in his bloodline, but he's Sha'almuireli, so I probably would be, too. If I turned out to be sidhe at all, that is. But being Sha'almuireli, however lowly a member, would probably keep me from being grabbed."

"I'm guessing that Sha'almuireli is one of the Hundred?" Seabourne said. When she nodded he added to the others, "There are a fixed number of sidhe surnames, which designate kinship groups similar to clans—though it's a great deal more complicated than the way we think of clans."

"It certainly is," she said with feeling. "I don't understand it all, but—" But she was trying to be brief. Not succeeding, but trying, so she wouldn't go into that. "Unfortunately, there isn't any way for me to be tested."

"You've never been to the sidhe realms, then?" Isen asked.

"Oh, no. Eledan can cross realms whenever he wants—and that's usually a middle sidhe ability, not low sidhe, but that's the thing about mixed bloods. Sometimes we're just a diluted version of a sidhe. Other times we don't have any sidhe skills at all, but the other parent's innate magic gets passed on, only stronger than usual. And sometimes we only get one or two of the sidhe abilities, but we get that full-strength. That's how it worked with Eledan, and with me, too."

"But he can cross, and he wants you to be tested, yet he's never taken you there for this testing."

"There's a mass limit to what he can carry when he crosses. I'm too big now. When I was little enough for him to take me, my mother wouldn't permit it. She thought he wouldn't watch out for me properly, or maybe he'd forget to bring me back. He might have. He's not very reliable."

Benedict spoke again. "I take it Eledan is your father's name."

She flushed. "Yes. I don't call him Father because, you know, he isn't. He's my genetic parent, and he's got some sense of duty toward me, but it isn't very highly developed."

Benedict's eyes were flat. So was his voice. "What did you mean about them breeding you?"

He looked scary again. He sounded scary, too. Why did all that grimness make her want to touch him? Right there, along that hard jaw . . . *Behave*, she told herself. "The sidhe realms are not uniform, no more than our realm is. Some governments in our world suck at civil rights. Some governments in the sidhe worlds do, too. There's one place that's rancid with slavery and other ugliness. According to Eledan, if I ended up there, I'd be used as breeding stock."

"And how would someone in this slavery realm know about you?"

"Like I said, my father registered my birth, so it wouldn't be all that hard to find out I exist and that this is my home realm. Especially because of Eledan's profession."

This time it was Isen who spoke. "Which is?"

"Um. We don't have an analog for it. He's unusually fertile for a sidhe, so basically he gets paid for impregnating women. Um—not my mother. She was a busman's holiday. He was in our realm and she drew his attention, and he *does* have a touch of the sidhe glamour, though even without it he's almost as beautiful as Mr. Seabourne."

"Cullen," Seabourne murmured. "Lovely ladies should always call me Cullen, not mister."

She awarded him a quick grin before continuing. "What I'm getting at is that Mom wasn't a paid job for Eledan, but he did come back to see if he'd impregnated her. That was partly duty, like I said, but also, the more offspring he registers, the better. Especially sidhe offspring, so we can't assume he's right about me testing as sidhe. I suspect he confuses what he wants with what is."

Benedict shoved back his chair and stood. "Excuse me." He strode away.

She started to rise, too. "What's wrong?"

Isen put a hand on her arm. "Give him a moment. "

"But—"

"He's angry. He doesn't like the way your father treated you."

She watched as, in three strides, Benedict reached the retaining wall and leaped almost straight up onto the upper deck. There he began pacing.

Arjenie frowned. Benedict was truly upset. His father seemed to think he should be left alone, but . . . "Do you always interpret him for people?" she asked Isen, then patted the hand he'd used to stop her. "Never mind. I think I'll go to the original text." She stood.

Seabourne spoke quickly. "That may not be a good idea."

"*Resides*," Isen murmured, but to Seabourne, not her. In this context that meant *calm down* or *subside*. "Benedict is not you."

Arjenie limped over to the stairs. Benedict stopped pacing and looked down at her, his expression not at all welcoming, so she was surprised when he jumped down to land beside her. "You're supposed to stay off your ankle."

"It's much better than it was." She tipped her head up, studying him. "What's wrong?"

"My father's interpretation is accurate."

"Oh. Well, Eledan may a bit of a prick by our standards—"

The muffled snort came from Seabourne back at the table.

"—and even for a sidhe I think he's careless. Of course, that's based on a sample of one and a half, so I could be wrong."

"Half? You sampled half a sidhe?"

She waved that aside. "I don't understand why you're so upset."

"Your father put you in danger of being enslaved and bled or bred in order to further his career as a professional stud."

"I like that." She smiled, pleased. "A professional stud. That's a good way to put it. But I may have made things sound too black-and-white. Registering my birth was partly self-interest, but not entirely. To Eledan, being sidhe is terribly important. In his eyes, he would have failed me in a fundamental way if he hadn't registered my birth. It wouldn't occur to him I might not want to be registered."

"Maybe because the danger isn't to him."

"Nooo . . . at least, I don't think so. I don't think he's cowardly. Self-interested and a bit lazy, but not cowardly. Anyway, I doubt the danger is very great. This is a big world. Someone who wanted to grab me would have to find me first, so I don't draw attention to myself." She shrugged. "Maybe no one's even looking. I'm just careful, that's all."

"No Facebook page, or Myspace, or Twitter. No Internet presence at all."

"You checked?"

"I can Google. I wonder if an out-realm kidnapper could."

"Who knows? My feeling is that if someone took the trouble to come here at all—and that's a big if—they wouldn't mind staying long enough to learn stuff like that. They couldn't just use a Find spell. My Gift protects me from that."

He looked so tight. Unhappy. Maybe that's why she did something unwise. She touched his cheek.

He went still. She skimmed the line of his jaw with her fingertips before reluctantly dropping her hand. "I get the feeling . . . are you a father?"

He nodded slowly, his eyes as wary as if he were the wolf instead of the man, uncertain about this human who'd dared touch him.

"So's my uncle Clay. He's a father to the children he had with Aunt Robin, and to me, too. I didn't grow up fatherless. I'm not hurting because my genetic parent isn't my dad."

His face softened. It wasn't quite a smile, but it came close. "I'm not to feel sorry for you."

"Absolutely not. And anger—well, I won't say that it's never useful, but in this case it's pointless. It won't change anything."

He didn't speak. His eyes were so intent, so focused on her . . . *He's going to kiss me.*

Arjenie's heartbeat picked up. Longing rose in her, sweet and warm as summer rain. She forgot about the people sitting at the table a few feet away. Her lips parted.

He put one hand on her shoulder . . . and slowly drew that hand down her arm to reach her hand, which he clasped. "Do you keep up with the news?" he asked.

"Oh. Um. Well." Was her radar that badly off, or had he changed his mind? She pulled her thoughts together. "I'm a bit of a news junkie, but real news, not the TV pundits who just talk and talk. Though I'm out of touch right now, what with traveling and, um, stuff. I haven't even checked the *Times* online lately."

He nodded. "Then maybe you haven't heard about Ruben Brooks or Lily."

"What?" Alarm pinged through her. "Ruben? Lily? What haven't I heard?"

"Yesterday Brooks had a heart attack. Last night Lily was shot."

"Shot!" She grabbed his arm. "Is she—no, you wouldn't be sitting around holding dinner parties if she . . . but she's all right? And Ruben? What about Ruben?"

"Lily's arm was damaged. We don't know yet how fully it will heal. Brooks lived through the heart attack and is considered stable. There is some question about whether it occurred naturally or was magically induced."

"Induced," she whispered. "Oh, no."

"You know something about this."

"Not about Lily getting shot." But about Ruben's heart attack . . . maybe she was wrong. Maybe there were other ways to magically induce a coronary infarction. Vodun? It could be a vodun spell. Maybe. "I need my laptop. And my phone. I've got to check in." And log in, do some research, and talk to someone, find out just how closely Ruben's symptoms mimicked those of a heart attack.

If it wasn't mimicry—if he'd actually had a heart attack—it wasn't vodun.

Isen came up behind his son. "Not just yet. You need to tell us what you know or suspect."

"I can't."

He shook his head. "I know we agreed you could withhold information on one subject, but there are lives at risk."

"No," Cullen said abruptly. "I think she's right." He shoved back from the table, strode up to her, and gripped her chin in one hand.

She tried to jerk away. Couldn't. "I don't like being grabbed."

"Hush." His fingers dug in enough to hold her head still.

"I don't like being told to hush, either."

"I'll remember that." But he didn't let go as he murmured something, his other hand shifting rapidly through the air. The first symbol he sketched was the Raetic *ka*, which was common to lots of spells, being a rune of seeking. The rest . . . his hand moved too fast. She couldn't see what they were.

And then she stopped breathing. Entirely.

It was only for a moment, but the terror was huge. She dragged in a deep breath as soon as her body would let her. "You—you—"

"I'm sorry. It was necessary." He looked at Isen, then Benedict. "When she says she can't talk about some things, she means it literally. There's a binding on her."

TWENTY-TWO

THE current crop of experts claimed that baby girls stare at faces while baby boys watch the mobile over their cribs. They extrapolated from this to conclude that women are inherently interested in people and men are inherently interested in objects.

Isen Turner supposed they might be right in a statistical sense, but numbers don't tell the whole story. If you have one foot in boiling water and one in a tub of dry ice, on the average you're comfortable. And maybe those experts hadn't included any lupi in their sampling. His mother used to say he'd begun studying people the moment he figured out how to focus his eyes.

He'd kept that up for the ninety-one years since. People fascinated him. Male people, female people . . . lupi, human, gnome, whatever. He never tired of studying them, figuring out what they were thinking and feeling, what they wanted, what they feared, how they had changed or were changing. That fascination worked out well. There was no more important subject for a Rho to devote himself to.

That's why it was his youngest son, not his eldest, who would become Rho one day. Benedict saw clearly when he looked, but it was a learned behavior, not innate. It was also why Isen's middle son hadn't been in the running. Mick had never learned to clear his eyes where others were concerned, his vision of them forever warped by his own wants and needs and obsessions. Eventually, this had killed him.

That was a grief Isen lived with daily, one that woke him some nights with his face wet. But Isen was well-acquainted with grief. It was the one opponent to whom even a Rho must submit.

Benedict understood and accepted why Isen had chosen Rule as heir. This was one of Benedict's most remarkable gifts—a deep and fluid acceptance of both his limits and his talents. Rule didn't understand, an odd blind spot in one who otherwise made good progress in his own study of self and others. But Isen knew his sons. Rule's blind spot would not hamper him as Rho, for Benedict would never take advantage of Rule's love and admiration for his big brother. He would, quite literally, die first.

On this sweet-smelling night in September, Isen didn't need his ninety-plus years of expertise. Arjenie Fox presented no challenge. A scent-blind ten-year-old boy could have read her face. She might be able to keep a factual secret, but emotionally she was transparent.

True, she wasn't purely human, and Isen had no real experience with the sidhe. That might be throwing him off. He didn't think so. When Seabourne had revealed her binding, Isen was convinced she felt a single, simple emotion.

Relief.

That certainly wasn't the emotion the others felt. Seabourne was suspicious and fascinated. Benedict remained fascinated, too, though in quite a different way, but he'd gone still, ready to counter if she suddenly attacked. As for their invisible company, why, Rule was silent at the moment. Probably typing out on his laptop what Seabourne had just said so Lily would know.

Technology was a marvel sometimes.

Rule had been listening in on their dinner table conversation via Isen's phone, typing a rough transcript of it for Lily, whose human ears would miss most of it. Benedict and Seabourne were undoubtedly aware of this. They would have heard Rule's occasional comments from Isen's earbud. Benedict had probably known from the moment Isen returned to the table with an open phone line. Even for a lupus, his hearing was unusually acute.

Isen's hearing wasn't exceptional, but it was easy for him to hear Lily's reaction. She wanted Isen to get away from Arjenie *right now*. Isen smiled. His youngest son's Chosen was wise and wary. Good traits. He had no intention of following her directions, but he approved of her caution. She was very like Benedict in some ways. "You can see this binding?" he asked Seabourne.

"I do now. It's a subtle thing, almost invisible unless it's active. I thought it a natural part of her aura at first."

Arjenie Fox looked from Benedict to Isen to Seabourne. No doubt it was clear from their faces they weren't experiencing the relief she felt. She spoke quickly. "Did you know that one kind of binding spell doesn't compel a person to *do* anything? It wouldn't even make them lie. It would just keep them from revealing something."

"Who did this to you?" Benedict demanded. "Friar?"

That deepened her anxiety, but she didn't speak. Probably couldn't.

Seabourne could and did. "Extremely unlikely. The spell is beyond anything I could do, and I refuse to believe he has that kind of skill and training. Plus it's hard as hell to use mind-magic on sidhe. Even someone only a quarter-sidhe would be resistant."

Isen spoke. "Could another sidhe do it?"

"It takes a sidhe to bind a sidhe?" Cullen shrugged. "Maybe."

Arjenie smiled brightly. "I don't think I told you that I was five when Eledan came to see me the first time. He was worried about me chattering the way kids do, so he put a spell on me so I couldn't speak about him or my heritage. I couldn't tell anyone about the spell, but fortunately my mother figured out what he'd done and made him remove it. Otherwise I couldn't tell you about it. Or him."

"Your father did this to you," Benedict said flatly.

Her smile stayed stuck tight to her face.

"You can't confirm or deny this binding," Isen said gently. "You can't speak of it at all, so you can't let us know if we guess right. But it doesn't make you lie, so you aren't forced to deny it. That's helpful."

She looked at him gratefully. "You remind me of my uncle Clay. I wish you could meet him. I wonder how you would feel if there was something you really wanted to let people know, but you couldn't speak of it."

Isen nodded, understanding. "You want to get rid of the binding."

She smiled like crazy.

Isen looked at Seabourne. "Can you do that?"

"Maybe, given time. The question is whether I can do it safely."

Rule spoke softly in Isen's ear. "Lily says Sam could."

Isen nodded thoughtfully. "I wonder if Sam would be willing to take a look at this binding."

Seabourne's expression sharpened. "Good idea. The binding is tied to her blood, so it's similar to what was done to me. Sam unsang that."

Arjenie looked from one of them to the other. "Who's Sam?"

"Sun Mzao. The black dragon."

Her eyes widened. Her mouth shaped a silent "oh."

Rule spoke so quietly Isen didn't know if even Benedict could hear him. "Sam is, ah, out of pocket at the moment. He won't be back for several days, and when he returns, he'll probably consider this a favor. Nokolai hasn't accumulated a favor from him yet. We'd have to bargain for this separately, and dragons tend to price their favors high."

Isen answered him while appearing to respond to Cullen. "It's worth finding out."

"Conversational breadcrumbs," Benedict said abruptly. His attention had never wavered from his Chosen. "You've been dropping some, haven't you? The potions are connected to whatever you can't reveal. Your father put this binding on you. Is your father connected to the potions?"

She started to say something, stopped, and began again. "When I was young I saw things much more in black-and-white than I do now."

"The connection is indirect."

She beamed at him.

"You said the potions wouldn't harm us."

"One of them was to mask my scent, like I said. The other one was intended to help, not harm."

"Did you make the potions?"

She all but sang her answer. "No!"

"Can you tell me who did?"

"I need to change the subject."

Benedict continued to circle around the forbidden topic with questions, trying to define its parameters. Arjenie looked harried and tense and tired. Seabourne had tuned the rest of them out and was frowning off into space. Rule was arguing with Lily. She wanted to check out of the hospital tomorrow and fly back here. Rule considered that incredibly foolish, though he didn't put it in quite those words.

It was nice to know his son had some sense. Isen sighed. Rule was not going to be happy with him. He agreed with Lily. "Arjenie, you're looking worn-out. Let's sit down again. Perhaps some more coffee?" He offered her his arm rather than taking hers. He'd noticed that she disliked being handled. Was that a sidhe characteristic? He'd have to ask Seabourne.

Benedict gave him a quick glance—wondering why he'd interrupted, probably. Arjenie took his arm, smiling at him in a much more natural way than her too-bright smiles earlier. "I'd love some coffee. You'd think I wouldn't be sleepy for hours after being unconscious for so long, but passing out doesn't seem to affect my sleep cycle at all, and back home it's midnight. Besides, I love coffee."

"Then we'll get you some." He patted her hand, then pulled his phone out of his shirt pocket. As they started for the table he added casually, "I believe it's time we all participated openly in this discussion. Rule, I'm putting you on speakerphone."

Arjenie stopped dead. "What? You don't mean—tell me you haven't—has Rule Turner been *listening*?"

"I'm afraid so. So has Lily, indirectly."

She blanched. "Oh, no. Oh, no. We agreed—"

"I agreed not to speak of your secret away from Clanhome," Isen said. "I haven't. Nor have those under my authority."

"But Friar can hear! If he's trying, he could have heard everything! Lily's Gift might block him from hearing her—I'm not sure about that, but it might. But it wouldn't keep him from hearing a phone near her! Someone . . . someone could be in terrible trouble."

Lily's voice came through clearly on the phone's speaker. "It shouldn't be a problem. I confirmed that he's in California now. I also checked with Cullen. No Listener can eavesdrop across that many miles."

Arjenie was anguished. "He can."

"You're claiming that Friar is the strongest clairaudient on record?"

"I *know* he can hear things in D.C. when he's in California, so he could Listen to you in Tennessee, too!"

"Well, even if you're right, he can't do it constantly, so the odds are good. And even if he beat those odds and was Listening to my hospital room, he didn't hear much. I know that because I didn't. Rule had his phone on speaker, so I heard Isen, but the rest of you weren't close enough to Isen's phone for it to pick up your voices much. Rule's been typing a rough transcript for me. If I hadn't had that, I wouldn't have been able to follow things at all, so I doubt Friar could have, either."

Arjenie was not placated. "You don't know what he could hear magically, not for sure. You don't have the right to risk someone else when there's so much you don't know."

"Arjenie, that's my job," Lily said, her voice weary. "That's what I do every day. I make decisions that either help or hurt people, and I almost always have way too little information."

Ah, poor Lily. Isen knew it wasn't really her injury dragging at her. That would frustrate and infuriate and worry her in the days and weeks to come—humans healed so slowly!—but it wouldn't flavor her voice with defeat. In her head she knew LeBron had not been under her authority, but in her heart he had been, and had therefore been hers to protect.

Isen understood her new burden all too well, but this wasn't the time for him to speak of it. It was time for clarity on another subject. He looked at Arjenie. "Lily believes there is an organized effort against the Unit. Ruben Brooks was nearly killed. He will be unable to resume his duties for some time, and may be unable to resume them at all, depending on the results of the healing performed on him. Then Lily was herself nearly killed. She has a responsibility to determine whether you were involved in the attack on Ruben Brooks or on her."

"Me?" Arjenie was dumbfounded. "But I've been here! Here in California, I mean."

"Isen," Lily said, warning clear in her voice, "don't—"

"I'm afraid you aren't entirely in charge," he told her gently. "Arjenie, Lily suspects a conspiracy that includes at least one perpetrator within the FBI. Who else could have reached Brooks to administer whatever caused his heart attack? But there could be more than one FBI agent or employee involved."

Arjenie chewed on her lip and thought that over. He liked that about her. She was as chatty and confiding as Benedict was silent and reserved, but she knew when to stop and think.

No one else spoke, either. Lily's silence was especially loud. Isen knew what she wanted to say: It was stupidly irresponsible to tell a suspect what you suspected.

She was right, of course. But whatever Arjenie Fox might be involved in, it did not include harming others. She knew or suspected something about the attack on Brooks, but she wasn't conspiring to bring down the Unit or anyone within it. Not intentionally, and not due to the binding. She was, he thought, a practicing Wiccan in the deepest sense, one whose heart embraced their core tenet: *and it harm none.* If her actions had caused clear harm—even if she'd been unable to direct those actions—she'd be consumed by guilt. She wasn't.

"I can't think of anyone who'd betray the Bureau," Arjenie said at last. She sounded almost as tired as Lily. "Of course, I might say that if I were part of a vast cell of traitors, all of whom I knew intimately, so that doesn't help. Is Mr. Croft in charge of the Unit right now?"

"He is," Lily said.

"Are you going to tell him about my Gift and my father and me being here at Clanhome and everything?"

"I haven't decided."

Arjenie sighed. Benedict moved closer to her, but not so he could counter a potential attack. Not this time. He wanted to hold her. Isen knew that as clearly as if Benedict had announced it.

After that involuntary movement, Benedict went still again, but Isen could almost taste his son's longing. It hurt his heart. There was so little he could do. He settled for patting Arjenie's hand. "If it helps, I don't suspect you of anything nefarious. Rule, Lily's right."

"Quite often," Rule agreed dryly. "But which specific instance did you mean?"

"She needs to come home. She is in serious and ongoing danger, and a hospital room is difficult to defend. In addition"—he put a subtle note in his voice so Rule would know his Rho spoke—"I need her and you here. Unless Nettie is utterly opposed, I want the three of you to return tomorrow. The meeting with the other North American clans is more vital than ever, and without Lily's presence as guarantee of our peaceful intentions, Ybirra will withdraw. Lily, I hope you don't object to my stating my wishes, since they agree with your own."

"Object? No. But you're up to something."

"Arjenie is right, too. There are some things that shouldn't be discussed over the phone. I'll say only that I disagree with you in one respect. I don't think your Unit is the target of a conspiracy."

"I'd be interested in hearing your reasoning."

"We'll discuss it when you return. I do believe there is a conspiracy."

"But not against the Unit."

"No. Against us. Lupi. All lupi, not just Nokolai, and all who might aid us or otherwise interfere in *her* plans. You can guess which enemy I'm thinking of."

Lily's breath caught. Rule didn't make a sound. Cullen Seabourne swung to face Isen, his eyes narrowing. And Isen's oldest son looked at him with dawning relief. "Of course."

TWENTY-THREE

ON the other side of the continent, Lily sat up in her hospital bed scowling at the computer screen. Rule sat on the bed beside her, his laptop balanced on his thighs. He'd just ended the call to Isen.

"I can't believe he told us that," Lily said, frustrated, "then wouldn't say why he thinks *she's* involved." She drummed the fingers of her good hand on her leg. "We'll find out tomorrow, I guess."

"We will not. You aren't flying across the country so I can attend that damned meeting a few days earlier than otherwise. You're barely out of surgery."

His jaw was set stubbornly. His eyes were dark, shadowed by sleeplessness, and brimming with emotion . . . emotion that for once she had no trouble reading.

Rule had been on high alert for over twenty-four hours. He was worn-out and wired up and afraid that wouldn't be enough. That *he* wouldn't be enough. That he'd miss something or sleep at the wrong time or be less than omniscient, and whoever wanted her dead would succeed.

Isen was right. A hospital room was hard to defend. There were too blasted many people around, and the other side of her door was public territory. Rule knew this. He was determined to keep her here anyway. He had some control over their small territory—more than he would in an airport, at least. But more importantly, her wound scared him.

She held out her hand. He took it. She let the contact ease them both, wishing he could climb into bed so she could hold him and be held. "I do heal, you know," she said gently. "I don't heal the way you do, but I do heal."

"You haven't healed yet. It's too soon."

"Rule, this isn't your decision." She let that sink in, then added, "I'm not an idiot. If Nettie nixes the trip, I'll stay here. My own opinion—which I confidently expect both you and Nettie to ignore—is that I can do it. I'll hurt, sure, but I'll hurt if I stay in this blasted bed, too. It won't harm me to sit in an airplane."

"We can't go strictly by what Nettie says. If my father tells her he wants you to return home, she—"

"You know better." She squeezed his hand. "Nettie won't adjust her medical opinion to suit Isen or anyone else."

He looked at their joined hands and sighed. "I don't like it."

"I know." It was her left hand he held, her right arm that was damaged, and that was a bitch. She was right-handed. But for that one instant, she was glad he could hold the hand that wore his ring. "You're going to wear one, too, you know."

Puzzled, he looked up. "One what?"

"Ring."

He smiled slightly. "I am, yes."

She took a breath and jumped. "I'll stay at Clanhome. Not the whole time I'm healing, because that's going to take way too long, but while I'm officially on sick leave. You can guard the hell out of me there."

His eyes searched hers. Some of the tension eased from his face. He lifted her hand and kissed it. "I love you at all times. Sometimes I like you tremendously, too. Thank you. I know you'd much rather be at our place. I also know you're planning to investigate as much as possible while you're there."

She didn't have a case. She'd been pulled from the Cobb

case and she couldn't just show up in D.C. to hunt for whoever had tried to kill Ruben and she was going to be on sick leave and . . . and did that matter?

Yes, she decided. But maybe not as much as it ought to. "Speaking of planning . . ." She glanced around, spotted her takeout cup, and disengaged her hand so she could pick it up. Then frowned at the few cold drops remaining in the bottom of the cup. "Maybe you could send the guard for more coffee."

"Or maybe not. It's nearly eleven, and you should sleep at some point tonight—especially if you're going to persuade Nettie you're well enough to fly home tomorrow."

She was tired, and she was tired of being tired, and he was right, and the whole thing sucked. "Do you buy Isen's idea? Do you think the Great Bitch is behind the attacks on me and Ruben?"

The twin slashes of Rule's brows drew down. "I don't know. Maybe more yes than no. Isen's right an awful lot of the time, and you've been *her* target before. You don't sound convinced."

Lily wobbled her hand back and forth, miming uncertainty. "Sure, it could be *her*, but we've thought that before and it wasn't. I don't think the attack on me really suggests *her*. When she went after me before, she wanted me alive so she could eat me or my magic or something. Last night's shooter wanted me dead."

Rule's face closed down, which meant he was upset. "You thwarted her earlier plans, not once but twice. *She* holds a grudge."

"Maybe, but surely she's imaginative enough to know that there are lots worse things she could do than kill me. If I was more useful to her alive a few months ago, why would killing me be a good idea all of a sudden?"

"Because her plans have changed. Not her goal. I doubt that has changed since she was defeated in the Great War. Three thousand some-odd years isn't a long time to an Old One."

"And that goal is—?"

"To possess the Earth. To remake it to suit *her* values, her notions of what is good and proper."

Lily drummed her fingers. "Having her avatar eaten by a hell lord may have set back her world conquest schedule."

"Unless that's what *she* intended. A year's delay in nothing. She may have needed that time to subjugate the demon lord who ingested whatever portion of her was held by her avatar. A demon lord would make a much more powerful avatar than one born human."

That was the problem with dealing with a perp who had, supposedly, been around since the universe kicked off—or maybe before that. The Great Bitch wasn't omnipotent or omniscient, but her knowledge, experience, and abilities were so far beyond the human it was impossible to guess her plans. "If the Old Ones fought a war to stop her once, wouldn't they step in now if *she* were trying to take over Earth?"

"Not directly. Neither they nor she can enter any realms where humans live. The Great War was fought, in part, so that those on my Lady's side could impose just that restriction."

"The good-guy Old Ones restricted themselves? Permanently?"

He spread his hands. "We are taught that they amended their reality in order to allow the younger races a chance to create their own."

That was too mystical entirely for Lily. She drummed her fingers again. "Why Ruben? Why would *she* want him taken out?"

"I don't know. I can speculate. His precognitive ability combined with his position may be a threat to her plans. But I don't know."

It was all too mushy. They had no real reason to suspect the Great Bitch's involvement, but almost anything could be made to fit that scenario when they knew so little about her plans, methods, and capabilities. It reminded Lily of the way people in medieval times thought the devil was behind every illness and misfortune. "If your milk cow dries up, blame it on *her*," she muttered.

"What?"

"Never mind." Maybe it was her brain that was mushy. Hot licks of pain kept grabbing her attention, disrupting her train of thought. Damned pain. Couldn't God or evolution or whatever have arranged things so pain didn't have to hurt quite this much?

Rule was frowning, more in thought than temper. "It's possible the attack on Ruben was her agent's idea and promotes his plans, not hers."

"What do you mean?"

"If Robert Friar is her agent—"

"Whoa. That's a giant step."

"She has to act through agents, just as my Lady does, since she's prohibited from acting directly. Why not Friar? He's cunning and wary and wealthy. He already has followers, an organization of sorts, and he hates us."

She looked at him, ruffled and irritated and not sure why. "You realize you've stepped off into pure speculation? There's a suggestion that Friar could be involved, but it's wispy. Enough to justify looking into the possibility, no more. We don't have even a wisp to say that *she's* involved, much less anything linking her to Friar."

"I'm entitled to a hunch," he said mildly, "even if I lack Ruben's accuracy."

She frowned at her hand. Her only useable hand. "I'm going to be a real bitch for a while, I think."

He touched her cheek lightly. "I'm tough. I can handle it."

She looked up. "You think *she's* involved, don't you?"

"Isen does. I won't adopt his conclusion without hearing his reasoning, but I respect his judgment. Also . . ." He got that far, then drifted into silence, frowning at his thoughts.

"Keep going."

"If *she* is moving, preparing an assault on us and our world," he said slowly, "our Lady would know this. She'd be working through her agents to stop her enemy." He paused, meeting Lily's eyes. "*We* are the Lady's agents. Lupi. It is very rare that she speaks to us directly through a Rhej, and she has not done that. But she has done something she hasn't done since she created us. She has gifted one of us with a second Chosen."

TWENTY-FOUR

ARJENIE was awake before the sun the next day. Her body was still on East Coast time, plus she'd ended up going to bed early—and without that second cup of coffee.

Shortly after Isen's announcement that some mysterious woman was conspiring against lupi, Arjenie had been informed she was tired. True, but more to the point, Benedict had wanted to talk with Isen privately. So it was Cullen Seabourne who'd escorted her to her room, and he'd refused to tell her anything about this mysterious female enemy Isen thought was conspiring against his people.

Cullen was still around when she woke up. So was her suitcase. She discovered the latter as soon as she put on her glasses. The former was obvious after she got dressed and opened her door. Then stood in the doorway, staring.

Cullen was out there, all right, walking down the hall . . . on his hands.

He glanced at her. His legs lowered with easy precision, arching his body into a perfect backbend. He rose from that as naturally as another person might rise from a chair. "Ready for breakfast?"

"Yes. Wow. That was amazing. Where's Benedict? And how did my suitcase get here?"

"Benedict's asleep. Even Superwolf needs sleep after skipping it two nights in a row. Your suitcase is here because he thought you'd need your things and sent someone to retrieve it for you. Isen wishes me to apologize on his behalf for removing a few items before giving it to you."

Like her athame and spell components. She'd noticed. "He may have meant well, but it was presumptuous to enter my hotel room without my permission."

"Benedict's good at presumption, not so good with asking permission. You'll have to work on that. I need to talk to Carl. He makes the second-best omelets in the world, and I'm hungry. Come on." He started down the hall.

"Wait a minute. I need to use the bathroom. And who makes the first-best omelets?"

He stopped, glancing back at her. The beautiful man hadn't shaved today. "A woman in a little village in the south of France. Her grandmother taught Carl how to cook, and she keeps chickens. Her eggs are fresher than Carl's. There's a bathroom near the kitchen. You can pee while Carl cooks."

She *hmphed*, but followed him down the hall to the great room or den. The kitchen, she'd discovered yesterday, opened off it at the other side of the house. "Does Carl actually talk to you?"

"Carl talks about food. Ask him about tarragon and he turns downright chatty."

"Are you going to tell me what Isen was talking about last night? About this enemy he thinks is behind everything?"

"Not my job to decide what you should or shouldn't be told, and it's easier to say no. I like easy. I like the T-shirt, too."

She smiled down at her chest, where white letters on a black background spelled out "no comment." "A friend gave it to me for my birthday. If I were prescient, I'd have worn it yesterday. I could have pointed to it when Isen was questioning me."

"No precog?"

She shook her head. "No more than the itsy hunches

everyone gets. Um . . . I consider precognition the Gift of the fifth element. I guess you know what I mean by that?"

"My original training was Wiccan, so yes."

In Wicca, the fifth element was spirit, which she'd been taught was available to all. The unGifted weren't able to use what spirit offered consciously or consistently, but now and then they tapped into it. That's why everyone had hunches, and even those without a trace of magic sometimes saw ghosts. It also explained the occasional miraculous cure.

Or so she believed. Other traditions—even other Wiccans—saw things differently. "What about you? Do you see precognition as tied to spirit?"

"Speaking literally? No. But that's probably because I don't see spirit."

"Really?" She stopped. "But that's fascinating! You see the other elements?"

"Of course. But not spirit, which makes me think that— with apologies to your faith—spirit is something other, not an elemental property of magic."

"Well, the pentagram is just a model, after all." But it made her feel pouty to think the model might not be right. They started walking again. "My aunt says the other elements are accessed through magic, but spirit is accessed through faith. Maybe that explains it. Do you have a faith?"

"No. That's an interesting distinction. What would . . . ah, Carl." They'd reached the kitchen, where the lanky Carl was wiping down a huge, restaurant-style stove. Cullen produced a charming smile. "Our Rho's guest is hoping for one of your superlative omelets."

They continued to talk shop while waiting for breakfast— minus a short bathroom break—and during the meal, where Cullen turned out to be right. Carl's omelets were incredible. After breakfast, they moved to the great room and kept on talking. They discussed theory and practice and tiptoed towards the possibility of trading a spell or two. Arjenie's coven had strict rules about that, so she'd have to get her High Priestess's permission before making a swap. But she had to call Aunt Robin today anyway.

Benedict and Isen didn't seem to be anywhere around.

The morning dragged. She felt wiggly and unsettled. Was it possible that after all these years she'd finally get the binding removed—and by a dragon? Who was this female enemy that had Isen spooked? She couldn't ask the first question. The cursed binding prevented it. Cullen wouldn't answer the second one. Maybe Benedict would, when he got back. From where? Cullen wouldn't say.

Arjenie wanted Benedict. Instead she was stuck with the most gorgeous man she's ever seen, a man who shared her interest in spellcraft and theory and could discuss them in an informed and intelligent—if occasionally sarcastic—way.

Some might say she was hard to please.

Clearly she was infatuated, but she wanted to see Benedict, talk to him, find out what his father had meant last night, why he didn't tell people his last name, and what his skin tasted like. Not necessarily in that order.

They were in the den when Cullen steered the talk to her Gift. She told him about the way glass affected it. "The glass in the windows doesn't bother you?" he asked.

Arjenie was curled into the corner of the big sectional about four feet from where Cullen sprawled in an armchair, and less than ten feet from the windows lining the back wall. "Nope. If I tried to use my Gift, though, it would . . . scratch at me. Interfere."

"Focus Fire, stop Air, seal Water, open Earth."

"Exactly. Now, if I were touching glass and pulled hard on my Gift, I'd pass out. So would . . ." Her voice drifted off. She'd seen something move outside. What—oh, it was just a dog. A yellow Lab, she thought. Not a wolf. Not a man who sometimes walked as wolf, either. "So would anyone nearby," she finished, "if it was a large piece of glass."

"Who are you watching for?"

"No one. Or, well . . ." She fluttered a hand. "I keep wondering where Isen is. He's been gone since before I got up, which was about five thirty your time. And you won't tell me where he is."

"He has many duties as Rho," Cullen said blandly. "And he doesn't need much sleep. Are you sure he's the one you're looking for?"

Her cheeks heated. Maybe she'd been a bit obvious about

her infatuation. "I guess Benedict has many duties, too. Does he live here? Here in this house, I mean."

"Here or at the barracks or at his cabin up in the mountains."

"Those are all places he stays, maybe, but where does he live? Where's home?"

"You're thinking like a human."

"Duh."

He grinned. "Point is, you think of this house as Isen's—and it is—but all of Clanhome is Isen's. Just as all of it, including this house, is ours. The clan's."

She frowned. "You don't draw lines between one person's property and another's?"

"We do, but not the way you're used to. Especially not when it comes to our Rho. He's ours. We're his. Everything he owns, we own. Everything we own, he owns."

Arjenie had known that the clan's holdings were in the Rho's name, but she hadn't grasped what that meant. She didn't think she grasped it now, either. "Okay, but . . . say you own something and another clansman wants it. Whose is it?"

"Mine. I might decide to give it to him, but it's my choice. He's unlikely to ask, of course, because status is involved. Remind me to tell you about the magpie game. Our kids and adolescents love it, and sometimes adults play it, too, though only among close friends. But if the clan itself needs something, then it's the clan's."

The magpie game? She shook her head, determined to stay on topic for once. "And your Rho gets to decide what the clan needs?"

"Of course."

"What if you've got a greedy Rho? One who confuses his own wants with the clan's needs?"

"A Rho who's perceived to be taking things selfishly would be Challenged. Eventually he wouldn't be Rho anymore."

"How does someone stop being Rho?"

"He dies."

She shivered. "These Challenges are to the death?"

"They can be."

"Has Isen ever—"

"No. Not for greed. I haven't been Nokolai long enough to know that in an absolute sense—internal Challenges aren't supposed to be spoken of outside the clan, so theoretically it could have happened without my knowing. But I can't imagine it. Nothing matters to Isen the way Nokolai does. His sons come close, but Nokolai comes first. Whatever Challenges he's faced, they weren't because he was greedy."

"What do you mean, you haven't been Nokolai long? I thought lupi were born into their clans."

"Stop asking so many questions."

She grinned. "Why?"

He snorted. "Back to the way glass affects you. Clearly your Gift is tied to Air. We can't rely too strongly on human models since it isn't a human Gift, but it seems that—"

A deep, growly voice spoke. "You're supposed to be guarding her. I could have taken you both out while you yammered on about Gifts and Challenges." Benedict stood in the doorway that opened onto the entry hall, his hands on his hips.

Cullen glanced over his shoulder, unruffled. "You could take us both out with or without warning, though I did know you were here. I warded the house last night."

The funny thing was, Arjenie hadn't been startled, either. She hadn't heard the front door open or close. She hadn't seen Benedict appear in the hall. No, it was as if she'd *known* Benedict was there. She just hadn't noticed that she knew until he spoke. "Hi," she said happily.

Benedict gave her a nod, but spoke to Cullen. "Cynna's ready to come home. She's pretty worn-out. This was a hard one."

Cullen left. He didn't say 'bye, nice talking to you, gotta go, or anything else. He just left, moving fast. This time she heard the front door open and slam closed. She looked at Benedict. "He's a sudden one, isn't he? Though I guess we have to expect that with a Fire-Gifted. Cynna's all right?"

"She will be. Where's your cane?"

"In my room. I don't need it anymore."

He frowned and started for her. "I need to check your ankle."

"Ask."

"If you object, I—"

"Giving me a chance to object is not the same as asking permission. You're used to telling people what to do. That works with those guards you're in charge of. You aren't in charge of me. You have to ask."

One corner of his mouth turned up. "It's more efficient my way."

"If your primary goal in life is efficiency, you should just die."

That startled him. His head actually jerked back. "What?"

"The most efficient way to live a life is to die a couple seconds after you're born. *Pfft.* Done." She dusted her hands to demonstrate that. "It's too late for you to achieve optimal efficiency, but you could still . . ."

Benedict was laughing. Silently. She couldn't hear a thing, but his face, his open mouth, his whole body said laughter. It only lasted a few seconds before dwindling to an audible chuckle. "You have a strange mind. I like it. I like you."

He sounded surprised. She was surprised, too. Also delighted. And turned on. Her cheeks heated.

"May I check your ankle now?" he asked courteously.

She gave permission, and he knelt in front of her to unwrap the elastic bandage, which made the flutters in her belly worse. The man said he liked her, and she reacted like a tween with a crush. It was almost as mortifying as it was wonderful.

He took her foot in one big hand and rotated it. "Good movement."

"I want to know who this enemy is Isen spoke about last night."

"You'll be told about *her*, but not now."

"Why not?"

"I'm taking the day off. Swelling's gone," he added, beginning to rewrap the ankle.

"You won't answer questions because you're on vacation?"

"More or less." His mouth turned up wryly, as if at some private joke. He tucked the end in securely. "A brief vacation. One day. How does your ankle feel?"

"Fine."

His eyebrows lifted. "A one-word answer?"

"I got tired of answering questions about my health twenty years ago."

"After the accident."

She nodded.

"I imagine there was a long recovery and therapy. You mentioned additional surgeries, as well, later on." He nodded as if he'd added up a column. "I may have to ask about your physical status sometimes, but I'll avoid it when possible." He rose. "Today I needed to know because I'd like to show you around Clanhome."

She beamed. "I'd like that. My ankle really does feel fine. There may be some lingering weakness I won't notice until I've been walking on it awhile, but Dr. Two Horses's treatment helped, plus I heal faster than most."

His eyebrows lifted. "The sidhe blood?"

She nodded. "Obviously I don't always heal completely, or at the rate your people do. But I heal fast for a human."

"I'll get your cane."

"I'm not taking it."

"It's a precaution, in case you need it later."

She stood and patted his arm reassuringly and smiled. "No."

TWENTY-FIVE

THE cane stayed behind.

Benedict worked this out logically. If he brought it along after that firm refusal, she'd be annoyed and more determined than ever not to use the thing, even if she needed it. More important, though, it was the wrong thing to do. Children needed to have limits set for them. Arjenie wasn't a child. She was his to protect, but not from herself. Not from the consequences of her own decisions.

That was the problem.

He'd dreamed of Claire last night. Once that had been common, but not these days. Still, he supposed it would have been more surprising if she hadn't shown up. In the dream, he'd been at his cabin, which had mysteriously sprouted a new room. A bedroom. Arjenie had been asleep in the new bedroom when Claire walked in.

Sometimes his subconscious was damned unsubtle. "I thought we'd look in at the center first," he said as he and his new Chosen left his father's house.

"What's that?"

"Our child care and community center. We don't get cable out here, so there's a satellite dish and a big-screen TV at the

center for those who want to watch HBO or Showtime." He
glanced at her. "But maybe you knew about that."

Arjenie looked apologetic. "The satellite dish does show
up on aerial photos. So does the playground equipment. But,
um, I haven't seen inside your center."

"Nice to know a few things aren't in the government's
files. We'll go to baby room first," he said, opening the front
door and stepping out ahead of her. The human courtesy of
waiting for the woman to go through a door was all flourish,
no sense. If any danger waited on the other side of a door,
he'd rather meet it himself, not send her into it.

"Baby room?"

She was moving easily, he noted. Just as she'd said, her
ankle wasn't bothering her. He kept his pace slow. "Where
the tenders mind the clan's babies. Any who are here, that is.
Obviously a lot of them won't be. Even when the father has
or shares custody, he may not live close enough to use the
center regularly."

She nodded seriously. "The courts haven't been exactly
friendly to lupus dads. I know Mr. Turner—Isen's son, I
mean, Rule Turner—wasn't able to have custody of his son
until recently."

Rule's custody hearing had made headlines—especially
since it coincided with a string of supernatural murders.
"Some mothers won't share custody with a lupus father, and
until recently there was no chance of pursuing legal remedies. Still not much point in it, in most places. And many of
the mothers who do share custody live too far away for their
babies to be tended here when they're at work." Of course,
some women—like Rule's mother—handed their babies
over to their lupus fathers as fast as they could. They didn't
want a child who was going to turn furry one day.

The gravel path didn't seem to be giving her any trouble.
"If I understand correctly," she said, "that would be girl babies and boy babies both, right? You consider your female
children part of the clan even though they can't Change."

They also couldn't be included in the mantle, but he
wasn't going to explain mantles yet. "Is that in the FBI's
files?"

"Well, yes."

"Your file's right. Our daughters are clan. Their children aren't, but are considered *ospi*, or friends of the clan. Several of the babies and younger children at the center are *ospi*."

"You provide child care for them, too? Even though they aren't clan?"

"Babies are babies." It was beyond Benedict's understanding that, in the human world, there were children who went unclaimed, unwanted. Logically he could see that a race as astonishingly fecund as humanity could afford to be careless with its young, but everything in him revolted at the idea.

To be fair, many humans were revolted by it, too.

She fell silent as they reached the road that circled the meeting field, a grassy swathe that anchored the little village at Clanhome's heart. The center was about two miles away, on the southeast corner of the meeting field; Isen's house was at the northern end, banked up against the mountains.

It was a typical fall day for their corner of the county—sunny and warm, the sky blue enough to raise an ache in the heart, spotted here and there with puffs of white. A breeze tugged at Benedict's shirt sleeves and tangled itself up in the riot of Arjenie's hair. She'd left it down today, and it shone in the sun like molten copper.

The wind smelled of cholla and pine, rabbit and dirt . . . of home.

It was good to be walking here on this hard-packed dirt road, smelling home and feeling the sun's warmth. Good to be alive to feel these things. Even after the overmastering pain had subsided, it had taken him years to be able to feel that simple joy, untainted by guilt. How, he had wondered, could he exult in life, when Claire would never feel these things again?

He'd finally understood that his grief and guilt added nothing to the short span of Claire's life. He'd had the question backward. The real question was: How could he not?

He was glad now that he'd lived. Life wasn't a burden taken up because his Rho insisted he was needed, and it hadn't been for a long time. Life was what it was. Short or long, bitter or sweet, life simply was.

As Claire had reminded him tartly last night. *Quit feeling sorry for yourself,* she'd said. *Good God. What's so special about pain? About fear? You know fear. Even back when we were together—and you know, you really weren't that bright about some things back then—you understood fear better than me. I went crashing around, smashing into everything so I wouldn't have to face my fear. You told me then I had to face it, accept it.*

She'd snorted. It had sounded just like her, too. *Some reason you want to make my mistakes instead of finding one of your own?*

Smart Claire.

Maybe it really had been her he spoke with in the dream, not just the promptings of some buried, wiser self. Maybe not. Benedict knew there was something beyond death. He didn't know if that something allowed a woman who'd been dead for forty-two years to drop in on him in his sleep. It seemed possible. And impossible to know for sure.

And it didn't matter. Benedict drew a deep breath, looking around at so much that he loved . . . none of which was guaranteed to last until tomorrow. He'd lay down his life to make it last, if necessary, but even then he didn't get any guarantees.

Fear could be helpful, if you learned the right things from it. Or it could make you helpless. He was tired of being helpless. "You're quiet," he said to the woman walking beside him. Walking, not limping.

"Every now and then," she agreed. "It doesn't happen often, but now and then I stop talking. I was wondering . . . you said you were a father."

"Yes." He might as well tell her. She would be learning a great many of their secrets. "What did you wonder?"

"Pretty much everything. Do you have a son or a daughter? Will we see him or her at the center, or is your child older, or not living nearby? What about the mother? Do you have custody, or . . . you're laughing at me."

Yes. Yes, he was. That felt good, too. "You've kept a lot of questions pent up."

"I was waiting for you to finish that thinking you were doing. It seemed to be making you feel better. Lighter."

He cocked his head, curious. Most people couldn't read

him at all. Especially humans, who couldn't use scent as a guide. "It did. I have one child, a daughter. Nettie Two Horses."

For some reason, that delighted her. "The doctor who treated me is your daughter?"

He nodded. "You may be surprised by her appearance when you meet her."

"She doesn't look like you?"

"Around the eyes she does. She's got her mother's chin and jaw, and her mouth is a feminine version of Isen's. But that wasn't what I meant." He paused. "She's fifty-two."

She blinked. "Oh. Oh! I was right! You don't age the way humans do."

He stopped, staring. "You know?"

"I didn't *know* until you said that, but I guessed. I mean, it's logical, isn't it? If you heal damage almost perfectly, you'd heal free radical damage, too, so you'd age more slowly. Oh! Is that why you don't use your original surname? Because it might give away your real age?"

Urgently he said, "Does the government—"

"No, no." She patted his arm reassuringly. "That isn't in any of the files I have access to. And I access Restricted and Confidential information routinely, and am cleared for Secret if I jump through the right hoops, and even Top Secret with specific authorization. Generally, if I run across a pertinent reference that involves Top Secret material—some of the Secret files are heavily redacted Top Secret material—I simply annotate it to that effect, and the agent making the inquiry can either request the complete file or not. But I've read pretty much everything the Bureau knows about your people. That information isn't in the files."

He wasn't reassured. "Who have you told?"

"No one. Like I said, I was just guessing, and I understand the need to keep some things secret. Even basically nice people might start envying lupi your longevity, and envy can be extremely toxic. Though I don't think you'll be able to keep it secret forever."

"Probably not," he said, his voice very dry. "If you can make that connection, others can, and will." They'd known the day was coming. From the moment Rule went public, it had been inevitable. Eventually people would notice that "the werewolf prince" looked the same in his recent photos as he had five years ago. Or ten.

"So how old are you?" She flushed. "I guess that's rude, but I'd really like to know."

"Seventy."

"Wow. That's just . . . wow. You were really young when Nettie was born."

"Young and foolish. No more so than most at that age, I suppose. I had a lot of help raising Nettie, both in her mother's tribe and here. I needed it."

"Nettie. That's such a pretty name. Old-fashioned. It comes from the German *nette*, I think, which means clean or nice."

His eyebrows climbed. "You know German?"

"I read it. I don't speak it very well. I can read a lot of languages I can't speak."

"How many?"

"Um . . . twelve?" She wrinkled her nose as if dissatisfied with her own answer. "More or less, and not fluently, except for the Latin languages. Just enough to see if a text has what I'm looking for, mostly. And it has to be a language using the Roman alphabet. Well, except for Greek, which I can wade through slowly, and I've got a teensy bit of Russian, which uses the Cyrillic alphabet. But I don't know hanzi or kanji at all."

His eyebrows climbed. "You're apologizing for only being able to read in three alphabets?"

She flushed. "I'm a little self-conscious about it. People think, wow, you know all those languages? You must be a brain and a half! But I'm not, as my grades in calculus proved. I just have a really good memory, especially for things I read. Not a photographic memory, which some experts think is strictly a savant ability, though I read this article that said . . . never mind. That's not pertinent. My point is, being able to remember things can be handy, but it isn't the same as being able to synthesize or draw accurate conclusions or come up with new ideas."

"Is an unusually good memory a sidhe characteristic?"

"Not as far as I know. I think it's just me."

He smiled suddenly. "I guess you remember the first words you said to me, then."

She rolled her eyes. "Oh, you're going to tease me."

"Nice doggie?"

"I was shook up," she said with dignity.

"You knew I wasn't a dog."

"I may not be a genius, but I'm not stupid."

And yet it was common for a lupus in wolf form to pass for one of their domesticated cousins. People saw what they expected to see. "What are the visible differences between a dog and a wolf?"

She snorted softly. "Aside from sheer size? You're a very large wolf, Benedict. But okay, I'll play. On the whole, wolves have longer legs, longer muzzles, and larger feet. The legs are a particular giveaway. Malamutes—who look more like wolves than most dogs—have curly tails, while wolves' tails are straight. There's a difference with the teeth, too, but I didn't see yours, so that doesn't count."

He smiled at having his guess confirmed. "You also knew I wasn't only a wolf."

"You didn't act like a wolf. You weren't upset by my nearness—and wolves aren't comfortable being around people, you know. Plus I was fairly close to your Clanhome, so that made it more likely you were a lupus. I'm ninety-five percent sure there aren't any wild wolves in the area."

"Ninety-five?"

"None have been sighted in recent years. I suspect other wolves avoid your territory. But while a lack of sightings might be highly suggestive, it isn't proof, so I couldn't be a hundred percent sure."

She'd figured out all that while crippled from a fall and scared half out of her mind. With armed militia in the area and an extremely large wolf watching her, she'd sorted through her prodigious memory and come up with logical possibilities. Benedict smiled. "You're wrong about your intelligence. You don't simply remember things. You apply what you know to your situation, even under strong stress."

She turned pink with pleasure or embarrassment. "I think I take more comfort from facts than a lot of people do, so when I'm under stress, my mind naturally zooms in that direction."

For whatever reason, she didn't like thinking of herself as unusually bright, though she clearly was. Maybe she already felt a little too different from everyone else, given her heritage. He held out his hand.

She blinked, then smiled shyly and took it.

That, too, felt good. Incredibly damned good. He wanted to . . . but he wouldn't. Not now. For now, it was enough to hold her hand, learn about her, walk with her. His Chosen. "Let's go look at the babies."

Arjenie liked the baby room, and she liked the babies. She knew how to hold them, too, how to make funny faces and tickle. One of her cousins, she said, had been a late-life baby, so she'd gotten some practice there, plus she used to babysit in high school. Benedict learned the name of that much-younger cousin, and of several others. He learned the names of her uncles and aunts, too—five uncles named Delacroix, one of them married to her mother's sister.

None of her uncles were related to her by blood. Most of her cousins weren't, either.

Arjenie came from a large and loving family, but only her aunt Robin and her aunt's children were family by blood. It didn't seem to matter to her. She claimed them and they claimed her. It was like clan, Benedict thought. Blood mattered, but the claiming mattered more.

They visited the toddlers, then headed to the barracks for lunch. Benedict made sure his people ate well; lunch was chili and cornbread today. She ate a big bowl and two pieces of cornbread, and chatted easily with men who'd helped capture her two nights ago. Then they checked out the new nursery, where Samuel was growing native plants to sell to local garden centers. She asked Samuel a lot of questions, no doubt sorting the new information away tidily in the encyclopedia in her head.

As Benedict stored away the sight, sound, and scent of her in his head. Each moment was clear and precious. He'd told her he was taking time off. That was true, as far as his duties were concerned. His second was handling drill and routine security. That wasn't unusual. Benedict left Pete in charge when he was up at his cabin or taking a new batch of youngsters into the wilderness for combat training.

But this wasn't a normal time. His Rho believed their ancient enemy was active in their world once more and moving against them.

That was seriously bad news, yet on a personal level, it was a relief. A huge relief. The Lady hadn't gifted Benedict with a second Chosen because of anything about him. It wasn't personal at all. She'd done it because, for whatever reasons, the clans needed Arjenie. The Lady needed Arjenie. This meant that by protecting Arjenie, Benedict acted on the Lady's side and for the good of his people.

He was free to protect her. Whatever it took.

Rule had called Benedict three times today. The first was to let him know that he and Lily would be returning today. They should arrive around supper, and would be staying at Clanhome for a while. The other two involved selecting the specific location for the heirs' circle. With the venue changed so abruptly, that was a scramble. Rule had to present the other Lu Nuncios with a choice of sites, then all five had to agree on one.

Amazingly, they had. Now it fell to Benedict to assure the security, first, of his own Lu Nuncio—and second, of all the others. He should be at that site now, reacquainting himself with it.

He wasn't. He was going to have to tell Arjenie about the mate bond, and soon. Everything would change then.

This wasn't time off. It was time stolen.

"*You're not supposed to just pick people up,*" she'd said when he first captured her. She'd offered several variations on that theme. He wasn't to pick her up without her permission.

"*I have a strong sense of privacy,*" she'd told him when she learned he'd opened the bathroom door a bit. "*I don't like having that intruded upon.*"

She hadn't liked it when he listened to her voice mail, either. And when Seabourne spotted the binding last night and held her still so he could study it, she'd told him, "*I don't like being grabbed.*"

Arjenie did not tolerate being physically forced or intruded upon. Just this morning she'd said it again. "*Ask. You have to ask.*"

Maybe that was a quality innate to the sidhe; he didn't know enough about them to say. Maybe it had developed because of multiple operations and long hours in the hospital when she'd had so little control over who touched her, what was done to her. Maybe it was just her, like her prodigious memory. Whatever the reason, Arjenie could not stand to be physically constrained.

At first he'd thought her reaction no more than what anyone would feel. She wasn't fiery, like Claire. She didn't scream or lose control. But after enough repetition, even he could get the point, however politely it was made. Arjenie did not want to be touched, held, or helped without permission. You had to ask first.

The Lady hadn't asked. Arjenie was bound to Benedict for the rest of her life—physically bound—and she'd been given no choice in the matter.

But "for the rest of her life" wasn't entirely accurate, was it?

It had always been within Benedict's power to release Claire from the mate bond. He'd hadn't once seriously considered it. And in truth, Nettie had been only nine, so he couldn't have offered that particular solution if he'd wanted to.

He hadn't wanted to. Back then, he'd never tasted real failure. Oh, he'd worked for success, not waited for it to fall in his lap. He might have been arrogant as hell, but he hadn't been an idiot. That had only served to convince him he deserved success. By the time he met Clare at the age of twenty-seven, he'd been spoken of by some as the top warrior of his generation—and by a few as the greatest warrior of the century. He had a daughter, his smart and shining Nettie, whom he'd sired when he was only eighteen, and she spent the school year with him, the summers with her mother. That had been a rare arrangement back then.

Not that he'd known how to fully appreciate Nettie. He'd loved her, sure—she'd been the central joy of his life. But he'd also figured it was only a matter of time before he had a son or two as well.

Then the Lady had gifted him with a Chosen.

A man who'd never failed sure as hell wasn't going to fail with such a precious gift. Sooner or later, he'd been sure, Claire would become reconciled to the bond. It wasn't as if she didn't care about him. She cared deeply, passionately. He just had to be patient, find ways to distract her, make the bond rest as lightly on her as possible. When that didn't work, he'd focused on keeping her from doing anything irrevocable.

Like driving her car off a cliff.

Benedict had never believed Claire did it on purpose. There had been a cop at the hospital who'd said . . . but Isen had held Benedict down. The officer had probably never guessed how close he'd come to dying that night.

Claire had always loved to take risks, to push herself, but when he first met her, those risks had been leavened by practicality, practice, and planning. She threw knives for a living, but she'd tried other acts, too—high-wire, trapeze. He'd taught her to skydive. She'd loved it.

Claire had always been restless, too. She'd grown up in the circus and was used to constant travel, but the mate bond wouldn't allow that. Not unless Benedict went with her. He'd gone with her as much as he could, but she'd hated knowing her freedom was forever limited by what he agreed to do.

The bond also meant that she couldn't marry. Ever. Wildly unconventional in so many ways, his Claire had wanted marriage, wanted it badly.

The coastal road had been slick with rain that night. Claire had been furious, frantic. And pregnant.

They'd fought when she told him. At least, she had. He'd tried to calm her down, but as usual, that only infuriated her. There was no guarantee he'd be able to give her a baby himself, so in spite of his sorrow that this baby wasn't his, he could rejoice that she would have a child of her own. He would gladly raise it with her.

That wasn't what she wanted. He wasn't sure she'd known herself what she wanted from him by then. Jealousy, maybe. She would have understood that. Or maybe she'd wanted exactly what she said she did. The demand she'd hurled at him had been simple enough: *Marry me or get out of my life.*

He couldn't do either one. And she couldn't understand why. Why couldn't he thumb his nose at the "lupi don't marry" dictum? Hadn't she thumbed her nose at everyone by taking up with him in the first place?

By then he'd been tired of explaining. Tired of her irrationality, her refusal to believe him or accept the reality of the bond. When she'd flung herself out the door and into the jazzy little convertible he'd bought her for her birthday, he hadn't called her back.

She'd died on the operating table.

As they left the nursery, a big yellow Lab came romping up, trying to coax them to play. Arjenie laughed and rumpled his ears, which reduced him to bliss. Benedict introduced them.

"Mondo?" Upon hearing his name, the dog immediately plopped down and offered his belly for a rub. She grinned, bent down, and complied. "What a perfect name for this big guy. He's huge, all right. Though I don't think he fits the Spanish meaning of 'clean.'"

"You know a lot about the meanings of names."

"It's sort of a hobby of mine. My name doesn't have a meaning."

Startled, he said, "None?"

"Not in our realm, anyway. It comes close to a lot of words or names in various languages, but I've never found an exact match." She straightened, much to Mondo's disappointment. "Just before he left, Eledan told my mother that if she did bear his child she was to name it Arjenie if it was a girl, Arjana if it was a boy. She always said it was a good thing I turned out to be female. Can you imagine naming some poor boy Arjana?"

"She named you to please your father?"

Arjenie looked wistful. "I don't know. Eledan told her that names affect the sidhe in ways they don't affect humans, and that seems to be true. Mom said she didn't know enough to name me properly herself, while Eledan had had a great deal of practice naming his babies."

He'd touched her cheek before he had time to remember that touching her was a bad idea. Her skin was so soft.

He stroked his thumb across that warm, smooth skin. "That makes you sad."

"It made her sad. Not all the time, but sometimes. Sometimes I'd see her sitting quietly, looking out the window, and I knew she was thinking of him. Remembering. Wanting him to come back, even though she knew he wouldn't stay. But he—he'd told her he'd come back one day. Not right away, because he was a foolish and distractible fellow. Those were his words, and when he said it he laughed in this way that always made her smile when she told the story. She wasn't to expect him on any particular day, for he was blasted if he could see how anyone knew what they'd do tomorrow, much less a year or ten from now. But one day he'd come back to check on her." She swallowed. "He did, too. He came to check on her . . . two years after she died."

He kissed her.

There was no thought to it, no plan, no reason. And every reason. She jolted when his lips touched hers, then went still. He kissed her softly, learning the taste and feel of her mouth, and then he made another mistake. With his lips touching hers, he breathed deeply of her scent.

Fire leaped in him, and need—need so strong it made his breath jerk in his throat and almost, almost, made him reach for her with his hands as well. But some dim remnant of reason told him that if he did that, he wouldn't stop.

And he had to stop. His head was light and empty, dizzy with hunger, when he lifted it, breaking the kiss. Her hands clutched his arms. She looked as undone as he felt.

"What . . ." She stopped. Swallowed. "What was that? I mean, I know it was a kiss, but it was—I never—"

"A summary," he told her, his voice hoarse. "You'll get the full report soon, but right now we both have to settle for a summary."

She shook her head. "You're not making sense. You aren't . . . you can't do a glamour, can you? Like the sidhe?"

Like her father had done to her mother, she meant. He looked at her wide, wary eyes, and sorrow took him by the throat and shook him like a terrier shakes a rat. "No." He forced that word out, then found a few more. "We'd better get back. Sun's on its way down. Rule and Lily will be here soon."

"Okay." But her brows remained pleated in a small, worried frown. "Are they going to answer some of my questions?"

He managed a wry smile. "I don't know. Can you wait until tomorrow to have them answered?"

Her chin tilted up. "I can. I don't want to."

When he held out his hand she looked more worried than shy. She hesitated for several long heartbeats. But she did take it.

His stolen time was ending. He'd known that it would. The sweetness of their afternoon together was marred now by all he wasn't telling her. And she sensed that.

Tonight, then. He would tell her tonight. But he would make it clear that if she couldn't tolerate the bond, there was an alternative. Not a good one, but sometimes all the choices were ill.

If everything went to hell, Benedict would release Arjenie in the only way he could. It was not a solution he liked, nor was it without risk for her. But if she grew frantic and miserable and dangerous to herself . . . well, Nettie was an adult now. He didn't fool himself that she'd understand. She wouldn't. She'd hurt, and so would his father and brother. But it was his decision to make, not theirs.

There was only one way to dissolve the mate bond, but it was one that lay within Benedict's power to grant. Death did the trick neatly. Only this time, he wouldn't be the one death left behind.

TWENTY-SIX

RULE rented a limousine to take them from the airport to Clanhome.

The flight itself wasn't as bad as Lily expected, probably because she didn't remember much of it. Nettie loaded her up on painkillers. Getting dressed for it had been a bitch, though. Most of Lily's tops were tanks and tees meant to be pulled on over her head. That didn't work now. Rule had bought her some button-down tanks that were much easier to get into, though she still needed help, dammit.

Much to Lily's surprise, Nettie hadn't argued when Lily told her she wanted to fly home. Oh, Nettie got her pound of flesh in the form of a promise—Lily was to stay off her feet on the day they traveled, and *we'll see* after that—but she didn't have a problem with the flight itself.

Dr. Skinny had. At first it had looked like he wouldn't release Lily, but Nettie had handled him. Most patients didn't have a personal physician in attendance for such a flight, after all. Lily might have felt pretty damn pampered if she'd been able to stay awake long enough.

A personal physician who was also a shaman and could put Lily *in* sleep whenever she woke up for two seconds.

Which she did, because of her bladder. Lily had been jumped in the ladies' room once and didn't want to repeat the experience, so she had Rule wake her up a couple times so she could use the facilities on the plane rather than at the airport after they landed.

Jeff flew back with them. The other Leidolf guards stayed behind . . . as did LeBron, in a very different way. Or maybe he didn't. Lily knew that something lasted beyond the body. Might as well call it a soul. She also knew that ghosts were real. A medium had told her once that a ghost was more like a side effect of dying—the shadow cast by a soul, not the soul itself, no more than a physical body was a soul. Ghosts winked out when the soul completed its transition, and most souls moved on pretty quickly.

Most, not all. Some ghosts lasted for days, weeks, even years.

Could LeBron's ghost have tagged along at thirty thousand feet?

Who knew?

The painkillers started wearing off shortly before they landed. Lily's arm throbbed as she was wheeled off the plane, then deposited in one of those motorized carts the airports use. But at least she was awake.

No one attacked them. They were met on the other side of security by five Nokolai guards with another wheelchair. Rule had taken her at her word when she said he could guard the hell out of her—and Nettie had meant it when she said Lily was to stay off her feet.

Lily gritted her teeth and put up with it. She hated being treated as incapable of taking care of herself, even if it was true right now. She hated the spectacle of being wheeled through the airport surrounded by bodyguards. Most of all, she hated the idea of anyone else dying because of her. For her.

It was a stretch limo.

That surprised a laugh out of her. It made her think of Grandmother, and that helped her put up with all the assistance Rule was determined to give her. She was capable of walking a few feet, dammit. Admittedly, she was annoyingly weak, but she could walk if anyone would let her do it.

She might have mentioned that a little too vehemently.

"Don't worry," Nettie said as she slid into the ridiculously long vehicle. "I'll have you up and walking. Just not today."

One of the bodyguards got up front with the driver. The others went with José, who would follow them in his car. Rule managed to climb into the limo while carrying Lily without banging her head or feet on anything, which probably ought to qualify him for an Olympic something-or-other.

He deposited her on the rear seat, then sat beside Nettie on the facing seat. There were pillows she could prop herself up with so she could stretch out without lying down. There was a cat carrier, too, on the floor. Inside, a thoroughly sedated Dirty Harry snoozed away.

"You're being perfect again," she told Rule as they pulled away. She gestured at the cat carrier. "Did anyone get hurt?"

"José is sure he can get the blood out of the carpet."

He wasn't kidding. She sighed. "I don't know how Harry will take to Clanhome. It must smell like wolf everywhere."

"Harry's tough. He'll adjust. Besides, Toby will be there."

She frowned. "Did you tell me that already and I was too doped up to notice?"

"Briefly. You asked if school was out already, but fell asleep again before I could answer."

"School isn't out."

"He'll be homeschooled for now. At least until we know for sure if *she* was behind the attack on you."

Toby wouldn't like that. Sure, he loved Clanhome. But he also loved school, little though he might admit it. He was a thoroughly social little being, thriving on having lots of kids around, and he was already finding ways to fit in at his new school in spite of the notoriety of being Rule's son. He'd tried out for soccer and been accepted. He was excited about that, and about the music program at the school. They'd bought him an oboe.

Public school had seemed safe enough. It didn't matter what enemies Rule might have himself. No lupus would harm a child. But *she* didn't play by the same rules. "Toby's at Clanhome already, then."

"He isn't happy about it, but he's there. If it's any consolation, he was mollified when he learned you'd be at Clanhome for a time, too. That helped him accept that the threat was serious."

That was something, she supposed. Another point in favor of Clanhome: her mother wouldn't be dropping by constantly. It was unfair, but Lily liked knowing her mother wanted to come fuss over her. She just didn't want her to actually do it.

"Has anyone talked to—" She cut herself off, frowning. If Friar could eavesdrop, she didn't want to mention Sam and the possibility of having a binding removed. Or did she? Would it matter?

Dammit, her head was still fuzzy from the drugs. And her back ached. Lily used her good arm to prop herself up better—and her other arm yelled at her to be still. She told it to shut up.

"You can have more pain medication," Nettie said.

"I don't want it," she snapped and shifted again, but slowly. This time the pain was more of an annoyed mutter than a shriek, and the new position did support her back better. "Um . . . was I rude just now?"

"Yes. You aren't the worst patient I've ever had, though."

Nettie's voice was dry, but her expression was abstracted, almost uncertain. That was unusual enough to get Lily's attention. "What is it?"

"You know Arjenie Fox?"

Oh. Lily glanced at Rule. Did Nettie know that Arjenie was Benedict's Chosen? Or that the woman had sidhe blood? "I've never met her in person. I've worked with her, but it's all been by phone or e-mail. I guess I'll be meeting her soon. She's staying with Isen, isn't she?"

Nettie nodded, her lips tight with worry or temper or both. "There's something Benedict hasn't told me about her. Something important. I'm not reading between the lines," she added dryly. "He told me there was, and that he would explain when I was at Clanhome, not over the phone. Security reasons, he said."

Lily was careful in her response. If Friar's clairaudience Gift was connected to *her*, the mantles Rule carried should create a sort of cone of silence. Even *she* couldn't spy on someone who carried a mantle. But they didn't know enough. They couldn't be sure, so they were being careful. "He talked to you about her?"

"If you mean do I know she's his new Chosen, the answer is yes." She glanced at Rule. "You told Lily."

"I did, yes. Benedict spoke accurately. I'm aware of the information he hasn't given you, but we're being careful what we say because there's reason to suspect Robert Friar is a Listener who is unable to eavesdrop at Clanhome."

"Friar?" Nettie said, startled.

"You know where and how Benedict first encountered Ms. Fox."

Nettie nodded, her face tight. "I'm worried. I'm worried about him."

Sometimes Lily almost forgot that Nettie was Benedict's daughter—probably because she looked five or ten years older than her father. "I can't tell you much about Arjenie. She asks good questions. She's quick but thorough, and probably brilliant in her way. And that isn't what you want to know, is it?"

"It all helps. All I know about her is what she looks like when she's unconscious."

Lily thought for a moment. "I've never heard her be bitchy, gossipy, or play the poor-me card. I guess I'd say she'd level. Not unemotional or stoic—just the opposite, really. More as if she got her balance years ago and held on to it."

Nettie's mouth curved up, but her eyes were bitter. "That would be a major improvement over Claire."

"I don't know much about Claire."

Nettie shrugged. "I don't suppose I really do, either. I was just a kid. I liked her when I first met her. She was one of those people who seem twice as alive as everyone else, who make you feel extra alive when you're around them. She was also a faithless bitch."

That startled Lily enough that she jolted physically. Her arm flashed a protest from fingers to collarbone.

"Benedict never held that against her," Rule said quietly.

"I did." Nettie's face and voice were stone.

Rule spread his hands. "I was a child at the time, too, so mostly I can only repeat what I've been told, not what I've put together for myself. But I believe it to be true. Claire couldn't accept the mate bond," he said to Lily. "At one point she tried to break it by sleeping with other men. She told Benedict what she was doing, and why. She didn't do it to hurt him, but to—as she saw it—save herself."

"That's what he believes," Nettie said. "That doesn't mean he didn't hurt."

"He was upset, yes. That much I did see for myself. But mostly because he feared she would damage herself emotionally, and for no reason, since her attempt would fail. He tried to get her to choose lupus partners because human men wouldn't treat her well if they saw her as easy. She refused." Rule looked at Lily. "This was over forty years ago, remember, in the 1960s. Attitudes toward women's sexuality were changing, but they had a long way to go."

Lily's brain was well and truly boggled. "That's . . . they discussed it? And his response was to advise her to only sleep with lupi?"

Rule's mouth quirked up, though his eyes remained troubled. "I've recently discovered that I am capable of jealousy. It's not knowledge I like, but it's true . . . of me. I don't think Benedict is. He's capable of possessiveness, certainly, but not in a sexual sense."

"He's capable of being hurt," Nettie said gruffly. "She hurt him plenty, long before she nearly destroyed him by killing herself."

Rule gave his niece a sharp look. "She didn't kill herself."

Nettie waved that away. "Maybe, maybe not. I don't know what was in her head that night, and you don't, either. Don't worry. I won't say that to Benedict. I wouldn't do that to him." She broke off, her eyes dark with emotion. "I wasn't there when she died. You were. I'd gone back to the reservation to stay with my mom. It was the usual time for me to go to her, so I wasn't there." She sighed, long and shaky. "You were. I resented that, you know, for a long time. That you were here when it happened, and I wasn't."

"I know," he said quietly, and reached for Nettie's hand.

She closed her fingers around his. "My mother wouldn't let me go to him. He was in bad shape, and she wouldn't let me go to Clanhome and be with him. She thought it would be too hard on me, seeing him like that. She didn't understand that it was worse, not being there."

"I know," Rule said again, this time with a small smile. "You got around that, eventually."

Nettie snorted. "It was a stupid thing to do. I was luckier than I deserved to be."

Rule turned that smile on Lily. "Nettie had just turned ten. Three months after Claire's death, she took matters into her own hands. She hitchhiked from New Mexico to California. Made it to Palo Verde unharmed, though she picked up a couple of scary memories before Benedict found her."

"He did? He knew she was coming?"

Rule shook his head. "Not ahead of time. Nettie left her mother a note. Her mother called Isen. She was pretty frantic, I gather. The authorities in her part of the state weren't exactly sympathetic to the Navajo population, and though she notified them, she wasn't sure they would look very hard. Isen . . . well, Benedict was in bad shape, and he wasn't getting better. Isen told him to either kill himself and get it over with, or go rescue his daughter."

"He did need me," Nettie said quietly. "Oh, not for what I thought. I was a kid. I thought he needed me to do things for him—sweep his floor, make sure he ate, whatever, so he'd remember he was loved. I was wrong about that, but I was right that he needed me. He needed to do things for me."

Kind of like Rule had needed to get Lily a limo . . . among other things. Guilt made her feel small. She hadn't had much energy to spare, it was true, but she could have made more of an effort to understand. The attack hadn't happened only to her. In a very real sense, it had happened to Rule, too.

Violence was like that. There was never just one victim.

He and Nettie were uncle and niece, but they were also close age-mates. Nettie had been ten when her father's Chosen died. That meant Rule had been eleven or twelve when he saw the big brother he idolized almost destroyed by the breaking of a mate bond. "I'm getting a better picture of how you felt when the mate bond hit," she said quietly.

He tipped her a wry smile, but his phone sounded before he could reply. She recognized the ring tone.

Rule's system for assigning musical ring tones baffled

Lily, but she knew most of them. His father got "Dueling Banjos." Benedict was "Eroica" by Ars Arcana. Those two sort of fit, but for Lily's ring tone he used piercingly sweet violin music, part of an old gypsy song. It was lovely, but it didn't sound like her. She'd asked him about it. He'd smiled and touched her cheek. "The music doesn't represent you, *nadia*, but how I feel about you."

He melted her sometimes.

This ring tone was the jangling intro to Hieronymus Bosch's "Nodus." That meant the caller was Alex, the Leidolf Lu Nuncio.

The call was short. Lily didn't need Rule's hearing to know it was bad news. Rule's face went straight into lockdown mode. "I see. No, I'll call him. I don't think so, but I'll let you know. Just a moment. I need to tell Lily."

He touched the mute button and spoke with icy precision. "At some point this afternoon, Raymond Cobb Changed and ripped out both anterior femoral arteries. He bled to death."

TWENTY-SEVEN

COBB had listed Alex—his Lu Nuncio—as his next of kin. That's the only reason Rule had found out, the only reason Lily knew about Cobb's death now. No one had called her. No one called her because it wasn't her case—but still, Croft should have let her know. Someone should have let her know.

Lily simmered on that, then twisted so she could reach her purse on the floor. She could call Sjorensen. The young agent would give her something, she was sure.

"No," Nettie said clearly.

"What do you mean, no?"

"You're not working now. You're resting."

"Like hell." Lily found her phone, pulled it out.

"You gave me your word."

Lily clamped down hard on a number of things she wanted to say. "Resting is not restful."

"Then you need to learn how to do it differently."

She wanted to throw something. It was childish, it was stupid, and only the ghostly remembered image of her mother's disapproving face kept Lily from doing it anyway. Which was also infuriating.

Rule was talking to Alex about Cobb's burial, which was

not the same as the ceremony—the *firnam*—she'd been invited to take part in. Burials were generally a private affair, attended only by the deceased's closest family. Both *firnam* and burial would have to wait, though—one for the body to be released. The other for Lily to be able to fly back to North Carolina.

Had Rule known this would happen? Expected it?

Maybe. Cobb had been on suicide watch. That was standard procedure with a lupus prisoner and one reason his cell had lacked so much as a cot. Lily hadn't known how easily a lupus could kill himself when denied access to any of the tools a human would need to do the job.

Rule had known. He must have.

She thought she understood. If Rule had granted Cobb's request but delayed acting on it, Cobb would have waited for someone to come give him the honorable death he longed for. He would have waited forever, because Rule couldn't get anyone in to do it without using Lily. He would have gone mad waiting.

Instead, with his silence Rule had left a door open for Cobb. Rule believed Cobb had killed due to some sudden, uncontrollable defect, that he wasn't responsible. In his eyes, Cobb wasn't to blame and deserved the grace of an honorable death. When Cobb took his own life without his Rho's permission, he lost that.

Lily looked at her lover. Her mate. Her friend. Weariness and worry grooved furrows along his mouth as he listened to whatever Alex was telling him. She reached for his free hand.

His eyes flashed to hers. She saw surprise there, a question. Had he expected her to be angry when she realized he could have prevented Cobb's death? Probably. She'd been angry a lot lately. Lily squeezed his hand and closed her eyes.

She was not dealing with this well. Any of it. Being injured, being taken off a case that mattered, being unable to do . . . anything. Any damned thing. Someone had nearly killed Ruben. Someone had killed LeBron. Cobb had killed himself. And she couldn't do a damned thing about any it.

With her eyes closed there was just the quiet murmur of Rule's voice, the red tide of her own anger . . . and the sick feeling in her gut, a roiling wrongness.

Lily had dreamed last night, but not of Helen. Of Sarah.

She and Sarah had been best friends. They'd teamed up in kindergarten, and stayed glued together up through third grade . . . when they'd done one last cool thing together. They'd played hooky.

They'd been snatched by a monster.

That monster had had a human face and drove a Buick with a big trunk. That's where he'd put them, in the trunk. She and Sarah had gone to the beach, just the two of them. It had been their big adventure, one they'd planned carefully because it wouldn't be at all fun to get caught. They'd both been good kids. Sarah had possessed a streak of mischief Lily lacked, but neither of them had cut school before.

Lily never did it again. Sarah never did anything again.

The monster had had a name, a perfectly ordinary name: George Anderson. George Anderson had driven around for hours with them in that big trunk, waiting for dark. Once it was dark enough to hide what he did, he'd carried them into his house, one at a time. Sarah had been a blue-eyed blonde, a pretty, pink and white little girl. George Anderson had raped her first. Sarah kept crying and crying, so he choked her to make her stop. He'd been surprised when she died, flustered, like a kid sneaking cookies who accidentally broke the cookie jar. Whoops.

It was a cop who saved Lily. He'd broken down George Anderson's front door. A jogger had seen the monster put them in his trunk and had even managed to get the Buick's license number. She'd called the police. But this was before cell phones, the Internet, Amber Alerts. Everything had taken time. Too much time for Sarah.

They called it survivor guilt. Lily understood the urge to tag something, label it, claim control by naming it. But that particular label had never helped. This roiling, murky wrongness was so much more than guilt. It was shame and terror and fury and loss, a world and a self turned equally strange and terrible.

Between one step and the next, the world could upend itself. Lily had known that since she was eight, but she hadn't felt like this in so long. So long.

It wasn't hard to see why she felt it now. She wanted desperately for the feeling to go away, but it wouldn't. Not all at once. That was the other thing she knew: it took time. Her arm wouldn't heal right away. Her self wouldn't, either.

But she wasn't eight years old anymore. And LeBron hadn't died because either of them broke the rules. He'd died because someone wanted Lily dead . . . and like Rule had said, LeBron had stopped the monster the only way he could.

Beneath her closed eyelids, Lily's eyes burned with salt, with blood transmuted to tears. And that was okay.

MOST Nokolai did not live at Clanhome, but they had to be welcomed and sheltered when they did visit. There were two barracks-style dormitories on the south side of the meeting field, each with a communal kitchen, communal showers, and multiple bathrooms. Together, they could house around four hundred lupi.

One of the dorm buildings was also used year-round as a group home for a few elderly clan who didn't want to live alone, and—when needed—for those who could no longer care for themselves. Even lupi eventually succumbed to the malfunctions and indignities of old age, but for them, the decline tended to be sudden and swift. An elderly lupus might be riding his Harley one week, bedridden the next, and dead the third.

Out-clan guests were rarer, but they also had to be accommodated. Two small cottages near the barracks were intended for out-clan guests. Often, though, they were used by clan, with the understanding that they might have to vacate the cottage if it was needed for a guest. No point in leaving them empty.

Lily had assumed that she and Rule would stay in one of the cottages. She blamed the drugs for that mistake.

Naturally, Rule's father wanted them to stay with him. Naturally, Rule wanted to stay there, too. It's where he'd grown up. It's where Toby stayed when he was at Clanhome. And there was plenty of room, even with Arjenie Fox in residence. Isen's sprawling home had lots of bedrooms . . . and she did not want to stay in any of them.

Why not? She didn't know. Neither she nor Rule would have to cook or clean, so while she was there she could focus on what she needed to do, start pulling together some of the threads their enemy had left dangling . . . whoever that enemy might be. Plus there were guards stationed around the house day and night, so Rule wouldn't be worried about her.

Staying with Isen made sense. But it bothered her, which meant she wasn't making sense, and she hated that.

By the time the big, black limousine pulled up in front of Isen's home, the sun was taking a curtsy before heading offstage. Flaming clouds spread like skirts around it as it dipped toward the western hills, and lights were on inside the sprawling stucco house. José and his pack of guards had peeled off when they reached the bunkhouse. Before they'd fully stopped, Toby shot out the door—pushing a wheelchair.

Lily gave Rule a dirty look. He returned it blandly.

The Toby-propelled wheelchair thumped merrily down the gravel path, full speed ahead, no pausing for the shallow steps. It did not—quite—ram into the limo. At the last second Toby swerved, the heels of his sneakers skidding in the gravel. Once stopped, he took a moment to position the chair, then reached for the door handle. Nettie leaned forward and hit the unlock button.

Toby swung the door open. "Oh, good! You got Harry. He's not gonna like it here at first, but I'll explain things to him. I don't know how much he understands when I explain, but I think he sorta does. Hi, Lily."

"Hi, Toby." She swung her legs off the seat. Rule had Harry's carrier and was already climbing out the other side.

"I'm really sorry you got hurt. Have you ever been shot before? How come you don't have a cast? Does it hurt a whole lot, kind of a lot, or only a little?"

"I was shot last year, but that bullet was nearly spent and didn't cause as much trouble as this one did. I may get a cast later, after the surface wounds have healed. They aren't sure yet." She eased off the seat, twisting so she could grip the frame of the doorway for support. Slowly she climbed out of the limo.

Whew. Dizzy for a second there, but it passed. She answered the last of the rapid-fire questions. "It hurt a whole lot at first. Now it's usually somewhere between a little and kind of a lot." Leaning toward a whole lot at the moment, but at least she'd gotten out of the car on her own. "I don't need the wheelchair, but thank you for bringing it."

"Don't worry—I'm not gonna push it. I guess Dad will. I wanted to, but Grandpa said no. He said it in that way that means you can't argue, even if you really want to."

Isen had left the house and was coming toward them. His beard had been burnt off last month, along with some skin. The skin had healed fast; regrowing a beard took longer. Lupi healed the skin that grew hair, but the hair itself took the normal time to grow.

"Lily?" Toby said.

Lily was glad Isen's face wasn't bare anymore. He hadn't looked right with a naked face. "Yes?"

"Did it hurt LeBron a lot when he got killed?"

She froze. Then gripped the door for balance and lowered herself—slowly, dammit, everything she did was slow—until she was on his level. "Nettie probably knows more about that than I do, but I can tell you what I think."

Toby's eyes were very dark, very serious. "Okay."

"Do you know how LeBron was killed?"

"He was guarding you when someone shot at you, and he saved your life but he got shot in the head. Grandpa says he died really fast, but lupi don't always die fast, even when their brain is hurt."

"That's true. But even lupi need their brains to feel pain. We—and I mean both humans and lupi—don't really feel pain with our bodies. Our bodies send the pain signals to our brains, and our brains say, wow, that hurts. If the brain doesn't get the signal, there's no pain. I don't think LeBron's brain had a chance to register any pain before he died. If it did, it was for just a second."

"Because his brain was all messed up from the bullet."

"Yeah." She swallowed. "Anyway, that's what I think."

"Grandpa says he gave his life to save yours."

Her throat closed up entirely. All she could do was nod.

When he frowned, he looked so much like Rule that her heart hurt. "LeBron's Leidolf. I mean, he *was* Leidolf, and they're the ones who hurt Grandpa, and they've been our enemies forever and they always try to get us, so I don't like them. But Dad says they aren't enemies anymore, and he's their Rho now, so I thought that meant he'd change them. But that wouldn't happen all at once, would it? They're a big clan. Only . . . I liked LeBron, even if he was Leidolf, and now he's dead, and he died saving you, and Dad wasn't there to make him. He just did it."

Rule had reached them. He rested a hand on Toby's shoulder. "It was a good death," he said quietly, "but we're still sad. We miss him and grieve for him."

Toby tipped his troubled face up to look at his father. "Even though he's Leidolf?"

"In grammar school, middle school, and high school, young humans pretend that everyone on their team is good, and those on the other team are bad and deserve to lose. Real life—adult life—isn't like that. Nokolai and Leidolf have been at odds for a long time, but Leidolf has many good men. LeBron was one of them. He had a great smile and a warm heart. He served well and he died with honor. How could we not miss him?"

Toby heaved a shuddering sigh. "I *hate* that he died. I hate whoever shot him."

Me, too, Lily thought, and began the process of getting herself erect. She got about halfway up when her head went light and fuzzy. Before she could wobble, Rule gripped her shoulders. "Steady there."

"My turn," Isen announced—and before the dizziness had quite faded, Rule's hands were gone. One burly arm swept beneath her knees, another circled her back, and Isen's beard brushed her temple as he swung her effortlessly up into the air.

"Isen, what are you *doing*?"

"Annoying you." He turned and set her gently in the wheelchair. "You and my son are determined to marry, which means I am not only your Rho, I am also your father-in-law-to-be. It permits me certain privileges." He put his hands on either arm of the wheelchair and leaned closer, his voice going soft. "You're worried about being here, yes? You're used to having your own space, you feel vulnerable in a way that's new to you, and you don't entirely trust me. You're afraid I'll take advantage in some way."

He straightened and beamed down at her. "You're right. I will. But we have the same goal, Lily *ma fille*. It will be okay."

In that moment, Isen looked like an older and hairier Toby. The smile was the same—open and merry and hard to resist. Lily found herself returning it, albeit wryly. "For what value of okay?"

"For a chicken and dumplings value," Toby told her seriously. "*Carl's* chicken and dumplings."

"I thought we'd eat early," Isen said. "I seem to recall you enjoy coffee. I'll make some after dinner."

Coffee. Coffee might save her life, her sanity, and her relationship with several of the people she loved. "Maybe we could have coffee with dinner."

Rule chuckled.

"Nettie!" Now that Lily was out of the way, Nettie had climbed out. Isen seized his granddaughter as if he hadn't seen her for weeks and gave her a quick hug, then held her at arms' length, studying her. "You need a nap almost as much as your patient does."

"I don't need a nap," Lily said. "I slept nonstop on the plane."

"No?" Isen said. "I could argue, and quite persuasively, I think, but you observe that I am not. However, you are supposed to stay off your feet today, according to your doctor."

That left her with very little to say, dammit. In the second's silence that followed she heard another voice, one she recognized.

". . . don't need to yip at anyone today?"

The second voice was even more familiar. "We're not on alert now," Benedict said, "so we don't need special means to identify ourselves."

Lily twisted around in the wheelchair, but couldn't see them. Rule moved behind her and turned the chair to face the two people coming down the road toward them—Benedict and a woman with black-rimmed glasses, thin legs encased in skinny jeans, and amazing red hair. She wore sneakers and a snug blue T-shirt with something written on it.

They were holding hands. "Hi, Lily," the woman said as they rounded the limousine's hood. "I know who you are, of course, because you've been on the news, and so has Rule Turner, so I know him. Maybe you recognize my voice? I'm Arjenie." She gave Isen a reproachful look. "I knew Benedict had a bad habit of picking people up without asking. I didn't know you were prone to it, too."

It was easy to develop the wrong mental image of someone you'd only e-mailed with or spoken to over the phone. Lily knew that. The sight of Arjenie Fox was still a surprise. The thinness somehow fit. So did the glasses and the expressive face, but the long, wild hair in that vehement red was totally unexpected. "Arjenie," she said. "It's good to meet you in person. And yes," she said as Arjenie and Benedict reached them, "the man lurking behind me is Rule." Lily held out her hand.

"You want to see what my magic feels like, I guess."

"Yes. Thank you for cooperating."

They clasped hands. The magic coating Arjenie Fox's skin wasn't quite like any Lily had touched before. It made her think of the iridescence inside a clamshell, rendered tactilely—slick, yet somehow plush, too. Like touching the shimmer in velvet and being surprised by its nap.

"Hello, Mr. Turner," Arjenie said politely . . . *so glad I did it so scary but these people are okay because I did it and how terrible awful if their beautiful bodies were hurt would be so terrible I'm glad I* . . . "It's good to meet you." . . . *look like your pictures only better makes my eyes happy only not Benedict Benedict makes me ache Benedict I love his name blessing or benediction I hope he kisses me again no I don't that was really scary and I don't understand but his mouth oh I* . . .

"Arjenie." Lily's heart pounded.

"Is something wrong?" . . . *with my magic? Still holding my hand does my magic feel weird why are you looking at me like*—

"What is it you can't tell us about?"

Arjenie's mouth turned up in an anxious smile. *Dya oh Dya I'm so worried why didn't you tell me more* . . . "If there were something I couldn't tell you, I couldn't tell you, could I?" *They'd help you if I could . . . but Friar's evil he . . . madness . . . if only* . . . "Could I have my hand back, please?"

Dammit, she was losing it. Whatever "it" was. "Who's Dya?"

Arjenie's eyes went huge. Her hand tightened on Lily's like she intended to juice it. *YOU CAN HEAR ME?*

That thought arrived in a single blast that nearly sent Lily's eyeballs rolling back in her head. She gasped and swayed.

"What is it?" Rule snapped. "Lily?"

Lily narrowed her eyes against the pain, which was generous enough to blot out any complaints her arm might be making. "She was mindspeaking me." Lily looked at her hand still gripped tightly in Arjenie's and listened to . . . nothing. "Emphasis on the 'was.'"

TWENTY-EIGHT

LILY'S eyelids lifted, and she was back. But in the wrong room.

No, that was stupid. Coming out of the light trance that was *in sleep* was as easy as opening your eyes—no sleepy brain-fuzz, no disorientation. She knew where she was—in Rule's old room—and how and why she got there.

She knew Rule was with her. And Harry. She heard him purring, felt him curled alongside her.

Her head didn't hurt.

Lily hadn't been able to get the mindspeech to happen again. They'd tried. It seemed clear that whoever Dya was, she was connected to everything Arjenie couldn't talk about, since she couldn't speak the name aloud. But whatever Lily had done when she took Arjenie's hand the first time, she couldn't do it with a jackhammer smashing rhythmically into her skull. So she hadn't argued when Nettie wanted to put her in sleep. There was no damn point. She hadn't been able to think, much less figure out an off-again, on-again new skill.

Or maybe it was Arjenie's skill, not hers. She hadn't figured any of it out yet.

"Better?" Rule asked quietly.

"Yeah." She moved her head tentatively on the pillow. "Lots better."

A dun-colored ceiling hung above her. It and the walls brightened to a soft gold in the glow of the reading lamp in one corner, the room's only illumination. That color was one of many things that had changed in this room since a much smaller Rule slept here every night. A few things remained from those years, though. Next to the window stood a mahogany bookcase. Benedict had built it before Rule was born, a baby gift for his youngest brother. The bookcase still held a few childhood trophies—a rock with a perfect trilobite fossil embedded on its surface; a mitt sized for a small hand; a ragged but complete set of E. E. "Doc" Smith's Lensmen series.

The rest of the furniture was newer, sized and styled for adults. Like the comfy armchair over by the reading light. It was large and worn and leather—what was it with guys and leather?—and the same cocoa color as the comforter.

Rule wasn't in the chair. He sat on the king size bed beside her, holding her hand. The chocolate comforter was folded back; only a sheet covered her. Dimly she heard voices coming from another part of the house. The loudest one sounded like Cullen.

She tried moving her head again, and smiled at the beautiful absence of pain. "I should send Nettie flowers or something. You haven't been just sitting here, have you?"

"No." He bent and kissed her forehead. "I'm devoted, but—"

"Not insane?"

"Carl makes excellent chicken and dumplings."

And Rule was too sensible to allow himself to remain hungry. "How long was I out?"

"It's after ten. Tuck-in with Toby took awhile."

"He's upset."

"He had questions about *her*."

"Jesus, Rule! You mean Isen told him—"

"Toby already knew about our enemy."

"He's only nine!"

"He knows our history. Not in detail, but he knows *she* is our Lady's enemy, and therefore ours."

"There's a difference between hearing ancient history and being told that a super-powerful Old One wants to kill you and everyone you love right *now*."

"Why would we not tell him the truth?"

"Maybe because it will scare the crap out of him?"

He paused for a handful of heartbeats. "Fear is part of living. I can't spare him that. Toby is a child, yes, so many decisions are made for him, but that doesn't mean he doesn't deserve honesty. If Isen is right—and Toby understands that we aren't certain of *her* involvement—Toby's life is in danger. That's why he has to stay at here—for the physical security, and because *her* magic can't penetrate Clanhome's borders."

Her magic can't penetrate . . . something clicked into place in Lily's mind. And oh, but she did not like how well it fit. "What about the other Nokolai children?" she said slowly. "If Toby's in danger . . ."

"Toby's danger is greatest because neither Nokolai nor Leidolf has another clear heir. He's an obvious target." Rule's mouth tightened. "But Isen is considering having all Nokolai's children brought to Clanhome and offering to take in the children of our subject clans. I'm not sure what I'll do. Leidolf doesn't have the funds or facilities Nokolai does." He squeezed her hand, then let go and stood. "You need fuel. I'll get you some chicken and dumplings."

"No, I'll get up." She threw back the sheet and sat up, making Harry grumble in protest. Not that sitting up was a simple matter. She had to roll to one side, grip the edge of the mattress in her left hand, and use it to lever herself up.

The good news was her arm took the movement pretty well. The bad news was she was a wrinkled mess. Rule had taken off her shoes, but otherwise she'd lain down fully clothed. She wanted—needed—a shower, but that wasn't allowed yet. Spit baths only. She grimaced.

"You look fine."

"I don't, but thanks for trying. Tell me Nettie doesn't want me use that damned chair to go to the bathroom."

"If you give me your word you're entirely steady, I won't mention it to her."

"Let's find out." She stood up. "Hey, not bad." She smiled.

She was back. She wasn't sure where she'd been, but she was back now.

Rule shook his head. "Does that mean you were dizzy when you fussed about us not letting you walk earlier?"

She patted his arm. "I'm not dizzy now."

"You're patronizing me."

"Only a little bit."

He smiled slowly. "You're steady now, though."

"I said I—"

He cut that off with his mouth.

This wasn't a soft kiss. It was declarative and definite, a kiss that knew what it meant—and it didn't mean "feel better" or "I care," the way his recent kisses had. This kiss said, "I want you," and said it loud and clear.

Lily's body woke up. The hum of desire was sweet, and she reached with her left hand to stroke his jaw. He hadn't shaved since this morning, and the hint of sandpaper on her fingertips aroused her. Oh, but her body felt *good* to be in, alive and zingy, like lemonade made with half the sugar—puckery and compelling. She hummed along with it, shifting, trying to get closer in spite of the sling caging her arm.

He took her bottom lip in his teeth and nipped. She shivered. Suddenly it wasn't enough. She couldn't get close enough, fast enough—the sling, his clothes, her clothes, everything was in her way. She slid her good hand up behind his head and pulled it down, needed the pressure. Harder. She needed this, needed both hands, dammit, needed to grab him and hold on, hold on, bring him into her and keep him, needed him—

Agony bloomed white-hot in her arm, an evil flower with quick-striking roots. She reeled back—less than a step, only a few inches, but enough to separate them.

"What did I do? Lily—"

"Not you," she managed. "I did it. My arm. I—I wasn't paying attention, and I moved it. Squeezed it." She let her head fall, her forehead touching his chest. Her breath came fast and ragged.

He slid one arm loosely around her waist. With his other hand he toyed with the hair at her nape. For a long moment neither of them spoke. Gradually her breathing returned to normal.

His voice was quiet. "What was that about?"

"I don't know." It had felt so good at first, but she'd turned desperate or greedy or something. She'd lost it. "Maybe I don't want to know. Maybe that's the problem."

He continued to sift her hair gently. "You'll figure it out when it's time. When you're ready."

Would she? For the first time since the shooting her head felt clear. No blurring from pain pills, none of the fog the body imposes when it's insisting on rest, rest, and more rest. Her arm was throbbing like a bad tooth, but the exhaustion, the sheer drag of recovery, had lifted. And mostly, what she found in her newly clear head was confusion . . . that, and a sense of dreadful change. As if more than her arm had been damaged.

She didn't understand. Was this guilt? Was she convinced on some deep but stupid level that she was wrong to have survived when LeBron didn't? She didn't think so. She'd gone over and over the shooting. Even with her brain fuzzed by drugs—maybe especially then—she hadn't been able to stop going over it, looking for what she'd done wrong. And there wasn't anything.

Oh, she could have skipped her run. She wished like hell that she had. But logically, reasonably, she'd had no way to know the danger was real and acute. Even Rule, protective as he was, had believed the only precaution she needed to take was a guard or two, and that was in San Diego, where the nutcases expected her to be.

No, once she and LeBron were out there on that sidewalk, there was nothing she could have done differently, no skill she'd failed to use, no trick of foreknowledge that would have protected them. They hadn't been too slow to react. There'd been nothing to react to until the bastard fired.

Besides, this didn't feel like guilt, the survivor's version or any other. It felt like . . . like dread. Fear writ large.

But she didn't see why, dammit. It wasn't the slap of a renewed faith in her own mortality. Lily knew death, knew it would happen to her someday. She wanted to put that day off as long as possible, sure, and danger lit up her back-brain the same as it would anyone else's. Getting shot was scary, but dying held no real terror for her.

Been there, done that, don't want the damn shirt.

She sighed and straightened and saw how worried Rule was, and how hard he was trying to hide it. So she smiled, and she made it a good one. "I need to do something with my hair and I need to pee." Gently she disengaged from his arms and started for the door. "Was that Cullen's voice I—damn, he got out."

Rule had opened the door for her—he was sneaky that way—and Harry had done his fast-cat bit, shooting through before even Rule could stop him.

"He's headed straight for Toby's room. No doubt he feels he'd done his duty by you and is needed to guard Toby now." Rule often spoke of Harry that way, as if the cat had plans and goals like a person. "And yes, Cullen's here. Cynna, too. They've been discussing matters with Arjenie, hoping to figure out the mindspeech you experienced with her."

She grinned. "Discussing" was Rule-speak for arguing, at least where those two were concerned. "I can tell you one thing about it. I have a new understanding of what Sam means when he complains about our muddy thinking."

"I take it Arjenie's 'speech' wasn't like Sam's."

"Only in the sense that a two-year-old's babble is like Hamlet's soliloquy." *Priorities*, she told herself. If she couldn't figure out what was wrong with her now, she'd have to figure it out later. Right now her first priority involved a bathroom. After that . . . "I hope they figured out enough that I can turn back on whatever I did when I touched her the first time."

"Do you?" he said calmly, reaching around her so he could open the bathroom door, too. "I don't."

Her eyes flashed to his. "It was a headache, Rule. A bad one, but it's gone, I'm fine, and there's no danger to me in trying to get the mindspeech working."

"No? And yet that's one of the things Cullen and Cynna have been arguing about."

He was going to hover, Lily told herself after she took care of her first priority. She looked in the large mirror over the bathroom sink and grimaced. She could at least wash her face. She turned on the tap.

Rule was going to hover, but she could live with it. She wet a washcloth and dragged it over her face and throat. She'd frightened him, frightened him badly, and . . .

Her heart gave a single, hard thump in her chest, a meaty gong sounding the alarm. Her mouth went dry. She started into her own wide eyes in the mirror. The washcloth, rung out imperfectly with her single hand, released a slow, cold runnel that ran down beneath her shirt, wending its chilly way between her breasts.

It could have been Rule running beside her instead of LeBron.

She saw it again—the bloody wreck where LeBron's eye had been, flesh and bone and brains blenderized by gunpowder and velocity, his other eye smeared with the placid scum of death.

Fear twisted sickly, a whole-body knife dragging disgust and weakness in its wake. Lily leaned against the vanity, closing her eyes as she swung between shame and terror and faced the thing she hadn't wanted to know: that she was glad. Glad it had been LeBron with her on the sidewalk. Glad it was him who'd died, and not Rule.

It could so easily have been Rule. Might be him tomorrow or the next day. Or Cullen or Cynna, her sisters, Toby, her parents, Isen, Nettie . . . she shuddered.

Funny. She'd thought death held no terror for her. But that was terror twisting her up right now, and it was all about death . . . from the other side. The side of the one left behind, the one who couldn't keep death from taking those she loved.

There'd been nothing she could have done to save LeBron. Nothing short of omniscience, and God knew she was short on that. And the *wrongness* in her, the weakness in her gut, blood, and bones, came from the certain knowledge that it could happen again. If not through a bullet, then through lightning, car crash, cancer, any of the freakish fits of fate and mortality.

She couldn't protect them all. She wasn't in charge of who lived and who died. She didn't think anyone was. And it didn't help, it didn't help at all, that she'd figured out why Isen believed *she* was actively moving against the lupi once more. Lily thought he might be right. Probably was right, if what Arjenie said about Friar being unable to Listen in at Clanhome was true.

How did she set that aside and go on as if she could count on having those she loved and needed with her tomorrow and tomorrow?

She used to know. Only three days ago, she'd known how to move through the day without gasping like a landed trout, terrified for those she loved. She couldn't remember how to do that.

Lily took a slow breath. All she could do was act, then. Act as if she could protect them, or they could protect themselves, or somehow fate would be kind. Act as if her heart wasn't pounding and pounding right now. As if she had the courage to risk them, because what choice did she have?

To risk Rule.

It could have been him.

Her head clear, her hands icy, Lily left the bathroom. She got in the wheelchair Rule had waiting for her and let him push her forward, since everyone was convinced she couldn't walk on her own.

They were right, weren't they?

TWENTY-NINE

LAUGHTER is not musical. Music is, by definition, an art form; real laughter is artless, unconstructed. Nor does laughter have the musical quality of some natural sounds—the rhythmic wash of waves, the patter of rain, or the hoot of an owl. It's contagious and appealing, but it's not music.

When Rule wheeled Lily into the great room, Arjenie was laughing, her head tipped back as if to open her throat better to let the laughter out. And it sounded musical.

Lily had noticed that before. Even over the phone, Arjenie's laugh had made Lily think of clichés about bells. She just hadn't associated it with the sidhe. Why would she? Sure, like a lot of six-graders, she'd been forced to memorize that stupid poem by Keats or Shelley or someone with the famous lines about elven laughter:

> . . . *a quiet music haunts my sleep*
> *nor rain, nor wind, nor night, were night to speak—*
> *yet a crescent moon, or a stag mid-leap*
> *a chuckle of clouds, the converse of blades*
> *recall the laughter of the elven maids.*

Huh. She actually remembered that bit. Point to Mrs. Mc-Cutcheon. The thing was, she'd never associated the poem with anything real, maybe because she'd never heard an elf laugh.

Only it turned out she had, and hadn't known it.

Isen and Nettie were at the rear of the room, seated on one of the big couches. Arjenie was curled up in an armchair near it. Isen rose when he saw her. "Lily." He was delighted. "You're feeling better."

"And you're in the damn wheelchair," Nettie said, amused. "Good for you." She stood, too.

Lily grimaced. "Rule persuaded me that was a better thank-you than flowers. Whatever you did this last time, it seems to have worked."

"I put you in sleep, that's all." Nettie came to them and crouched. "That's all I can do with you. Your Gift doesn't let me in." She took Lily's hand, turned it up, and laid her fingers on the pulse at the wrist.

Lily understood why Nettie couldn't heal her directly the way she could one of the lupi. Lily's Gift blocked magic, period—even the good sort. What she didn't understand was why Nettie *could* put her in sleep, or how that worked. Nettie said *in sleep* let her body do its own healing, only faster and more fully than it could on its own. This had something to do with the difference between magical and spiritual energies. According to Nettie, the "in sleep" trick was a spiritual practice, not a magical one, so it wasn't blocked by Lily's Gift. That's also why Lily had to give permission before Nettie put her in sleep.

Lily could repeat this explanation. She knew from experience it was true—spiritual energy did affect her. She just had no idea what that meant.

"Good news," Nettie said, releasing Lily's hand. "You're alive."

"Always nice to have a hunch confirmed. Can I get out of the chair now?"

"No." Nettie patted her shoulder. "But if you're good, I'll give you a cookie."

"You're enjoying this way too much."

Nettie had a lovely smile when she used it. "I take my

moments where I find them. You should be glad I'm not insisting on bed rest."

Lily shuddered. "Oh, I am. Trust me."

Cynna, Cullen, and Benedict were sitting around the patio-sized dining table at the other end of the room. It was getting louder down there. ". . . no friggin' way you can equate the Etruscan *kah* to the Raetic *ktah*!" Cullen said. "The similarity of sound has nothing to do with their runic function, which you ought to—"

"And you," Cynna said, pushing to her feet, "have a sadly simplistic grasp of runic magic. Plus you don't listen. I didn't say they were identical. I said the *kah* could be replaced by the *ktah* in that particular spell to increase congruity. Clearly you'd have to rework the placement."

"Placement." Cullen's brows snapped together. He looked down at the table, muttering under his breath, and began sketching with one finger . . . a finger that left a glowing line behind. "Right. Higher, you mean? In the line invoking Air?"

"You're the one who can see magic. You figure it out." The words were curt. The look on Cynna's face was fond, amused. She scrubbed a hand from the base of Cullen's skull to the crown, making his hair stand up.

"Hey!" He looked up, grinned, and grabbed her hand, then tickled her palm with one finger. Lily couldn't hear his murmured words, but she saw the wicked look he gave his wife.

She grinned back. "Later, you romantic fool." She withdrew her hand and started toward the rest of them. "Hey, Lily. You look like crap."

"Gee, thanks."

"It's almost like you'd been shot and then operated on and then insisted on flying across the country."

Cynna was tall and buff, with strong shoulders, shapely arms, and long, muscular legs that Lily envied. She was also stacked—at least, Lily assumed that somewhere beneath the shapeless dress and mound of nearly due baby Cynna's usual shape lay waiting to reassert itself. Her blond hair used to be short and spiky. It was still short, but lately she'd been leaving off the gel and letting it frame her face more softly. That face, like much of her body, was decorated by lacy whorls and patterns drawn in spiderweb-thin ink.

Well, not exactly ink. Cynna wore her magic on her skin. Beneath that filigree, though, she looked pale and tired.

"You don't look full of vigor and vim yourself," Lily said when Cynna reached her. "You okay?"

Cynna snorted as she bent to give Lily a hug. "I'm pregnant, for God's sake, not ill."

"Grouchy, too." Lily hugged back quickly so Cynna could straighten. It wasn't easy for her to bend these days. "But I was thinking about the memories, not your pregnancy. You've been . . . what's the right word? Assimilating or absorbing them awfully quickly."

"Oh." Cynna grimaced. "That. I'm . . . this was the last batch from the early days, you see. The Great War and just after. Those are really important memories, and really awful."

"A lot of death," Rule said quietly.

Cynna nodded, a crease between her brows, her eyes unfocused. As if she still saw something terrible that had happened three thousand years ago, though from what Lily understood, the memories were supposed to be packed away somehow.

"That's the last of them until after the little rider makes his appearance," Cullen said firmly, coming up behind Cynna and slipping an arm around what used to be her waist. "Cynna's got one hell of a good elevator—"

"She what?"

"It's symbolism for how I store the memories," Cynna explained.

"But she has to live the memories before she can put them away, which leaves her exhausted and heartsore. She needs distraction, which you have thoughtfully supplied with your mind-reading trick."

Lily frowned. "It was not mind-reading. I'm no telepath."

"Whatever." He waved that aside. "Admittedly, you probably couldn't have done it if Arjenie weren't a broadcaster."

"Is that what that was—broadcasting?" Lily looked over at Arjenie, who'd been oddly silent. Lily didn't know her well, but *silent* wasn't an adjective she associated with Arjenie. "It felt like you'd turned the volume up to sonic boom."

Arjenie spread her hands apologetically. "The broadcasting happens all the time, whether I want it to or not, but normally it doesn't matter. The extra boost—I thought I was supposed to do that. Of course, I also thought the only person who could hear me was Eledan."

"I'm getting this scattershot," Lily said, and looked at Benedict, who still sat at the table. He was good with reports. "Can you give me a summary?"

For some reason that made Arjenie giggle.

NETTIE didn't join them for the summarizing. She was tired and wanted her bed, she said, and Lily didn't need her, so she'd head home. Since the combination clinic and cottage where she lived was only a mile away, she left on foot.

Everyone else gathered at the table. Lily decided she liked it there. With everyone sitting, she could almost forget what kind of chair she sat in. Not about her arm, though. She couldn't make notes left-handed. It bugged her intensely.

It was interesting to see how everyone grouped themselves. Isen sat at the head of the table. The chair to his right was for Rule, who'd gone to the kitchen to make coffee. Lily's chair was wheeled into place next to his. Isen motioned for Cynna—the Rhej's apprentice had high status—to take the spot on his left. Cullen sat next to Cynna, of course, and Arjenie took the seat on his left. Benedict sat next to Arjenie, leaving Lily and Rule alone on their side of the table.

What does Arjenie know? Lily wondered. Not just about those potions and Robert Friar, but about why Benedict stayed close to her, why he kept watching her. Did she know about the mate bond? Lily was pretty sure she didn't. But they were all speaking openly in front of Arjenie, as if she were already clan, and trusted.

Was that wise? Something—someone—had bound her. They were assuming it was her father, but they didn't know that, did they? Lily tapped her fingers on the table, thinking.

"Ready?" Benedict said.

"Go for it." Rule would be able to hear just fine from the kitchen.

"All right. Arjenie possesses half of an ability the sidhe call by a word that translates as *kinspeech*. Though it is mind-to-mind contact, they don't consider it mindspeech because of its limitations. Kinspeech requires physical contact and occurs only between close kin, most often parent and child. It's common among middle sidhe; less common but not unusual in low sidhe. Her father can both send and receive. Arjenie can only send, like a radio transmitter without a receiver."

Lily glanced at the woman who'd been her favorite researcher at the Bureau. She was watching Benedict as closely as if she'd never heard any of this before. She must have felt Lily's eyes on her, because she turned a wry smile on Lily. "It took me thirty minutes to say that. I don't know how to boil things down."

"It's a learned talent," Lily said. "Is that true for this kinspeech?"

She shook her head, but it was Benedict who answered. "No, it's an innate ability. Though she did have to learn how to put more power behind her thoughts for her father to 'hear' them."

"He wanted her to yell like that?" Lily asked, startled.

"Essentially, yes. When she realized you were picking up her thoughts she boosted the output, as she'd been taught. This was apparently too much power for the form of mindspeech you use."

"No kidding," she said dryly.

"I didn't know," Arjenie said earnestly. "I had no idea it would hurt you."

"No, you couldn't have, could you? Why didn't you mention this ability?"

She shrugged. "I never think about it. I mean, the only time I ever experienced it was when Eledan visited me years and years ago, and I didn't really experience anything then. He did, because when he touched me he could hear me, just a little, so he taught me how to turn up the volume. But I've never heard anyone's thoughts, and as far as I knew Eledan was the only person in all the realms who could hear mine. Well, except for dragons, but that wouldn't be me doing it. That would be them."

"If you . . . ah." Lily broke off with a smile.

Rule entered bearing a thermos-style pot and a fistful of

mugs. He set the mugs down and poured one of them full of hot, fragrant coffee and set it in front of Lily.

"Thanks." She grabbed the mug and inhaled the scented steam, then sipped, gesturing for Benedict to continue.

He did. "The first question, obviously, is why you were able to receive what Arjenie broadcast. Clearly it has to do with your potential for mindspeech. Beyond that, our various experts disagree—though they do all believe that kinspeech must require a good deal more power than the dragon form of mindspeech you've inherited."

"You've explained to her that I can't actually use mindspeech yet?"

"Several people explained," he said dryly. "Frequently all at the same time, on different topics. But yes, that was touched on. The second question is whether and how you can repeat the event or connection. The third question is whether it would be safe to do so."

Lily glanced at Rule, who'd poured his own cup and was sipping it. His eyes met hers over the rim of the mug. They were about the same color as the coffee he sipped. About that revealing, too. "It didn't hurt until Arjenie turned the power up. I don't see a problem."

Cullen leaned forward. "If kinspeech draws on a fundamentally different form of—"

"Cullen," Isen said mildly.

Cullen scowled but fell silent. Benedict continued. "There are three clear differences between the two forms of mental contact. One is, as I said, the amount of power involved. The other two involve the way contact is achieved. Kinspeech requires physical contact, but doesn't require training. With mindspeech, the requirements are reversed. Or so we've assumed?" He raised his brows.

"You assumed right," Lily said. "Sam won't tell me much because, according to him, I'd try to fit my experience into his words. Apparently that would be bad. But yeah, while the ability to use mindspeech is inherited, actually using it has to be learned." Slowly. Very slowly.

Benedict nodded. "Seabourne believes this means that mindspeech doesn't function like a Gift, but kinspeech does."

"We don't know that," Cynna muttered.

Benedict slid her an opaque glance. "We've arrived at a point of disagreement. Seabourne believes the two forms of mental speech may be fundamentally different—enough so that you risk being harmed when you attempt to 'listen' to Arjenie. Using the radio analogy, he says the frequencies may be so different that kinspeech could damage you. That, in fact, you may have already sustained damage, and that's why you couldn't repeat the experience. Cynna disagrees. She believes the two are essentially the same, but kinspeech is far less efficient, thus requiring more power and the added boost of physical contact. She thinks you unconsciously threw up a shield when Arjenie's broadcast caused pain, and that's why you weren't able to 'hear' her anymore."

"Huh." Lily frowned at her mug and took another sip.

"They agree more than they disagree," Benedict said dryly, "but they disagree loudly. Because they do agree that both theories are possible, they've been attempting to modify a spell that would measure some aspect of kinspeech. I'm unclear on the details."

"Not measure," Cullen said. "Magnify. If Arjenie is continually broadcasting, she's using power, though at a very low level. I've got a spell I call my magnifying glass. I use it to enhance the focus on faint or intricate components when I'm deconstructing a spell. We're trying to modify it to work on a particular aspect of an innate ability—which is not simple. The section dealing with congruity alone has to be—"

"Not now," Lily said firmly. "I take it you think that magnifying this, uh, aspect of an innate ability would tell you if it was safe for me to make that kind of contact with Arjenie again?"

"Not definitively, but if the energies involved look highly dissimilar, that would suggest a greater risk. If they look fairly similar, it suggests less risk."

"Hmm." She looked at Benedict. "Does Arjenie have an opinion?"

"Not on this. She feels she lacks sufficient data. She has never experienced mindspeech herself and knows only what little her father told her about kinspeech. "

"Okay." The fingers on Lily's right hand twitched. She

wanted to jot things down. She settled for drumming the fingers of her other hand on the table. "Have you asked her about Dya again?

"She still can't speak that name, or respond in any way to questions about him or her."

"Her," Lily said, then frowned. "I think. I'm not sure why I said that." She glanced at Arjenie, who offered an apologetic smile.

Rule spoke for the first time since sitting down. "I'll offer a summary of my own. If Cullen's right, you shouldn't try to open a channel with Arjenie. The danger is real. Unquantifiable because we don't know enough, but too real to risk it. If Cynna's right, there's little danger in trying, though you may be blocked by the shield you unconsciously created."

Lily looked at him. Did he feel what she did? Not just fear. She'd feared for him before. This was fear on steroids with the volume turned up to a scream, like Arjenie's mental shout. Rule looked calm enough, but he was good at hiding fear. That had been a large part of his training. Wolves freak if they sense their leader is frightened.

She looked at the others. "The one thing—"

"Dumplings," said a gravelly voice behind her. "Made 'em fresh. Soggy dumplings are no good. Also scones for everyone." Carl came up beside Lily and set a steaming bowl in front of her. Wordlessly he added a large basket full of scones to the center of the table, then began pulling things out of his apron pockets—a napkin-wrapped set of silverware for Lily. Salt and pepper shakers. A jar of marmalade, and a small, lidded tub that might hold butter. Several butter knives. A roll of paper towels.

"You're not to have wine, I'm told," he said in his slow, grave way. "What do you want to drink?"

"Just some water. And maybe more coffee?"

"I've got water heating. The sprout here can make coffee when you're ready. Or Isen. They make decent coffee. Not Benedict. He doesn't. Ice?"

She blinked. Oh—he meant for her water. "Yes, please."

"Your cat wanted chicken. Gave him some. He liked it." With that he turned and stumped back to the kitchen.

Chicken apparently trumped guard duty. Not that Harry

really guarded Toby. That was just Rule's way of talking. Cats didn't have that kind of instinct the way dogs did.

Arjenie leaned forward and whispered, "He's very quiet, isn't he?"

Isen smiled. "Carl speaks fluent math. None of us can carry on a conversation in his tongue, but he doesn't hold it against us. Try one of the scones."

The bowl in front of Lily smelled wonderful. Her stomach surprised her by rumbling. She was hungry. That shouldn't come as a surprise this late in the day, but this was the first time she'd been really hungry since getting shot. She dug in.

The dumplings were a surprise, too. Lily had expected the heavy, greasy lumps of dough she associated with American-style dumplings, but Carl's were different. Light and fluffy, slightly savory with herbs, they swam in a thickened sauce chunky with chicken and carrots.

Hunger and the sheer deliciousness of the meal held her attention at first. Arjenie asked Isen what kind of math Carl spoke and seemed to understand his answer, which was more than Lily could say. Interdimensional degeneracies? A quantum-isolated four-body system?

Isen was right. She didn't speak Carl's language. But he made incredible dumplings, and they were easy to eat with one hand. Maybe he'd planned it that way. She beamed at him when he returned to set a glass of ice water at her place. He answered with the usual nod, but the solemn creases of his face lifted briefly in what was nearly a smile.

"Good?" Rule said.

She gave him a smile, too. He gave her a scone.

It was comforting, this meal. Familiar. Cynna announced that the little rider was dancing on her poor, squished bladder and left the table, heading for the bathroom. Isen asked Cullen about the project he'd been working on, trying to create a cheaply replicable insulation against the rising levels of ambient magic. According to Rule, If Cullen could pull that off neither he nor Nokolai—who was funding his efforts—would ever have to worry about money again.

Everything was normal, safe, peaceful. Any one of them could be dead tomorrow.

Rule passed the little tub—which turned out to hold clotted cream, not butter—to Arjenic. She said something Lily didn't catch, and he laughed.

Lily would risk herself for Rule in a heartbeat. He knew it. He'd do the same for her, and she knew that with sick certainty. But why? Why did that make her shaky and scared now? It never used to.

Death was a constant. It always had been, and Lily supposed her current hypersensitivity to that reality would ease in time, and she'd return to the normal human state of semiblindness. God, she hoped so. But she was weird and shaky now, and it made her doubt her judgment. How did she decide what risks were justified?

Lily put down her spoon and sipped the ice water Carl had provided. It was cold, like her insides. *I'll be careful with myself*, she wanted to tell Rule. *I don't want to scare you. I'll be careful for your sake.*

How careful? What did she owe him in that way? Why had that always been obvious before?

Because of her job. Understanding hit, as clear and icy as the water. She'd known what risks were justified because she knew what her job required of her. Rule had the same sort of guidance. He knew what was required of him as Lu Nuncio to Nokolai, as Rho to Leidolf. They each understood duty. But whatever she was doing now, it wasn't about the job. As far as the Bureau was concerned, she had no investigation. She was on sick leave.

But they had to find out what Arjenie knew. Didn't they?

Lily ate slowly and thought about duty, about Robert Friar, mindspeech, mysterious potions, Arjenie Fox, and three attacks. One by bullet. One by magic. One by madness.

THIRTY

ARJENIE wasn't hungry, but the scones were too good to pass up. Especially with clotted cream. Maybe, she thought as she bit into her second one, if she stayed here long enough she'd actually put on a little weight.

But she wouldn't be staying, would she?

She snuck a quick peek at Benedict, who was listening carefully to what Cullen the Beautiful said about enhancing the insulating properties of silk. Benedict's eyes were steady and dark and turned away from her, so she indulged herself by watching him beneath her lashes.

She loved his skin, the color of it, the texture . . . such a warm, coppery shade, not *chocolate* or *tea* or *cinnamon* or any of the food names people often used for skin, but a living color, as infused by sun as it was by blood. She loved his body, bulky with muscle, yet he moved lightly in it, adept as a dancer. Then there were his hands, with their flat, square nails . . .

Thoughtfully she applied more of the clotted cream to what remained of her scone. Maybe it was just as well she wouldn't be here much longer . . . or just as well if she could convince herself it was just as well. Arjenie had nothing against a quick, hot interlude. She was pretty sure she could have the quick and hot with Benedict—pretty sure she would have that if she was here much longer. But she had the uneasy feeling the interlude part of the equation might not end cleanly. It might hurt her, haunt her, afterward.

But you could be haunted by the things you didn't do, too.

"There's probably more stew in the kitchen," Rule said to Lily on the other side of the table. "No? Dessert, then." He tried to hand her the last scone.

She shook her head, her mouth quirking up. "Am I a goose? Stop feeding me."

Arjenie liked watching the two of them together. The Bureau's files held all sorts of facts, but they weren't always the ones she wanted. Everyone knew that these two were engaged, but what did that mean to a lupus? Would Rule Turner really commit himself to a single woman?

Sure looked like it from where Arjenie sat. They weren't obvious about it. They didn't hang all over each other. But they kept track of each other in a lovely, unthinking way. Rule had been talking to Isen, but he'd known it when Lily finished her stew.

They touched easily and often . . . eleven times in ten minutes.

Arjenie counted touches. She hadn't mentioned this hobby to anyone in years, since most people found it peculiar. But the way people touched said so much about a relationship. This was true with sisters and friends, with mothers and children, but it was especially true with couples.

She'd started counting with her aunt and uncle. After thirty years, they still averaged five touches in ten minutes when they sat next to each other. Less when they'd been fighting. More when they were planning for intimate touches as soon as they could be alone.

There were those afflicted with glued-at-the-hip syndrome. Most teens and some new couples fell into that category. The inability to *stop* touching wasn't a sign of soul mates, but of need, insecurity, or hormones. Then there were couples who seemed to have a great marriage, who never fought, whose friends believed they were solid and forever . . . but who seldom touched except at the expected times. He'd help her on with her coat. She'd peck his cheek to say " 'bye."

Arjenie had sadly but successfully predicted a couple of divorces based on that kind of touching.

The couples who worried her were the ones where one partner touched and the other didn't. Sometimes that was a power thing—a man who wanted to keep his woman physically under his thumb, and reminded her constantly with little touches. Or maybe the woman exerted control with constant, vaguely sexual touches. And sometimes, sadly, one partner was simply indifferent.

New couples touched more often than established ones, of course, and it meant less. Sex was a form of intimacy, but it said little about long-term prospects. And admittedly, a few established couples defied the touch rule. But most of the time, Arjenie's touch-counting gave her a pretty good idea of how a couple was doing.

Not that it was any of her business, of course. Which was another reason not to mention her touch-counting.

Benedict leaned close enough that his arm brushed hers. Heat swept through her and she forgot about anyone else's touches.

"You're staring," he rumbled very softly. "And you look gooey. Do you have a crush on Rule? Or maybe on Lily?"

"On . . . oh!" She flushed, ducked her head, and grinned inside the privacy of the curtain formed by her hair. "No. No, I'm just nosy, and they're so sweet together. I'm about an eighty on the hetero scale. Maybe eighty-five. I gave it a try in college, because you can't really know otherwise, can you? And there was this sweet lesbian girl who wanted to date me, but we never got past a kiss or two. I'm just not turned on by breasts, even real pretty ones."

Dead silence. She tilted her head to look at him. "You're shocked. I didn't think lupi got shocked."

"Surprised," he said dryly. "I expected to fluster or annoy you."

"I'm Wiccan. I fluster about lots of things, but sex isn't one of them. Why did you want me flustered or annoyed?"

His mouth turned wry. "The same reason I would have

pulled your hair a few decades ago. Or turned cartwheels, or lifted something impressively heavy."

"You want my attention." Delighted, she propped her chin on one hand, elbow on the table, so she could look straight at him. "Okay. You've got it."

He hesitated. "I think I'm flustered."

That made her laugh.

At the head of the table, Isen tapped the coffeepot on the table like a gavel. "There's a couple cups left. Anyone want some before we give Lily the floor? Unless I'm mistaken, she's ready to get us all lined up."

"I wouldn't go that far," Lily said wryly, "but I've got my own thinking lined up. I've got a couple of ideas to share and some questions."

For some reason that made everyone chuckle or grin. Everyone but Arjenie. There were much more important things going on than a bit of flirtation . . . but she'd wanted the flirtation.

"Okay," Lily said. "Three topics up for discussion: the Great Bitch, Friar, and Arjenie. First question." She looked at Isen. "Are we speaking openly about *her* and related matters? Arjenie isn't clan."

"We are." Isen's smile was placid. "With one exception." His gaze flicked to Benedict so fast Arjenie wasn't sure that's who he'd indicated—until Lily looked at Benedict, too. She didn't speak, just raised her eyebrows.

"Not yet," he said. His voice was level. Was she imagining it was also grim?

Lily looked at Arjenie next. "Have they told you about *her*?"

"I don't know what *her* you mean."

"That means they haven't. I'll give you . . . let's call it the cover blurb of the CliffsNotes version. You can ask questions later. When lupi refer to *her*—sometimes known as the Great Bitch, though that's unfair to female dogs—they mean the Old One they were created to oppose. We don't use her name, any of her names, because she's reputed to be able to hear it. She is powerful beyond our understanding, so it's a good thing she can't reach into our realm directly. For something around three thousand years she's been penned up, or weakened, or busy elsewhere. We don't know, but she hasn't been meddling here. Until last year. She was behind the hell-gate the Azá tried to open. You'll know about that. She also tried to send me to hell, and partly succeeded—"

"What?" Arjenie exclaimed. "I didn't—"

"You didn't hear or read anything about it, and you won't. Ruben knows the story, but it's not in the Bureau's files. *She* suffered a setback there, but we have reason to think she may have made one of the lords of hell into her avatar."

Arjenie's heart beat too fast. Her mouth was dry. In a small voice she said, "Old Ones are real? And this one . . ." She looked at Isen. "*This* is who you think is behind the attacks on Ruben and Lily?"

He smiled gently. "Oh, yes."

Lily looked at her again. "You'll have questions. I'm asking you to hold them for later. You said Friar can't Listen here at Clanhome."

Baffled, Arjenie nodded.

Lily looked at Isen. "That's why you're convinced *she's* involved, isn't it?"

He spread his hands. "I can think of no other reason Friar's Gift would be blocked here. Can you?"

"Son of a bitch," Rule said suddenly. One of his hands rested on the table. It fisted. "Of course."

Benedict leaned closer to Arjenie and spoke softly. "*She* isn't omniscient, but she's clairaudient and clairvoyant even across realms. She can hear or see what happens on Earth, but not around lupi. Our nature blocks her. If Friar's Gift came from *her*, it would explain why he can't Listen here."

"This is not established fact," Lily warned them. "Maybe *she* has recruited Friar. It fits what we know, but we don't know much. We haven't confirmed that Friar is a Listener or that he can't eavesdrop here."

Arjenie squirmed. She so wanted to tell them. "That's— it's just—" Too much. She shoved to her feet. "Excuse me. I need a minute."

FEAR comes in many flavors. Tonight's flavor was bitter with a twist of misery. She left the table, not caring where she went—just *away*, someplace where she could be terrified in private.

Someplace turned out to be the kitchen. But it didn't work. She stood at the kitchen counter with her arms wrapped around herself and somehow, even without looking, she knew Benedict had followed her. Her heart fluttered with fear and other things.

They could all die. Benedict, too. She couldn't stand it. "You're talking about an *Old One*," she whispered, not turning to face him. "That's like a little *g* god. An Old One who's out to get all of you."

He stopped close enough for her to feel the warmth from his body along her back. Two big hands came to rest on her shoulders. They were even warmer. "We don't have to stop *her*. She can't come here or act directly. We only have to stop her agents."

"Only? It's *scary*. Why is everyone so calm? Isen keeps smiling. Why would he smile like that?" Her breath huffed out. "I hate being scared. I hate being a coward."

Benedict chuckled. She wrenched around to face him. "You're *laughing*." She wanted to hit him.

He kept on smiling. "A coward who invades Friar's land in spite of armed militia goons. One who invades lupus territory the next night—and I can promise you, most people are more afraid of us than they are of any human, with or without guns. A coward who doesn't want me to make a big deal about the chance that evil elves might try to kidnap her so they can bleed and breed her." He wound one of her curls around one finger. "Such a coward."

"I'm used to the possibility of being grabbed," she said, "and it's never happened, so I'm careful, not terrified. But I was scared the whole time I was sneaking around. More scared at Friar's because I was pretty sure you lupi wouldn't kill me, but I was scared here, too, even though I knew no one could see me. Though it turned out you could, and I don't understand that, but I didn't know that and I was scared anyway. And I *know* that courage is supposed to be acting in the face of fear, not the lack of fear, but no one at that table just now was quivering with terror. Lily's been *shot* and she wasn't shaking. I am." She held up one hand and showed him.

He took her hand in both of his. Wordlessly he began rubbing it, as if fear were a cramp he could dispel.

It worked. She stared at him in astonishment. "How did you do that?"

"I dislike fear, too," he murmured. "I dislike the way it feels. I dislike the way it tries to control me. But a large part of fear is physical. It's possible to learn how to control some of the physical aspects."

"But I haven't learned how to do that. How can you—"

"Later." He brushed her shoulder with his fingertips—just her shoulder, and she barely felt it through her clothes. Yet that simple touch brushed heat through her. "I owe you a full explanation, but later. Lily wants to ask you some questions."

THIRTY-ONE

WHILE they waited for Benedict and Arjenie to rejoin them, Lily took another cup of that coffee Isen had been waving around. And argued with Cullen.

"In learning mindspeech," Cullen insisted, "you must have learned how to turn off the main function of your Gift."

"No." Lily looked over her shoulder. Benedict and Arjenie came in, holding hands again. Well, she knew how comforting that could be, and it looked like Arjenie needed the comfort. She was still pale. "You okay?"

"No," Arjenie said, circling the table to return to her chair. "I mean yes, I'm okay in the not-falling-apart sense, but I might fall apart again." She sighed. "There's a reason I never tried to be a field agent. Even if I could have made it through the training with my . . ." She shot Benedict a glance. He was holding her chair for her. "With my physical limitations, I wouldn't have been a good agent. I scare too easily."

"It would have been a waste," Cynna announced. "You're a top-notch researcher. You love research. Why would you want to be an agent?"

Arjenie smiled ruefully and sat. "Why did you?"

"I didn't. I wanted to help people. To Find people who were missing. The rest just sort of happened."

Lily waited until Benedict sat, too, then said, "Arjenie, I want to try to do the mindspeech thing again. Or kinspeech. Whatever we call it, it's pretty intrusive. Are you willing?"

"Do you think it's safe?"

"We were just talking about that." She glanced at Cullen. "There's a problem with both the theories I've heard. They don't explain how something magical could affect me in the first place."

Surprise lightened Arjenie's expression. "Of course. You're a sensitive. Magic shouldn't hurt you, should it? But somehow it did."

Cullen shook his head. "Because she's doing things with it she couldn't do before. Lily, it seems obvious that when you use your Gift differently, it leaves you less than completely impermeable to magic. Most Gifts aren't stuck in the 'on' position, after all. Cynna doesn't Find things unless she looks for them. I don't spray fire around all the time. Arjenie isn't using her Gift now, so we all see her. You must be—"

"No," Lily said again. "There's a lot I don't know about my Gift, but I'm clear on one thing. I can't turn it off. It isn't like those shields of yours—and that's what Sam says, not my own, uninformed opinion."

Cullen scowled at her. "Explain your headache, then."

"The only way I can see for magic to hurt me is if it's *my* magic."

Cullen's scowl slid into a frown—a thinking sort of frown, not the angry sort. That was one of his saving graces. Cullen might argue at the drop of a vowel, but he didn't take offense if you disagreed. He just kept arguing . . . unless he decided you had a point. He was capable of turning around and agreeing with you, because getting it right was more important to him than being right.

"I don't see it," Cynna said. "I don't see how your magic could be doing a number on you. It sure looks like it was Arjenie's magic that did it." She shrugged. "But then, I don't get mindspeech."

Cullen spoke slowly. "What you did to the Chimei last month . . ."

"Yes?" Lily wished she could use mindspeech right then so she could think "shut up" at him. She didn't want him to mention her ability to soak up someone else's magic.

Either he got the warning, or he was tactful, for once. "In a way, that's a logical extension of your Gift. You soak up magic. Normally you absorb such a tiny mote of power that the loss isn't noticeable. Your Gift translates that mote into your own form of magic—and in the process, gives you information about what you touched. You experience that information as a tactile sensation."

"Yeah," she said, not seeing where he was going.

"Mindspeech doesn't fit with that model—"

"I noticed that."

"—unless we stipulate that receiving thoughts is simply another way of experiencing information. Thought and magic are closely linked."

Lily's brows drew down. "I almost understood that."

"I think I get it," Arjenie burst out. She looked at Cullen. "It's the 'thought given form' dictum you're thinking of, right?"

His eyebrows lifted. "That's right."

Arjenie turned to Lily, her thin face alight with enthusiasm. "It's a Wiccan teaching. Spells are 'thought given form.' By that we mean the caster's intent is translated into an external statement using spell components, but the spell can't function unless the caster's thoughts are aligned with the statement of the spell. Which means, basically, that you can't cast a spell that doesn't make sense to you. But some take the expression farther. They believe that thoughts are *part* of the statement, just as much an external component as a sprig of rue."

"I'm sorry," Lily said, "but if that was supposed to explain something, I'm missing it."

"It's the difference between thoughts happening strictly inside our heads or being somehow 'out there' as well, like radio waves. Though I don't think radio waves are a good model because that's a space-time phenomena and I'm not sure—"

Benedict laid a hand over Arjenie's. "Later, perhaps, for that."

"Oh. I suppose so." She looked at Lily earnestly. "If this model is accurate, thoughts are always external as well as internal, and mindspeech would be a sort of magical translator. Like your touch sensitivity, it soaks up a bit of something that's out there and puts it in a form your brain understands. Only instead of tactile sensations, you get words. So it *would* be your magic giving you the information, not mine."

"Okay," Lily said slowly. "But that doesn't explain two things. Sam sends as well as receives thoughts. If mindspeech just translates external stuff, how could he do that? And I still don't see why really loud kinspeech would give me the mother of all headaches."

Cullen shrugged. "I can't answer your first question. I could speculate, but not helpfully. But as for your headache . . . we don't really understand what happens in the brain when we think, but we know it involves electrical impulses and the way neurons fire together. I'd guess the 'really loud kinspeech' used your own magic to create new neural pathways in a really loud way."

That didn't sound good. But Nettie had said she was fine. She felt fine.

"The point is, if that's the correct model for what happens when you touch Arjenie, it won't be dangerous for you to try again. You might not be able to repeat what you did earlier, but there wouldn't be any danger in trying."

"Glad to hear that," she said, "because clearly I have to try." She looked at Rule. "If it hurts, I'll stop. Promise." Their eyes met. For a second her mind went light and dizzy in an echo of that free-fall moment when the mate bond had first clicked in place. It was like having your skull vanish. It came back, but for a second, it wasn't there.

Rule smiled, his eyes swimming in mystery as if he'd felt it, too. *"Nadia."* He touched her cheek. "I accept your promise."

Lily nodded, swallowed, and held out her hand to Arjenie.

Slowly Arjenie reached across the table and clasped it.

. . . wish I could tell them! The . . .

She had it. Then she didn't. This time, though, Lily didn't try harder. She didn't try at all. Instead she breathed slowly and thought about candle flame and skin, about the cool, complex feel of Arjenie's magic. "I'm not getting much, but I got something," she murmured. "I'm going to ask questions. Answer out loud when you're able to. And, ah, think softly. Don't put any power into it, okay?"

Arjenie's smile sketched uncertain agreement. She added a nod to that.

"Why do you believe Robert Friar is a Listener?"

"Someone told me." *Dya warned me when she called. Wish I knew how she could do that, if it was magic or . . . snuck into his house? but she . . . Friar can Listen across the country, she said. Be careful. There wasn't time to . . . worried about her. If he . . .*

"I know you can't talk about Dya. Think about her—who she is, how you know her."

She's my sister. That arrived as clearly as spoken words, but trailed a confusing mélange of thoughts and memories. Something to do with Dya staying with Arjenie when Arjenie was young. Staying up talking and talking all night. *Love you, little fox.* Their father didn't want Arjenie talking about Dya . . . didn't want Dya put to the tears so young . . .

"Your father brought Dya to you."

Yes, he wanted them to wait a few years before they gave her the tears. Her elders didn't agree and the contract . . . she's a professional daughter, not like me, but the contract doesn't . . . it's the best thing I know of him, that he wanted to . . . the tears. I hate them. Addict their daughters on purpose so . . . her duty, but she's so different but I . . .

"These tears are an addictive substance."

She goes crazy without them. Brain damage that can't be healed and that's how Friar controls her but she thinks he's broken contract which is a very big deal to the Binai but Queens' Law even bigger I don't know . . .

Little by little, Lily pulled together the story. Arjenie was thinking in sentences more often this time, aware that Lily was "hearing" her and trying to be clear, but it was still nothing like the crisp mindspeech Sam used. Plus Lily's ability faded in and out, and she had to go back and ask again. And again.

"But you believe Dya could have crafted such a potion. One that would cause a heart attack."

*Oh, yes, humans are easy to . . . Binai make incredibly
sophisticated potions that can't be detected . . . why they're
feared and coveted says her people couldn't survive without . . . but her lord holds her contract don't know what
realm he's in but sure not here don't see how Friar got hold
of it. Of her.*

"I have an idea about that." Lily was vaguely aware of her
head throbbing and wished she could rub her neck, but she
needed her one useable hand to . . . oh. Shit.

She looked at Arjenie, who was thinking about a complex jumble of rules called Queens' Laws, then at Rule. And
sighed. "I'm getting the beginning of a headache. It feels like
a normal headache, nothing spooky, but I promised." She let
go of Arjenie's hand.

The sudden silence in her head was wonderful. Did Sam
pick up everyone's mental chatter all the time? Surely not.
She'd ask, though.

"Lily?" Rule looked worried.

"It's a tension headache." She could feel the tightness all
across her shoulders and neck and scalp. "I'm okay. Now,"
she said, looking around at the others. "You probably picked
up some ideas from what I asked, but with lots of gaps. Plus
we jumped around some. I'll see if I can put it in order.

"The binding is all about Dya. Dya is Arjenie's half sister,
and the result of a contract job for Eledan. Her other half is
Binai, a non-sidhe race who live in one of the sidhe realms.
When Arjenie was fourteen, Eledan showed up suddenly
with Arjenie's half sister in tow. She's small enough for him
to take with him when he crosses, apparently. He wanted
Arjenie's family to keep Dya for a while.

"Eledan explained that Dya's people—her elders—
wanted to start her on something called the tears. Eledan
thought she was too young for that. Ah . . . I didn't understand all of this, but there was something about a contract
that allowed him to negotiate for Dya. Or maybe he could do
that because he was her father. Anyway, when Arjenie's aunt
and uncle learned what the tears were like, they agreed. Dya
stayed with them for over a year. She learned our language
and other Earthly things—like how to use a phone.

"That's how she contacted Arjenie about a week ago.

Friar is keeping her at a little guest cottage behind his house. She's sort of on loan to him—there's a big-deal sidhe lord who holds her contract."

"What does this contract cover?" Isen asked.

Lily shrugged. "Arjenie doesn't know specifics. She believes the Binai hold contracts as sacred, inviolable. Um, when I asked, she thought that the closest analogue we have would be the kind of contracts signed by indentured servants back when we were a colony, only a lot more important. Anyway, Dya managed to make a phone call to Arjenie, who flew out here to see her, but secretly. Arjenie's afraid of what Friar would do to Dya if he found out. The night Benedict ran into Arjenie at Friar's was the first time she'd seen her sister since she was sixteen. They talked. Dya gave Arjenie the two potions and told her what to do with them."

"And these potions were supposed to do—what?" Isen asked

"One was to nullify Arjenie's scent, so she wouldn't leave a scent trail. The other . . . Dya called it an undoer. Supposedly it would undo any other potion she'd made—and one of her potions had already been dumped into Nokolai's water supply."

Benedict made a small sound. Lily paused, giving him a chance to speak, but he waved for her to continue. "I wondered about that. If Friar is one of *her* agents, he couldn't come into Clanhome without the Rho and the Rhej being aware of it. Or something like that. Or so I've been told?"

Isen answered. "You were told correctly. If Friar has been touched—changed—by *her*, the mantle would react to his presence on Clanhome. But he could send someone who didn't bear *her* taint. Most or all of his people probably don't."

Arjenie spoke for the first time in quite awhile. "Mantle? What's a—"

"Later," Benedict told her.

Mantles were not to be spoken of around out-clan . . . but a Chosen was clan, even if she didn't know it yet. Lily felt a pang for all Arjenie had yet to learn, but went on. "It seems that Dya's people, the Binai, are famous for their potions. I get the idea there aren't many Binai, and the ones who can make top-grade potions are rare. They don't make them in the usual way, though. The women—only the women—manufacture them in their bodies. They can do this because of the tears. The Binai have this gland that makes a nasty poison like a snake's venom. The tears change them, body and brain, so they can control what kind of substance they excrete, tailor it and give it magical properties. But they also render the Binai permanently dependent. Dya has to receive the tears daily. Friar controls her supply.

"These potions are special. Highly targeted. They—the Binai—are used as healers sometimes, and for other things, but most of all—well, the potions are undetectable once they've done their work. That makes them the best damn poisoners in the business."

"Ruben's heart attack," Cynna said.

"Oh, yeah." Though proving it was going to be one helluva challenge.

"And the first potion someone emptied into our water?" Isen said, his voice dropping to a growl. "What was it?"

"Dya wouldn't tell Arjenie what that one was supposed to do, just that it would be very bad. She—Arjenie—thinks it had to reach critical mass before it took effect. People had to drink the tainted water for several days for enough of the 'very bad' potion to build up in their bodies before anything happened. Arjenie emptied the undoer into the well nearest the road before the bad potion took effect. She's certain there's no danger from the original potion now."

Lily glanced at Arjenie, who was silent and tense. "Arjenie wanted me to tell you that her sister isn't evil. She's constrained by her contract to do what Friar wants. She's been taught from infancy that contracts are inviolable. She's also been taught that providing a weapon is not the same, morally, as using a weapon. If wrong is done by Friar, that's on his head, not hers. Plus, of course, Friar has the tears."

Silence. Rule broke it to say, "You believe what she's told you. Or thought at you, I suppose I should say."

Lily hesitated. "I don't know if it's possible to lie in this kind of mindspeech. It isn't like when Sam talks to us. Arjenie's thoughts trail all this—this stuff along with them. Not feelings—I don't pick up those. More like snatches of memory and meaning. I think if she tried to lie with her thoughts, the trailing stuff would tip me off."

"That's a yes, then," Cullen said. "Next question. How do we get Dya away from Friar?"

"Oh," Arjenie said. Her eyes filled. "Oh."

Lily didn't want Arjenie thinking it would be that simple. "We can't just rush in and grab her. We don't have cause for a warrant yet."

Isen smiled. "You would need a warrant. We do not."

"Don't *say* stuff like that." Lily dropped her head and ran her hand through her hair. "Look, Arjenie isn't sure Dya would even come with us if we tried to smuggle her out. Even if we got the tears, too—and we'd have to—Arjenie doesn't know if Dya would leave because of the contract. She's got a different set of ethics and imperatives than we do, and we can't assume she'd do what looks logical to us. Plus Dya doesn't think she's in danger, so we've got time to do this right. *Right* means more than getting Dya away from Friar. It means stopping him. To do that, we need evidence. I've got some ideas about that."

"Yet Dya acted against her contract already, didn't she?" Rule said. "When she sent Arjenie with the, ah, undoer, surely that was a contract violation."

"Dya thinks Friar's broken something called Queens' Law, which would invalidate the contract. It's complicated, and no, I don't know what this Queens' Law is."

"I can talk about that," Arjenie said, leaning forward. "Not that I know much, but Eledan did teach me the basics. The sidhe have lots of rulers, but the two Queens are over them all. The Queens outlaw the seriously bad magical stuff: death magic, binders—um, that doesn't mean regular binding spells, but something much worse—genocide, the two banned Names and the three banned Words . . . not that I know those names or those words. I don't know what the last one means, either: interfering with the dead. Eledan shuddered when I asked and told me to wait until I was older."

Isen and Rule exchanged a look. "Genocide," Isen said thoughtfully.

"Very likely," Rule agreed. "If Friar is working for *her*. She wants us dead."

Arjenie shivered. "All of you? That's . . . hugely bad."

Lily agreed, but they needed to get back on topic. "The first thing we have to do is figure out how to get word of this to Croft or Karonski. Karonski's heading the investigation into the attack on Ruben. He and Croft both need to know what we've learned, but we can't call them. Not if Friar can potentially listen at their end. I'm not sure if e-mail is safe. If whoever tried for Ruben can—"

"No," Benedict said, "the first thing we need to do is to make sure Dya is still there and okay. Then we can ask her if she'd come away with us once we secure her supply of these tears." He looked at Isen. "I'm thinking Seabourne."

Isen nodded. "Give him Danny for backup. He's almost as fast and he knows the terrain well."

Benedict turned to Arjenie. "Dya will need some reason to listen to Seabourne. Please give me your ring."

Arjenie rolled her eyes. "That's an order with 'please' tacked on, but at least you're trying." She pulled the ring off and handed it to him.

"Lily." While Benedict gave Cullen instructions, Rule leaned close, his voice low. "I'm thinking of Raymond Cobb."

"What? Oh. Oh, shit." She rubbed her neck. She should have thought of that. "It's possible, isn't it? He was at a public party, drinking a Coke or something. It would have been simple enough for someone to dose him with a potion."

"It would explain why he suddenly went insane. Why it looked and felt much like falling into the fury, but wasn't." His voice even softer, he added, "I'm wondering if Cobb was a test. A test of the dose and effectiveness."

"Jesus." She shivered. "If that's what the potion Arjenie countered was supposed to do to every lupus at Clanhome . . . but how did they know he was lupus?"

"Friar keeps files on us. It's one of the things he uses Humans First for—to assemble files on known and suspected lupi. Cobb only had to slip up once in front of the wrong person to give himself away."

It made a horrible sort of sense. Friar would have wanted to try out his potion, see what it did. Why Cobb, out of all the lupi in the country? Maybe he was simply convenient.

Maybe Friar had an agent in place in the city—like whoever had shot her—and Cobb hung out with humans often enough to make it easy to dose him.

Cullen shoved back from the table. "Got it," he told Benedict and bent to give Cynna a quick kiss. "Don't go into labor."

"Yet," she said. "You need to put 'yet' on the end of that sentence. I have every intention of going into labor, just not tonight."

He grinned, ruffled her hair, and left.

"Now that the first thing's been dealt with," Lily said dryly, "let's move on to the second thing. How do we let Croft know about Friar's guest and her capabilities? E-mail's safer than phone, but I'm not sure it's safe enough. We don't know who at the Bureau is a traitor. We don't know if Friar has a means of hacking into the system, either. We may need to send someone to report in person."

"Someone from the local FBI office?" Rule asked. "Or someone from Nokolai?"

Arjenie jumped in, her face lighting up. "I could do it. It wouldn't look odd if I cut my vacation short by a couple days, not with everything that's going on. It would have to be a written report, of course, but if you gave me a written report, I could deliver it."

Lily hesitated. If she said no, Arjenie would think they were back to distrusting her. But she couldn't go jetting across the country. Not without Benedict. Lily met the young woman's eyes. "I'm not sure a written report is the best way to go." *And Benedict needs to tell you about the mate bond really, really soon.*

Arjenie's eyes widened. "Ohmygosh. That was so weird. What's a mate bond?"

THIRTY-TWO

"I'M sorry," Lily said helplessly. "Benedict, I didn't mean to . . . I don't know how I did that."

"What's going on?" Arjenie looked from Lily to Benedict, then on to every other face at the table. Then back at Benedict again. His face was smoothed out, blank, but his eyes . . . storms swirled there. Her heart began to pound. "Everyone's upset. Why is everyone upset?"

Benedict shoved to his feet. "Arjenie, will you come into the kitchen with me?"

"Now?" She blinked. "The kitchen?"

"Or we could go outside."

He meant that they should be alone to talk about this. Her stomach turned queasy. She didn't know why. "You're scaring me."

"That's appropriate. I'm terrified."

CARL'S kitchen was not going to need much cleaning, Arjenie thought as she looked around. There was a pot on the stove that probably held what was left of the chicken and dumplings. The two cookie sheets in the sink must have been for the scones.

She headed there. "Okay," she said, turning on the water to get it hot. "Start talking."

"You're washing dishes?"

"I'm nervous. It's easier to be nervous if I'm busy."

"Arjenie." He turned off the water and put his hands on her arms and turned her to face him. "I don't think I can do this while you wash dishes."

His face wasn't all smoothed out anymore. She still couldn't read it. He'd said he was terrified, but what she saw was urgency. She licked her lips. "Lily thinks you need to tell me about the mate bond really soon. Soon would be now."

"You know that my people do not believe in marriage or monogamy."

This was not the lead-in she'd expected. She nodded.

"There is one exception. Rarely—very rarely—our Lady gifts one of us with a Chosen. We call her that because she is chosen for us. A lupus gifted with a Chosen will be faithful to her unto death."

Disappointment swamped her. "Is that why Rule and Lily are getting married? Not because they love each other, but because they've got this mate bond thing? And Cullen and Cynna, too—"

"Cullen and Cynna don't share a mate bond. Rule and Lily do. They also love each other. I don't understand why they're marrying. It's a meaningless flourish when they are irrevocably bound together. It will cause no end of problems."

Irrevocably? Her heart was pounding harder. "I don't understand. I don't see why Lily wanted you to tell me this. If she was worried that . . . well, I guess it's obvious I'm attracted to you, but if she or you are thinking I don't understand how lupi are about sex, that I'm going to get my feelings hurt because you aren't going to make a commitment—"

"That isn't what anyone is thinking." His hands tightened on her arms. "Arjenie, I will be faithful to you unto death."

Her heart leaped into her throat. Her hand flew there, trying to keep it from jumping right out of her body. "No. No, you're mistaken."

"The mate bond snapped into place the moment our eyes met. I was wolf at the time, but it didn't matter."

"You can't be right." She tugged at one of his hands. "Let go. Let go of me."

His hands dropped. "It's why your Gift doesn't work on me. It's why we take comfort from touching each other, why we know where the other is at all times."

"I don't know that. I had to ask Cullen where you were this morning. I didn't know."

"Didn't you? I knew where you were. I felt it. That sense will grow stronger after we cement the bond. It's why we want each other so badly. I think about your skin, your scent. I want to feel your hair against my skin. I want inside you. I don't know how I managed to stop when I kissed you this afternoon."

Her stomach churned. "My mother was beguiled into sex. She never got over it. She never—"

"This isn't anything like faerie glamour. There's no illusion involved. The connection is real and physical. Lily wanted me to tell you so you would understand why you can't fly back to D.C."

"I *live* in D.C.! My career is there. My family's in Virginia. I'm not going to—"

"We'll have to work that out. I don't know how yet, but we can't live on opposite coasts. We can't put that much distance between us. The mate bond won't allow it, especially now when—"

"I don't believe you! This can't be true. You have to be mistaken. Or—or there's some way to make it go away. To remove it."

"Arjenie." His eyes were frantic. His hands were clenched fists at his sides. "The bond can't be removed. You have to believe me. Don't fight the bond. Please. I beg you not to fight it."

He begged her? This man didn't beg. He didn't. She wanted to hold him, soothe him. She wanted to do other things, too, that wouldn't be at all soothing. Was this ache, this need, not really hers? Had it been imposed on her? "I don't understand," she whispered. "I don't understand any of this." She took a step back. Another. "Do you want it? Did you want this mate bond?"

"When it hit, it was the last thing I wanted in this world."

The words were wrenched from his gut. She believed him. Benedict hadn't wanted this, hadn't done it to her. To them. "Okay." She nodded. "I have to think. I have to get away and think."

"Don't go. Stay. Talk to me. Ask me questions."

"I'm going to take a walk." *Yes.* Yes, that felt right. "I won't go far. You tell me I *can't* go far, so I won't, but I have to think. There must be a way to fix this. I have to think, figure out how to fix this."

His hand rose . . . and fell again. "There is one possible fix. It's a last resort. It would be painful and dangerous for you, and it's . . . forbidden to me, but I won't let you suffer. If you try but you can't adapt to the mate bond, can't live with it, tell me."

She stared at him a moment, her head boiling with thoughts that rose and popped before she could grasp a single one. She nodded slowly, then turned and fled.

"'I didn't mean to.' " Lily quoted herself bitterly. "Those are the most useless words in the world."

"But you *didn't* mean to." Rule drew the brush through her wet hair. He'd washed it for her. "You didn't know it was possible, so how could you have guarded against it?"

They sat together in the center of Rule's bed, her back to his front. She wore one of his button-down shirts since she didn't feel right about sleeping naked here like she did at home. He wore what he always slept in. Skin.

Dirty Harry was back, running his motor and allowing Lily to pet him. That brought a faint smile to her lips. While Rule petted her, she petted the cat. "I was already mindspeaking her, though it only worked one way. I should have considered the possibility that I could send a thought as well."

"As clever as you are, you might give a thought to world peace. I'm sure if you considered the possibility—"

"I'm too tired to hit you."

"Not too tired to beat up on yourself, however."

"No, that's actually easier to do when I'm tired." It was a

hair short of midnight and Lily was in the unwelcome state of being deeply weary but wide awake. The wide-awake part may have had something to do with the coffee she'd enjoyed so much. The weary part she blamed on her arm. Pain made her tired.

Lily leaned back against him. His arms came around her as automatically as breathing.

Neither Benedict nor Arjenie had come back after Lily forced Benedict's hand. Lily wanted that to mean they'd gone off to have mind-blowing sex in private. She was pretty sure the real reason for their absence was a lot more complicated and unhappy.

She couldn't fix things for Benedict, so her mind veered toward something she might be able to fix. They'd talked out the situation after Benedict and Arjenie left—not the Benedict and Arjenie situation, but the one with Friar and the Old One they suspected was his new mistress.

There were two immediate concerns. One, as Lily had said, was getting word to Croft. Friar had risked a lot with his attempt to kill Ruben. Lily figured that meant the last thing Friar and/or the Great Bitch wanted was for the government to be aware of them—so she'd better make damn sure it was.

Even encrypted, e-mail was too risky. Friar couldn't Listen to that, but there was a traitor in the Bureau, possibly within the Unit itself. A mole. Lily didn't dare assume that mole was unable to access e-mail accounts.

The question, then, was who to send? Cynna was too close to D-Day to fly across the country, and Cullen wouldn't leave her. Lily could appropriate someone from the local FBI office, but that might tip off their enemies. *She* wasn't omniscient, but she could observe multiple locations on Earth simultaneously, probably while painting her nails and playing *Grand Theft Auto*—or whatever beings the age of the universe did for fun and relaxation. Her main limitation was communication. It was extremely hard for *her* to communicate with her agents here on Earth, but *hard* did not equal *impossible*. Another nutty telepath like Helen would do the trick nicely.

In the end, Lily had settled on Jeff. He could fly home to

North Carolina without sending up any warning flags. One he arrived in Raleigh, though, instead of heading for Leidolf Clanhome he'd drive up to D.C. to hand-deliver Lily's report.

There was the little problem of getting Jeff in to see Croft without anyone else seeing the report. So Lily would call Croft when Jeff was on his doorstep and tell him, "Code 300. Courier Jeffrey Merrick Lane has information for your eyes only."

"Code 300" meant that *all* channels were possibly compromised, and sensitive information was to be conveyed in person only. Lily couldn't actually declare a Code 300—only Ruben or the director had that authority. But using it ought to get Croft's attention.

It was slow, convoluted, and downright paranoid, but they were up against an Old One. Paranoid made sense.

The other issue—one Lily hadn't thought of until Rule brought it up—was the meeting taking place the day after tomorrow. They had to assume Friar was aware of it. He couldn't Listen to conversations at any of the clanhomes, but none of them had been careful to speak only when at their respective clanhomes. Wouldn't a meeting of the heirs of seven clans strike him as a dandy target? "You're sure you want to hold this meeting still?" she said.

"It's a risk. But without the heirs' circle, we aren't going to get an All-Clan. We need the All-Clan. We'll hope Friar's failure has him sufficiently off-balance to give us the edge."

"Hmm." The failure Rule referred to was the first potion, the one Arjenie had undone. Friar had no way of knowing what had gone wrong, so he ought to be rethinking his plans. Whatever they were. "I wonder if . . . what is it?"

He'd turned his head to look at the door. So, she noticed, had Harry. A second later, someone knocked on it. "Lily?" Arjenie said softly. "Your light's on, so I was hoping . . . I know it's late and if you're hurting I'll just go away, but if not, I'd really like to talk."

Lily nodded at Rule, who slid off the bed. "Pants," she hissed at him, then said more loudly, "Just a minute."

"Lily insists I cover certain bits," Rule told the door as he stepped into the trousers he'd tossed on the floor earlier.

"There." He zipped them and opened the door on a pale, tense Arjenie. "I'll go raid the refrigerator, I think."

Arjenie pinked up. "I didn't mean to . . . no, actually, I did. Thank you. I would appreciate a chance to talk to Lily privately."

"Of course. I'm told you don't care to be touched without permission. This is awkward for me, as I'm accustomed to touching those I care about."

"I don't like to be grabbed without permission. Touching's okay. You don't really know me, though."

He smiled suddenly. "You are the closest thing to a sister I'll have in this life. I'm learning you. What I know so far is very easy to care about." He bent and kissed her cheek, then eased out the door without quite touching her.

Arjenie watched him for a moment, her eyes large and her cheeks pink. She looked at Lily. "Is he always like that?"

"Pretty much." Lily had scooted up to the head of the bed so she could prop herself up. Harry gave her a dirty look. She hadn't asked his permission to move. She patted the bed. "Have a seat."

Arjenie closed the door and came closer, then hesitated. "Are you uncomfortable? I am. I want to ask you about—about deeply personal matters, but I don't know you all that well. We've talked a lot, but it was always about facts."

"We can start with facts. I'm comfortable with facts myself. Sit," Lily said again.

Arjenie flashed a wry smile and perched on the edge of the bed, her shoulders held stiffly as if she were sitting to attention. "Is this your cat? He's a big one." She held out her hand.

"Ah, I wouldn't—"

But Harry decided to accept Arjenie's tribute with nary a growl or scratch. He allowed her to rub his head as she spoke. "I'm not sure where to start. I have a list of questions all made up in my head, but I don't know where to start."

"Benedict told you about the mate bond."

She nodded. "He said you and Rule have one. He said you love each other, too, which is what I thought, watching you, only then I didn't know what was this bond and what was just . . . well, love."

"I had a hard time figuring that out at first. What it comes down to, I think, is that the mate bond affects the physical stuff. The bond is . . . hmm. Have you ever lusted after someone you didn't much like? Or didn't know well enough to say if you liked him or not?"

"Yes!" Arjenie's shoulders relaxed slightly. "So the mate bond is great at lust, but it didn't make you fall in love?"

"You might say it got my attention." In spades. Lily had to smile. "But I managed the falling in love part on my own."

"Okay. Okay, that helps. Um . . . the other thing I was wondering is . . ." Her voice drifted off. She paid a great deal of attention to stroking Dirty Harry. "Benedict said the bond won't let us be separated very much. What happens if we're too far apart?"

"You get dizzy. If you don't close the distance, you'll pass out. He didn't tell you?"

"He would have, but I freaked." She grimaced. "He wanted me to stay and talk, but I had to get out, get my head straight. I had to think things through. I was trying so hard not to believe him, you see. My sense of reality was messed up. I had to find some objective points to consider."

"What kind of objective points?"

"Like when he said the bond made us know where each other was. I told him that wasn't true for me, but when I thought about it, I realized I did have a fuzzy idea of where he was. Not exactly, but I felt as if I could find him if I needed to. Right now, he's . . ." She closed her eyes and waved a hand in the general direction of the great room. "That way."

"How far away is he?"

Arjenie's eyes popped open. "I don't know. Am I supposed to know?"

"Right now, I know that Rule is roughly twenty yards that way." She pointed the same direction Arjenie had. "That puts him out back on the deck, I think."

Arjenie shook her head. "I can't tell that much."

"You haven't had sex with Benedict yet."

"Well . . . no."

"The first time you have sex, it cements the bond. You'll know where the other one is a lot more clearly than you do now. And for a few days you'll have to stay very close to each other. For me and Rule it was forty-seven feet." She had, of course, measured. "That was just the first couple days. The bond relaxes with time, but at first you have to stay very close."

Arjenie's eyes widened. "You mean that the bond isn't cemented yet?"

"No. No, I used the wrong word. The mate bond's permanent from the get-go. Sex strengthens it, but if you were somehow stubborn and strong-willed enough to avoid getting naked with Benedict for the next thirty years, you'd still be bound to him. Also insane from frustration."

A smile flickered over Arjenie's mouth. "I can't imagine going thirty years without . . . never mind. The most important thing I needed to ask is how to remove the bond."

"You can't."

"There must be a way. Something, maybe, that's painful? Or dangerous? Or even forbidden?"

Lily shook her head. "The only thing that ends the bond is death. I know this for a fact, Arjenie. If there were some way to remove it, I'd have tried it back when the bond was new." Her smile was wry. "And messed up my life big-time, but I didn't know that then. When the bond first hit, I did not think it was a good thing."

Arjenie grimaced. "Neither did Benedict."

"Would you expect him to, after losing Claire like . . . oh, shit," she said when she saw the look on Arjenie's face. She'd just blown it on Benedict's behalf a second time. "He didn't tell you about Claire."

"No." Arjenie leaned forward. "But you will, won't you?"

THIRTY-THREE

THE night air was cool and silky. Stars spattered the darkness overhead as if some celestial dog had gone swimming in them, then shaken himself dry. The upper deck was still warm from the day's heat. It felt good beneath Benedict's bare feet.

His brother had joined him out here for a while. He and Rule hadn't talked beyond exchanging basic information: Arjenie was talking with Lily. Yes, Benedict had followed her when she went for a walk to get her head straight. It was his duty to keep track of her. She'd walked slowly along the road for about a mile, then sat in the grass of the meeting field. She'd sat there for about half an hour, then returned. She hadn't limped. She hadn't seemed overwhelmed by emotion. She'd seemed to be doing just what she'd said she needed to do. Thinking.

A couple minutes ago, Rule had gone back inside. Those weren't his footsteps coming up behind Benedict now.

"I guess I do have a Benedict-locating sense now. I found you."

He turned slowly. "Did Lily answer your questions?"

Her nod was brief. He couldn't see her face well. The

moon was up, but she stood beneath the patchy shade of the big eucalyptus tree. Her hair was as loud and boisterous as ever. He just wasn't sure what it was shouting about.

"You will not do it," she told him.

He blinked. "What?"

She came closer and jabbed a finger at him. She poked him in the chest with it. "There is only one way to remove a mate bond, *and you will not do that*! I want your word. Right now."

"What did Lily tell you?" he demanded.

"That there's only one way to break a mate bond. Death. When I added that to what she said about Claire—"

"She told you about Claire?" *Damn meddling female!*

"*You* should have told me." She poked him again. "Lily thought you *had*. She assumed you had the sense God gave a goose." Poke. "She didn't realize that you are such a complete *guy*!"

"You're angry." In the past two days she'd been captured, scared, worried, aroused, curious, delighted, hungry, annoyed, and frustrated. She hadn't been angry. Not until now. "Really angry."

"Pissed! I am pissed! When you tell someone that you're romantically bound together—and I don't care how unconventional that binding is!—you have to tell them about it if the last person you were bound to died and *you* almost died of grief." She stopped poking to seize his arms, both of his arms, as if she was going to shake him. As if she could have. "I want your promise. Now."

"I know you can't tolerate being physically held against your will. The bond is physical. I don't want you to be frantic because—"

She put her fingers on his lips. Just rested them there. "Shut up, Benedict. Shut up and promise."

He smiled. Her fingers didn't prevent that, but he gently removed them from his mouth anyway. "All right. I promise I won't kill myself." Not directly, at least. He kissed the fingers he was holding.

He knew her pulse stuttered. He heard it, smelled it in the renewed wash of her scent. Her voice didn't. "Or do stupid, reckless things that lead to your death."

His Chosen was much too bright sometimes. "I can't promise to never risk myself." Tenderly he brushed her fingers back from her palm so he could kiss that, too. "Sometimes there's a need for risk."

"Then promise you'll be as careful with yourself as you would be with any of your men."

"Are we bargaining?" He tickled her palm with the tip of his tongue.

"Yes."

"Then you must be prepared to offer me something in return."

Her sudden smile was pure pixie. Mischief with a hint of sex. "Sure. I'll stop yelling at you. About this, anyway. I don't promise I'll never yell at you. I've got a feeling you'll need it from time to time."

She was talking about the future. About their future, as if it were settled and agreed upon that they would be together. As if she'd accepted the mate bond.

The hard crust of time moved inside him—calcified years shifting, shifting, threatening to break apart under the assault of this new flood of feeling. He didn't move. Didn't breathe. Didn't allow his fingers to tighten on the hand he held. He was too strong. He could crush it, could quite literally crush her bones if he gripped too hard. He could hurt her.

He wouldn't. Easier to stop breathing than to take that chance. But she wanted his promise, didn't she? To give her that, he needed air.

Benedict's chest heaved. The breath he drew was ragged. He felt it all the way down. "All right. But you have to promise the same. That you'll be as careful with yourself as you would be with—with any other who you were responsible for."

Her face was still and solemn, her eyes large. It was too dark to see their beautiful ocean color, yet he could feel the ocean in them washing over him. Her voice was quiet. "I do so vow."

Those were the right words. The perfect words. Were they Wiccan? Part of some sidhe ritual? It didn't matter. He gave them back to her. "And I, too, do so vow."

She smiled—deep, secret, mysterious. And reached up to cup his face in her hands. "Now you're supposed to kiss me. I'd do it myself, but I can't go up on tiptoe, so—"

Benedict was no fool. He followed instructions.

Her arms went around him tightly. Her mouth was sweet and her scent flooded him, as if even his pores had opened to absorb it. He stroked her back, her butt, running his hands up and down, savoring the feel of her. She shivered.

Urgency bit. He tried to go slow. He couldn't. The sweetness of her mouth deserved an hour or two to appreciate, but already he was urging her deeper into the shadows beneath the tree. He put his back to the smooth trunk of the old eucalyptus and tunneled his fingers into the insane mass of her hair, tipping her head so he could kiss and suck on her neck.

She liked that. Her body moved in a slow undulation. When she hummed down low in her throat, he felt the vibration in his lips. Her hands dug in at his waist and he shuddered and straightened and reached for the hem of her T-shirt.

"Wait, wait—can they see from the house? I can't see the house from here, but—"

"They can't see." Neither could the guards. He'd chosen this spot because he knew it was hidden from view.

"You're shaking."

"I thought you wouldn't like it if I ripped your clothes. I'm trying not to."

"Oh. Good. I've thought about this, and I think you need to court me."

"Okay." He pulled the T-shirt off over her head. This excited her hair.

"That isn't what I—oh!"

He'd fastened his mouth on one nipple without waiting to remove her bra. This was stupid because he wanted her bra gone. Only he'd have to stop in order to remove it, and—

"Benedict." Her voice was breathy.

He made a noise low in his throat and reluctantly released her nipple. "I'm sorry. I know how to go slow. I'd love to go slow, but I don't think I can right now. If you—"

"Pay attention." Her hands dived for his waistband. She unsnapped his jeans. "I'm not sure how we're going to do this out here, but I do *not* want you to go slow. I'm pretty sure I'd go insane if you tried." Carefully she eased the zipper down.

He flung back his head and gritted his teeth and thanked God she was careful. He wasn't wearing underwear. "Like this," he said thickly, and as quickly as possible he stripped off her jeans and panties, cupped her bottom in his hands, and lifted her off her feet. "We do it like this."

Her legs circled his waist. "Yes," she whispered, nuzzling his neck. He probed and found her wet and ready and just as he was about to thrust inside, she thrust forward, and they were joined.

He wanted to stay there forever. His body had other plans. So did she. She bit his neck and he growled and began to move, using the trunk to hold his upper body steady as his hips thrust and his hands held her to him.

It wasn't slow. It was more like grabbing on to a high-speed train headed straight for the edge of a cliff—if riding a train could flood every neuron in your body with need and pleasure so demanding you had no choice but to hold on, hold on . . .

Until she bucked against him, crying out. And he could leap off that cliff after her.

His legs buckled. He turned that into a controlled slide, lowering the two of them to the ground. His chest heaved. Her face was buried in the side of his neck, her hair spilling over his shoulder and chest.

Benedict stroked that hair. His hand still trembled, but for a different reason.

"Wow," she whispered into his skin, then lifted her head. "You've got such big hands." Her voice was soft and dreamy. "I never knew that was possible, what we just did. Such big hands."

Her face was a pale oval in the darkness. His hands smelled like her now. So did his body. His heart still thudded strongly in his chest, its earlier gallop slowed to a canter . . . and at peace. He smoothed her hair back from her face. "If I live another hundred years, this moment will remain clear and vivid for me."

She didn't say anything, but she smiled.

"What kind of flowers do you like?"

"What?"

"You want to be courted. I need to know . . ." He stiffened, his head turning.

"What is it?"

She hadn't heard, of course. "My father. No, don't panic, he's not coming here. Shh." He listened.

Silence was not Arjenie's strong point. Mostly she managed it only when a magical binding would not allow her to speak. But she distracted herself from talking by grabbing frantically for her jeans.

But as Benedict had told her, Isen wasn't approaching. He stood at the back door of the house and spoke softly, knowing Benedict could hear. First he apologized for the interruption, then he explained it.

Benedict sighed. "Seabourne's back."

Arjenie quit trying to wiggle into her jeans without standing up. "What did he find out?"

"Not what we wanted him to." Benedict hated having to tell her. "He couldn't find your sister. The guest cottage behind Friar's house is empty."

THIRTY-FOUR

ARJENIE had told Benedict that sex didn't fluster her. That was mostly true, but it occurred to her as she put various pieces of clothes back where they belonged that everyone in that house would be able to smell what she'd just been up to. That was a level of sharing she was not used to.

Everyone but one. Cynna had left, but as soon as Arjenie and Benedict went back inside, Lily and Rule emerged from the bedroom wing. She wore the man's shirt she'd had on earlier with a pair of wrinkled slacks. And, of course, her sling.

Isen looked at Lily and shook his head. "You did not hear Seabourne return."

"No, but Rule did."

Isen bent a look on his younger son. "I had hoped Lily would sleep."

"So had I," Rule said dryly.

"I will. Just not yet." Lily turned a wide-awake look on Cullen and began asking quick, to-the-point questions.

Arjenie paid anxious attention to his replies, but part of her noted that, in a room brimming with really bright alpha males, Lily was still somehow in charge. At least, she considered herself in charge—maybe not of the people, but of the questioning—and no one disputed her assumption.

That was deeply interesting, but she couldn't think about it now. She sat beside Benedict on one of the couches while Cullen explained what he'd seen, done, and smelled.

Apparently Cullen had been studying Friar's wards off and on for some time. He knew about the weak spot Arjenie had used, and that's where he'd crossed, too, though his method was different. It involved him being able to see the wards and manipulate them directly, which was a very neat trick. He'd arranged to reach the little cabin unseen by having Danny intentionally set off the wards some distance away, drawing Friar's soldier wannabes away.

He was good with locks, he said, so when Dya didn't respond to his soft call at her window, he'd gone inside the cabin. She wasn't there. He didn't find her clothes or other items that might have belonged to her . . . but her scent was all over the place. A clearly nonhuman scent. He'd Changed to better register it.

The lupi all perked up as if that was important. What did she smell like?

Rather like an otter might if you added cloves and subtracted fur. Also oily, he said. Oily like olive oil, with its bright green notes, though she was definitely a meat-eater.

No, he didn't smell spilled blood. Nor did he see any.

Benedict squeezed Arjenie's hand gently when he said that.

Cullen had tried to track Dya's scent. The strongest scent trail, he said, seemed to head to Friar's house, but he couldn't follow it far without being seen. He did not find a recent scent trail leading away from the cabin in any other direction. He'd waited in the cabin for an hour, hoping she might return. But when Danny set off the wards again as planned, he'd had to leave while he had the chance.

Lily drummed her fingers on her leg. "The obvious assumption is that Friar moved her into his house. Sometimes the obvious is accurate. There was no sign of foul play." She looked at Arjenie when she said that. "We've no reason to believe she's been harmed."

Arjenie swallowed. She couldn't even nod. The stupid

binding wouldn't let her agree with the fact that her sister existed.

"That's the obvious assumption," Isen agreed, "and it may be what's happened. However, there's information you lack. I've had Friar's place watched for several months." He looked at his older son. "Benedict?"

"Originally," Benedict rumbled in his beautiful, deep voice, "we simply watched from the road to keep track of who came and went, particularly on nights when he held Humans First meetings there. It pays to know who your enemies are. When I looked over the lists my men kept, however, I noticed some anomalies. That's when we decided to keep a closer watch." He glanced at Arjenie. "A decision that led to my marking the location of the wards three nights ago."

"What anomalies?" Lily asked.

"Twice someone left Friar's place who hadn't been seen arriving. Once one of his lieutenants arrived—and was never seen to leave again, though he later showed up in Sacramento. It might be that my men screwed up either in observing or in recording what they saw. Or it might be they were right."

Rule spoke slowly. "You think he has some secret means of egress." He gave his father a hard look. "I wasn't told about these anomalies. About Friar being watched, yes—"

"Which you hadn't mentioned to me," Lily said.

"Which," Isen said, "is one reason I didn't tell Rule about the anomalies. He dislikes withholding information from you. Also, it seemed vaguely ridiculous. Why would Friar be sneaking people in and out through the wilderness? We were curious, so Benedict set additional watchers. We've had men observing Friar's neighbors as well and the dirt road at the rear of the property."

"Last week, it happened again," Benedict said. "Paul Chittenden left Friar's house with Friar shortly before ten P.M. on a Tuesday. He was not seen to have ever arrived at Friar's. It's clearly possible to come and go from Friar's without being seen—it's rough country, with plenty of opportunities to hide. But you must make an effort to go unseen. Why would Chittenden enter in great stealth, then leave openly with Friar?"

"What are you suggesting?" Lily asked, frowning. "That he's got some sort of secret tunnel?"

"Yes."

"You're kidding." She frowned harder. "You're not kidding."

"I consider it one possibility. A somewhat remote one, I thought, until now." He paused. "*She* has an affinity for underground places. Under some of *her* names, she was a goddess whose worshipers built altars to her in caves."

Lily had a funny look on her face, as if she'd bitten into something nasty and wanted to spit it out. And couldn't. "But we're talking about Friar. *She's* not here, so whether he's hanging out aboveground or below wouldn't affect *her*."

Isen spoke gently. "But *she* affects those with whom she has contact."

"She makes them start burrowing in the ground like moles?"

"The Azá did, didn't they?"

"At the end, yes—because the node was *in* a cave. Plus they didn't want to be seen opening a hellgate. Plus they had that whole religious fanatic thing going, so—"

"Her agents may have solid, rational reasons for operating beneath the earth. That doesn't mean they weren't influenced by *her*."

Rule spoke. "If Friar has some sort of underground passage, we need to know about it, and we need to know why—because I'm betting that, *her* influence aside, he'd have a solid, rational reason. Something that advances his goals. We don't know what those goals are." He glanced at Lily. "The specific ones, that is. His general goal involves destroying us and probably the Gifted and others of the Blood."

All lupi? Everyone of the Blood, and all of the Gifted? That was a big step off a steep cliff. Arjenie had trouble getting her mind around that level of megalomania and malice.

"You're right that we need to know more," Lily said. "I've got some ideas about how to go about that, starting tomorrow. Arjenie, we could use your skills, if you're willing to help."

"Yes," she said quickly. If it helped them find Dya, helped

Dya, she'd do it. "That is—are you talking about my research skills, or my sneaking skills?"

Lily smiled. "Research, for now. Here's what I have in mind."

BY the time they broke up it was after one A.M. Arjenie was equal parts tired, worried, exhilarated, scared, confused . . . and eager to dive into what she knew best. *This is what I need*, she thought as Benedict escorted her to her bedroom. A day spent with facts, with her computer, would give her space to let some of this . . . this emotional overload . . . settle. She had plenty of ideas for how to find out some of the things they needed to know, and she had access to some kick-ass databases.

"This meeting you were talking about," she said as they stopped outside her room. "It's a big deal, I guess, if you and Rule have to spend tomorrow getting ready for it instead of investigating Friar."

Benedict seemed abstracted. A frown lingered between his eyebrows as if it had drifted there awhile back without him noticing. "Isen has called an All-Clan. That's a meeting of all lupi clans. Traditionally, we hold an All-Clan every decade or two. We aren't due for one yet, but last year when the Great Bitch became active in the world again, Isen called for one."

"But the meeting day after tomorrow isn't an All-Clan, is it?"

"No. The meeting on Monday is between the Lu Nuncios of the dominant North American clans. Our neighbors, in a sense. If we can't persuade our neighbors of the need for an All-clan, we're unlikely to get one."

"Don't they see the need? If there's an Old One who wants to destroy you, surely they see the need to act together."

"There's suspicion of Nokolai because of Rule's unexpected elevation to Leidolf Rho. It creates a severe power imbalance. Nokolai and Leidolf are arguably the two most powerful clans, and have long been enemies. Think of how it would have looked to the rest of the world if, at the end of the Cold War when the USSR collapsed, the U.S. vice president suddenly became the Russian prime minister."

"China would have freaked. Are some of the clans freaking?"

"A few. Even some of those who have long been friends of Nokolai are uneasy."

"How many clans are there?"

"Twenty-four altogether. Eleven dominants, seven of them in North America—Nokolai, Leidolf, Ybirra, Szøs, Etorri, Wythe, and Kyffin. Kyffin is subordinate to Nokolai for a year and a day, which means until mid-November, so they'll do as we bid. But they're a dominant, so their Lu Nuncio must be included in the circle."

Arjenie had a feeling she didn't use the word *dominant* quite the same way he was, but she let that go for now. That slight frown clung to his face as if he'd carried some worry for so long he'd forgotten how to stop. "You need to stop thinking for a while." She took his hand. "Where do you sleep?"

Now, that was a real, intentional frown—brows drawn down, his attention suddenly focused like a laser. "I have a place up on Little Sister. When I'm down here, I usually stay at the bunkhouse with my men."

She was going to have to lead him by the hand, wasn't she? "Where do you want to sleep tonight?"

"I don't want to put pressure on you."

"I'm guessing you don't want to insult me, either." She gestured with her free hand. "I don't know what this mate bond means to you. I don't know what it means to me. I don't know what it's going to mean, or what I'm going to do. I do know we've got a problem if you don't want to sleep with me." She looked at him sternly. "And I'm talking sleep, not just sex. Though *just* is a silly word to use for what we did up against that tree."

His eyes kindled a smile that spread everywhere, smoothing his forehead, tipping his lips up, relaxing his shoulders. He smiled down at her like she'd just fixed world hunger . . . while begetting another type of hunger. He stroked her cheek, not saying a word. Smiling.

She smiled back. She might have a huge list of things she didn't understand, but knew one thing quite clearly: mate bond or no mate bond, she was in love.

Arjenie tugged her lover into her room. And shut the door.

THIRTY-FIVE

"YOU'RE sure about this." Lily clicked her seat belt in place.

Cynna's seat belt barely fit around her. She barely fit behind the steering wheel. "I asked Nettie months ago about driving. She told me not to hit anything and to pull over if I go into labor."

"Labor." Lily took a deep breath. "I may hyperventilate."

Cynna chuckled. "Lily, pregnant women drive all the time."

"Okay. I just feel like I should be the one . . ."

"Driving? In charge?" Cynna started the engine and put the car—Rule's Mercedes—in gear. "This is not news."

"I'm still in charge."

"Keep telling yourself that. You know how to use the GPS thingee?"

"Sure. I sent the car the directions from Googlemaps. You just have to download it." Lily leaned forward and pushed the "i" button. They were headed for Del Cielo, a tiny little mountain town. The quickest way there from Clanhome involved twisty blacktop roads. Lily had Googled their route earlier.

"That is crazy cool," Cynna announced. "Are you going to call Mariah Friar and let her know we're coming?"

"I did that, too." Lily pulled her laptop onto her lap and

opened it. "She's waiting for us." She could do a lot of things one-handed, like tapping out instructions for the computer. It was disconcerting, though, how often she started to do something and discovered she couldn't. Or had to do it in a weird-ass, annoying way.

Like getting dressed. Forget about wearing a jacket or her shoulder rig. The weapon she couldn't shoot worth a damn left-handed was in her purse. But she could do most of the rest of it herself, except for her bra and putting her bad arm through the sleeve of a shirt. For today she was skipping the bra and wearing another of Rule's shirts to conceal that omission. Rule had threaded her arm into the shirt's sleeve for her.

Showers were out. Washing her hair by herself was out. She could brush her teeth left-handed, but first she had to get the toothpaste on the toothbrush. She did still have a right hand, so she managed that, but she had to do it differently.

Lily had experienced some of this last year, but it had been her left shoulder, not her right, and the damage hadn't been nearly as bad. Maybe what was getting to her was not knowing how much function she'd regain.

With one finger Lily tapped in her password and waited for the computer to offer her the file she wanted. *Everything* had to be done differently, and she kept forgetting to allow for that. Last night, when she decided to send Jeff to D.C. with a written report, she'd forgotten that she couldn't type it. She ended up dictating it to Cynna. . . . who was acting as her chauffeur as well. Lily could drive one-handed, but she had to admit that would be stupid. Especially since she'd taken half a pain pill earlier, before Nettie arrived.

Nettie would be cleaning Lily's wound and changing the dressing on it every morning for a week or so. Having experienced that in the hospital, Lily hadn't tried to go without some kind of chemical buffer.

Lily glanced in the side mirror. They were being tailed by a white sedan slightly newer than Lily's personal vehicle. She knew both the men in the car. Rule had insisted on guards. Lily considered an attack highly unlikely—Friar would have to be able to track her magically, and tracking a moving target was extremely hard if you weren't a Finder. So, she was told, was Listening; chances were Friar couldn't eavesdrop on them in motion. To be sure, Cullen had given her a charm that was supposed to be putting out magical static.

So she had the charm and the guards for just in case. She'd told Rule he could guard her, after all, and Cynna would be with her. Cynna was trained and armed, but she was also pregnant—and potentially a target. They didn't know what Friar knew and what he didn't. They didn't know how he chose his targets, whether he was guided by *her* or had some other metric.

Rule couldn't do the guarding himself. He and Benedict and Isen were working on details for tomorrow's meeting. Cullen was busy making charms for that meeting. And Arjenie was doing what she did best: research.

"So what are you hoping to learn from Mariah Friar about her dad?" Cynna asked.

"First, if she had any inkling about his clairaudience. Second, dates." Lily skimmed the report she'd filed last April, looking for the transcript of her interview with Friar's estranged daughter. "We might get more, but I'm hoping for dates. Specifically, the date when Friar suddenly acquired shields. Mariah said he was gone for a while, then bam! When he turned up again he had these handy-dandy shields. Or maybe it's a single shield. I didn't get a date from her at the time." Should have. Didn't think of it.

"And Mariah knows about shields because . . . ?"

"I didn't tell you about that?" Cynna had been gone when Lily met Mariah Friar in the course of an investigation. Way gone. She'd been kidnapped into another realm. "Mariah's an empath. Completely unblocked."

"Aw . . . that's rough. Nearly as bad as having Friar for a father."

True. "It's important to her to keep her Gift secret."

"Sure, I can see that. What will the date Friar got shielded tell us?"

"It suggests that's when *she* recruited him. It's probably when he became a Listener, too. If he had a clairaudience Gift before that, Mariah wasn't aware of it. I think she would have been, considering her Gift. She was wary of him, kept track of him until she moved out."

"You can't turn a null into a Gifted."

"We don't know what an Old One can do."

Cynna was silent a moment. "You think Friar left our realm to go see *her*?"

"I sure as hell hope he left our realm. I'd hate to think someone here on Earth could turn a null or a near-null into the strongest Listener on the planet."

"Me, too. But what about Dya? How does she fit? The G.B.—"

"G.B.?"

"Great Bitch. *She* doesn't hold that contract Dya is bound by. Some elf bigwig does."

"Sidhe. We don't know if he's an elf, just that he's a sidhe lord of some sort." Lily had tried to ask Arjenie more questions about Dya's lord this morning . . . and gotten nothing. *Nada*. Zilch. It was intensely frustrating. "So maybe Friar wasn't contacted by the Great Bitch directly. Maybe this mysterious sidhe lord showed up here and made him an offer he couldn't refuse. Sidhe lords can cross into our realm. I'm guessing one of them could take Friar traveling with him if he wanted to."

"You think this sidhe lord is hooked up with *her* and brought Friar to *her*?"

"Maybe." This morning Lily wasn't sure of her earlier reasoning. Was the fact that Friar couldn't Listen at Clan-home reason enough to implicate the Great Bitch? There could be other explanations. Just because she couldn't come up with one didn't mean it didn't exist. She couldn't explain color televisions, either. Or how her own Gift worked.

TURN RIGHT AT THE NEXT INTERSECTION, an automated voice said.

"You think it knows what it's talking about?" Cynna said, slowing as they approached a stop sign marking an intersection with another winding mountain road.

"Yes. Ah . . . can I ask you something?"

"When people say that, they always mean 'ask something personal.' But sure. Shoot."

"There's a mental component to spellcasting, right?"

"Of course. You know that."

"What I was wondering . . . is there an emotional component, too?"

Cynna turned onto the other road and gave Lily a look she couldn't read. "You can't separate mental and emotional into neat little boxes. Emotions affect what you think. What you think affects your emotions. It's all tied together."

"So guilt might interfere with you casting a spell?"

"Maybe you should tell me what you really want to know."

Lily looked down and shut her laptop. "I, uh, dreamed about Helen last night."

"The nutty telepath who tried to open the hellgate?"

"Yeah." The investigation that led to Helen and the Azá and Lily's first encounter with both Rule and the Great Bitch had happened before Lily met Cynna, but Cynna knew the basics. "I've been dreaming about her lately, generally after a session with Sam. I dreamed about her last night, after mindspeaking Arjenie, and I couldn't mindspeak at all this morning."

"You feel guilty for killing Helen."

"No. I didn't have a lot of choice about that—not unless I was willing to let her kill me, Rule, and a bunch of other people, then let a godawful lot of demons into our world." Lily bent and put the laptop on the floor. It was awkward to do it one-handed. Everything was awkward. Especially this conversation. "Never mind."

"Uh-uh. You don't get to stop now. Quit thinking so much. When you dreamed about Helen, what did you feel?"

"While I was dreaming?" Lily flashed back to the dream. "Rage. I wanted her dead. She was going to kill Rule. She'd killed his brother and she was going to kill him, and I wanted her dead."

"You didn't feel guilty in the dream?"

"No." She'd felt angry. Killing mad. She wasn't sure anymore if she'd felt that way last year when she actually killed Helen. Was the dream making her face a truth she didn't like? Or had it distorted the truth, replacing her real memory with a dream version?

"How about after you woke up? How did you feel then?"

She'd felt the way she always did after a Helen dream. Drained. Tainted. Ugly. "Not good. Not angry. More like . . . smeared."

"Well, guilt can create blocks. Most empaths who're blocked . . . it isn't just self-protection, or they'd all be blocked. It's guilt. But guilt can affect anyone, not just empaths. Some Gifted—especially those who were raised in a hellfire and brimstone theology—are never able to cast a spell. It makes them feel unclean. The feeling keeps them blocked."

"I'm blocked? I'll never be able to do it?"

"No, you've already done it, and more than once! Lily, you're used to going at something you want to learn head-on. This isn't a head-on kind of learning. It's more circling back at something over and over until you get it."

"I don't know how to do that kind of learning." Staring at a candle flame to find Sam there? That wasn't her.

Cynna snorted. "It's what you do every day. Investigations are all about circling in on a perp. Investigate mindspeech."

But mindspeech wasn't the perp. She was.

Lily turned that thought over in her mind. It felt right. It gave her the same kind of click she got when an investigation suddenly made sense, when she knew she was on the right track. She didn't think she was guilty. She didn't feel guilty. But some part of her was obscuring the trail, hiding things from the rest of her.

She'd track it down. Cynna was right—that's what she did. "You're pretty smart."

"This is true."

Lily looked at her friend's smiling, decorated face. "Smug, too."

"Pregnant women get to do smug. It's part of the package, compensation for having our bladders reduced to the size of a pea. Speaking of which . . ."

"You need to go already? We just left!"

"Size of a pea," Cynna said firmly, and pulled into a gas station on the outskirts of Del Cielo. Mariah Friar's hometown.

"YOU'RE sure about this." Rule leaned over Arjenie's shoulder to look at the computer screen.

He'd spent some time with Toby early that morning, then

sent the boy off to lessons. For now, Harold Spanner would homeschool him. Harold had taught Rule at one time, and he had a student already—Mike Rose's son, Sean. Toby would spend the night with Sean tonight . . . and Rule already missed him. It was foolish, but he'd gotten used to having Toby with him every morning and evening. But with everything that was going on, it was simpler for Toby to stay with a friend. This way Rule didn't have to keep sending Toby out of the room when they discussed things the boy shouldn't hear.

He and Benedict had been going over security details for the meeting when Isen summoned them to his study, where Arjenie was ensconced with her computer.

"Not at all," Arjenie answered. "Well, I'm sure that Friar had his old swimming pool taken out and a new one put in last year. The permits for that are clear. I'm also sure Friar made some odd purchases about that time and did his best to hide them, using a dummy corporation. I'm not sure all of that adds up to some underground tunnel or hidey-hole, but it's suggestive."

Rule looked over Arjenie's head at Benedict, who stood on her other side. Their eyes met. "Can you show me those purchases?"

"Okay. What I've got is a single invoice, though. I, uh, sort of snuck in someone's back door to find it."

"Hacked in?"

"Hacking is *illegal*. I simply know how to find back doors sometimes . . . and some people don't have much protection." Her fingers flew over the keyboard. A new screen popped up. "Here it is."

The invoice didn't tell Rule a great deal. Some of the materials could have been for a swimming pool—there was a lot of cement—while others clearly weren't. "I'll have Jimmy look at this. He's a contractor," he added to Arjenie. "He'll be able to give us an idea of what those steel beams might be used for."

Isen stood behind Arjenie, smiling. "She does good work, doesn't she? Did you notice the name of Friar's dummy corporation?"

"Why?"

"Hernando, Hyde, and Way." His father paused, his eyebrows wagging. "You don't get it?"

"No, I don't recognize . . ." Rule's voice trailed off when his father hummed a few bars from an old song. "You've got to be kidding."

Isen's smile split his beard like a knife. "Our enemy has a sense of humor. He named his dummy corporation after 'Hernando's Hideaway.' "

"YOU were really good with Mariah," Lily said, closing the door and reaching for her seat belt. "She liked you."

Cynna patted her belly. "The little rider makes friends for me everywhere. Plus it turned out we had a lot in common." She drew the seat belt back around her. "We head into the city now, right?"

"Right." Lily's arm hurt way more than she thought it should. She felt like crap. She did her best to ignore it.

"You going to take a pain pill? You look like you need one."

"Not yet. They make me sleepy. I need to stay awake."

"You also need to not keel over. I can't help if you keel over."

"I'll be okay. I didn't know you were a pole dancer back in your young-and-wild days."

Cynna chuckled. "Hey, where I grew up, pole dancing was considered a great job, as long as you didn't do it butt-naked. Butt-naked would be tacky, but as long as you had that G-string you were cool."

"Hmm." Lily dug out her iPhone. "I guess you have that in common with Cullen, too. He wore a G-string when he was dancing for a living. Not that he considers 'naked' to have any connection to 'tacky.' "

"With a body like that, why would he? Besides, lupi don't have the body issues we do."

"No kidding." Lily couldn't make notes, but she needed to make a record of the interview, so she used the "record" feature on her phone. "Interview with Mariah Friar on September twenty-fifth. Subject was cooperative when questioned about her previous report concerning the unexplained absence of her father, Robert Friar, four years ago. At the time in question, subject was sixteen and was living with her father, who was gone from their shared residence from March thirteenth until March thirty-first of that year. Subject was told of his planned departure the night before he left. She was not told where he was going or when he would return, which was contrary to Friar's usual habit.

"Subject received no explanation for this absence. Upon Friar's return, subject questioned him about it. He became angry and she desisted. Subject arrived at these dates through reference to an old diary she kept at that time. She allowed me to look at it to confirm the dates, but she did not wish to release it to me."

"Can't blame her for that," Cynna said.

Lily shot her a "hush" look. "Subject is convinced that, prior to this absence, her father did not possess significant magical abilities, and believes he was entirely unGifted. After his return, however, he possessed a shield or shields. Ah—due to the nature of subject's Gift, Robert Friar's new ability to shield was immediately apparent to her." Lily had been careful not to mention the nature of Mariah's Gift in official documents during her earlier investigation. She wasn't sure if today's oral notes would make it into an official report, but she wasn't taking any chances.

"Subject was unaware of the nature of Robert Friar's magical abilities, if any, aside from the shield or shields," she concluded. "When it was suggested that those abilities might include clairaudience, however, she remembered events from that period in her life which seemed to support this possibility." Lily touched the "end" button and paused before putting her phone up. "Anything you can think of that I should add?"

"Subject is one brave chick," Cynna said promptly. "Subject's father is one sicko bastard."

"True, but not appropriate for a report." Lily bent to stuff her phone back in her purse's outside pocket. Bending hurt her arm. Everything hurt her damned arm. The purse was a problem, too. She needed it, but she had to wear it over her good arm, which hampered her. She could try using a fanny pack, but aside from the ugly factor, they didn't hold much. Like her gun.

Not that she could shoot worth a damn left-handed. Maybe she should learn. "What else don't I know about your wild and woolly youth?"

"All sorts of things. Like the time Abel arrested me."

"Abel Karonski? He *arrested* you?"

"Yes, and no, I'm not telling—not until you tell me about this Cody Beck dude you're going to see after you talk to the task force dude."

"Why did you ask me that?" Lily demanded. "Who told you about Cody?"

"I know all, see all—"

"No, you don't."

Cynna grinned. "Maybe not, but you made a point of telling Rule you'd be tipping Beck off personally. You didn't tell him the name of the task force dude you're meeting with, but you told him Beck's name in such a careful, casual way. Then there was the way he looked at you when you told him, as if—"

"That is deeply annoying."

"Yeah, but you still want to know why Abel arrested me, so talk. Who's Beck?"

"A good cop. And, yes, we had a thing years ago. But it's the first part that counts."

"That was a ridiculously skinny spilling of the beans. Don't think you're getting away with it, but first tell me why you're tipping Beck off when you're also passing that fat file to Task Force Dude."

Lily drummed her fingers, hunting words for what was mostly a hunch, stringing together an assortment of conjectures.

The meet she'd set up with the DEA component of the task force wasn't hunch. She'd take Mark Burke to lunch and tell him about a tip she had from a reliable informant, and she'd give him a dossier on Friar and his chief lieutenants. Because once Lily learned what Arjenie's sister could do, she'd thought of the new, untraceable date rape drug with a magical component. The drug they called Do Me.

Friar was spending a lot of money setting up Humans First. The militia he'd co-opted, for example. Rule doubted they were working for free. Friar and his lieutenants did a lot of traveling, too. He had money, sure, but he was no Bill Gates. Maybe he needed deeper pockets. Maybe he got a kick out of selling Do Me to finance his operation.

To rescue Dya, they needed a reason to search Friar's properties. Suspicion of the manufacture and distribution of a banned substance would do the trick, but they needed evidence, something to take to a judge.

Lily didn't have that. She was on the multidepartmental task force coordinating the efforts of various agencies, but the actual investigating was done by the DEA and by local law enforcement . . . like the San Diego County Sheriff's Office. Where Cody Beck was a deputy.

"The longer you're silent, the more you get my imagination going," Cynna said. "Like maybe you don't trust Task Force Dude."

"No, Burke seems like a good cop," Lily said. "I think he's committed to finding and stopping whoever's making Do Me, but . . . I don't know. He's a careful sort, and he's overworked, and I can't give him a solid link between Friar and Do Me. That's what I want him to find. I think he'll check out my tip, but if he doesn't find something pretty fast to hold his interest, it'll go on the back burner."

"He'll listen, but he'll grain-of-salt it. Beck's your backup plan because he'll believe you."

"Pretty much, yeah." She grinned suddenly. "Cody and I do have that history you're so curious about. He'll take what I say seriously."

"Speaking of history, tell me about—"

"Just a sec." Lily's phone had beeped. That meant a text message, which she didn't usually check immediately. But she didn't object to an interruption right now, so she bent and retrieved her phone.

It didn't take long to read. "Son of a bitch."

"What?" Then Cynna's phone dinged.

"That will be a message from Croft," Lily said. "Looks like Jeff made it in to see Croft okay. The MCD is operating under Code 300 until further notice."

THE next time Rule was summoned to Isen's office, Cullen went with him. He'd just finished the charms they needed for tomorrow—and, being Cullen, he was curious.

Benedict was already there, leaning over Arjenie's shoulder. "Good," he said. "Take a look."

Arjenie began explaining before Rule reached her. "I've

been running searches of several databases using Friar's name and those of his key people. Breck's popped up because Paul Chittenden purchased it last year."

"Friar's West Coast lieutenant." Rule peered at the screen, which showed another invoice. This one showed that Breck's Disposal had purchased a high-end security system last April.

"Now, Breck's is a pretty small outfit." She brought up another window, which showed a tax return. "They grossed a couple hundred thousand last year, and, as you can see, they actually had a net loss. So it seemed odd for them to buy such an expensive security system. It took some digging, but I found the address where that system was delivered." The next window she clicked on showed an aerial map. "Right there." She pointed at the red marker Googlemaps put at the address. "It's a small house in the middle of nowhere. According to county records, that house is unoccupied . . . but it's the only structure on the western edge of the mountain bordering Friar's property. Or hill," she added. "I don't know if you call that a mountain or a hill."

"First clue," Cullen said. "It's in the mountains."

"That makes sense," Arjenie said, "Only the elevation isn't . . ." She glanced up at Benedict, who'd rested one hand on her shoulder. "And that's not relevant."

No, it wasn't. "Good find," Rule said. "It looks like whatever Friar built under the guise of replacing his swimming pool, he's got it wired against intruders."

"So it seems. Naturally, I wondered what Breck's Disposal disposes of. Turns out it's medical waste. And in the past year, they've particularly focused on disposing of unused portions of an intravenously administered MRI contrast agent that, until recently, was used to enhance images in MRI and MRA procedures."

He looked at her blankly.

Patiently she said, "When the government began phasing out the use of gadolinium in MRI imaging agents, it also regulated the disposal of existing stocks of such solutions. *That* is the type of medical waste Breck's has been handling lately."

Gadolinium. The key ingredient in . . . "Gado. The bastard is extracting the gadolinium and using it to make gado."

She nodded and pushed her glasses up. "Yes, I think he must be. The question is, why?"

Rule's eyebrows lifted. "Because gado renders us weak and unable to Change."

"I *know* that. But why does he need it? Um . . ." She looked at Benedict.

He said it for her. "Why does he need gado if he's got Dya to make potions for him?"

Rule thought a moment, then said grimly, "Quantity."

Benedict got it immediately. "If Friar's having Dya make the magical part of that Do Me drug the way Lily was talking about earlier, she probably can't make a large amount of gado, too. Which brings up some interesting questions. Why does he want a large amount of it?"

"And how much might he have?" Rule looked down at Arjenie. "How much gadolinum has he been able to access?"

"I don't know." Her fingers sped over the keyboard again. "But I'll see if I can find out."

THIRTY-SIX

THERE were times when Rule wished his *nadia* wasn't such a damnably stubborn woman.

The two of them rode in the backseat of Isen's seven-year-old Lincoln with Cullen in the middle—a seating arrangement that pleased none of them, but served a purpose. At least there was plenty of room. They'd taken the shiny behemoth today because it possessed useful modifications. Technically the glass was bullet-resistant rather than bulletproof, but it would stop a slug from almost any handgun and most rifles.

Benedict was driving. Arjenie sat in the front seat beside him. Having her at the circle was far from ideal, but with their mate bond so freshly sealed there was little choice. Benedict had wanted her to remain in the car, using her Gift to go unnoticed, but the thick bulletproof glass interfered with her Gift too much.

Not that she was in danger from the other clans, although this particular bonding would come as a shock. No, it was Friar who worried Benedict. He worried Rule. Lily, too, of course, for she wasn't stupid. Just stubborn.

Rule's wolf liked riding in his father's car. It smelled faintly of Isen and more strongly of his big brother and his *nadia*. Cullen's scent was known and comforting; Arjenie's was new, but so overlaid with Benedict's that she seemed familiar already.

Rule the man was less comfortable.

When he had first called for the heirs' circle, he'd asked Lily to attend. Her injury should have changed that, but Ybirra had agreed to the new location only on the condition that the Chosen would still be present. Lily had insisted she could easily—as she put it—stand around symbolically. Reluctantly, Rule had agreed.

But the situation had changed again now that they knew about Friar's clairaudience and his alliance with their great enemy. Lily herself said that while Friar might have had to change his plans when the potion dumped in Nokolai's well didn't work, that didn't mean he didn't have plans. Those might well center on today's meeting.

Yet there she sat between him and Cullen. Rule knew she was needed. Without her, Ybirra would withdraw and there would be no circle. They'd have to begin negotiations all over again.

And in spite of that, this morning he'd tried to talk her out of it. He'd told her that her presence increased his danger. Normally he knew she could act swiftly, but she wasn't normal now. If they were attacked, he'd be focused on her safety, not his own. She'd looked at him for a long moment, then leaned forward and kissed him lightly. "Good try," she'd said. "Help me with this stupid sleeve, will you?"

His stubborn love was currently speaking on her phone with Aaron Gray from the local FBI office. She'd had to hand off her open cases after she was shot. One had gone to Gray—a case involving the theft of gadolinum.

Lily believed Friar was behind that theft. Proving it was the trick.

Whatever Friar was planning, he meant to move on a large scale. Arjenie had made a rough estimate of how much gadolinum might have been extracted from the imaging solution. Add that to what Friar may have obtained through outright theft, and he had enough gadolinum to make upward of four hundred doses of gado.

The problem was that gado had to be administered

through injection. Neither oral nor topical application had any effect. Rule doubted that Friar planned to trap lupi one by one and inject them with gado, but administering it en masse was supposed to be impossible.

But Friar had Dya. Was Arjenie's sister capable of creating a potion that could make gado effective orally? Was that what Friar had tried dumping into Nokolai's well?

Lily had tried asking Arjenie those questions last night. Unfortunately, Arjenie didn't know. According to Lily, Arjenie's lack of knowledge was expressed with a great deal of technical thinking about the difference between potions and other magical agents, with a side excursion into her theory about why gado worked as it did. Lily had claimed it was the tech talk—"like mainlining Cullen," she'd said—that had given her a headache.

Since this headache had arrived after fourteen minutes of mindspeech, just like the last one, Rule thought otherwise. Actually, so did Lily, however much she might like to blame it on something else. Fourteen minutes was probably the limit for how long Lily could tolerate kinspeech.

"All right," Lily said. "Let me know." She disconnected and grimaced. "Frustrating. I'm going to text him some of what I couldn't say."

They didn't know if Friar could Listen now that they'd left Clanhome. Probably not—Rule's mantle should shut him out—but they were watching what they said anyway. That had made for a good deal of silence during the drive.

Once they formed the circle, of course, they wouldn't have to worry. That's why Cullen was here. He would set the circle and act as Gatekeeper. This was usually done by the Rhej of the clan who called for the circle, but everyone knew the Nokolai Rhej was blind and didn't leave Clanhome. They'd accepted Cullen as substitute—with some grumbling, but recognizing necessity. The circle might lack a Rhej to encourage good conduct, but there would be a Lady-touched present. Lily.

Two Lady-touched, actually, but the others didn't know about Arjenie. Rule was rather looking forward to their reaction to the news.

Lily tapped away on her text screen. Benedict slowed for the turn. Nearly there.

One of the conditions Wythe had insisted on was that the circle be held out of doors. This was an old tradition, frequently set aside these days, but it wasn't unreasonable. Wolves dislike small spaces. Meeting outdoors lessened the tension. After some discussion, the others had accepted Rule's suggestion of Los Penasquitos Canyon Reserve.

The Reserve was a crooked arm of wilderness reaching up into San Diego's city boundaries. It was a great spot for a run in human form—even on four legs, now and then, if one slipped in after hours—and was popular with mountain bikers, horseback riders, and dog walkers. But they wouldn't be meeting down in the canyon. They'd hold their circle on top of the mesa overlooking it. No one could sneak up on them on that flat, open stretch of grass dotted with the occasional sage or sumac. Especially with Benedict minding the perimeter.

Plus a few others. Each Lu Nuncio was allowed to bring one guard to act as escort and to secure the circle from without. The exception was Etorri. Rather than one guard, Stephen had brought five. Etorri had been asked to secure the site, and had camped on the mesa last night. Secretly, of course, for the human world had rules against that sort of thing.

There were several entrances to the canyon trails. They would use the one closest to the mesa. It meant a short trek through the parking lot of an apartment complex, followed by a hike up a steep trail. Normally, Lily would have had no trouble with that. Since she was far from normal, Rule had wrung one concession from her: she would allow him to carry her up the worst of it.

"Benedict," Arjenie said suddenly, "I'm pretty sure that someone's following us. That white SUV has been behind us for the last mile at least, and they turned when you did."

Benedict nodded approvingly. "Yes, it has. I'm glad you're paying attention."

"If you're talking about the Hyundai," Lily said, still tapping out her message, "that's Scott, Rule's Leidolf guard."

"Oh." She was disgruntled. "I guess everyone here knew about him."

"I should have told you." Benedict flicked a glance her way. "The others are a short distance behind him. Save for Etorri, of course."

"They, uh, the Etorri are the clan everyone trusts. That's why they got there first. They're sort of holding the ground for everyone else."

"That's right."

"Well, why? You all seem pretty suspicious of each other. Why are they exempt?"

"It's a long story and an old one. "

"You're good at summaries."

Rule heard the smile in his brother's voice. "I'll attempt it. Have you heard of Horatio at the bridge?"

"Of course. Though his name was really Horatius. He and two other generals held off invading Etruscans until the bridge could be destroyed, then he leaped into the river in his armor and swam to safety despite a spear wound. He actually lived through it. I don't think the other two did."

"Etorri performed a similar feat, though in worse circumstances and with far worse casualties. Their Rho sacrificed his entire clan holding off the *dworg* at a narrow pass. Had he retreated, as it seemed he must, the *dworg* would have attacked the rest of the force from the rear during a pivotal battle. The clans would have been decimated or destroyed, and our world might well have fallen to the Great Bitch."

Arjenie digested that a moment. *"Dworg?"*

"Imagine the offspring of a troll and a demon."

Cullen snorted. "Only not as mellow and harder to kill. Happily, there aren't any *dworg* left. At least not in our realm, and I hope not anywhere. Here." He held something out to Lily. "We're nearly there. Time to take up charms against the foe."

Lily accepted the small silver disk, etched on one side. "All I have to do is lick it?"

"Or dunk it in any liquid—water, blood, lemonade. Doesn't matter. Wetting it activates it, then slap it against someone's skin. Got to be flesh to flesh to work."

Weapons were strictly prohibited at the circle . . . but a

sleep charm was not a weapon. Cullen had made one for each of them, holding on to Lily's until the last minute because her Gift would slowly leach power from it. A very small amount, true, but Cullen had fashioned the charms to hold very little power—so little that they wouldn't trigger a charm designed to detect magic, if anyone bothered to check.

Arjenie was still focused on Etorri. "So you trust them because of what one man did a long time ago?"

Rule answered this time. "We honor them for that, and always will. We trust them because, in the three millennia since, their honor remains unstained." He did not glance at Cullen. "It's not that they're saints. An individual Etorri can be selfish, misguided, self-righteous., prickly, arrogant . . . but he will not break honor. Etorri agreed to camp on the mesa last night and hold it as neutral ground for the rest of us. They will have done so."

Arjenie frowned. "Isn't Nokolai honorable?"

Cullen chuckled. "Sure. But Nokolai is taking sleep charms to an heirs' circle."

"What he means," Lily said, slipping her phone back in her purse, "is that Nokolai likes to be tricky. We don't intend to use the charms. They're a last resort. But we're sure as hell exploiting a loophole in the 'no weapons' rule by carrying them. I guess Etorri wouldn't do that."

We. She'd spoken of Nokolai as "we" quite automatically. Warmth flooded Rule. "I doubt it would occur to Frederick or Stephen to do such a thing."

"Honorable and thickheaded," Cullen said. "That's Etorri. I prefer a clan known for thinking. Looks like we've arrived," he added.

Benedict had pulled to a stop in the turnaround, but not at the curb. He got out, leaving the motor running, and moved several orange traffic cones out of the street, then climbed back in and parked so that those in the car had a view of the street leading to the turnaround.

The traffic cones had not been placed with the approval of the California Department of Transportation. Lily had winced when she learned how Nokolai intended to secure parking spaces for everyone, but she hadn't argued. She understood the need to keep innocent bystanders at a distance.

Rule pulled his phone from his shirt pocket and placed a call. "Scott," he said, "as soon as you've parked, take my compliments to Stephen and tell him Leidolf and Nokolai are here and await the rest."

"Will do. Kyffin's a block behind me," Scott said as the white Hyundai pulled up behind their car. "I think Ybirra's a few cars behind them."

"Excellent." Rule disconnected and looked over his shoulder. A wiry man with short hair and gold-framed glasses climbed out of the Hyundai and set off at an easy lope for the apartment complex to the north. The glasses were an affectation—there was nothing wrong with Scott's vision. He liked the geek look. It helped him pass for human.

"Why don't you just call the Etorri guy?" Arjenie asked. "Doesn't he have a mobile phone?"

Rule had done that, of course, earlier. He was confident the others had, also. But . . . "There's a political and a practical reason," he said, settling back against the seat to wait. "The political reason is that the other clans have insisted on following old protocols, developed when travel was time-consuming and arduous, for this meeting. I observe that respect for the formality of the past by using another old protocol and notifying Etorri personally."

"That's sarcasm, lupi style," Lily added. "What he means is that Wythe and Ybirra have been jackasses, so he'll make them wait while we do things ceremonially."

Rule flashed her a grin. "More or less, yes."

"And the practical reason?"

Benedict answered tersely. "Friar. We don't know what he's capable of. Best to have someone check on Etorri in person. Kyffin has arrived."

"I noticed." A black Impala was easing into the turnaround. When Rule saw who was behind the wheel, he couldn't help grinning. In defiance of all protocol, Myron had driven himself to the meeting, leaving his guard to ride shotgun. There was some logic to this. Myron—in spite of being Lu Nuncio—was a terrible fighter. Best to leave his guard's hands and eyes free for any threats, because Myron was not the man to counter them.

When the Kyffin Rho had assumed his clan's mantle, his

son had still been diapers. But he'd had two cousins who clearly carried the founder's blood; both good fighters with good control, obvious candidates for Lu Nuncio.

Instead Jason had named his uncle, a very clever man but a poor fighter . . . who would rejoice when the time came to transfer the heirship to his great-nephew. A few decades back, Myron had been an enthusiastic hippie, participating in peace demonstrations and civil rights marches. Today he was a reluctant and irreverent Lu Nuncio.

Jason could get away with a less than combat-ready Lu Nuncio because he was young, popular with his clan, and an excellent fighter himself. Plus Kyffin was one of the least combative clans. Rule had heard of only one Challenge within Kyffin since Jason became Rho, and Jason had fought it himself.

Kyffin's technique would not work with Leidolf. Especially not with Rule as Rho.

As the Impala parked behind Scott's Hyundai, a red Camry slowed for the turnaround. Rule got a glimpse of the passenger in the rear seat. Javier Mendoza, Ybirra Lu Nuncio. He reached for Lily's hand, but spoke to his brother. "We'll wait on Wythe. They'll be right behind."

Sure enough, a second Camry—this one silver—glided into the turnaround before the first had parked. The windows were heavily tinted, but Rule was betting that was Edgar's son, Brian.

Rule waited until that car, too, had parked. Then he waited another few minutes, until a red Ford joined their parked cavalcade.

"Showtime," he said, and reached for the handle of his door. Benedict reached for his. Together they opened their doors and got out.

THIRTY-SEVEN

IT was almost as if they'd rehearsed it, Lily thought, amused in spite of herself. Maybe because they had.

Rule and Benedict got out on the same side at the same second. Each walked around the Lincoln—Benedict circling the front, Rule the rear—at exactly the same pace. Benedict reached the front seat passenger door precisely when Rule reached the rear door. The two men opened them in unison.

Benedict helped Arjenie out. Rule helped Lily.

She'd resisted this bit of staging. "You are a Chosen, a woman, and injured," Isen had said last night when they were going over their roles in today's drama. "We want them to be very aware of that."

Because they were lupi and therefore nuts about protecting women, he meant. Maybe they'd feel guilty for dragging her out of her sickbed. Maybe they'd *listen* when Lily told them their great enemy was moving against them. She understood what Isen wanted and why, but it went against the grain. She was a cop. Cops didn't wait around for someone else to open the door.

Isen had smiled. "What would Madame Yu advise?"

"Unfair," she'd said. "Grandmother loves to have people

wait on her. She'd say . . ." That Lily was fighting the wrong battle. That her authority in this situation didn't come from her badge, and her autonomy didn't depend on opening a car door. That the president of the United States permitted others to open doors for him, and perhaps he knew more than Lily about the visual display of power and authority.

Grandmother could be exquisitely sarcastic even when she was all in Lily's head.

In the end, Lily had agreed. Rule had taken damnably quick advantage of her agreement to expand on the theme. Somehow she'd agreed to let him carry her up the steepest part of the track.

She only wished that part was only staging. Very likely she'd need it.

She and Rule stepped up onto a wide strip of scruffy grass next to the road. Arjenie and Benedict moved to stand beside them. There was just enough room for the four of them to form a receiving line of sorts. Cullen remained in the car; this part of the show belonged to the two Chosens and their mates.

Doors opened in the four vehicles strung linearly along the curb behind theirs. Fit, attractive men got out.

It was hot. The reserve was far enough from the ocean to get little of its cooling benefit. The sun was high, well into the sweaty part of the day—not the optimal time for a run at Los Penaquitos. That, of course, was why they'd chosen this time. Fewer runners, dog walkers, and such would be around. But the warmth felt good on Lily's bare legs.

It was funny, really. Lupi were big on formality, but they were also practical. They needed to blend in, so everyone was in shorts and tees and running shoes. Not that a woman with one arm in a sling looked ready for a good run, but she was blending in as hard as she could.

The two closest men were those from the Impala. One—six foot, two-ten, buzzed hair—looked like a rent-a-thug. He remained by the car, his eyes as quick and observant as a cop's. The other strode around the hood of the Impala quickly. He was tall with grizzled dark hair down to his shoulders and the sly, merry smile of a toddler snitching a cookie. He wore the raggediest pair of cutoffs imaginable—

the threads looked ready to give up the struggle to remain intact—with a bright Hawaiian shirt, left open. His chest was narrow, but nicely muscled. There was a faded button pinned to the collar of his shirt: *make love, not war.*

He looked over forty, which meant he was at least sixty and probably more. His voice was resonant as an actor's. "This is your Chosen! Rule, you will introduce me at once so I can kiss her and make her forget all about you for a few beautiful moments."

"Lily, the eternal adolescent in front of you is Myron Baker, Lu Nuncio of Kyffin," Rule said. "Myron, I recommend you check with Lily first about any kissing."

"My dear?" he said, eyebrows raised as he extended one hand.

Lily never objected to shaking hands. She encouraged it. So far all lupi felt pretty much the same to her Gift, save for the ever-exceptional Cullen—rather like fur and pine needles. Some were pinier, some furrier, and Rhos were distinctly warmer. But you never knew, did you? "Good to meet you, Myron." She took his hand. Fur-and-pine, nothing more.

Instead of shaking it, Myron bowed with European grace, brushing his lips over the back of her hand. "Such a pleasure, Lily. And such a lovely name! Lilies are the most beautiful flowers in the garden." He released her hand a second before she grew uncomfortable enough to tug it away and turned toward Benedict and Arjenie. "Benedict. Indomitable as always. But who is the lovely lady with you? Such hair!"

"Good question," one of the men coming up behind him growled.

There were three of them, with their bodyguards fanned out several feet to their rear. Lily recognized two from photos Rule had shown her. The shortest and youngest one would be Javier Mendoza of Ybirra. He bore watching, and not because of his startling good looks—kind of like a Mexican Brad Pitt—but because of the intensity he radiated. Short fuse?

The man on his right was as average-looking as any lupus could be: five-ten, one-sixty, brown and brown, pale skin, apparent age maybe thirty. Lucas Demeny of Szøs looked like he would want to sell you insurance. The only striking thing about him was the beautiful way he moved.

According to Rule, Lucas was one of the top two-legged fighters in the clans. Also according to Rule, he was as different as it was possible to be from his brother Rikard—who had died last year in a fight with a couple dozen armed gangbangers who held Lily's sister hostage.

The gangbangers hadn't been a problem for the lupi. It was the ancient staff wielded by their leader that had done it for Rikard.

The man who'd spoken, though—who was he? Older than the rest, yes, she was pretty sure of that, though with lupi it was easy to get the age wrong. He was sandy all over—tan shorts, tan tank, and weathered skin a shade darker than his sand-colored hair. His eyes were a brilliant blue, unfaded by age. He was built like a battering ram, square and solid, with a beak of a nose, a pugnacious jaw, and thin lips currently twisted in a scowl.

"Well?" Sandyman demanded as he came to a stop. "Who is that woman? Why is she here? Why is Benedict standing at your side instead of falling back decently?"

Rule didn't answer. Benedict did. "Edgar," he rumbled, "I will not require your apology, but do not speak of Arjenie as if she weren't standing in front of you."

"What?" Edgar Whitman—the Wythe *Rho*, not the Lu Nuncio—stared at Benedict incredulously. Guards were supposed to be seen and not heard.

Benedict's expression didn't change. "I have the honor to present to all of you my Chosen, Arjenie Fox."

"Hi," Arjenie said brightly. "It's good to meet you. We, uh . . . Benedict and I . . . the mate bond is very new, which I'm told means we can't be apart by much distance at all, so I had to come, too. I do apologize for the intrusion."

"Benedict!" Myron cried happily. He strode forward and slapped Benedict on the back. "This is marvelous! Fantastic!" He beamed at Arjenie. "Arjenie Fox, and with that hair! Amazing! You will allow me to welcome you properly."

Arjenie beamed back. "I liked the way you greeted Lily." She held out her hand.

As Myron bowed over it, Javier said in a low, angry voice, "You don't expect us to believe that—"

"Javier," Rule said softly, "pause and think before you say more."

Amazingly, he did—though his expression retained more of volcano than thoughtful consideration.

Rule had told Lily that none would seriously doubt Benedict when he introduced Arjenie as his Chosen. They might be shocked—two Chosens for one man?—but it was unthinkable for any lupus to lie about that. Looked like Javier had gotten the memo, but needed to be reminded about the thinking part.

Edgar was still staring, gape-mouthed. Lucas spoke in a voice as calm as the others were not. "I'm delighted to meet you, Arjenie. A new Chosen is a blessing to us all." He glanced at the simmering volcano beside him and added with a faintly chiding note, "Is that not true, Javier?"

Javier defeated Lily's expectations by giving his head a little shake, which served to smooth his face into a smile. He'd been gorgeous before. The smile kicked him up nearly into Cullen territory. "Of course." He offered Arjenie that smile. "Ybirra welcomes you, Ms. Fox." He then turned it on Lily. "I'm afraid this unexpected gift from the Lady caused me to lose what poor manners I possess." He glanced at Rule, one eyebrow cocked.

Rule performed introductions. Javier wanted Lily to know that Ybirra stood ready to avenge her injury. Lucas murmured conventional wishes for her speedy return to health. Lily thanked him and said she was sorry for the loss of his brother last year.

He smiled briefly. "My loss has been eased by time, and Rikard would have been delighted to go out in such a way. He lived large. It must have suited him to die large, also."

The last one Rule introduced—and that must have been intentional—was Sandyman: "Edgar Whitman, Wythe's Rho. Which brings us to an important question."

Edgar waved that aside to tell Lily brusquely that Wythe did not tolerate violence to a Chosen, and he hoped she would recover quickly. He added curtly to Arjenie that Wythe rejoiced in the Lady's gift. Arjenie looked incredulous, but nodded politely. Myron immediately reclaimed her attention.

"Two Chosens," Edgar muttered, shaking his head. "No-kolai claims two Chosens."

Rule was using his polite voice, the one so ostentatiously courteous it reminded Lily of Grandmother accepting tribute on her birthday. "We are amazed by the honor the Lady has done us. I am amazed by something else as well, Edgar. I hope Brian is well."

"He will heal." Edgar made a brushing gesture. "It's a clan matter."

Lily's eyebrows rose. She was pretty sure she wasn't supposed to ask questions. She was also pretty sure a Chosen could get away with it. "Does that mean he was Challenged?"

Edgar flushed. Anger or embarrassment? Rule glanced at the car, nodded at Benedict, and gave a little jerk of his head.

Cullen climbed out of the Lincoln. Lucas greeted him with a single nod; the rest ignored him. Arjenie whispered quite audibly to Myron, "If you'll excuse me? That means we have to go stand somewhere else now."

Myron chuckled. "I believe you're right. Silly custom, isn't it?"

Benedict took Arjenie's hand and led her to the spot he'd decided she should occupy between Lily and Cullen. Then he strode toward the other guards.

No one answered Lily's question. She was about to repeat it when Lucas said mildly, "It would be very odd for a Lu Nuncio to fight a Challenge just before an heirs' circle."

Edgar's color stayed high. "I do not discuss Wythe matters."

"None of us would pry into an internal clan matter," Javier said. "Unless someone means to call Edgar liar, we should drop the subject and proceed to the circle's location."

"But how odd it is," Myron said, cocking his head to one side, "that Edgar didn't inform us of this change ahead of time. Phone not working properly, Edgar?"

Javier frowned. "What does it matter? Rule has established most convincingly that a Rho may attend an heirs' circle if his heir is unable to. He can't very well turn around and protest Edgar's presence now."

"Nokolai is not the only clan here," Lucas said in his mild way. "I, too, am puzzled at Edgar's omission. Almost it seems he sought to take advantage of us with this . . . surprise."

Edgar looked like he was going to explode. Instead he ducked his head a single time—not far, but baring the nape was an important cue for lupi. "I apologize. I apologize to all of you. I should have notified you I'd be replacing Brian, but I did not want any questions, you see? I am embarrassed." He spread his hands widely. "Brian handled things poorly. You are right," he said directly to Lucas. "No Challenge match should have been fought just before an heirs' circle. If Brian placed me in the wrong with his actions, well, I compounded the wrong."

"Is Brian well?" Rule asked again, but this time there was some warmth in his voice.

"He will heal," Edgar said as he had before. "Enough about my scapegrace brother. We aren't here to discuss him. Shall we proceed to the meeting place?"

"The man I sent to inform Etorri of our arrival hasn't returned yet," Rule said. "He should be here soon, though, and I prefer to hear from him before we go to the mesa." He sent a long glance around the lot of them. "You will recall what I said about an enemy who may be aware of our meeting."

"Certainly." Javier had himself all smoothed out now. "You wanted the guards to be permitted weapons." He shrugged. "It's against tradition, and for little benefit. The mesa is the high ground. Even if your mysterious enemy is or can employ a sharpshooter, there will be nowhere for him to hide."

"This mysterious enemy has a name. I shared it with you: Robert Friar. Among other things, I believe he was behind the attack on my Chosen. Because of one man's sacrifice, the shooter failed. Friar dislikes failure. I believe he will try again."

Every eye went to Lily.

Rule added quietly, "And while the mesa is the high ground, we have to get there."

"We will keep Lily and Arjenie in our center," Edgar said gruffly, "surrounded by bodies able to heal damage much better than theirs. If there really is any danger, both Chosens will be protected."

Javier nodded. "Excellent idea, Edgar. Probably unnecessary, but none of us want to risk a Chosen. While we wait for the return of the Leidolf guard, we should make sure that all of us have honored the conditions of this meeting."

Rule went still. "What do you mean?"

"I suggest our guards be searched."

Rule's eyes turned hard as glass. His upper lip lifted in a snarl. "I have had enough of poorly disguised insults. Call me liar or be quiet."

Javier spread his hands. "I do not ask that *you* be searched, Rule. Lu Nuncios—and, of course, Edgar—will give our words that we are unarmed. That is for form only. None of us would go armed into a circle, I'm sure. But any of our guards might have grown worried, given your constant murmurings of danger, and decided to arm himself without our knowledge. Let us make sure, I say, that is all."

For a moment Lily thought Rule would refuse. Or maybe punch Javier in the nose. Why this was a nearly intolerable insult when he'd taken other demands in stride, she didn't know. Maybe the man smelled bad. "Very well," he said at last, his voice cold enough to freeze the sweat on any sensible person. "Nokolai agrees, if the rest do." He continued with arctic dryness, "I give my word I have no weapons on my person other than those bequeathed by the Lady."

Cullen broke his long, uncharacteristic silence. "Excellent notion," he said in a bright and silky voice. "I have a suggestion. We should all strip. Then no one need wonder what we might be hiding. I'll go first." Quick as a flash, he'd pulled his tank top off. It landed in the dirt. He toed off one of the disreputable Nikes he wore, then the other—no socks—and smiled sweetly as his hands went to the snap on his shorts. "Myron? Lucas? Javier? Who's going to—"

"Call off your madman," Edgar growled, "before he gets us all arrested."

"Cullen." Rule's voice continued dry—but dry and amused now. "Perhaps that's far enough."

"Are you sure? I might have a grenade up my ass, after all. No way for anyone to know unless—"

"Enough." Javier rolled his eyes. "As you stand in for the Rhej in the circle, we will accept your word, also."

Cullen's smile remained, but grew edges. You could cut yourself on a smile like that. "But not the guards' words."

"What does it matter?" Edgar demanded. "Wythe has nothing to hide. Robert!" He turned to face the guards spread out behind them. "Allow Benedict to search you."

A lean blond man well over six feet with a hooked nose turned to face Benedict and held his arms straight out. Benedict didn't move, didn't so much as glance at him.

"If we're going to do this," Rule said, "best do it quickly. Wythe and Nokolai guards will search each other. Kyffin and Ybirra will do the same. When Scott returns, he and Lucas's guard may ensure their mutual compliance. Agreed?"

"Foolishness," Lucas said, "but very well. "

"Oh, all right," Myron said. "Though Lucas is right—it's a foolish sacrifice of dignity, which Billy possesses in much greater quantity than I, so I suppose he can spare a morsel of it. Billy! Please allow—ah, I think your name is Gil? Allow Gil to pat you down, then do the same for him."

The man with the buzzed hair—who looked like he should be called Crusher or Bull, not Billy—moved toward the dark-skinned man on his left. Rule gave Benedict a nod.

George had waited with his arms outstretched. Benedict went to him. He was quick, efficient, and as thorough as one can be without the body cavity search Cullen had mockingly suggested. Within moments Benedict straightened. "Unless his phone transforms into a laser gun, he's clean."

"Permit him to assure himself that the same is true for you."

Benedict looked bored. He tugged his T-shirt off over his head and held it out. "You'll want to check that."

The man took it, shook it, shrugged, and tossed it over his shoulder.

Benedict hadn't left him many places to look. His shorts were knee-length khaki. Unlike most of the others, he wore a belt with them. His phone was clipped to it. George patted Benedict's hips and butt, paying attention to the pockets, and ran a couple fingers inside the waist of his shorts, then knelt on one knee. Apparently he meant to check Benedict's socks and shoes, but Lily didn't see what he actually did. George's body blocked her from seeing his hands.

She saw Benedict's face change, a subtle disturbance rippling through his features. Then Benedict roared.

And things went to hell really fast.

THIRTY-EIGHT

BENEDICT slammed his fist into George's face. George flew backward several feet. He hadn't yet landed when Benedict leaped at the man closest to him—Gil, Javier's guard, who'd just finished patting down Myron's Billy. Benedict didn't land on Gil. He jumped past the man—seizing his head and twisting it as he did.

Gil never had a chance to cry out. His body slumped to the ground like an under-filled bag of sand.

Benedict landed on his toes already bending into his next move. He spun on one leg, the other one swinging through the air, his torso lined up perfectly with the outstretched leg to balance the kick.

Billy was in motion, too—rushing into the attack, trying to redirect the kick and upset Benedict's balance.

Billy was lupus. He was fast.

Not fast enough.

Somehow Benedict altered the kick in midmotion, bending his knee and twisting his body to change the trajectory. Had he misjudged even a fraction, it would have been his knee rather than his thigh that smacked into Billy's head—

probably crippling Benedict, however much damage it did to
Billy. Instead Billy fell to the ground, stunned or dead.

All that took three seconds.

Lily was slow to react. Sheer disbelief held her motion-
less. The lupi around her were a split-second faster. Even as
Billy fell, Rule threw himself into a run. So did Edgar and
Lucas. Javier howled and jumped . . . on Rule. From behind.

The two tumbled to the ground, rolled. Myron, who had
just started forward, jerked to a halt near them.

"*Furo!*" cried the one remaining guard, dodging frantically as Benedict charged him. "He stinks of the fury!"

The fury? Oh, gods, this was bad. Lily started to reach
inside her sling. Stopped.

"Circle him!" That was Cullen—who wasn't a trained
fighter, but he was blindingly quick. Maybe the only one
faster than Benedict. He didn't obey his own order. He
rushed Benedict, moving so fast Lily couldn't quite see what
happened—but it resulted in Cullen veering at the last second when Benedict's arm flashed out.

The sleep charms. Cullen had tried to use one. He
couldn't get close enough.

Lucas dashed in just as Cullen veered away. The flurry of
motion was too quick to follow, but it ended with Benedict's
mouth bleeding freely and Lucas flying a dozen feet through
the air. Edgar charged Benedict from behind. Benedict spun
and slammed both fists on Edgar's head. Edgar went down
hard.

They needed Rule, who might be able to use the portion
of the Nokolai mantle he held to stop Benedict. Maybe.

There was a solid smack of fist on flesh. Rule nearly
won free, but Javier snaked out a foot, tripping him. Lucas
and Cullen were distracting Benedict, giving him two fast-
moving targets. Lily hesitated for one more second, looking
over at Arjenie. The woman stood stock-still, eyes huge with
horror. "Get in the car," Lily snapped. "Lock the doors."

"*Furo?*" Those huge eyes turned to Lily. "The fury?
What's that? What's happening?"

"Madness. In the car. Now." Lily didn't wait to see if she
obeyed, but raced toward Rule and Javier. Twenty feet away,

Cullen danced and darted around Benedict like a rodeo clown keeping an enraged bull away from his target—Edgar, who was trying to rise. Lucas was down again, on hands and knees, shaking his head. The remaining guard cradled one arm close to his body and moved sluggishly, as if dazed.

In the second or two Lily had looked away, Benedict had struck again.

Myron had stayed near Rule and Javier. He jumped back as the entangled fighters rolled. "Javier! Stop it! We need Rule to—oh, damn," he said, sliding sideways quickly to avoid them. "Not going to listen, are you?" He grimaced, drew back his foot, and kicked Javier in the head.

Javier went limp. Rule sprang to his feet and dashed toward the madman who was his brother. Lily followed as fast as she could.

"Benedict!" Rule shouted. "Freeze!"

For a split second, he did. For one shutter-click moment, he didn't move. But only for that long. Then he charged Rule.

Rule danced aside at the last second. "Circle him! I'll keep him busy while—"

"Hell, no, you won't!" Cullen yelled back. "I'm faster." As if to prove that he darted in—then back, ducking and dodging, giving Rule a chance to move closer while he weaved around blows that didn't quite land.

Until one did. Cullen sailed backward, skidding across the dry grass in a cloud of dust to end up next to one of those terribly still bodies. Lily stopped just as Rule leaped on his brother's back. Benedict threw himself backward. The two of them landed in a tangled pile, but Benedict had managed to twist himself around as they fell, landing with one knee in Rule's back.

For a sickening second, Rule was still. Benedict reached for Rule's head or maybe his throat—

A rock sailed in and hit him in the head.

He rolled off and in one smooth motion regained his feet, growling in a way no human throat should be able to do. Cullen stood ten feet away, another rock in his hand, grinning like a maniac. Half his face was covered in blood. He swayed slightly where he stood and his eyes looked fuzzy, as if they weren't tracking right. "Want some more? C'mon. Come here." He made a beckoning gesture. "Let's dance, big boy."

Benedict's face contorted in fury—but instead of launching himself at Cullen, he moved sideways, his head swinging between Cullen and Rule—who'd gotten to his feet. As Benedict retreated, Lucas shoved to his feet and his guard moved closer, making part of a loose circle around Benedict. That guard still clutched one arm to his chest. Broken, probably.

He'd be the weak point. He must know it. Benedict would, too. He might be mad with rage, but even a fear-maddened beast knows which predator is injured and weakened.

Lily held back. She for damn sure couldn't fight Benedict, and if she—

"Benedict." Rule's voice was low, so deep it could almost have been Isen speaking. "Submit. Now."

Again Benedict froze. It lasted a full second this time.

It might have lasted longer if Javier hadn't shot in from one side and tackled him.

They went down together. Rule dove in, seizing one of his brother's hands with both of his even as Javier reached for Benedict's throat—and took a blow to his ribs from Benedict's other hand. Lucas skidded onto his knees on Benedict's other side, reaching for that arm. Rule shifted quickly, using his knee to pin Benedict's forearm. He dug into his pocket, popped something in his mouth, took it out and reached for Benedict's bare skin.

Benedict bucked so strongly he toppled Javier, who bumped into Rule, knocking him away. And something small and silver went spinning off to land near Billy's motionless body.

With Javier dislodged and Rule off-balance, Benedict's legs were free. He used them to kick to his feet in spite of Lucas's grip—or maybe Lucas helped, because he used the motion to flip Benedict.

Benedict landed well, though, and was on his feet before Lucas could close. Rule had regained his feet, too, and the two of them circled Benedict.

"Stop it!" Arjenie cried from back at the car. "Stop now!"

Myron came up beside Lily. He imitated Cullen by lobbing a rock at Benedict. This one, though, Benedict simply caught—and hurled back.

Lily ducked. Myron yelled something. Benedict charged. Arjenie slapped her hand against the car's rear window.

Lily *felt* the magic as it rolled past her, quick as a flash fire but somehow bruised, a hot, squishy sort of power prickling her skin. As it hit, people fell—Myron, Rule, Benedict, Lucas, the lone remaining guard. Arjenie, too. She collapsed into a small heap beside the car. Everyone but Lily—and Cullen. Who had shields, excellent shields, and who was staring at her in the same astonishment she felt.

Lily shook that off, took four running steps, and slid to her knees beside Benedict, who was supposed to be immune to his Chosen's magic. Turned out that was wrong. Whatever Arjenie did when she combined her Gift with glass, it had hit Benedict along with the rest.

She licked the silver disk Cullen had given her and slapped it against Benedict's bare chest. Then, for a moment, she just breathed . . . and noticed what she was touching. Mixed with the pine-and-fur of lupus magic was something oily. "Okay," she said, looking around. Bodies everywhere. "Cullen? You okay?"

"Not seeing double anymore, which is a good sign." He'd knelt beside one of the fallen. "Billy's alive, but I think his neck's broken. Potentially healable. Depends on his innate healing and the care he gets."

"The others?"

"Gil's dead. Checking on the rest." He stood.

At some point in the past, Cullen had gone to medical school. Lily hoped he remembered enough. "Check the injured first. The ones knocked out by magic should . . ." Movement in her peripheral vision had her head swinging around.

The Leidolf guard had returned. Scott stood staring in horror about ten yards away—too distant to be affected by the blast from the glass, she guessed. "Check on Arjenie," she snapped. "She's next to the Lincoln. If she didn't break anything when she fell"—unlikely, but best to check—"put her in the car and make her as comfortable as possible."

"I—my Rho—"

"Is okay." She thought. She hoped. "Move!"

He ran up to Arjenie.

"Edgar's dead," Cullen said flatly, rising from Edgar's still body. "I think George twitched earlier, before Arjenie knocked everyone out."

Oh, shit, oh, shit. The Wythe Rho. This was going to be bad. "We need to ask George some questions. Benedict didn't go into the fury all by himself."

"Didn't think he did," Cullen said curtly, moving to kneel beside George.

"She seems okay," Scott called. "Out cold, but I didn't find any injuries. Heartbeat's strong."

"Good. Soon as she's settled in the car, come here and hold this charm on Benedict's chest. Cullen, how long will it work?"

"Twenty to thirty minutes. He'll come out slow, give us a chance to switch to a fresh one." Cullen nodded at George, who wasn't twitching now. "Broken jaw. Probably a concussion, too, but his pupils match. Good thing Benedict wasn't trying to kill us."

"Not funny. Do you have any idea how long Rule and the others will be out?"

"No. Rule should come around first, though." Cullen rose. "He heals quick, and he's got a full mantle, unlike the rest of them. That will help." He headed for the Lincoln. "And I wasn't joking. If Benedict had intended to kill instead of damage, we'd have more than two dead."

"He didn't have time," Lily said dryly. Her arm was hurting. She hadn't noticed it much in the middle of everything, but now it pulsed with pain in time with her heartbeat.

Stupid arm. It hadn't done a damn thing.

"Cullen's right," said a groggy but welcome voice. Rule sat up slowly. "I believe you haven't seen Benedict fight before."

Lily had been told often that Benedict was the best fighter in the clans. That he was something special. She hadn't known what that meant, not really. It was still hard to believe she'd seen what she'd seen. "Ten to one will keep even the best fighter busy." Even if he cut it down to seven-to-one in the first three seconds.

"I wouldn't say that he held back, exactly." Rule grunted as he rose. "Damn, those ribs feel a lot worse now than they did with the adrenaline going."

"Your ribs? Rule, if they're broken—"

He waved that away with the hand that wasn't clutching his side. "They're not badly enough displaced to put my lungs in danger. He could have broken my back instead. He didn't. He didn't hold back, but some part of him found nonlethal blows."

"Not in every case," Cullen said grimly. He'd popped the trunk and was pulling out a large white case with a red cross on the front.

"Sir," Scott said, trotting toward Rule. "Lily said to—"

"Then do as she told you." Rule glanced at Cullen. "How many died?"

"Gil and Edgar."

Rule's face went tight. After a moment he said, "George is alive?"

"Unless he's got injuries I didn't spot, he should make it."

"We need to talk to him."

It sounded like Rule's mind was running along the same track as Lily's. "He did something, all right." Scott settled to the ground on the other side of Benedict's peacefully sleeping body. She let him take over as holder-of-the-charm and used her freed hand to reach into her shorts' pocket. "Benedict's coated in some kind of oily magic. I'm guessing it's from one of Dya's potions. It's what was done to Cobb, but not administered in a drink." She glanced at Cullen as she pulled out her phone. "Is there such a thing as a tactile potion?"

"Probably." He set the backboard down beside Billy but headed to George.

"Lily." Rule's voice was sharp. "Who do you mean to call?"

"9-1-1. We need ambulances, stat."

"9-1-1 will give us police, also. If you call this in, Benedict goes to prison—probably for life, though only if they allow us to continue applying the sleep charm. If not, he'll probably kill more people and they'll shoot him. If he lives, Arjenie will have to take the cell next to his. She'll spend her life in prison as well. The mate bond will no longer be secret."

Lily scowled. "There are two people dead. There are others in need of immediate medical attention. We'll have to sort it out later, prove that Benedict wasn't acting under his own volition." Using magic in the commission of a felony was a felony. Investigating that, finding the real perp—that's what her job was *about*.

Rule just looked at her. "Arjenie said her sister's potions were undetectable. How will you prove Benedict's innocence to the law's satisfaction?"

"I—" She wanted to say the potion was not undetectable, dammit. She was detecting it right now. But her word wasn't evidence. No doubt there'd be screams about conflict of interest again, too. She might not be allowed to handle the investigation. "I don't know yet. That doesn't mean I won't figure it out."

And someone could die while they argued about it. Lily flicked on her phone.

"Lily." Rule moved with that eerie speed he seldom used when he wasn't fighting. He crouched next to her and placed one hand on her wrist. "I had to make a difficult decision in Nashville when we spoke with Cobb. I'm asking you to make a difficult decision now."

"You're asking me to cover up a crime."

"Yes."

She looked at his hand on her wrist. He applied no pressure. He could have easily wrested her phone away, taken the decision from her. He could have said that if she failed to prove Benedict innocent, he'd be convicted and given gado. He might survive with his sanity intact . . . for the first few years. Rule could have pointed out how little Benedict deserved that, no more than Arjenie deserved what would happen to her. Or that with the Great Bitch active in their world, Nokolai and all the lupi needed Benedict.

He could have told her he couldn't stand to lose his brother.

Instead he waited. He trusted her to know these things. He trusted her to make the right decision.

Lily put her phone back to sleep and slipped it in her

pocket. Nausea twisted in her belly. She didn't know if she'd made the right decision. She didn't know. "We need medical help. And someone could have seen the fight and called it in already."

"I'm the medical help, for now." Cullen studied the unconscious George. "I think I got his jaw back in place, but I should tape it up."

"You can't set a jaw that way."

"You can't. I can. I'm not saying I did it right, but the bones are lined up better than they were. Wouldn't try it on a . . ." His voice drifted off. He bent closer, then looked at Rule. "Rule."

Rule moved quickly to crouch next to Cullen. His back was to her, and the two men kept her from seeing George. "Is he—"

"Awake," Rule said curtly. He bent lower as if the man had said something, though Lily didn't hear anything. "No. Edgar is dead."

This time Lily heard George. He keened, a high-pitched sound of grief.

One of the other bodies groaned. Lily looked over and saw Myron stirring. She pushed to her feet and headed to him, arriving just as he sat up, holding his head in both hands.

"If this is what humans feel with a hangover, I don't see why any of them would drink. What happened?"

"I believe George used some kind of topical potion on Benedict that induced the fury."

Myron's eyebrows flew up. "You do? Ah, that would explain things. But what I meant was what knocked us all out?"

"Oh. That was Arjenie. She's Gifted. She knocked herself out, too, doing it. Rule woke up a couple minutes ago."

"That's quite a trick. Wish she'd used it earlier." He looked around, his eyes bleary. "How many of those bodies are dead?"

"Edgar and Gil."

Myron winced. "Poor Gil. I never liked him much—he's always been a bit of an ass, to tell the truth, but . . . I suppose you're thinking Edgar was an ass, too. He wasn't really. Just stubborn. Once he got hold of an idea—"

"Myron, I'm sorry to interrupt, but we have to move

quickly. I don't have Stephen's number. Do you? Can you call him, get him to bring his men?"

"Guess we'd better tidy up before your compatriots arrive, hadn't we?" Myron got to his feet. "I'll call."

Myron assumed she'd want to "tidy up" instead of cooperating with her compatriots. That bothered her. Everything about this bothered her. She looked around. "Everyone else is still out."

Myron flipped his phone open and offered her the sickly cousin of his charming smile. "I may be a lousy fighter, but I'm a fast healer. If—"

"Myron," Rule said. "I need you over here. I need you to listen to what George has to say. To serve as witness."

"You'd do better to wait for Lucas," Myron said, but he started toward Rule. Lily kept pace with him.

"You're awake. He isn't."

George lay flat on the ground. Cullen had straightened him, Lily supposed. His face was tight with pain, but his color was good and his eyes tracked them, so he was focusing.

"Maybe," Myron said, "but no one will be amazed if Kyffin backs you up when . . . yes, Stephen. This is Myron. We've got a situation. The circle won't be happening and you're needed here with your men." A pause. "Well, you can talk to Rule, but everyone else is either unconscious or dead. Except Lily, of course, because the knockout was delivered magically, but that was after Benedict went into the fury. Lily says he was dosed with some sort of potion, and George is the likely culprit. We could use some help getting . . . certainly." He held out the phone to Rule. "Here."

Rule grimaced but took it. "Stephen. We have two seriously injured and two dead. We need to get everyone away before—*shit*."

George had blanched suddenly, his face turning pale and sweaty. His eyes went frantic. Cullen laid his fingers on George's neck, scowling.

"Cullen, what's—"

"Shut up." He bent and rested his ear on George's chest. He stayed there a few seconds, then straightened. "Acute myocardial infarction. Maybe."

"Brian," George gasped. "Brian. You have to . . ." He reached out weakly.

Rule gripped that seeking hand. "We'll rescue him. Be still." Without looking around, he held the phone out to Lily. Automatically she took it. "You're having a heart attack. You need to lie quietly."

George's head turned toward Rule. "Benedict. Tell him . . . sorry. Had to. Had . . ."

"I know," Rule said soothingly. "I'll tell him. Don't try to—"

"Watch out!" Myron yelled—a second before someone slammed into Lily, knocking her down. The phone went flying. She landed badly on her hip and her elbow. The elbow of her bad arm. Shock waves whited out her brain.

"Whoops," a vaguely familiar voice said, and a pair of hands seized her rib cage just below her arms and hauled her several feet backward. "There. Out of the way now."

Lily blinked her eyes back into focus. Javier and Rule were faced off, crouched and circling. Rule had a new trickle of blood from a cut lip.

"Traitor," Javier spat. "Oath-broke coward. You won't walk away from this."

Myron—it was Myron who'd dragged Lily away from the fight—said reassuringly, "Don't worry. I'm sure Rule can clear everything up. Though it may be hard to make Javier listen. He and Gil were close."

"Son of a bitch," Cullen said. He'd thrown his body over George to shield him when Javier jumped Rule, but now jerked upright. "Son of a sorry mongrel bitch."

George's eyes were blank and staring.

"I've had enough of this shit." Lily held up her hand. "Get me on my feet."

"Do you think you ought to—"

Lily snarled. "Now!"

He took her hand and tugged her easily to her feet. She reached inside her sling and pulled out the little Smith & Wesson Airweight Snubnose she'd hidden there.

Shooting left-handed, Lily was pretty sure she'd miss any target less stationary than the proverbial side of a barn. That's why she hadn't tried to use it earlier. Benedict hadn't seemed interested in holding still. God only knew who she might have hit.

But Javier didn't know she was right-handed, did he?

"As soon as I've done for you," Javier snarled, "I'll have the life of your brother as well in payment for Gil."

"No," Rule said, "you won't. I'm tired of making allowances for your age. We don't have time for this."

Lily clicked off the safety and began moving.

Javier's voice was low, throbbing with anger. "I'll help you make time."

She picked a spot on Rule's left. Not too close, since he needed room to react, but well within Javier's line of sight—and saw that Javier's eyes had bled to black. All-over black, the whites subsumed by darkness. So not a good sign. His wolf was trying to force the Change. Lily sited carefully. Unfamiliar weapon, left hand . . . she'd best be sure. "You're going to listen before you leap this time."

He barely glanced at her. "A *puta* with a toy gun."

"It shoots real bullets."

He sneered at Rule as if she hadn't spoken. "You have your woman fight for you now, Rule?"

If Rule was surprised by her weapon—and he should have been—it didn't show. "My *nadia* has killed demons. I don't think you can say the same."

"Listen to me," Lily said. "Benedict isn't responsible. Neither is Rule. Robert Friar set this up. Somehow he got George to dope Benedict, induce the fury in him. You need to back off. There are wounded. You need to stop this now."

Javier crouched a little lower, as if about to spring.

"Javier," Myron said sternly, "get your wolf under control."

"Myron's right." Lucas limped toward them. "This is a public place, man. I'm surprised we don't hear a siren yet." He looked at Lily, then Rule. "Not that I buy this nonsense about Friar. A human wouldn't even know about the fury, much less how to induce it. But that's for later. We need to be out of here."

Javier had gone still in the way lupi did sometimes. Inhumanly still. Suddenly he drew himself up straight. The black receded from his eyes. The anger didn't. "You told me earlier to call you liar or be quiet. I call you liar now." He spat at the ground. "I call on Szøs and Kyffin to witness. Nokolai has dealt in deceit and death. For this, Ybirra Challenges Nokolai. Single combat."

For a second no one moved or spoke. Then Lucas said quietly, "Szøs witnesses the Challenge."

Myron sighed. "Idiot. Kyffin witnesses the Challenge."

Rule's voice was cold and weary. "Nokolai accepts the Challenge. I exercise my right as Challenged to pick the location. I choose the abandoned mine near Hole-in-the-Wall where our clans last met to discuss boundaries."

"Accepted." Javier bit that off as if it galled him to accept anything Rule said. "Ybirra exercises its right to choose the time. This Challenge will be fought at ten o'clock tonight."

"Accepted. I propose we ask Etorri to handle the arrangements. I further propose that we limit attendance."

"Two," Javier said. "That is customary. Nokolai and Ybirra may each have two witnesses present. Other clans may have two witnesses there as well, if they wish."

"Save Etorri," Rule said, "who will bring as many as they deem right. That stipulated, Nokolai accepts these terms."

"Ybirra accepts these terms."

"I call on Szøs and Kyffin to witness."

"So witnessed."

"So witnessed."

"Shit," said Lily.

THIRTY-NINE

RULE climbed stiffly behind the wheel of the Lincoln and slammed the door. His ribs hurt like fire. Cullen had wrapped them hurriedly with an elastic bandage, but that was mainly to remind him not to bend.

Lily looked at him. "I can't believe you accepted a Challenge. Your ribs are broken. You can't fight tonight."

Did she think he had a choice? "They'll be partially healed by then." Not healed enough, and he knew it. So did Javier, damn and blast him.

Rule turned the key, slid the car into gear, and got the hell out of there.

Etorri had arrived seconds after Rule accepted Javier's Challenge. Stephen had been informed of the Challenge, and had agreed to serve as caller and witness.

With Etorri's help the rest of the bodies, living and dead, had been quickly removed. Stephen and four of his people had simply taken off at a run back into the reserve; their cars were parked elsewhere. The fifth Etorri guard would return Edgar's rental car discreetly.

Rule and Lily were the last to leave. Javier had been the first, screeching away with the body of his friend in his rental car. Myron was taking Billy to a hospital, where they'd both lie about how he'd been injured. Rule had promised to send Nettie to them as soon as possible . . . assuming Cullen was right, and Billy survived to be treated. Lucas's man had still been unconscious when the two of them left, but that was probably because he'd been the closest to Arjenie when she pulled her knockout trick. Otherwise, he'd seemed the least injured of the guards, with only a broken arm.

Cullen and Benedict were in the back of Scott's white SUV. Benedict was bound with a plastic restraint and out cold. Cullen was keeping him that way.

Arjenie was still passed out on the backseat of the Lincoln . . . which also had two bodies in its spacious trunk.

To be doubly sure Benedict didn't wake up, Rule would take the long way home, allowing Scott to put plenty of distance between them. Even if Cullen suddenly passed out and dropped the charm, Benedict would remain unconscious because his mate was too far away.

Rule was numb with disaster. He felt as if he were moving through a mind-dulling fog, able to see a single step ahead, and no more. That step was calling his Rho . . . who he could not think of as his father. Not now. Not with his brother locked in madness as tightly as he was in plastic and sleep. Rule reached for his phone . . . and realized he didn't have it.

Shit. Had he left it back there?

"Here." Lily held out an iPhone.

"Is that mine or yours?"

"Yours. Javier knocked it out of my hand, but I found it before we left."

Thank God one of them was thinking. "Thank you. I'd like to know about the gun you pulled on Javier."

"It seemed to me I'd been left out of the ban on weapons, since I wasn't a principal or a guard. I asked Isen about it last night. He said that if I were asked, I'd have to say I had a gun, but otherwise, I was free to carry a gun if I wanted to. And, ah, he offered to loan me one."

"You saw no need to tell me? No, never mind. Isen would have wanted me kept in the dark."

"He suggested that, yes."

Isen would have wanted to leave Rule free to honestly deny that any Nokolai had come armed to the meeting. Oh, yes—as Lily had said earlier, Nokolai was known to be tricky. And largely because of the man who'd been its Rho for so many years.

Rule hadn't expected the question to even be raised. He for damn sure hadn't expected it to come from Javier. Despite the occasional clash, he'd considered Javier a friend. Tonight his hotheaded friend would try to kill him.

Rule placed the call he dreaded making.

Immediately he got a busy signal. "Damn it. The house line's tied up. You'd think he'd keep it open when . . . I'll try his cell, but half the time he forgets to turn it on." He did try, and was sent straight to voice mail. "This is Rule. It's urgent. Call me."

He tossed the phone on the seat and tried to relax his grip on the steering wheel. He was tense and scared and hurting, and his wolf wanted *out*. Out of this luxurious box on wheels. Out of this stupid two-legged form so he could howl.

Javier had Challenged *him*. His wolf felt betrayed and furious, eager to answer that challenge. Which told Rule why Javier had issued it in the first place. Too much wolf, not enough thinking. Surely if that young hothead had paused to think he'd have seen that Rule hadn't somehow sent his own brother into the fury in order to stage an act as monumentally stupid as it was treacherous.

Though Lucas had doubts, too, didn't he? And Lucas was as coolheaded as they came.

Rule glanced at the phone on the seat beside him as he slowed for the light. Grimaced. Better try again. Or maybe Lily could. He glanced at her, about to ask . . . and saw her face clearly.

He reached for her hand. "Are you okay?"

"I should be asking you that."

"That doesn't answer my question." He stretched out his hand. After a moment, she took it. He focused on the feel of her skin, the way her fingers wrapped around his, the sheer comfort of the connection. "I'm sorry," he said quietly. "Sorry I had to ask you to make such a choice. Are you okay?"

She surprised him with a soft huff of a laugh. "Okay? I'm a mess. I've been a mess ever since I saw LeBron's brains up way too close and personal."

"We're quite a pair at the moment, aren't we? Banged up, mixed up . . ." He squeezed her hand. "I know you hate messes."

"Especially when the mess is in my head. I made the best call I could at the time, but I don't . . ." She shook her head. "I don't have time to sort it out now. I still don't hear any sirens. Do you?"

Subject closed, he thought. For now. "Apparently no one saw the fight." The traffic cones they'd used to block the street had kept cars away, and of course the fight hadn't lasted as long as it seemed. Under ten minutes, surely, though the aftermath had taken that long again, and more. And several of the apartments in the nearby complex had a view of the turnaround. Those on upper floors wouldn't have had that view blocked by everyone's cars. If someone had looked out a window at the wrong time . . . "We were lucky."

"I wonder why?"

"Luck isn't defined by reason."

"No, but if you're smart you minimize how much is left up to luck. Friar's smart. Why didn't he have a reporter or two tipped to be there? Or have one of his people hanging around, ready to call it in anonymously when Benedict freaked?"

"Maybe he did and something went wrong."

"Which makes us awfully damn lucky, doesn't it?"

She was right. "Your brain's working better than mine at the moment. Maybe you can come up with a reason. I'm drawing a blank." The light changed to green. As he accelerated he frowned and released her hand. "Would you try calling Isen again?"

She answered by picking up his phone and doing as he'd asked. "So what did George tell you before . . . Isen. It's Lily. Things went badly. Three dead, none of them Nokolai. We never made it to the circle. I'm putting you on speaker so Rule and I can both speak."

Good idea. Rule inhaled carefully. Talking wasn't comfortable. It required a lot of breath, and breathing hurt. "I'll start at the end," he said. "Ybirra has issued a formal Challenge, properly witnessed."

Isen hissed. It was an oddly feline sound from a man who wasn't at all catlike. "When?"

"Tonight at ten. Single combat at the abandoned mine near Hole-in-the-Wall."

"In a hurry, was he? If that's the ending, I'd better hear the beginning and middle."

Rule gestured for Lily to begin.

"The beginning," she said. "was when Javier insisted all the guards be checked for weapons before we left the rendezvous point. During this process Edgar's guard, George, apparently dosed Benedict with something that sent him into the fury."

Rule heard his father's quick indrawn breath. Lily probably didn't.

"There were multiple casualties," she continued, "including two initial dead—Edgar of Wythe and Javier's guard, Gil. Benedict was extremely difficult to stop or subdue, so Arjenie knocked everyone out—"

"She *what*?"

"That's my assumption. I saw her slap the windshield of the car. I felt magic move out across the area. I saw everyone but Cullen collapse. I believe she drew strongly on her Gift, and the interference from the armored windshield knocked her out. Somehow she broadcast the effect."

"I see," Isen said. "No, actually I don't, but I'll save my questions for later. Benedict's condition?"

"He took less damage than anyone, I think. He's sleeping in the back of Scott's car. Cullen's keeping a sleep charm on him. Arjenie is with us. Um . . . summary of injuries. Rule has cracked or broken ribs, which is probably why he's letting me do a lot of the talking. Cullen has a concussion, but his vision cleared quickly. I think Lucas's guard has a broken arm. Billy—Myron's guard—has a broken neck, but Cullen thinks he can heal it if he receives proper medical care. I think Lucas got bumps and bruises but no breaks."

"You don't mention yourself."

"I stayed back. I couldn't help. I didn't trust myself to shoot left-handed, not with everyone moving so fast."

"She's got a bruised hip," Rule said, "and may have incurred damage to her arm. Javier knocked her down on his way to me."

She slid him a look he couldn't interpret, but there seemed a hint of surprise in it. Had she thought he hadn't noticed her being hurt?

Isen spoke. "You've accounted for only two deaths."

"George, Edgar's man, had a broken jaw and probably a concussion, but he didn't die from his injuries. He had a heart attack."

"A heart attack."

"I'll take it from here," Rule said. "George was farther from Arjenie than most of us, which is probably why he woke before the others. He was able to subvocalize despite his jaw, and confirmed that he'd used a potion on Benedict, expecting it to knock him out. Edgar ordered this. He believed it to be the price of his brother's life. Brian—" His voice caught. *Hold it together*, he told himself. "Brian is being held captive. George didn't know who held him, but I can guess. At any rate, Edgar felt he had no choice. He did order George to stand over Benedict and defend him if we were attacked."

Lily was frowning. "Edgar believed that? The kidnapper tells him it's a knockout potion, and he believes it?"

Rule gave a small shrug. "I don't know what assurances he was given or why he found them credible. There wasn't time for me to learn more. Isen, after I heard this much, I called Myron to come and bear witness. He was the only other Lu Nuncio awake at that point. Before he could, however, George suffered a heart attack."

"That's what Lily said. I find it hard to believe."

"Whatever happened, it killed him."

"Cullen called it a heart attack," Lily said. "I'm thinking he was given some kind of delayed action potion. Something to make sure he didn't live long enough to tell us much."

"Hmm." Isen could stuff a lot of doubt into a single sound. "How could such a potion be timed to work at exactly the right moment?"

"Maybe it wasn't triggered by the elapsed time, but by some other factor. Like when his healing went into overdrive because he was injured. I don't know diddly about potions, but supposedly Dya's people are really good at causing heart attacks."

"You're thinking of Ruben Brooks," Isen said. "But Brooks's heart attack didn't kill him. It's a stretch to believe that he's tougher than a lupus."

"Dya wouldn't have known that Ruben has a trace of sidhe blood. That could make a difference."

Rule was hit by a thought. "Edgar didn't die right away."

Lily looked at him. "What do you mean?"

"He took a blow to the head, a hard one. But he was moving, trying to get up, shortly after that. Maybe it wasn't the blow to the head that killed him. His injury would have triggered his healing. Maybe that in turn triggered a potion he'd been given. Maybe he died from a heart attack, too."

"Do you have his body?" Isen asked.

"Yes. George's, also."

"I assume Nettie will be able to tell if there's heart damage. I'm getting an idea I don't like."

Rule started to laugh, but stopped because it hurt. "I haven't liked much about today so far."

"So far, our enemy has held the high cards," Isen agreed. "But there may be a joker in the deck. Shortly before Lily called, I received a call from a young woman who wouldn't give her name. She spoke English with an odd accent and claimed that Brian of Wythe asked her to call me. No doubt you're making the same leap I did—that my mysterious caller was Arjenie's mysterious sister. I believe we're right about that. I kept a log, of course—"

"A log?" Lily said.

Rule answered briefly. "Shorthand." Isen might routinely forget he owned a cell phone, but he was excellent with older information technology. He routinely jotted notes in Gregg shorthand during a call. "Go on," he told his father.

"First she asked me to confirm that I was Isen Turner. I did. Next she asked me not to interrupt or ask questions because she didn't know how long the telephone lines would cooperate. I didn't. She then said she'd been trying to call for some time, but . . . I'll give her exact phrasing. 'Phones and magic do not agree. Easy enough to disrupt, hard to make

clear.' She then said Brian named me because I was nearby
and an ally, and was this true? I told her yes, and slipped in
one question: Who was she? She said she was a friend of
Brian's who didn't want him to die."

"Friar," Lily said. "Robert Friar has him."

"You interrupt again—but then, unlike her, I didn't ask
you not to. Yes. She said it would be best if Robert Friar died
instead of Brian, and perhaps I would kill him, and I was not
to tell the authorities about Brian because Friar would very
likely know and would kill him and possibly her, also. She
said that if I act, I must act quickly. I will quote her again.
'Friar does not listen to me. He makes his own experiments,
and I think Brian is dying too quickly for my potions to help.
Tomorrow I think will be too late. We are . . .' Unfortunately,
the call ended then in a burst of static."

No one spoke for a moment. "Well," Lily said, "that's
definitely a joker. The big question is whether Friar dealt it
to us."

Rule glanced quickly at her. "Her story agrees with
George's."

"Which could mean it's true. Or it could mean Friar fed
Edgar that story and made sure Dya pitched hers to match."

"You credit him with an amazing degree of cleverness."

"So far he's winning. He probably did grab Brian, but we
don't know that Brian's still alive. If—"

"Of course we do," Isen said. "If Friar had killed him
instead of kidnapping him, the heir's portion of the mantle
would have returned to Edgar, who could not then have been
blackmailed. We know, therefore, that Brian was alive at the
time of Edgar's death, because Edgar wouldn't have staged
things the way he did if his heir was dead. Now that Edgar
is dead, Brian has inherited the full mantle. If anything happens to him, the Wythe mantle is lost forever."

Vexation crossed Lily's face. "I should have thought of
that."

"Such knowledge is not yet instinctive for you. Knowing
that Brian is alive, our duty is clear. We can't allow Wythe
lupi to descend into pack-lost beasts. Also, Brian's testimony
will persuade the other clans as nothing else could."

"Dammit." Rule's hands tightened on the steering wheel

as if he had Javier's neck there to wring. "I don't see any way out of the Challenge. Javier won't believe anything we tell him, so he won't agree to a postponement. Maybe his father would listen to you." The Ybirra Rho, Manuel, was as calm as Javier was fiery.

"Hmm. I could try speaking with Manuel, but . . . no, I think not. We'll want to make sure Friar is aware of the Challenge. It will provide an excellent distraction for us to rescue Brian."

"How?" Rule demanded. "Hole-in-the-Wall is too far from Friar's place for me to do both, and I don't know if Benedict will be in any shape to lead a rescue party tonight."

"We'll need Lucas, I think," Isen said thoughtfully. "I've an idea how we can encourage him to help, despite whatever doubts he may have about Nokolai's integrity. And Stephen, of course. I imagine he's agreed to witness?"

"Yes, but—"

"With or without Benedict, you'll have to lead the rescue party."

His throat closed up. He forced out two words: "Father. No."

Lily looked worried. "I don't understand."

Isen said what Rule could not bring himself to. "Javier Challenged Nokolai, not Rule. Such Challenges are usually settled by the two Lu Nuncios, but there is another way. I will fight Javier."

FORTY

❦

ARJENIE woke up as they passed Clanhome's gates. Lily gave her the high points—or low points—of what they knew as quickly as possible, but she wasn't sure how much Arjenie took in. She was quiet, anxious, maybe shocky.

Many people went through most of their lives without ever seeing someone die, much less by violence. Arjenie had watched her lover kill. It was going to affect her, it was going to affect Benedict, and it would damn sure affect how they were with each other. Lily didn't know how and was trying not to think about it. None of her guesses came out happy.

Nettie met them at door. She checked Cullen out briefly, told him his head would stop hurting sooner or later, then began unwrapping the elastic bandage around Rule's ribs. While she did, Lily checked on Benedict.

They'd put him on a couch in the living room, with two guards—one who made sure a sleep charm stayed in contact with his skin, the other ten feet away with a weapon drawn. Just in case. Interestingly, none of the lupi smelled the fury on him now, and hadn't since he was knocked out. Whatever chemical exudation their noses picked up, it only kicked in when he was awake. But when Lily touched him, she still felt that oily magic.

Less of it, though. That was a relief. Cobb had apparently thrown off the effects of the potion within a couple hours, but a sample of one didn't guarantee anything. Of course, Cobb had also woken up suicidal.

Sample of one, Lily reminded herself. Probably not applicable. Benedict wouldn't be waking up in a tiny cell with no hope of freedom.

When she straightened, Arjenie was talking to Isen, who'd put an arm around her. Nettie was standing in front of Rule with both hands on his bare rib cage, her eyes closed, muttering a chant.

Lupi heal some things faster than others. Their bodies eliminate invading agents—poisons, drugs, bacteria—so quickly that the invader never has a chance to do any damage. When there is actual damage—from a knife, a bullet, a kick—healing takes longer. How long depends on the injury and the lupus.

Rule was a fast healer, even for his people. Lily waited to hear just how fast.

Nettie's eyes opened. "That's all I can give you right now," she told him. "If I'm going to help Billy, I have to save some for him. You said he's at Alvarado?"

Rule smiled, bent, and kissed her cheek. "You've eased me considerably, Nettie. Thank you. Yes, I told Myron to take him to Alvarado. It was close, and you've spoken favorably of their treatment of spinal injuries. I'll send Myron's contact info to your phone so you can call him if you need to."

"Good. I'm going to wrap you again." She retrieved the elastic bandage and began winding. "Compression will keep you more comfortable, and you don't have to worry about pneumonia. Two of your ribs are cracked, not badly. They'll be eighty percent healed by tonight. The third one was broken and displaced and poking your damn lung." Her lips tightened as she fastened the binding. Nettie was offended by damage to her people. "No puncture, but it was abrading the surface, which your body kept having to heal. I got the ends lined up and there's soft callus forming now. By tonight there will probably be some hard callus, but hard callus does not equal healed. That rib will still be fragile. You'll be careful."

"As careful as I can." Rule glanced at his father, who'd headed for the big dining table.

It wasn't until then that Lily noticed who else sat at the table—which just proved how distracted she'd been. A round, cheerful old woman sat at the table knitting. Her dress was full, fuchsia, and floral, sprouting blooms in a half dozen unlikely colors. Her hair was white. So were her eyes.

Lily didn't know what had caused the Nokolai Rhej's blindness. Whatever it was, her lack of vision was more excuse than cause, Lily thought, for the woman's habit of seldom leaving her cabin. Blindness was a loss for anyone, but less restrictive for her than for others. She was a highly Gifted physical empath, able to sense objects around her.

But how did it let her knit? "Sera," Lily said, using the title lupi gave her. Lily had been given permission to use her name, but she didn't understand the rules for when it was and wasn't okay, so she seldom used it. "I'm surprised to see you here."

"You'll be talking about our great enemy," the Rhej said, her head tilted down as if she were watching the needles busily clicking together. Whatever she was knitting was a much calmer color than she wore, a soft blue gray. "I'm needed for that." She lifted her head for the world as if she were looking straight at Arjenie, who stood uncertain and alone several feet away. "Arjenie, isn't it? Come sit by me. You and I will need to talk later."

NETTIE left—with, much to her disgust, an armed escort. Isen informed her she was potentially a target and she wasn't going alone. The rest of them—save Benedict—sat down at the long dining table to plan.

When Lily first became Nokolai, she'd thought of Isen as the clan's CEO, setting general policies and goals, but handing off the implementation to others. The Council of Elders might be considered his board of directors. Rule was CFO;

he handled the overall finances and investments. Benedict handled security. In all honesty, she'd thought Isen didn't work as hard as his two sons. It had taken months for her perspective to shift enough for her to understand what his job really was.

Isen handled the people.

It was a full-time, hands-on job. Kind of like being a stay-at-home mom, she thought, a lot of what he did was invisible, with success measured in absences. Fights that didn't break out. Arguments that didn't deepen into enmity. Daughters who weren't ignored. Sons who didn't go wild. Men who didn't stay stuck and angry in jobs they hated. And a lack of Challenges.

Little *c* challenges were common in the clans. Lupi settled grievances and established status that way. They were fought either two-legged or four-legged, and with varying degrees of formality. Killing was not allowed. If you killed your opponent in a little *c* challenge, you could be put to death yourself if your Rho determined it was intentional. If the death was clearly an accident, you'd still be in big trouble.

Big *C* Challenges were fought only in wolf-form. Internal Challenges could be issued to another clan member, to the Lu Nuncio, or to the Rho. There was a complex code for Challenging the Lu Nuncio or the Rho, and such Challenges were rare in most clans, most of the time. If a Challenge was issued between clan members, the Rho had to give consent. There was a good chance he'd lose one of his clan if he allowed it to proceed.

In any Challenge, if a combatant submitted, his life must be spared. But by submitting he acknowledged himself in the wrong and bound himself to fulfill whatever penance or payment the victor decreed.

A clan Challenge was like an internal Challenge that way. But since it was fought to settle differences between clans rather than individuals, if one Lu Nuncio submitted to the other, his entire clan had to accept whatever terms the other Lu Nuncio imposed. If the Rho of the losing clan refused the terms, he had two choices: repudiate his heir and remove him from the clan. Or war.

That's why Clan Challenges were rare and almost always

to the death. Lu Nuncios were lousy at submitting and unlikely to give their enemy a blank check.

Lily had learned some of this from Rule, some from the Rhej, whose job included teaching a new clan member what she needed to know. She wasn't sure how it changed things when a Rho decided to answer a Challenge personally, but it was bound to raise the stakes.

Rule's father was over ninety years old. Those were lupi years, of course, but even in lupi years, that put him into middle age. Javier was young, quick, strong, and considered a very good fighter. Isen was rolling dice at an extremely high-stakes game, and the odds were against him.

From what Lily could tell, he was delighted with himself.

Oh, he was brisk enough as he opened by informing them he'd spoken with Manuel, who'd said that he backed his son's decisions. No one seemed surprised by that. But there was a merry glint in his eyes.

"I asked Cynna if she could confirm Brian's presence at Friar's," Isen said. "She said she could certainly Find a lupus, if one was there. Earth doesn't block her. Since it seems unlikely Friar is entertaining multiple lupi guests, I thought that would be enough. Given the quality and strength of her Gift, she didn't think she'd have to get close enough to be in danger, but I sent Paul and Jason with her to be sure."

Cullen grunted. Clearly he didn't like having Cynna anywhere near Friar, but he didn't say so. "I'd like to know how Arjenie could knock out her bonded mate."

Arjenie looked wan and worried. "I don't know. I don't understand this mate bond thing, but I thought . . . I was told my magic couldn't affect Benedict. That's why I waited so long. I had to think it out. I expected to knock out everyone but him and Lily and maybe Cullen. He—Benedict left the ones who'd fallen alone. I was scared he'd go after Lily if she was the only one standing, but I didn't know what else to do."

"You did the right thing," Lily said firmly. "I've an idea about why it worked the way it did. When a mate bond is new, it's really tight. The obvious result is that you can't be far apart, but with Rule and me, it also meant we got some . . . call it overlap. Not all the time, but when things were really tense, I got a bit of his hearing and he got a bit of my imperviousness to magic. It didn't last." She glanced at Rule, remembering where they'd been when she heard almost like he did. "Maybe when Arjenie knocked herself out, Benedict was tapped into her Gift, so it affected him, too."

"Hmm." Isen was thoughtful. "So Benedict was vulnerable to what happened to Arjenie because of the mate bond, not in spite of it."

"I'm just guessing, but yeah."

He turned to Arjenie and spoke gently. "Arjenie, what do you want to do?"

She blinked. "I'm sorry?"

"You've had a difficult experience. Do you need a sedative or some privacy to think or meditate?"

"You don't want me to hear what you're planning?"

"I need your help in another way, if you're able to offer it. We need to know more about what Friar built underground. Specifically, there has to be a back door. People have left through his house who didn't come in through his house. I'm hoping you can find it."

Arjenie bit her lip, then thrust her hand out to Lily.

Lily took it—winced, and let go. "You're shouting."

"Sorry. I get anxious and try too hard, and . . . please."

Lily tried again. Arjenie may have been trying to think in clear sentences, but she was too agitated. Her thoughts tumbled over each other so quickly it took Lily a moment to sort out what Arjenie desperately wanted to say. "Isen, she wants you to promise you'll rescue Dya, too, which means you have to get the tears for her. Arjenie can't tell you what they look like, but Dya will be able to. She thinks Dya will be willing to leave now. Ah . . . she thinks Dya refused to leave earlier out of fear for her—Dya didn't think Arjenie could get the tears without being caught—and because Brian needed her. That he needed the healing potions she made."

Isen nodded. "I can't promise results. I can promise we will try as hard to retrieve Dya and the tears as we would to reclaim one of our own."

"I wasn't asked to promise," Lily added, "but there's no way I'm leaving Dya there."

Arjenie sighed in relief and let go of Lily's hand. "I'll do anything I can to help. I don't know what more I can find, but I'll do my best." Her mouth twitched into a quick smile, there-and-gone. "Research will settle me better than meditation, so I'll get started right away." She pushed her chair back and darted a glance at Benedict, sleeping peacefully on a couch at the other end of the long room . . . with a .38 trained on him. "What's going to happen with him?"

Isen answered. "Lily will keep checking. Once the potion is out of his system, we'll let him wake. After that, we'll see what kind of shape he's in."

Emotions flitted over her face in a cascade too quick and jumbled to read. Lily wondered if she smelled as confused and unhappy as she looked. She left without saying anything more.

Rule leaned closer to say, low-voiced, "You weren't asked to promise because there is no way you are taking part in this rescue."

"Arjenie made an assumption. You are, too."

"You're wounded, unable to fight, and we are not going in legally. You can't be part of it."

Lily had thought this through on the way here. She knew she had a tough sales job ahead—but Rule wasn't the one she most needed to convince. "Until recently, the law hurt and hindered lupi instead of offering the protection it's supposed to provide. You're accustomed to working around it or outside it." She looked at Rule, Cullen, the Rhej, Isen. "That's your default. Go in, get it done, don't get caught. If Friar were the only enemy involved, that might work. But he isn't."

"If you're planning to arrest Her Bitchness," Cullen said dryly, "I'm going to think it was you instead of me who got knocked in the head."

"Think about who *her* agent is. Robert Friar is determined to rouse public opinion against lupi. That's been *her* theme, too. When she first moved against lupi last year, she tried to get Rule framed for murder. Bad press for you. More distrust between you and the law in general. Now think about who's been attacked—and how. Think about what the potion was designed to do."

"Hmm." Isen fingered his beard. "I do believe you've

spotted a pattern. The attacks on lupi haven't been designed to kill us. Killing is a by-product. *She* wants to turn humans against us."

"Devil's advocate here," Cullen said. "We don't know what the potion dumped in our water supply would have done."

"Which means we can't factor it in," Lily said. "Either for or against."

"It doesn't fit *her* previous strategies," Rule said slowly. "During the Great War, she pitted one group of humans against another. She didn't try to turn all humans against us. I'm not saying she couldn't have learned a new trick, but—"

"Eriodus," the Rhej murmured without looking up from the yarn in her lap. "The Twins."

That must have meant something to Rule. "Ah. Yes, it worked with the Twins, didn't it?" He looked at Lily. "By giving the humans of a small but strategic kingdom a common enemy to unite against—the king's twin sons, who were accused of dabbling in death magic—she was able to insinuate her worship into the highest councils. Eventually her agents controlled the kingdom."

"So we're agreed?" Lily asked, looking around. "She doesn't just want to destroy lupi. She wants to use your destruction to increase her power among the general population. She wants a pogrom, a witch hunt, a second Purge, with lupi as the target."

"I'll agree that's one of *her* plans," Isen said. "She plans in multiples. You may have noted that she was setting this up with Friar well before the Azá attempted to open that hellgate. If they'd succeeded, she wouldn't have needed Friar."

"Wouldn't she?" Rule said. "Let's speculate. Say the hellgate had opened and the world is at war with demons. Friar would be talking the same 'us against them' rant he spews now—and he'd have an even bigger, angrier, more frightened audience. How hard would it be to extend the fear of demons to fear of all nonhumans? Perhaps that was her original plan. Or one of them."

A chill ran down Lily's spine. The Great Bitch had so nearly succeeded . . . "Now think about who she wanted just plain dead, no tricky PR campaign needed. First, the head of the federal Unit that investigates crimes connected to magic. Second, the federal agent closely allied with lupi."

Isen's eyebrows lifted. "You're thinking that *she* wants to cut us off from the support and protection of our government."

"I'm thinking she doesn't want the lupi and the government working together. That's what she's trying to prevent, which means that together we threaten her plans. Which means you can't afford to burn any legal bridges tonight."

Isen shook his head. "It could just as easily mean it will take both legal agents and those acting outside the law to stop her. The human world doesn't know about her. They can't and won't react to what she does quickly and decisively enough to stop her. We can."

"Sure," Cullen muttered. "If we ever stop fighting each other."

"Here's a clue," the Rhej said, her needles busy. "You have two Chosens now. One is an FBI agent. The other works for the FBI. I'm sure there were many reasons Lily and Arjenie were Chosen. The Lady is efficient—she layers many purposes into a single gift. But I think it's no coincidence you have two Lady-touched who are connected to the law."

Isen frowned and didn't respond.

"Look, I know why you have to get Brian out," Lily said. "But I have to ask—what if the tip about him was deliberate? Maybe Dya had orders to call you. Maybe she's sincere, but has been tricked or manipulated. What if that's why no one called the cops today? Because Friar wants you free to invade his place, and get caught doing it."

"I'm not buying it," Rule said. "I don't know why no reporter showed up, but I don't think that's the reason. Friar's smart, but I don't think he's capable of the sort of devious, layers-within-layers planning you're talking about. *She* is, but she's limited by her tools."

"Friar has some kind of deal with the sidhe lord who provided Dya. I'm no expert on the sidhe, but they've got a rep for the devious and the subtle. Layers-within-layers, like you said."

Isen's eyebrows shot up. Rule started to say something. Stopped.

"Son of a bitch," Cullen said. "She's right. The sidhe

adore subtlety, and we don't know jack shit about this elf. Maybe he isn't involved at all. He hands over Dya for some unknown consideration, then heads back to work on his own plots back home. Or maybe he's the boss of this operation and pops in for a cup of tea and a status update twice a week. We don't know."

Rule summed that possibility up nicely. "Shit."

Isen spoke. "You convince me that we'll have to be especially wary. But trap or no, we have to rescue Brian, and I don't see how your participation would help. You're injured and not up to a fight. Your presence would divide Rule's attention."

Lily drummed her fingers once, impatient. "I don't go in as part of a lupi SWAT team. Kidnapping is a federal crime. We've received a tip about a kidnap victim that I judge to be valid. I go to Friar's front door and present him with a search warrant. The rest of you need to find a back door."

It wasn't that simple, of course.

Normally, kidnappings were investigated by regular FBI, not the Unit. But add in gado, a lupus victim, potions, and an out-realm being, and Lily could easily argue that this particular kidnapping required a Unit agent. Normally, too, a kidnapping was treated as a hostage situation—you went in with your weapon drawn, not with a search warrant. But the warrant would be as much legal sleight-of-hand as it was a serious search tool.

One more "normally" she wasn't observing: her backup. Oh, she wasn't going in alone. The warrant made a good lifeline; if she vanished, there'd be a judge who'd point a finger in the right direction. But Friar could decide that a pointed finger was the lesser of two evils, compared to getting arrested right then and there. Criminals were like that. So backup, yes, but not regular FBI. The situation was too volatile, with too much she couldn't tell them. Just asking the wrong question at the wrong time could land them all in "oh, fuck." Instead, she wanted to take Cullen and Cynna.

Cynna would not go into the tunnel with them. She'd Find it. As for Cullen—well, his presence might come back to bite her later. Unit agents were allowed wide discretion in employing Gifted consultants, and a few months ago, she wouldn't have thought twice about using Cullen in a search. But that was then, this was now, and it was Robert Friar's home they'd be searching. He would claim that Cullen planted anything they found. They'd be lucky if he didn't sue.

And it was absurd to worry about that when the thing that would really get her ass handed to her was outsourcing a break-in by lupi.

By the time Cynna returned, they'd agreed on the basic plan. "The bad news," she said, tossing her purse on a chair, "is that there is no lupus in or beneath Friar's place."

Cullen scowled. "Does that mean there's good news?"

"More like not-quite-so-bad," she said, digging in her purse. "There is a tunnel. I mapped it as closely as I could by Finding for air beneath the ground—which is not as easy as it sounds, believe me. No underground rooms that I could Find, but I couldn't follow it very far. No good cover to hide from the guys with guns." She pulled out an aerial map, unfolded it, and spread it on the table. "Here's Friar's house, see? I've drawn the location of the tunnel in red."

"Heads up into the mountains," Rule said. "Or under them, I guess."

Lily frowned. "Why would he go to so much trouble and expense to create a tunnel into the mountains? An underground shrine or dungeon or drug-making lab I can see. But this?"

"A node?" Cullen tipped his head, considering his own suggestion. "If you want your elf buddy to be able to drop by, you need a node."

"Wouldn't you have noticed a node near Friar's place?"

"Not if it's far enough below ground. The power gets absorbed or dispersed by that much earth pretty thoroughly." He frowned. "Seems to be a pretty long tunnel, though. That's both expensive and hard to hide while in process."

"I found something," Arjenie called from the other side of the room. She was heading toward them, carrying a laptop. "It's not exactly what we're looking for, but I thought you ought to have a look." She reached them, hesitated. "Something's up?"

Rule explained briefly.

"Let's see." She leaned over the table, looking at Cynna's map. "Yes, this makes sense. Let me show you." She set the laptop down and touched a key, waking it from sleep. The screen lit with a puzzling diagram. "This idea kept nibbling at me. It was sort of wild goose-ish, but I wasn't having much luck looking for the back door, so I gave it a try. Lily, you probably remember that after the Azá created all that trouble at that underground node, the USGS got tasked with mapping that cave system."

Lily shook her head. "I never heard about that."

"Oh. Well, Ruben did, and he had me check on the progress every so often. One of his hunches, I think. They never finished—first there were budget cuts, then the gnomes applied to have the cave system added to their Underways, which is why the partial map got classified Secret. You know how gnomes are about privacy. But I remembered looking at a schematic of the part that did get mapped, and I thought . . . well, here it is."

It looked like spaghetti to Lily. Radioactive spaghetti. Wiggly white lines glowed against a black background with a few glowing blobs—caves, caverns?—strung along some of the loops.

"Of course, you can't tell much from this," Arjenie said. "Here's the 3-D view." She hit a few keys and the lines separated, becoming a 3-D representation. "They tied a bunch of key points to GPS, so I was able to transpose it onto an aerial map. I'll show you." She moved the cursor, clicked. Glowing spaghetti suddenly overlay the tan, gray, and dull green of mountains. "This is the tunnel we're interested in."

She shifted the screen to follow one particular strand of spaghetti that stretched out straighter and farther than most . . . and the aerial view was suddenly familiar. A whole lot like Cynna's map, in fact, complete with a view of Friar's roof and swimming pool.

Lily felt cold. Then hot. "Are you telling us that Friar's tunnel connects to the cave system the Azá used?" On the list of places she never wanted to see again, that one would be number two. Right after hell.

"I can't say for sure. My tunnel ends more than a quarter mile from the one Cynna found, and I don't know if that's because it really ends or if that's just where the mapping stopped. Plus I'll have to check the notations about depth to see if the two tunnels are in the same plane. But it looks like they could connect, doesn't it?"

It sure as hell did. "Arjenie, you said the gnomes petitioned to have this added to their Underways. Was their petition granted?"

"I don't know," she said apologetically. "I didn't check."

"Find out. Unless the petition was refused out of hand, I'm betting it's still pending. It's been less than a year, and if the gnomes claimed that cave system, they wouldn't tolerate Friar's little tunnel."

"Okay." She looked puzzled. "You sound really cheerful about that."

Isen smiled. "I believe I know why. Once the government agrees to consider such a petition, it becomes the custodian of the caves in question."

Lily shot him a grin. "Exactly. In which case, we've not only found our back door—it's on federal property."

FORTY-ONE

DUSK. Air cooling in the slide from light to dark. A world wrapped in gray, its edges fuzzed and uncertain. Birds quiet, lights coming on inside houses . . . and, here at Clanhome, the occasional howl off in the mountains. Or closer.

Lily stepped out on the rear deck and paused, letting her eyes adjust to the incomplete light. Then she headed for the tall, dark-haired man leaning on the railing at the far end of the deck.

He turned. "You got the warrant?"

"Finally." The judge had taken some persuading. The terms of the search were unconventional, and she hadn't liked the idea of discussing matters in her chambers in a circle drawn by a sorcerer. The circle had been necessary to make sure Friar didn't eavesdrop. The Code 300 the Bureau was operating under had persuaded the judge to accept the precaution.

"And you wanted me to know right away."

"Not exactly. I . . ." Lily finger-combed her hair back from her face. "This wasn't my idea. I thought Isen should talk to you. He thought I should. He won. I'm not sure how. Something about how he thinks you and I are so alike."

Benedict's eyebrows lifted. "My father's understanding
of people is uncanny, but . . ."

"I don't get it, either." She frowned up at him. "I don't
know what he thinks I can say. I'm not a talk-it-out person,
so I don't know how to get someone else to do that. Unless
I'm interviewing," she added, "but that's different, isn't it?"

He smiled slightly. "Is that what this is? An attempt to get
me to work through my trauma?"

"No. I can listen if you want to—"

"No."

She nodded, understanding perfectly. "How you deal
with what happened isn't any of my business as long as it
doesn't interfere with the mission tonight. The potion's out
of your system, so that's not a problem. You told Isen you
were okay to go tonight, and he took you at your word. I'm
trusting his judgment."

"And yet you're here."

"I talked to Arjenie a few minutes ago. Or tried to. I'm
not a talk-it-out person, but she is, and she's not talking."

He turned away, laying his hands on the railing again.
"You don't want to go there."

"My wants have nothing to do with it. She's avoiding
you. You're avoiding her. That isn't going to work."

"You're a couples therapist now?"

"It isn't going to work because in a couple hours you'll
both be underground with your lives and a lot of others depending on how well you function together."

"You discussed this with my father."

"Damn right. With Rule, too. Rule thinks I should stay
out of it. He's willing to gamble his life that neither of you
will screw up because you're tied up in knots about the other
one. I'm not."

His hands tightened. She heard the wood creak in protest.
"I'm not going to force my presence on her. She's afraid of
me."

"She—"

He slashed the air, quick, and definite, with one hand,
cutting her off. "Don't try to feed me comforting lies. I smell
it on her."

"Maybe she is. She also thinks you blame her for what happened."

He turned—quicker this time, not so deliberately. "How could she possibly—"

"She couldn't say it, of course. She can't speak of her sister. But I held her hand and I know what she thinks. It was her sister's potion that turned you into a killer."

"I am a killer."

That stopped her—but only for a moment. "Wolves kill, yeah. Warriors kill, too—when we have to. When that's required. You didn't kill today because of your wolf or your will. You were used. Viciously used."

He made an impatient noise. "You see that. I see it. But while Arjenie might agree with you in her head, she doesn't feel that way about it. She doesn't understand violence."

"You're right. She doesn't have a context for it. She's trying to build one, but you staying away doesn't help. She saw you freak out . . ." Lily paused, remembering. "That was incredible. Until today I would have said no single person, human or lupus or whatever, could take down one of those red-eye demons without major firepower." She'd seen Rule try once with the help of another lupus, and with Lily shooting it every so often. "I'm betting you could."

His voice was desert-dry. "I doubt Arjenie shares your admiration."

Annoyed with herself for getting sidetracked, she brushed that away. "My point is, she saw you freak. She knows you didn't act by your own will, but knowing that doesn't erase the images. You need to remind her of who you are. We're what our choices make us. What you didn't choose isn't part of you. What you do about it will be."

He was still. Silent. After a long moment, his mouth crooked up on one side. "My father is right again. How annoying of . . ." His voice drifted off. So did his attention, drawn to something behind her.

Lily turned. Arjenie had stepped out onto the deck. And for the first time, Lily saw the woman's sidhe heritage.

Maybe it was the quality of the light, the shifting dimness somehow transmuting Arjenie's careful gait into an instant of pure grace. She wore her usual tee and jeans, yet Lily could almost see the filmy sort of gowns elves wore. See how right that would look, anyway, flowing around long, thin limbs, with the wild rumpus of her hair falling loose around pale shoulders.

Lily blinked. The almost-seen vision was gone. It was thoroughly a normal woman coming toward them—thin, uncertain, her glasses hiding her eyes in the failing light. Lily glanced at Benedict.

He stood utterly still, as entranced as they say humans sometimes were by the sight of an elfin maid. Maybe he saw Arjenie as Lily had for a moment. Or maybe what he saw didn't matter, eclipsed by what he felt.

"I'll be going now," she said dryly, sure he wouldn't notice.

But he did. He looked straight at her. "Lily." He paused. "Most advice is useless because it's shaped to the giver, so it is an ill fit for anyone else. But my father did send you to me, so I'll give you my hardest-won lesson, for whatever good it may do you. For some of us, it's easier to understand what we would die for or kill for than what we will live for. What we live for can change." He nodded. "Thank you."

ARJENIE was desperately unsure if she was doing the right thing. Maybe she should turn around and go back inside immediately. Benedict didn't want to see her, and she wasn't at all sure she wanted to see him, and . . . and he was looking at her as if she were the only thing left to see in the whole world. Her heart fluttered.

Foolish heart. Maybe she was a fool. She could live with that. She kept walking toward him. It wasn't until he turned his head and said something to Lily that she realized Lily was present. Her feet stopped. She should go back inside. This wasn't the right time.

If not now, when? They weren't guaranteed to live through tonight. She thought they would. Hoped they would. But no guarantees. She got her poor, frightened feet moving again.

Lily left, pausing briefly on her way inside to give Arjenie a nod and a smile. Bless her. Arjenie let her feet carry her up to within a couple feet of Benedict. She managed a smile. She managed to say, "Hi." Then her brain shut down.

A wisp of amusement ghosted across his hard features. "Hi?"

"You think I know what to say? I don't know what to say, except that I'd be a big mess if I were you. No, I mean I'd be a mess if I'd had done to me what was done to you." She cocked her head. "You don't look like a mess."

"I'm functional. I . . . have a context for what happened. You don't."

"It's still pinging through me. Little aftershocks. I'll get shaky all of a sudden, as if . . . I don't know why. None of that was aimed at me."

"The first time I saw someone killed, I threw up."

She smiled. "That's a very human reaction."

"I was ten, so my wolf was still asleep."

Only ten. Dear gods. "And the first time you killed someone?" Because this wasn't his first. She was sure of that. Not sure why she asked, what she needed to know, but sure this wasn't the first time for him.

He was silent so long she thought he wouldn't answer. "His name was Brad Mettinger. I didn't know that when I killed him. My father used to leave Clanhome more often. He went to the symphony one night. He was restless afterward, so we headed for the park. We were jumped by a Leidolf strike squad. I killed the one with the gun and disabled two others. My father killed the fourth one. He—the fourth Leidolf—was in wolf form," Benedict added as if he didn't want her to think poorly of Isen. "It's harder to kill a wolf than a man."

"How did you feel?"

"At the time, satisfied. I hadn't failed. I was glad I'd refrained from killing all of them. It was best to allow Leidolf to clean up their own mess."

The bodies, he meant. He'd refrained from killing all of them so the survivors could remove the bodies. "Afterward? How did you feel afterward?"

Again he was silent for a long moment. "I was young, but I've never . . . Rule says that I live close to my wolf. That's not how I think of it. I don't feel the division between myself as wolf and myself as man that most do. Wolves don't regret killing. I didn't regret it, but it made space between the man and the wolf. I was uncomfortable with that space. Isen told me to learn about the man I'd killed."

"So you found out his name."

"His name, his age, that he had had two daughters, no sons. His father was still alive at the time. I learned his name, too. And his uncle's."

"Did that help?"

"It allowed me to grieve his death. Wolves don't, not when it's an enemy they've killed. Men need to, or they get twisted up."

"You're grieving now."

"Yes." He hesitated. "Isen says humans have a hard time being glad they're alive when others died, even when those others weren't close to them. They feel guilty for their joy at surviving. They have trouble grieving those deaths because of the guilt. I understand this in a way. My grief for Claire was muddied and snarled by guilt. Do you feel this way now?"

A sound broke from her, something between a laugh and a sob. "Yes—no—I feel confused! When it was happening—it all happened so fast! I couldn't believe how quick it all was. And you—" She stopped abruptly.

"I went insane. You saw that. You're frightened of me now."

"Lily said you're angry at what was done to you. She assured me anger doesn't make you crazy, that it isn't what I saw today, and you would never fall into the fury if you hadn't—if someone hadn't . . . the fury's different from regular anger. Isn't it?"

"They're alike in the way a puddle is like the ocean."

She shivered. "It must have been horrible to feel that way."

"They say women often forget the pain of childbirth. That the mind protects them from a too-keen recall. I remember what I did. What I felt has already begun to fade. Arjenie, I don't blame you. I don't blame your sister. I blame Robert Friar."

In that last, flat statement she heard and saw the anger

Lily had regretted mentioning. Deep anger. She couldn't speak—but not because of his anger. Because what she wanted to say involved Dya.

"You're frightened of me. Standing here with me scares you."

"Well, of course. Not because I think you're going to hurt me, because you're not doped up by some terrible potion now, so you wouldn't. It's more that I saw how much I don't know about you, and while I guess that's true for anyone when they fall in love, I—"

"In love?" He started to reach for her. Stopped. His face shifted from anger to hope to . . . fear? Yes, that was it. Hope and fear were conjoined twins, after all. "You think you love me?"

"Maybe it's just the mate bond thing for you, so you don't want to hear the L-word, but I know 'in love' when I feel it. Not that I've ever felt it this strongly, and I don't know if the mate bond makes it stronger, or if that's because of who you are. I'm still at the falling-in-love stage, and there's so much I don't know about you, which is scaring me. You have to really know someone to really, deeply love them, don't you?"

"I know you." His voice thrummed with certitude.

Her heart was pounding hard. So hard. "Only a few days of knowing. That's not much."

"There will be more to learn, but I know you. You're stubborn and pragmatic and caring. You like people. That liking is genuine and constant, with very few exceptions, so it's no surprise that people like you back. You delight in the pleasures of the mind and of the body. You think of yourself as fearful, but don't allow fear to stop you, which is the definition of courage. You're deeply accepting and deeply loyal. When the half sister you knew for two years nearly twenty years ago calls, you drop everything, risk everything, for her. You feel deeply, see clearly, and talk a lot. You don't care for wine. You love sweets. You have a strong sense of privacy. You treasure your family. You hate lying and avoid it if you possibly can. I don't know what it would take to make you really angry. You're clear and pure, and there are no stagnant places in you."

Her face was wet. When had she started crying? She

stepped forward, into his arms. They closed around her and she held on to him. Held on.

"I didn't think you'd let me hold you again." His voice was rough, broken. He pressed his cheek to the top of her head. "Not for a long time. Maybe not ever. Not after what you saw me do."

"I won't say that doesn't matter, because it does, but I don't know how and why and what it means . . ." She sighed. "I'm all-over confused. You made me sound so much more together than I am."

He began stroking her hair. "*Together* sounds like *finished*. You're too alive to be finished. I hope to have fifty or sixty years to watch you try out all sorts of ways to put the pieces of Arjenie together."

Her breath broke on a small laugh. "Maybe more." Honesty made her add, "Probably quite a bit more. Part-sidhe, remember? I don't know how long I'll live, but almost certainly more than that, and from what you've said about the mate bond, that means you'll be putting up with me a long time."

He went still. He stayed that way so long that she had to lean back so she could see him . . . and then couldn't, not clearly, because of her wet eyes, so she wiped them. Met his eyes.

And saw joy. Stark, bone-deep, glowing like the heart of the sun.

He reached up, cupped her face. "You will live a long time." There was wonder in his voice.

She nodded. "Most low sidhe live to a hundred, easy. A few live several centuries like the elves do, but they're the ones who heal really quick, which I don't. But I do heal faster than straight humans, so . . ." Suddenly she understood. Wonder seeped into her own voice as she said, "You love me. It isn't just the mate bond. You love *me*."

"So much." He smoothed her hair back. "So very much."

FORTY-TWO

IT was a whippy wind, a darting, daring, sand-in-the-face wind. Perhaps, Isen thought as he listened to it slapping at the car, the wind was annoyed with them for intruding on the empty places it frequented. Or perhaps it was delighted to find a new target for its mischief.

All personification aside, the wind was one more factor to consider when he fought for his life tonight . . . and, if he could manage it, fought to spare the life of the foolish, whippy young wolf he would face.

He had no desire to kill Javier. He had even less desire to be killed. Pity the odds were against him achieving both desires . . . or even just the last one.

Sixty-forty. That's where he put his chances. Though if his hunch was right, the odds would change drastically . . . but one couldn't count on an enemy to take the bait, however temptingly it might be offered. So if he were betting on the outcome tonight, he'd give himself a forty percent chance of seeing the dawn.

He suspected his sons put his chances somewhat lower, though they'd done their best to hold their fear hidden. They were good at concealing fear. They'd learned well.

Fine lupi, both of them. Exceptionally fine. Isen took a moment to enjoy the pride and humility of having such sons. He knew they'd survive and do well tonight. He didn't worry. Oh, he gave lip service to the idea that they could die, but he didn't believe it. Years ago, he had understood that sanity lay in a single, committed point of irrationality. Nature, circumstance, and duty would put his sons in danger at times—at times through his own orders. In order to do what he must, he had to believe they would live. And so he did. Mostly. Determinedly.

He didn't want to bring them grief tonight, but every son lost his father someday. Either the father died, as his had, or the son did. As three of his father's had. As one of his own sons had as well, defying Isen's deliberate, irrational certainty.

Mick had always been one to defy his father's expectations.

Strange. It was that lost son, the one he'd failed so thoroughly, who rode with him through the darkness now. Maybe because the dead drew closer when one faced death. Maybe because a tangled love bound more tightly, and the love between him and Mick had certainly been tangled. Maybe simply because regrets always hitched a ride when one traveled to death.

Not that he intended to die. How morbid he was! Isen chuckled at himself, earning a quick glance from Jason, one of his two living companions on this ride. He smiled and shook his head, letting the boy know he didn't wish for conversation.

Would Jason tell the clan that their Rho had gone to the Challenge in high good humor, chuckling at the prospect? Probably. That wouldn't hurt.

Isen had the reputation of being an excellent fighter when he was younger. This was part training and skill, part calculation. He'd needed that reputation, so he'd chosen his fights carefully, just as he'd chosen the events he participated in at All-Clans. His father had been a hundred and thirty when he was born—such a late-come babe he'd been! But much cherished, and desperately needed.

His father had lost three sons by then. A bullet took one. Another was killed in Challenge. The third, they had always believed, fell to a Leidolf assassin, though there was no proof. Isen had grown up knowing he would have his father for only a short time, and that he'd be taking up the mantle while still young.

Those youthful battles were long ago, but his strengths remained the same. He was an exceptionally fast healer, a quality enhanced by the mantle. He could take a lot of damage and keep fighting. He possessed both strength and endurance—not as much as he once had, true, but above average. And he fought best as wolf.

This was not as common as it might be. Young lupi fought and trained in wolf-form, certainly, but they either fought instinctively, or they were defeated. A wolf's instincts for battle were excellent, and if the man attempted to control the wolf instead of relying on him, it interfered with his reactions. But there were useful moves that wolves did not instinctively use, and lupi who fought purely on instinct missed opportunities to use them. This was where age aided Isen. It took many years and a great deal of training to seamlessly blend the two natures in a battle, combining a wolf's instincts with a man's canniness.

Isen had only one real weakness. He lacked speed. He always had.

That, alas, had only become truer with age. No matter how clever and canny the fighter, if he was too much slower than his opponent, he would get bloodied. Look at how well Seabourne had done against Benedict today. Benedict was twenty times the fighter Seabourne was—but Seabourne was ungodly fast, and smart enough to rely wholly on his speed. From what Isen had been told, Seabourne had done his damnedest not to close with Benedict.

And still the super-quick Seabourne had ended up concussed. It was a cheering thought.

Not that Isen was in the same league as Benedict. No one was. His oldest son had it all—speed, agility, strength, healing, training, instinct, control, guts. Isen doubted there had been such a fighter in a thousand years. That was sheer speculation, of course, as there was no way to pit Benedict against, say, Armand, who had been legendary among the clans in the sixteenth century.

But it was good to remember that speed didn't always win. And Javier, thankfully, was no Benedict.

Just young. And fast. And probably lacking Isen's desire to spare his opponent's life.

Ah, well. Too much thinking, according to his wolf. Isen smiled and settled himself to wait, but underneath, his wolf was excited and eager. It had been a long time.

"THE wind's chilly," Benedict said, tucking Arjenie's jacket closer around her. "Are you sure you're warm enough?"

"I'm fine."

"I'd better get those kneepads on you, then."

"I can do that."

"I'd be pleased if you allowed me to do this for you."

Her smile flickered like a lightbulb with a poor connection. "That's not exactly asking, but you're doing much better. All right." She handed him the kneepads.

They were in the state lands that butted up against Friar's land—and one corner of Clanhome. That afternoon, Cynna had gone back out to try and Find Brian again, searching close to the underground node. She'd failed in that, but reported that she also couldn't Find the node. Three possible reasons for that, she'd said. One, it could have closed. That was rare, but possible. Two, she might not be strong enough. Dirt and stone usually didn't block her Gift, but large amounts of quartz could. Three, the node could be warded in some way she'd never encountered before.

Given the sophistication of the wards around Friar's property, they were betting on door number three. They were also betting that Brian was being held near the node. The plan was to go in, find him and Dya, subdue whatever militia-types were guarding Brian—and Friar, too, if he was there—and get Brian and Dya out through the tunnel to Friar's house. Preferably they'd accomplish this before midnight, which was as long as Lily had been willing to wait before she came looking for them. Assuming Cynna Found the tunnel's entrance by then, that is.

Who knows? It might even work out that way.

The tumble of rock on their immediate right hid a crevice that opened onto a tunnel connected to the cave system. Benedict had sent José in earlier to check out the first part of their descent. It would be steep, twisty, and tight.

Most of them would Change and descend on four feet, except for Sammy and Arjenie. Sammy was the slightest of them. He'd remain two-footed so he could carry their weapons and a pack with some of their clothes. And Arjenie, of course, had to remain two-footed. She'd have a backpack, too, but would have to crawl in places.

Thus the kneepads. They'd found a pair of gloves for her, too.

Benedict knelt and wrapped a pad around Arjenie's left knee. She bent and whispered, "I'm kind of worried about Lucas. It seems like you gave him an awfully big incentive to not believe you."

Benedict tightened the pad, checked to make sure it was secure, looked up, and smiled. He whispered back, "He can hear us."

"Oh." She flushed and looked over at the tall, quiet man standing beside Rule—who was looking at her now, one eyebrow raised. "I'm sorry. I didn't realize . . . but since I've already got my foot in my mouth, I might as well explain."

"No need," Lucas said pleasantly. "I realize humans have different standards."

"Did you just insult me back? If so, I probably deserved it."

Benedict fastened the second kneepad in place and stood. "You're afraid Lucas or his father will prefer keeping the apartment building to publicly acknowledging that Nokolai has been blameless, and that the clans are in danger from *her*."

"Um . . . yes."

Lucas's presence was Isen's idea. He was a superb fighter, coolheaded and experienced, and so made a valuable addition to their team. But the main reason Isen wanted him along was to bear witness to the other clans. To obtain his Rho's consent to this, Isen had applied what Rule called blunt force bribery: he'd given the other clan Rule's apartment building. Temporarily.

It would serve as a monetary hostage. A very large monetary hostage. Benedict didn't know what the building was worth—that was Rule's department—but he'd heard Rule assure Andor that Nokolai's equity exceeded ten million. If anything happened to Lucas, that equity belonged to Szøs. If Lucas lived but still didn't believe Nokolai was right about *her*, that equity belonged to Szøs. Only if what Lucas saw tonight convinced him that Nokolai was right would his Rho sell the building back to Isen for a token amount.

"If this were a business deal," Rule said, exchanging a smile with Lucas, "I'd be suitably wary. In such a case I'd expect Andor and Lucas to take any advantage they could of Nokolai—short of outright lying, that is. That would be discourteous. But this isn't business. It's a matter of honor."

Arjenie nodded seriously. "In many tribal societies, honor is more important than wealth. A Cherokee brave's status wasn't dependent on what he owned, for example, because he didn't own anything. Family property all belonged to the wife. Then there's the potlach, which is . . ."

Benedict stopped listening as he bent and pulled off his shoes, then stuffed them in the backpack Arjenie would carry. The lecture on tribal customs was her way of coping with nerves. Facts comforted her, and she was very nervous. Benedict pulled his T-shirt off and wished fiercely and futilely she wasn't here. Wasn't going to be part of this. It was too dangerous, and she was no warrior. But the mate bond meant that where he went, she had to go. And reason and the dictates of the mission said she would be extremely useful, given her Gift.

To hell with the mission. That's what he'd wanted to say earlier when they were planning this. He hadn't.

Her voice drifted off in the middle of something about Australian Aborigines. A frown creased her brows. "I guess it's time."

"Yes." As his hands went to the snap on his jeans, Rule and Lucas began stripping. Arjenie hadn't batted an eye earlier when the others stripped before Changing. Her coven, she said, conducted many rituals sky-clad. Group nudity didn't unsettle her the way it did most humans. Benedict removed his jeans and rolled them up. They'd travel in Arjenie's backpack.

He paused and looked at her. For a moment he just looked. She'd braided her hair to keep it out of the way, rendering it temporarily more orderly than he'd ever seen it. Her eyes were large and worried. She smelled like heaven and home and he wanted badly to say something, to give her something to take down into the dark.

He touched her cheek. "You'll be careful."

"That's what I'm supposed to say to you. Benedict . . ." She laid her hand over his. "You didn't want me along, but I need to do this. I can help. I know it."

"Yes." He accepted that. Hated it, but accepted it, just as he accepted his fear for her. He wished he knew what to say . . . oh. Of course. He smiled. "I love you," he told her, and smiled, and dropped his hand. And Changed.

A frisky breeze blew in the open windows of Lily's government Ford. They were parked about a mile from Friar's house. Waiting.

Cullen was behind the wheel with Cynna in the front seat beside him. Lily didn't think she'd ever ridden in her own backseat before, and she didn't like it. She'd wanted to drive, but had succumbed to reason. The guy with two working arms and no baby in the tummy should do the steering and braking.

Waiting sucked.

They'd settled on ten o'clock—the onset of the Challenge—as the best time for Lily to present Friar with the warrant. Rule would fit his party's efforts into that timeline, if he could. They wanted Friar as distracted as possible during the retrieval.

As soon as they'd parked, Cullen had started fidgeting like a three-year-old. Cynna had dug a crossword puzzle magazine out of her purse. He'd been working it ever since. In the dark.

Lily couldn't do that, dammit, or much of anything else. If this had been a stakeout, at least she'd have had a focus. But someone else had that duty—one of Benedict's guards. She'd checked with him when she arrived. Friar hadn't left his house since he returned late yesterday afternoon.

Robert Friar lived at the end of a short gravel lane off a narrow county road. There was a gate and a sign warning people that the lane was private, but according to Benedict, the gate was usually left open. It was open tonight. She'd had Cullen drive by so she could check before parking on the shoulder of the county road to wait.

Waiting gave her way too much time to think.

She was afraid for Rule. It rode in her gut, that fear, like a ball of maggots. Every now and then one of those maggots wormed its way up to her brain and she started thinking about all the things that could go wrong . . . about Rule trapped beneath the earth and how he hated small, tight spaces, and how shaky this whole plan was when they knew so damn little . . .

Shut up, she told herself, and stuffed those maggot-thoughts back down. "Are you napping?" she asked Cynna.

"Huh?" Cynna's head jolted up from the headrest. "Oh—guess I did doze off. Happens all the time these days." She twisted around to look at Lily. "I'd offer you a crossword puzzle book, too, but . . ."

"Since I can't read in the dark, it wouldn't be much of a distraction."

Her arm itched horribly. Not on the wound, but between it and her elbow—a spot she could not possibly reach. The wound itself wasn't hurting much. After talking to Benedict, Lily had asked Nettie to put her in sleep for a bit, knowing she needed to be as rested and alert as possible. Then they'd all eaten a light supper, then she'd stolen a few minutes alone with Rule, then he'd had to leave, then Isen did, then at last it had been time for her, Cullen, and Cynna to leave. So they could sit here. And wait.

Maybe she should have brought someone else with her. Cullen's quasi-official status was a plus for her, but Rule might need him. Sure, Arjenie could sense wards, but she couldn't see them or throw fire or fight or . . .

Did she really want to make herself crazy? Second-guessing everything was a great way to do that. She drummed on her thigh.

"What's a nine-letter word for flawed?" the man in the front seat asked.

"Seabourne."

"You're good." He flashed her a grin. "But not quite accurate. If we're talking morals, then yes, that is sadly true. But if we're talking sexual prowess and creativity—"

"Let's not."

Cynna chuckled. "He's had to be creative, as big as I am now. The upside is that I'm really sensitive down there. The sensations get intense. It's the one time I don't fall asleep these days."

"If talking about sex helps you pass the time . . ." Lily gave in and looked at her watch. "Never mind. It's time."

"Thank God." Cullen tossed the magazine on the floor and reached for the key in the ignition. "Have I mentioned that I'm not a patient person?"

"Being a trained and careful observer, I'd already noticed that."

At last they were moving, air streaming in through the windows. Lily wondered just how uncomfortable Rule was right now.

FORTY-THREE

RULE hated the air underground. It was still and dead and there never seemed to be enough of it. The last, of course, was all in his head. He knew that, just as he knew it was being underground that got to him, not the quality of the air.

Didn't matter. He still hated it.

At least that first, hellishly tight stretch was well behind them. And while Rule's ribs ached, the pain wasn't bad. Nettie had helped with that. And Arjenie was holding up well. She'd made it through the worst of the squeezes without a murmur of complaint. She wasn't bothered by small spaces, she said.

Just bugs. Rule smiled slightly. Caves held more fauna than one might suspect—mostly creepy-crawlies. Arjenie's Gift was a drawback there. She was drawing lightly on her power, just enough to be sure she'd sense a ward if they drew near one. That was more than enough to confuse vermin. A spider the size of Rule's fist had failed to notice her even as it scampered over her foot.

Arjenie had certainly noticed the spider.

Otherwise, she was doing well for someone who claimed to be fearful. Oh, she was afraid—Rule smelled it on her—but what of it? So was he. So were they all, to varying degrees. Fear wasn't the problem. What the mind did with that fear was. Arjenie was coping with her fear, and with the uneven footing and darkness.

Not that the blackness was absolute. Even lupi can't see in the utter absence of light. Light made them too damn visible in this thick darkness, but they had to see. Aside from the literal pitfalls, like that crevice they'd passed earlier, they couldn't risk getting lost down here. Earlier, Cullen had taught Arjenie the trick of making mage lights, and bobbing along with them were two faint globes of light. Very faint. Their hope was that anyone else down here would be using much brighter lights, which might blind them to such a dim glow.

So far it hadn't mattered. Their route was clearly not used by Friar's people. There was no trace of human scent . . . which, he told himself, was good. It did *not* mean they were wandering far afield, lost beneath the earth.

That was the sort of trick fear could play on the mind—creating scenarios and weighting them with too much likelihood. If Lily were here, he could have taken her hand and soothed his discomfort. He'd grown accustomed to that, hadn't he? But he was glad she wasn't here. For once she'd be away from the worst danger.

His wolf disagreed. Wolves hunted with their mates, and that part of him disapproved of going on this hunt without her. He could have kept her safe.

Good thing the man was in charge. Lily was in no shape for these rough, twisty tunnels. He glanced at his watch. Almost ten. He thought of his father—then shut that thought off. Concentrate on what he could affect, not what was outside his control. They had about two hours to find Brian and Dya and remove them before Lily would start down Friar's tunnel.

Benedict lifted a hand in the universal signal to stop. Rule did, lifting his own hand to make sure those behind saw. They were drawn out single file at the moment because the walls along here varied from skin-scraping to narrow. Benedict first, then Arjenie, followed by Rule, Lucas, Sammy, and Paul, with José at their rear. Benedict had the lead because his ears were the best and he had an uncanny sense of direction. Arjenie had to be close to the front so she'd sense any wards—and her remarkable memory was a help, too. They'd all studied the 3-D map, and had brought printouts of its 2-D version, but Arjenie could recite their route, complete with depth notations.

Benedict had frozen, studying something ahead. He held up his hand again, emphasizing that they should stay put, and eased ahead until he was swallowed by darkness.

Rule saw nothing, heard nothing, for what seemed a very long time, but was probably five minutes. Finally his brother reemerged from the blackness ahead. Once Benedict reached them he made the signs for *trail*, *jump*, and *down*, paused, then added the sign for *water*.

Lucas tapped Rule's arm. Rule leaned close and subvocalized. "There's a drop-off ahead. And water."

Benedict put his mouth next to Arjenie's ear, no doubt telling her the same thing. Like Lucas, she didn't know ASL. Rule wasn't fluent in it, but everyone who trained under Benedict learned a few basics. Subvocalizing was useful if you were close enough, but with sign you could speak to the whole team without making a sound as long as you were in their visual range.

They continued single file, and within a few feet he picked up the damp scent of water. Rule's heartbeat quickened in anticipation. There was a twenty-two-foot drop-off marked on the USGC map of their route. The map hadn't indicated anything about water, but there were a number of things it didn't include.

They'd chosen their route not because it was the quickest or shortest, but because there were fewer branchings where they could take a wrong turn. Since they'd passed the mouths of two tunnels that weren't on the map, Rule wanted to conclude that the mapmakers had been less than thorough. The alternative would be that they were lost.

He hadn't entirely convinced himself. If this drop-off was the expected twenty-two feet, he'd feel much more cheerful. It would also mean they were getting close to their destination.

That was a too-familiar spot. The last time Rule had been there he'd been a prisoner. So had Lily and Cullen.

He'd watched his bother die, sacrificing himself for Rule. And Lily had fought and killed Helen. Oh, yes, he thought fiercely. He was very glad she wasn't here. She didn't need to revisit the place of her nightmares.

Benedict stopped and turned.

Rope? Rule signed. At Benedict's nod, Rule turned and signed to Sammy, who passed up the coil of rope he'd been carrying.

Rule moved close to Arjenie and whispered barely above a breath next to her ear. "Pull harder on your Gift and see if you sense anything below."

She nodded, paused, then shook her head, mouthing a silent "no." He nodded, gave her a smile, and moved to the edge.

This time, Rule would take the lead. They'd known that at least one point would require a climb, so had planned for it. Arjenie couldn't fight, so she needed to be the last down, just in case. Once Rule reached the bottom and signaled, the rest would take turns belaying each other, leaving Benedict and Arjenie for last. Her skills did not include shimmying down a rope or rock climbing. If there was a place to tie off the rope, Benedict would use it to descend with Arjenie riding piggyback. If not, Benedict would lower her, and Rule and the rest would form a pyramid to catch her. Then Benedict would climb down.

That was assuming the drop wasn't more than, say, twenty-two feet.

Lucas took the other end of the Rope as Rule lowered himself over the edge.

It would have been an easy descent if his ribs hadn't been sore. As it was, he had no real difficulty. He simply hurt more than he liked. Arjenie sent one of the dim mage lights with him, which helped. The smell of water strengthened as he descended. Stagnant water, he decided. A pool of some sort . . . yes, he could see it dimly reflecting the mage light—a small pool in the center of a small rocky chamber. High ceiling, he noted with relief. Thirty feet or more.

The ground, when he reached it, was dry. That was good. Even better, his estimate for the descent was about twenty feet. Best of all, he saw light.

More accurately, he saw a patch of dimness rather than stark black at the mouth of a tunnel to his left, just where memory told him the map had shown it. He bent his attention to his ears, but didn't hear anything. But what was that smell? Not airborne, he thought. The air remained deadly still. He crouched, lowering his face close to the ground.

Something warm-blooded had passed this way in the last week or so. Not a human, he thought, though in this form he couldn't be sure. He straightened. Once the others were down, he'd have Sammy Change and see what he could learn. But now it was time to get them down. He tugged once on the rope.

One by one they came. No need to form a pyramid; once down, Sammy told Rule—subvocalizing—that Benedict had tied off the rope. As soon as those two were down, Rule signed *smell* and *Change* and pointed to Sammy. The young redhead had an excellent nose and could Change twice in a row without needing to rest.

A moment later, a tawny wolf stood on the empty clothes that had fallen to the ground when he blended himself into and through an unreal dimension. He shook his head once as if to clear it, then started sniffing at the ground. He took a step, then looked at Rule.

Track, Rule signed.

Sammy nodded and padded silently around the pool, nose down, heading for the dim maw of the tunnel. He paused there, looking over his shoulder.

Rule held up a hand to stop him, about to sign *Change*. Vertigo struck like a hammer a split second before the darkness all around swarmed in and swallowed him.

ROBERT Friar's house was as large and unlikely as Lily remembered: two stories of wood and glass with a staggered veranda—God forbid you should call it a porch—three gables, and camera-ready landscaping. Lights were on inside, she noted as they pulled up in front, and the landscape lighting glowed discreetly, but he'd forgotten to leave the porch light on for callers.

Lily climbed out as soon as Cullen shut off the engine. Cynna's door slammed on the other side, and Cullen climbed out on hers. As they started for the door, Lily half expected to see some of the militia types Friar had running around everywhere.

Sometimes half-assed expectations come true. A burly cliché in fatigues, complete with blond, buzz-cut hair and shoulder-slung AK-47, stepped off the porch. "Mr. Friar isn't available right now."

"Pity, but we'll be going in anyway. Agent Lily Yu, Unit Twelve, FBI." She held out her badge, and damned if he didn't take it and study it. "I'd like to see your ID, also."

"Looks genuine, but I've seen some good fakes." He handed it back.

"You travel in interesting circles, Mr. . . ."

"Brewster, Calvin." He reached in his back pocket. "I'm complying with your request for ID, Special Agent, but after that I have to ask you and your companions to leave."

"Can't do that." She managed to brush his fingers as she took the driver's license he pulled from his pocket. No tingle of magic. She handed the license to Cynna. "Jot down the number, would you?"

"Sure." Cynna dug in her purse.

"The open gate gave you legal access to the property," Calvin said, stony but polite. "But you have to leave when asked."

"Not when I've got a search warrant."

"I'll need to see that."

"Actually, you don't. Robert Friar does. You aren't Friar."

"I'm responsible for the security of Mr. Friar's place."

"You a relative of Friar's? A member of his household?" She shook her head. "The law's funny, Calvin. If you'd been inside the house when we arrived, I'd have to show you the warrant. But you aren't. I have no reason to believe you have access to the house, which means you have no right to see the warrant. Got to protect Mr. Friar's privacy."

His lips tightened into invisibility. He stepped back a grudging pace and pulled a phone from his shirt pocket. "Sergeant, I've got a situation here," he said as Lily walked around him, with Cullen and Cynna right behind.

She rang the bell. Waited. Rang it again, adding a firm knock.

Nothing. No sound of footsteps, no television noise . . .
"You hear anything inside?" she asked Cullen.

"Not even a mouse."

She considered a moment. Glanced over her shoulder.
Another militia guy was rounding the corner of the house,
headed their way. She moved so that she blocked Cal's view
of Cullen, raising her voice slightly. "Odd that someone as
security conscious as Mr. Friar would leave his front door
ajar, isn't it?"

Cullen grinned. "Damn weird, if you ask me."

Cynna nodded. "Makes me think something's wrong. We
should check."

Calvin spoke sharply. "That door's closed and locked."

"Was it closed earlier?" She turned to look at him. "Because it isn't now. Is Mr. Friar in the habit of leaving his front
door ajar?"

"It's not—"

"Sure it is," Cynna said. "See?" She gave the door a shove
and it swung open.

And that was another reason Lily had wanted Cullen
along. He was very good with locks. "Looks like you're
wrong, Calvin."

"I'm going in with you." He started toward her.

"Nope." She moved to block him, giving Cullen and
Cynna a chance to go in. "Same deal. Not a relative, not a
member of the household, so you stay out here."

"I'm going in with you."

She cocked her head. "Those allergies give you a lot of
trouble?"

"What the hell are you—"

"Gesundheit," Cullen said, pointing at him.

Calvin sneezed. Sneezed again, and again—a paroxysm
of sneezes that left him bent over.

It was Cullen's newest trick, one he was quite proud of.
He and Cynna had cooked up the spell together, but she had
trouble executing it—something to do with the difference
between runic charms and spoken spells. Lily grinned and
slipped inside, locking the door behind her.

Her grin slid away. She listened a moment, then called
out, "Mr. Friar? Special Agent Lily Yu here. I have a

warrant to search your house and physically connected structures."

No answer. She looked at Cullen. He shook his head. "Can't hear a thing. Either he's playing hide-and-seek, or he isn't here. If he isn't here, I bet I know where he is."

So did she. Belowground someplace, either in his tunnel or at the node. Where Rule was headed. "Cynna?"

"Ready, set, go," the taller woman said, and shook out her arms. "I warned you this could take awhile. If he's warded the entrance to the tunnel, it'll be hard for me to Find."

"Understood." Maybe Rule would be knocking on the other side of the tunnel's entry before they found it. Maybe not. Either way, they had the best Finder on the planet looking for it. And while Cynna hunted her way, she and Cullen could try more common methods. Hands and eyes. "Let's get started."

THE moon was half full. Plenty of light for lupus eyes on a clear night, enough to see the looming wooden ghosts of the mining operation that had died here over twenty years ago. Also the vehicles pulled up in the dusty yard in front of what had once been the office. And the men gathered to one side of the vehicles, near a fire pit complete with a small blaze.

The wind was having fun with that fire, Isen noted, though they'd dug the pit deeper than usual. One of Stephen's men hovered near it with a bucket and a blanket. Fire was traditional at a Challenge, and tradition carried great weight for Stephen.

Isen's driver pulled up at the end of the row of vehicles nearest the gathered men. He glanced at his watch and nodded. Two hairs past ten o'clock. Excellent.

He did enjoy making an entrance.

Jason got out on the far side of the car. The driver got out on her side . . . the driver being Nettie. Isen heard the exclamations from those waiting and grinned and opened his own door.

The noise cut off. Eight startled faces stared at him—five Etorri, including Stephen; Myron from Kyffin; and the two Ybirra clansmen who'd driven in to support their Lu Nuncio and bear witness. Plus a ninth, furious face. Javier was not pleased to see him.

"You seem surprised," he murmured, moving forward. "Myron, how is Billy?"

"Well enough, though he'll—"

"What trick is this?" Javier demanded. "Why are you here? And that woman. Who is she?"

Isen paused, eyebrows lifted gently. "I believe Nokolai has been Challenged. Did you think I would allow my heir—who was injured today, as you must know—to fight in his condition?"

Javier scowled. "He didn't plead injury as a reason to delay."

Isen said nothing, but he allowed rebuke to enter his gaze.

Myron snorted. "As if he could. You'd have screamed to high heaven that he was up to something. It's Rule's ribs were hurt, I think?" he asked Isen.

Isen nodded. "They'll mend, but not in time for the Challenge. You said Billy is doing all right?"

"Didn't even need surgery, though he'll wear a collar for a while. Thanks for sending Nettie." He smiled at her. "How interesting to see you again so soon."

"Ah, that's right," Isen said. "I believe Javier asked about her." He gestured for Nettie to step forward. "This is my granddaughter, Nettie Two Horses."

Stephen of Etorri spoke for the first time. "It's irregular to bring a woman to a Challenge."

"Irregular, perhaps, but no one stipulated that we only bring male clan. Nettie is Nokolai. She's also a doctor, healer, and shaman." Isen beamed at them. "I expect to need her services, and hope that Javier will, also. I've no desire to kill you for being an idiot, boy."

"I've no desire to kill you, either, old man. Feel free to cry loss and submit."

Isen chuckled. "That's telling me. Well." He pulled off his shirt and handed it to Jason. The wind chose that moment to kick up its heels, stinging his bare chest with sand. "I assume the circle's been drawn?"

"It has," Stephen said. "As mediator, I ask if there is any way your clans can reconcile this difference without Challenge."

"Nokolai owes a blood debt for their betrayal." Javier's eyes glittered in the firelight. "Ybirra means to claim it."

Isen's good humor fell away. He looked at Javier and allowed his mantle to rise. "Rule has explained what happened. You will not listen, blinded by anger and grief and the unwillingness to know yourself wrong. In your blindness and arrogance, you aid our ancient enemy. Our Lady's enemy." He paused, letting his voice drop to a growl. "When we step into that circle, know that you will have to kill me to win. I will not submit. Nokolai will not abase itself, submit to a lie, to satisfy your refusal to deal in reality instead of rage."

For a moment, doubt flickered in Javier's eyes. Uncertainty. Isen smiled grimly. "I will bleed you, boy, but I'll only kill you if you give me no choice. I don't want Manuel to lose a son. I don't want our people to lose a fighter—for believe me, the time is coming when we will need every fighter. Come. Our Lady needs us, all of us. You can still withdraw your Challenge."

That was a step too far. Javier's head jerked back, as if Isen had struck him. "I do not withdraw."

Bloody young idiot, thinking withdrawal meant cowardice. And a bloody old fool he was for mishandling the boy. Ah, well. He looked at Stephen. "Ybirra will not withdraw. Nokolai will not submit. It looks as if we had better get started, doesn't it?"

FORTY-FOUR

RULE came to with the same suddenness he'd passed out. He lay utterly still, allowing no muscle to tighten, using his other senses to gather information before opening his eyes.

Piss. That smell was so strong it took a second to sort out the rest, but Benedict was close. José, too, was near. And Sammy, Paul, Lucas . . . was that Brian? Yes, though his scent was so smeared with the stink of illness it was almost unrecognizable. He heard a heartbeat . . . no, two heartbeats, both of them unnaturally languid, but strong and steady.

He was lying on a hard, rough surface. The air was chilly and calm. His ribs ached, but nothing else hurt. Benedict was on his left, also lying down. José was on his right. Either they were still unconscious or they were faking it well. Better than he was, for he was sure his own heartbeat had speeded up.

"Rule? You awake?"

Brian's voice. Rule opened his eyes. "So it seems."

He was in a cage. No, only one wall was barred; the others were rock. Someone had made use of a handy cubbyhole in the rock to form a cell. The stone of the ceiling glowed—mage light, but fixed to a surface instead of floating free.

That ceiling was much too close. Only two feet from Rule's head when he sat up. Too low to stand.

Panic twitched at him, a puppeteer demanding that he move, run. He breathed in slowly, deliberately, and looked around.

The stink of urine came from a bucket at the back of the cell, not far from where Brian sat, leaning against the stony wall The sanitary facilities, it seemed. Their cell was about twelve by eight, just enough room for their captors to lay everyone out neatly and naked . . . no, not everyone. Only the lupi. And not entirely naked. Rule touched his ribs. They'd left his elastic bandage on. How thoughtful.

On the other side of those bars . . . "Someone's redecorated," he murmured. He couldn't see the whole place. His cell was at one end of the long, narrow cavern . . . a cavern he recognized, though the altar, the chanting Azá, and the electric lights strung on cables were missing.

In their place were mage lights and elves.

One, two, three, four of them . . . they had to be elves. One stood quite close, about fifteen feet from the bars, watching them with a drawn sword in one hand. His hair was blue. The others . . . Rule moved closer to the bars, crouched to avoid the low ceiling, to get a better look.

Their hair was long, too—white hair on one; the soft, taupey gray of a dove on another; yellow on the third. Not blond. Pale yellow, like freshly churned butter. They wore sleeveless tunics and trousers in bright colors. The tunics were belted at the waist; from this angle Rule could see that at least two of them had sheathed knives hanging from those belts. Thin and lovely, graceful and androgynous, those three were absorbed in what they were doing. Whatever that was.

One sat, eyes closed, lips moving. Another crouched ten feet from the first, patting the ground rhythmically, as if it were a drum. The third moved one step, stopped. Moved one step. Stopped. The three formed a rough triangle around . . . "Is that a gate?"

Rule had never actually seen one. He'd been zapped to the hell realm by other means, returned while unconscious, and hadn't visited the one official gate on Earth in D.C. But he'd heard them described as a shimmer in the air, like heat waves. That's what he saw over the spot that had once held the Azá's altar.

"Yeah, afraid so."

Brian's voice was weak, strained. Rule turned.

Brian wasn't a large man, no more than five-ten, and had always been slim, full of energy. Now he looked gaunt, his cheekbones jutting out sharply.

Rule crawled over the unconscious José to reach Brian. He gripped his friend's hand. The stink of illness was so wrong, blended with a lupi's scent. "You're hurting."

"Dya's kept me going, but I think . . . not much longer. Oh. She's Friar's servant or slave or something. She doesn't like being called a slave, but he for damn sure controls her. She's, uh, she's not from our realm."

Rule nodded neutrally. Best, maybe, if he didn't mention Arjenie. She wasn't with them. He prayed that meant she'd somehow escaped whatever knocked them out, that she was okay. There were other possibilities, worse ones. For now, he wasn't going to think about them. "Is she the one who called Isen?"

"I shouldn't have asked her to. She got caught, and you . . ." His face spasmed. Sweat popped out on his upper lip and forehead.

"The pain's bad."

"Comes and goes." His voice had sunk to a thread. "More coming than going lately. Rethna likes to experiment. Gado and . . . variations. He wants to control the Change. Not just shut it off, but call it up when he pleases."

"Rethna?" Rule said sharply, glancing over his shoulder. The elves were still busy with their odd tasks. "What about Friar?"

"Friar's around. Rethna's bigger and badder, though. He's an elf. Not one of those three—they're flunkies. He's some kind of big muckety-muck. Likes to be called 'my lord.' I told him he wasn't my lord."

Rule smiled. It hurt, but he did it. "Bet he didn't like that."

"Not much." The ghost of Brian's usual cocky smile crossed his face.

"How long have you been here?"

"I think . . . ten days? Hard to tell, underground." He squeezed Rule's hand. "There's things I need to tell you. Rethna and Friar aren't exactly partners, but they're working together. They've both made deals with *her*. The Lady's enemy."

"I knew about Friar and *her*. I've been trying to convince the others . . ." He thought of his most recent attempt. Of his father, who must be fighting for his life by now. Of Brian's older brother, who'd fallen to a complicated madness. "I'm so sorry about your brother, Brian."

Brian closed his eyes. "Felt it, of course. When what Edgar carried came to me, I knew he was gone. I haven't told them about that." He opened his eyes. They glowed with sudden intensity. "About the Lady's secret. They've done things to me, but I haven't told them the Lady's secret."

The mantles, he meant. "Good. You've done well."

Brain snorted, sounding so much like he always had that it pinched Rule's heart. "No, I haven't. I told them too much, but he—the elf—Rethna can do things you wouldn't believe. He calls it body magic. Mostly it's pain. Good thing he doesn't have much mind-magic, or . . ." He shook his head. "Never mind. I need to tell you before they come. The deal Friar made—he gets paid tonight. They're setting up this big ritual to give him some kind of major Gift. I don't know what. Once that's done, Rethna will clear out. Now that he's got you, he'll go home. He means to take you—all of you he caught—with him. To sell."

Nastiness twisted in Rule's gut. "It was a trap, then. Dya's phone call. They were ready for us."

"No! Dya didn't . . . she's a friend. She didn't trick you. But Friar knew about the call somehow . . . maybe one of Soshi's pets. Soshi's one of Rethna's flunkies. They'd planned to lure some of you down here soon. Dya didn't know how, but she thought if you got here quickly they wouldn't be ready yet." He grimaced. "They were."

"Soshi's pets?"

"Spiders. They're big, the size of a tarantula, but they aren't from our realm. Soshi links with them, sees from their eyes."

The spider that had run across Arjenie's foot—had it been

watching them? "You're sure this Rethna plans to sell us? We, ah—we had reason to think Friar and a sidhe allied with him were breaking something called Queens' Law. The one about genocide."

Brian's eyebrows lifted. "You know about Queens' Law?"

"Cullen knows a little about all sorts of things he shouldn't." True enough, but a lie in the way he meant it to be taken.

"Oh, Seabourne. Sure. No, genocide's the one they don't want to break. Don't want to attract the Queens' attention. Keep a few of us alive and it isn't genocide when they kill the rest." He licked his lips. "The law Rethna's breaking involves a name. Call on that name and the Queens get totally pissed. It's a name we don't use, either."

Rule's eyebrows lifted. "Our ancient enemy is anathema to the two Queens?"

Brian nodded weakly. "It's all about power. Rethna wants more. He thinks he can get it from *her*, but he has to cut his realm off from the Queens. I don't really know what that means, but it takes time and planning and if the Queens find out, he's toast. That's why they won't kill all of us. Someone might notice." He licked his lips again. "Sorry. I need . . ." He fumbled for something at his side—a hide sack with a metal nozzle.

"You're thirsty." Rule picked up the primitive canteen and held the nozzle to Brian's lips. Brian drank greedily.

"Thanks," he said when Rule lowered it. "Hate that you're here, but it's been hard, thinking I'd die alone. Only now, Wythe . . ." His face twisted with worry or grief. He spoke subvocally. "When I die, the mantle's lost. There's no one else, only my son, and he's too young. Much too young."

Losing both Rho and heir almost always meant losing the mantle. Clan history said that twice a Rho had died without an heir and the mantle had passed to someone from the founder's bloodline anyway, but the Spanish massacre in the seventeenth century proved how rare that was. And a mantle couldn't pass to one who hadn't yet Changed. Rule squeezed Brian's shoulder gently. "You're not dead yet. With what you received from your brother, you may postpone that moment quite awhile."

"Rethna won't take me with him. I'm too damaged to sell. When he leaves, Friar cuts my throat. I'm no use to him." He swallowed. "We have to try."

"Try . . . ?"

Lucas's voice was drowsy. "Knocked out twice in one day. No offense, Rule, but I have to stop hanging out with you. What happened?"

"Sleep spell," Brian said. "Rethna set them himself along the routes to this place. They're targeted to us—to lupi—and to humans, so his people don't trigger them accidentally."

Would a sleep spell intended for humans and lupi leave a part-sidhe woman unaffected? Had Arjenie managed to escape?

"Rethna?" Lucas sat up. "Who the hell is . . ." His gaze locked on Brian. "Brian. Shit, man."

Brian tried to grin. "Look that bad, do I?"

"You've looked better." He switched his gaze to Rule. "I guess we got where we meant to go."

"If not quite the way we meant to arrive. We're near the node. Our hosts have added a new touch to it—a gate. I'm guessing it goes to the home realm of the elves you see out there."

"Elves." Lucas said flatly as if forcing himself not to sound incredulous. Then he looked out through the bars. "Elves. Son of a bitch."

"The chief son of a bitch seems to be a fellow named Rethna, a sidhe lord who's fallen in with bad company. So bad we don't name her. He wants to take us home with him . . . as merchandise."

Benedict growled, "I don't much care for travel."

Rule's breath sucked in. Benedict was awake—and not screaming or howling at the severance of his mate bond. No, he was looking out through the bars. Rule spoke carefully. "I imagine your sweetheart would miss you."

"Yeah." Benedict sat up and smiled faintly at Rule. "We're very close."

Arjenie was alive—and close? Rule couldn't see her, couldn't see anything that suggested she was there. His view of the cavern wasn't impeded. He didn't have any sense he was being urged to look away from some spot. "You met

Benedict's sweetheart earlier today," he told Lucas, who looked puzzled. "She's shy."

"A real wallflower around strangers," Benedict said. "Hates drawing attention to herself."

She was near the wall, Rule concluded.

"Of course," Lucas murmured. "I remember her."

"Brian," Rule said, "do you have an idea of how long we were out?"

"Not so good at guessing time lately. Maybe an hour?"

Arjenie was here now. In about an hour, Lily would be coming . . . and wasn't that a fine bit of irony? He'd wanted to spare her the worst of the danger, but she would walk right into the trap just as he had. If any of them were to get out of this, she had to be warned about Rethna—and those damned spiders. "Perhaps," he said softly to Benedict, "your sweetheart and my *nadia* will console each other."

Benedict nodded. "The sooner the better, I think."

The rest were waking—stirring, looking around. José rolled up on one arm and looked at Rule. "Not what we had in mind."

"No. Explanations—"

"Shh," Brian said urgently. "He's coming."

Yes, Rule had noticed a new scent. He looked at Brian. "That smell—a bit like human, but not as meaty, a hint of cardamom. That's how elves smell?"

"Shh." Brian's eyes were wide.

A tall elf sauntered into view a few feet back from the bars. His hair was the blue black of a raven's wing, so shiny it was almost iridescent. It hung to his waist in back, but was arranged in elaborate braids on the sides. He wore a similar outfit to the others—red tunic, black trousers. He'd added a knee-length vest in gauzy black silk. His belt was black, too, as was the hilt of the knife protruding from the sheath on that belt. His boots were dark red. He liked jewelry. Rule saw two rubies in one ear, a diamond in the other, plus armbands and two pendants: a short one with a silver disc and a longer one with a large black stone.

He stood there with his head tipped to one side, studying them. "Which of you is the leader?" He spoke news-anchor English.

"I am," Rule said.

"Has Brian told you who I am?"

"If you are Rethna, a lord of the sidhe, he has."

The elf nodded. "I will speak only with you. The others are to remain silent at all times in my presence. If they do not, I will hurt you. You will speak only when I ask you a question. You will answer fully and truthfully. If you do not, I will hurt one of yours. Like this." He pointed at Rule and clicked his tongue.

Every nerve in Rule's body fired with agony. He convulsed, mouth agape, too stunned by pain even to scream. Pain ate his skin, his eyeballs, his genitals, and burned from inside as if he'd breathed it in.

It passed. Between one moment and the next, it passed. His chest shuddered in relief.

"Rule." Benedict's voice. Benedict's hand on his shoulder. "Rule, can you talk?"

It wasn't until he opened his eyes that he realized he'd closed them. He was shaky, weak, flat on the ground again . . . and unharmed, aside from his ribs. They disapproved of convulsions. Benedict hovered over him, worried. He managed to nod—then realized that Benedict had spoken, which that bastard had threatened to punish them for.

Rule pushed himself up on one elbow. The bastard was gone. He'd introduced himself, told them his damned rules, given Rule more pain than he'd ever felt outside of the Change . . . and left. "I'm okay. But something tells me Rethna and I are not going to get along."

FORTY-FIVE

"**GIN,**" Cynna said, spreading her cards.

"Again?" Lily tossed her cards down, disgusted. She didn't mind losing. She hated being useless, especially when she thought something had gone wrong.

She couldn't call Rule and he couldn't call her, not when he was a few hundred feet below ground. But nothing blocked the mate bond. She knew roughly where he was right now . . . and that he hadn't moved for the last hour. He could be hurt or trapped . . . or, she admitted, he could be simply waiting for the right moment to make his move.

They were in Friar's kitchen, where oceans of granite and islands of stainless steel floated on solid oak flooring. Cynna and Lily sat at the table; Cullen was sitting tailor-style in front of the open broom closet, staring at the floor.

Cynna had Found the secret door pretty fast. The house was lousy with doors, of course, but she could eliminate those on the upper floor, and one by one she'd removed those on the lower floor from the pattern she used to search, leaving only the one they wanted.

The broom closet held a mop, broom, and carpet sweeper suspended off the floor by grippers fixed to the wall. The opposite wall had shelves for cleaning supplies. The floor held a trapdoor.

It was snugly fitted, almost invisible, but close examination revealed a hairline crack outlining a tidy square in the polished oak flooring. As for how to open it—there were two switches on the plate just outside the closet. One turned on the light. The other activated the trapdoor . . . or so they thought. They couldn't check because the damn thing was warded to hell and gone. Open it and they notified Friar they were on their way.

Unless it fried them instead. Cullen said it was a nasty piece of work, not like any ward he'd ever seen. He could neutralize it, sure, but doing that without tipping off its caster was a slow, tedious business.

Funny how Cullen always claimed to be impatient. He'd been sitting there for an hour studying the damn thing. Now and then he muttered something or sketched in the air with his finger. Then he went back to staring.

Cynna collected the cards and began shuffling. "You want to switch to poker?"

"I want—" Lily's phone rang. It wasn't Rule's ring tone, but she lunged for her purse anyway. It might be Nettie with word about the Challenge, or maybe Rule had sent someone aboveground for some . . .

The caller ID had her frowning, puzzled. "Lily Yu here."

"As if I wouldn't know your sweet voice," Cody Beck said. "Hope you don't mind me calling so late. It's important, verging on oh-my-God."

Lily's focus tightened instantly. "What's up?"

He told her. When she disconnected, Cynna was frowning at her. "I didn't catch all of that, but I gather you want me to Find something."

"Yeah. Cody discovered a very odd purchase made by Friar's hazardous waste disposal company. Two days ago, they bought fifteen pounds of RN40."

"I don't speak acronym."

"It's a high-grade plastic explosive, new to the market. Fifteen pounds is a lot. A single pound of the stuff, applied right, can take down an office building."

Cynna's eyes widened. "Isn't stuff like that regulated? How could they get hold of that much?"

"It sure as hell isn't something a hazardous waste company ought to be able to buy. I don't know how they got it or how Cody found out—he didn't give me details. You said you can Find something if you have a piece of it, right? Well, they've got a piece from the same block of RN40 that Friar bought. Cody's bringing it here."

"I can use that, sure,"

Cullen's head whipped around. He glared at Lily. "You want Cynna to play with high-grade explosives?"

She could have sworn he'd been too absorbed to hear a word. "It's safe to handle unless you pop it in the oven or hold a match to it. And we might be in a hurry here."

"Why?"

Because her gut said so. Not that she was a precog, but . . . "This buy of the explosive—it's clumsy compared to his other tricks. Sure, he doesn't know we know about his dummy company, but he's left a trail this time. When something blows, that trail's going to point to him."

Cynna asked, "You think he's getting hasty and stupid?"

"I don't know. He wants to make something go boom, though. Maybe Rule's apartment or the FBI building or some place I don't have a clue about. But we know his usual target—lupi, specifically Nokolai lupi—and we know he got someone into Clanhome once to pour a potion in the wells. That attempt failed, and he's a man who likes to win. Maybe he's given up on subtlety."

AT a deserted mining camp, two wolves circled in the moon-cast shadow of a wooden gantry. The gray wolf was the taller, the reddish one had a more powerful build. A low growl rumbled continuously from the gray wolf's chest. His ears were flat to his skull, his lips peeled back in a snarl.

The red wolf's ears were flat, too, yet somehow the gaze he pinned on his opponent seemed more jaundiced than enraged.

A scattering of silent men formed a circle around them. The dirt in that circle was trampled, gouged in places from claws scrabbling for purchase, muddy in places where blood hadn't fully soaked into the parched ground. Wind whipped at their fur, tails, and ears ... three ears between the two wolves. The fur of the gray wolf was black with dried blood where one ear had been ripped off. The fur was dark on one haunch, too, and around his muzzle.

The reddish wolf moved as smoothly as the gray one, though he used only three feet, holding one foreleg off the ground for obvious reasons. Blood dripped sluggishly from the mangled leg.

The gray wolf charged. His opponent dropped and turned belly up—and thrust with his hind legs, flipping the other wolf, who thudded to the ground and rolled, nearly colliding with one of the watching men.

It would end soon.

Isen knew this. He'd trained three-legged, which might keep him alive a bit longer. But he hadn't trained while pain radiated in huge waves from the broken limb.

Twice he'd held back from the kill. Once when he removed Javier's ear instead of crushing his skull. Once when he had Javier pinned and stepped back, refusing the kill. Oh, but that had infuriated the young wolf—being made a gift of his life by his enemy.

Anger was Javier's weakness. Isen had taken advantage of that, using body language to taunt the youngster into rashness. It had paid off, helping Isen drag things out, hoping that Rule would manage to rescue Brian quickly and a call—a single phone call—would allow them to stop spilling each other's blood.

That hadn't happened, and the pup was fast, damn him. The moment Isen had felt his leg bone snap beneath his enemy's teeth, he'd known he could delay no longer. Either he finished things, or Javier would.

Javier righted himself quickly. Isen hadn't tried to take advantage of his brief disarray. He couldn't move fast enough, and he knew it. He would have to draw the other wolf in close, perhaps by feigning ...

Fifty feet away, a wolf yipped three times.

Son of a bitch. The enemy had taken the bait after all. Isen lifted his nose, but the sentry's call had come from downwind, so scent told him nothing. He looked that way.

Javier's hard, heavy body slammed into him, jaws gaping. Flip him and go for the belly, that was the idea. Isen twisted frantically, avoiding disembowelment but rolling onto his shattered leg. Pain paralyzed him for a second—a second too long as Javier lunged again.

And was knocked away by another wolf. Stephen. Who crouched between Isen and Javier, growling a warning at the younger wolf.

Stephen might be overly tied to tradition, but he could be counted on for fairness and good sense. The Challenge had ended the moment the sentry sounded the alert. Panting with pain, Isen struggled to his feet and took in the situation quickly. He'd warned Stephen they might be attacked, so Stephen had posted all four of his guards as four-footed sentries. They yipped at each other now in a code Isen didn't know. His own people had followed orders and were racing for . . .

Isen heard the rifle. He never felt the bullet.

LILY called Pete, Benedict's second. Clanhome was already on alert, but she wanted him to know about the RN40—which she'd been told had a distinctive smell. A bit like almonds, at least to a human nose. She also wanted to find out if there'd been any word about the Challenge. None, he said.

Cynna was pacing, waiting for Cody to get there with the sample of explosive.

Cullen still sat on the floor by the broom closet. "Lily. I need you here."

"Got to go," she told Pete, and put her phone up. "What?" she asked as she went to him.

He didn't look up. "I'm not going to unravel this thing tonight. It's beyond anything I've ever seen. But I've isolated the thread that powers it."

She crouched beside him, but the sling made that awkward, so she went to one knee. "Okay. Does that mean you can cut the thread and it won't have any juice?"

"That's what I want you for."

"Me?" She couldn't have been more surprised if he'd told her he needed her to dance naked. Actually, the dance naked bit sounded like something Cullen might suggest.

"I called it a thread deliberately. Thread's twisted to strengthen it. This has a twist to it . . . I've never seen that before, but I'm pretty sure it means that if the thread's cut, it comes uncoiled. That releases the inherent energy from the twisting. I can't cut it right next to the ward—don't ask why, I don't have time to explain—so the remnant of thread nearest the ward would release a bit of power into the ward, triggering it."

"Okay," she said dubiously. "But what do you want me for?"

"To soak up that bit of power."

She opened her mouth . . . and closed it without saying anything.

Twice she'd actively absorbed magic from a person. Apparently she did the same thing passively all the time, only in very tiny amounts. That was the essence of her Gift—the ability to soak up tiny amounts of magic, which her brain then interpreted as a texture. "Am I supposed to try to soak it up?"

"Yes, but don't pull hard. The thread's tied to the node—that much I'm sure of. Nothing else is that clear and pure. If you pull too hard, you'll draw too much energy up through the thread and it will break."

"How do I know how hard is too hard? I'm not even sure I can do this!"

"I'll monitor you. Here's what we'll do. I'll put your finger where I want you to pull. You do your thing. I should see the bit of thread between your finger and the ward go dim. When it does, I'll cut it. If I've figured it right, the ward will evaporate."

"And if you're wrong?"

"We'll find out exactly what this ward's supposed to do. Which reminds me." He raised his voice slightly without looking away from that fascinating floor. "Cynna, go pace in the living room."

"If it's too dangerous for me to stay here," she began.

"I don't think it's dangerous or I wouldn't do it. I intend for our child to have a father. Even if the ward does trigger, I doubt it will do more than knock us out. Friar wouldn't want a fireball going off in his kitchen. That's why you need to be

in the other room. Worst comes to worst, you can drag Lily
and me away from the trapdoor before Friar comes to see
who tampered with his ward."

Cynna bit her lip, frowning.

Lily looked at her watch, considered her options, and
nodded. "Okay. Cynna, having you in the other room makes
sense."

"You're going to do it, then?"

She'd try. Whether she could do it or not remained to be
seen. "It's nearly eleven."

"Which means you'll still have another hour to wait once
you get that thing open."

"I'm not sure waiting is a good idea."

Cullen chuckled. "What will it be? You had your fingers
crossed when you agreed to wait for midnight?"

"That would be childish." She paused. "We didn't say
midnight in this time zone, though, did we?"

ARJENIE'S heart pounded. Her mouth was dry. She leaned
against the rough stone beside the cell and thought about
fear.

Terror was the top of the fear scale. That's what she'd
felt when she saw everyone dropping around her even as
a wave of vertigo swamped her, sending her to her knees.
She'd fought off the dizziness by the time she heard people
coming. The terror had taken longer to go away. It was probably the sheer passage of time—or exhaustion of her adrenal
glands—that muted it to simple fear.

She'd followed the elves here and watched as one of them
opened the barred gate to the cell by pressing his palm to
a silver plate where you'd expect to see a knob or handle.
She'd watched as they laid her friends and her lover in the
cell. Then she'd gone exploring, creeping around the walls
of the cavern like a frightened mouse.

Arjenie looked at the blue-haired elf standing guard fifteen feet away. He never moved, just stood there watching
the cell, his thin, lovely face as still as a statue's. She looked
past him and to the right, at the dark mouths of the tunnels
separated by about twenty feet of tumbled stone. Then she

looked at the far end of the cavern. That's where Dya was, curled up in a nest of exotic bedding. They'd put a collar on her with a long leather lead clipped to a ring in the wall. Tethered her there, like an animal.

Working out how to talk to Dya without being noticed had taken longer than it should have. Fear might be great for helping someone run faster, but it sure fogged the brain. Fogged her brain, anyway. Finally she'd realized she could hunker down behind one of the trunks—the elves were messy, leaving their stuff all in a jumble— and let go of the pull on her Gift.

Dya had not been glad to see her.

Her lord—the black-haired Rethna—was punishing her. He knew about the call she'd made to Isen—Arjenie had guessed that much—and when it was time for Dya to take the tears, they'd given her only half what she needed. Enough to keep her from permanent damage. Too little to keep her from going into withdrawal.

It had taken several minutes for Dya to calm down enough to tell Arjenie this. Then she wasted several more minutes trying to persuade Arjenie to leave, get out. When Arjenie finally persuaded her she wouldn't, Dya had wept and asked Arjenie to get the tears for her. She knew where the rest of her dose was—in the blue vial sitting on another trunk. It was two feet beyond Dya's reach with her tether stretched as far as it could go.

That, too, was part of the punishment.

Arjenie had given Dya the vial. She'd left her sister passed out in a pile of fur and silk and crept carefully back to the cell. An endless time later, Rule had woken. Then Lucas. Then Benedict. When Benedict opened his eyes and looked right at her, for a moment she'd *known* they would be okay. She'd been able to touch him, to reach through the bars and touch his fingers with hers.

A few minutes ago, that black-haired elf had come up. Rethna, who'd tied her sister up like an animal and left her to suffer. Arjenie had discovered her adrenals had managed to restock all those shriek-and-flee hormones. Elves were more resistant to magic than humans, and he was an elf lord. She'd been sure he'd notice her sitting only a few feet away.

He hadn't. He'd spoken only to Rule. And then he'd hurt him.

She'd thought about creeping up behind Rethna and hitting him over the head, but what if she didn't knock him out? She'd never hit anyone over the head. She didn't know how hard you had to hit. Besides, that wouldn't get Benedict and the rest out of their cell, so she'd eased back in front of the bars so she could see if Rule was okay.

He said he was. He was sitting up, talking about the bars with Benedict. Her heart hadn't gotten back to normal yet. She watched as Benedict, Rule, and the one named Paul crowded up together. What were they—oh, they were testing the bars. After a minute Rule said, "We'll break our hands before we bend these. You were right, Brian." Then he did something with his fingers down low. Sign language. Why hadn't she ever learned to sign?

Benedict scooted over to where he'd sat before and put his hand where she could touch it, so she did. "If only I knew where my sweetheart was," he said, looking right at her. "It would help to know she was safe."

What did he . . . oh. She pulled hard on her Gift and whispered, "You want me to go to Lily, tell her about Rethna."

He hummed a soft, approving sound.

"There are too many tunnels."

He lifted both brows questioningly.

"While you were unconscious, I snuck around and—and looked. There are three tunnels leading out of here. I know which one we came in from, but there are two more, and they're close together. You can see one of them from in there, I think. The other's about twenty feet away. One must go to Friar's house. The other must be the one on the USGS map. But they're too close to each other. I don't know which is which. And they're both warded." She paused. "Really strong wards."

His fingers stroked hers, then he turned away and signed something to Rule. She couldn't see it, but she supposed Rule signed back, because a moment later he looked at her and mouthed one word: wait.

Wait? That was it? She had to bite her lip to keep from giggling hysterically. She was good at waiting, but this was not the *time* for that. Surely there was something she could do.

He mouthed two more words. She couldn't quite tell . . .

"The bond," he whispered very softly, hardly moving his lips at all. "Rule will know."

Oh. He meant that Rule would know which tunnel Lily was in, because of their mate bond. She nodded and . . . uh-oh. "Someone's coming," she whispered, and eased away from the comfort of Benedict's touch so the dark-haired man in the long white dress—it was sort of like an Arab *thobe* only more loose and flowing—wouldn't stumble over her.

FORTY-SIX

RULE was examining the way the bars had been fitted into the rock when their next visitor arrived. He was a husky man with black hair streaked dramatically with white near one temple. His long white robe looked striking next to his deeply tanned skin.

He was most definitely not an elf.

"I do hope this isn't a bad time," Friar said, smiling.

Rule barely glanced at him. "That's a new look for you, Robert. You've grown quite daring in your fashion choices."

"I would have dropped by sooner, but I've been preparing for the ceremony. They're almost ready for me." He bared his teeth in another smile. "If you crowd up to the bars, you'll be able to watch."

"What ceremony is this?"

"One in which I am consecrated to her."

Friar sounded suddenly different—fervent and sincere, like a bridegroom aching for his wedding night, or a jihadist yearning for martyrdom. Rule stopped pretending interest in the bars and looked at his enemy. "*She's* converted you, hasn't she? Or rather, messed with your mind so you have no choice but to serve her. You're no longer your own man, Robert."

The barb slid off, unable to penetrate Friar's zealotry. "Any man would change, faced with such purity. But you wouldn't know about that, would you? Neither *her* purity, not what it is to be a true man." Abruptly the naked longing was gone, hidden behind the man's usual sophisticated gloss. "You're wasting your time with those bars, you know."

"Oh? You could just give me the key."

Friar chuckled. "There is no key. The bars are set with magic, not cement. And it takes magic to open the cell. You are well and truly trapped."

The words flicked Rule in the place where panic waited. He gave himself the space of a breath to be sure it didn't show in his voice. "But alive. Were you disappointed when you learned you weren't allowed to kill me?"

"At first. I admit it. At first I didn't care for that at all. *She* deserves full tribute. But I'm only human, sadly shortsighted compared to *her*. You will keep your life." He smiled maliciously. "But you will lose everything else. Already you've lost your freedom. And your father."

Rule lifted one brow. "Sure about that, are you?"

"My men went hunting out near Hole-in-the-Wall. If he survived his fight—you call it a Challenge, I believe—if that didn't kill him, a bullet in the brain will have done the job by now. Tell me, is Lily waiting for you at your clanhome?"

"I'm sure she told me her plans. Pity, but I can't remember at the moment."

"I hope she's gone to see her parents or one of her sisters. I doubt it, but I would prefer that she live awhile longer. I was quite disappointed she wasn't with you, but the poor thing is injured, isn't she?"

Anger flowed into Rule—cold anger, settling like ice in his veins. He didn't speak.

Friar took a step closer. His eyes gleamed with malice and pleasure. "While you're lying in some other cell in some other realm—no doubt in pain, for you won't bend easily, will you? Though you won't be able to hold on to your pride too long. Not with what Rethna can do. He's got plenty of gado, and he's learning how to tailor it to his needs. He doesn't want you unable to Change, you see. He wants you to Change on his command. And fight at his command—

dance, kill, fuck—he'll control you utterly." Friar paused, savoring the moment. "What, you're silent? No witticisms?"

"You were speaking of Lily," he said softly.

"So I was." Friar smiled. "Such a pretty thing. If she isn't at your clanhome, I'll be bringing her here. Have you heard of a drug called Do Me? I have a nice supply. I'll fuck her right there in that cell. And over on the furs the elves enjoy sleeping on. And anywhere else I want, and she won't object. She'll be quite desperately eager, in fact."

The icy anger built to a flood, washing away the last traces of claustrophobic panic, bringing clarity. He was sliding into *certa*. A battle state. What Friar said was data, no more and no less. "And if she's at Clanhome?"

"Ah, well, then, I won't have the pleasure of getting to know her as intimately as I'd like." Friar pulled something from the pocket of his loose, robelike dress. "This is a radio transmitter. It won't transmit well from down here, of course. But after my consecration, I'll return to my house to celebrate. I'll push this little button." He showed it to Rule. "And boom! No more Clanhome. No more Nokolai."

Toby. Toby was at Clanhome. That one thought loomed so large there was room for no other thought at all. Rule stared at his enemy in silence.

Friar dropped his gaze. It was a quick, involuntary reaction, and he caught himself and looked at Rule again. "I'll stop by to see you again after the ceremony. You may find me . . . *powerfully* changed." He chuckled at his cleverness and walked away.

As soon as the man was well out of earshot, Rule turned to Benedict to make sure he'd noticed that Friar, in his eagerness to cause maximum suffering, had said too much. First, he didn't know where Lily was. That was excellent news. Second, if the bars couldn't be bent or loosened and the lock required magic to open, that left one potential weak spot in their cage. They could concentrate on that.

He subvocalized. "The hinges."

WHAT kind of a paranoid idiot puts wards at both ends of his secret tunnel?

Lily leaned against the wall of the tunnel, frustrated beyond belief. Cullen had snaked ahead on his belly to examine the ward he'd seen . . . right at the well-lit exit from the tunnel.

Beyond that, she saw a rocky cavern. And an elf.

The elf had long, flowing hair the color of bluebells. He—or maybe she—wore loose trousers in buttercup yellow with a white sleeveless top. The sword he carried was pretty, too. The four feet of blade she saw was made of some shiny metal—did elves use steel?—and was held steady at his side. Lily couldn't see his face because his back was to her. He was watching something out of her line of sight.

Rule's cell, according to Arjenie, who was pressed to the wall beside her. According to the mate bond, too. Lily could feel him there.

Plan A was for Cullen to take down the ward. They'd sneak in, with Cullen and Lily using cover from a couple of boulders near the tunnel. Arjenie would use her Gift to approach the guard nearest the tunnel and knock him out, if she could. Lily would shoot—or shoot at—the blue-haired elf while Cullen raced to the cell, which had to be unlocked magically.

If Cullen couldn't take down the ward, they'd use Plan B—which looked a lot like Plan A, only without the sneaking in. Arjenie would have to go first. As soon as she knocked out the nearest guard, Cullen and Lily would rush in.

Lily suspected that either way, their plan would fall apart pretty fast. But you go with what you've got.

Lily and Arjenie were in deep shadow. Cullen was all too visible up at the tunnel's mouth. The light in the cavern flashed brighter for a second, turning orange. It had been doing that for a while, changing colors, as if someone was setting off silent fireworks.

There were seven elves in there and one human—Robert Friar. The good news was that none of them seemed to have projectile weapons, according to Arjenie—unless they were really good at throwing knives. More likely they were good at throwing spells. That wouldn't affect Lily, but Cullen and Arjenie would be vulnerable.

At the moment, Rethna and four of the elves were busy

with a major ritual that was supposed to give Friar big magical mojo. That's what the light show was about. One of the remaining two was the blue-haired guard Lily could see. The second was on guard, too—standing between the mouth of this tunnel and one about twenty feet away.

Lily's arm ached. Her head ached. Arjenie had been eager to tell her everything, both in whispers and directly. She'd gotten a little "loud" in places.

The elf lord who held Rule and Benedict and the others was one of the ones Arjenie's father had warned her about. One who dealt in slaves. That's what he planned for his captives. That's what he'd be only too happy to do with Arjenie, if he got his hands on her.

Lily wanted to kill him.

That desire was stark and clear in her mind. It wasn't the muddy wish that some bastard would drop dead, or even the urge to violence, the impulse to strike back, to hurt. She wanted to kill Rethna.

Part of her found this eminently logical. She'd expected to be dealing with Friar and his militia goons. Humans, in other words, who used human weapons and were susceptible to the same, and to human law. This Rethna was near the top of the elf food chain, power-wise. Even away from his territory—sidhe lords drew on their land, their territory, for power—Cullen couldn't handle him. He'd said so. Not without gambling on mage fire.

Since they didn't know if any of that RN40 was stored in the cavern, fire was a no-no.

Rethna wasn't human. As the law stood, Lily could deal with him as if he were one of the creatures that had been blown in by the power winds during the Turning. She could step out there and shoot every elf in the place.

Except, of course, that she couldn't. Even if she'd been willing to go down that road, she'd be shooting left-handed. *Good luck with that.*

Did elves know what a gun was? Human perps would see her drawn weapon as a threat. Elves might not. Even if they knew intellectually what a gun did, they hadn't been watching crime shows and the news all their lives. They wouldn't react to her weapon viscerally. Made it hard to bluff.

Cullen began wiggling back, staying flat on the ground. Lily waited. Her mouth was dry. Funny. She didn't feel afraid, but her body thought she was.

Endless seconds later, Cullen reached the shadows where they waited and stood. He whispered, "Looks like we're going with Plan B."

Lily looked at Arjenie. It was too dark to see much but a pale blob where her face was. Very softly she whispered, "You okay to do this?"

Arjenie might have nodded. The pale blob moved anyway. "I'm pretty sure I won't set the ward off."

Lily leaned close to whisper, "Pretty sure?"

"It's a really strong ward and I'm a little tired."

Lily looked at Cullen, but couldn't see his expression. What choice did they have, though? They had to act before Rethna finished his big ritual. Cullen said that sort of major working could not be put on pause while the elves dealt with intruders. Not quickly, anyway—they'd have to either finish it or ground the energy, which took time.

And it was a lot of energy. They were working directly with the node. "Got your rock?" she whispered at Arjenie.

Another movement of the pale blob.

"Okay. Good luck."

Cullen wished Arjenie luck his own way, by planting a sudden kiss on her mouth. He whispered something in her ear that Lily couldn't hear. Then Arjenie was walking toward the tunnel opening. The closer she got, the better Lily could see her. It was hard to believe no one would notice her. She clutched a good-size rock in one hand.

She'd armed the woman with a rock, for God's sake. But Arjenie had never shot a gun, so—

Arjenie stepped out into the cavern—in a dazzling flash of light.

Shit. No sneaking for anyone—go for surprise. "Go," Lily said, slapping Cullen on the back. He shot off at a run. Lily was right behind him, her SIG out and ready.

The ward flashed again as Cullen crossed it. It was hellish bright, but she thought he'd veered right. Lily ran straight through it, each footfall sending a bolt of pain from arm to brain. And stopped without taking cover.

She couldn't shoot straight. She couldn't fight one-on-one. But she made a damn fine target for spells.

The plan had already disintegrated. Arjenie jogged toward the blue-haired guard, looking scared and determined. Lily didn't dare try to shoot him—too much chance of hitting Arjenie. She swung her gaze to the other guard just in time to see him doubled over and Cullen's locked-together fists landing on his neck. He collapsed. She looked at the node-end of the cavern.

Magic prickled over her skin, hot and tight like a sunburn.

Five elves—one in front of the gate, back to the room, arms held out as if embracing the air. His long black hair streamed back as if a wind were blowing. The other four were arrayed on either side of him, two and two. The nearest two knelt, thumping the ground rhythmically. The two closer to the gate stood stock-still, their eyes closed, lips moving.

Friar was *in* the gate. He hung there, spread-eagled a good foot off the ground, as if he'd been stuck to the air with superglue. Wavy ripples of distortion flowed over him. Lily couldn't see his face clearly, but it looked like he'd frozen in midscream.

Light lanced from the up-thrust hands of the black-haired elf directing the show. Blue light this time. He made a perfect target, standing there motionless with his back to her. She couldn't accept that invitation. Kill him now and there was no telling what would happen with all the power he was handling.

A *thud-rattle* sound came from the barred cell twenty feet or more to her left.

The two sitting elves stood smoothly, in unison. One pointed off to Lily's side. One pointed at her.

She pointed back with her gun. "Freeze!" she yelled, even as a creepy-crawly sort of magic swept over her and she sited . . . squeezed . . .

Off to her right, Cullen screamed. Her hand jerked the tiniest bit as she snapped off the shot. The blast of sound was ungodly loud. Her target didn't fall. She darted a glance to her right. Cullen was on the ground, body and face contorted in pain.

The other elf was still pointing at him. Shoot that bastard, then. Lily moved her arm smoothly. Thirty feet wasn't all that far. She could do this. She squeezed.

Hot damn. She hit him. He looked as surprised as she felt as his hand dropped and red bloomed just below his collarbone.

"Behind you!!" Rule yelled.

Lily spun. Blue-hair was almost on top of her, with four feet of shiny sword swinging through the air right at her neck.

She ducked and damned if she didn't hear that blade swoosh through the air way too close to the top of her head. She backed up fast, bringing up her gun up, but Blue-hair was almost as quick as a lupus, sliding toward her in a loose, slinky way, his sword moving in a blur as—

Arjenie tackled him from behind.

He went down face-first, still clutching the sword. Arjenie went down, too, clutching his legs. He must have noticed her finally, because he kicked her off, his foot catching her in the shoulder. Lily darted in and stamped on his sword-hand. Something crunched. She kicked the sword away. He rolled. She aimed. "Freeze, asshole!"

Faceup now, he pointed at her, muttering something through lips white with pain. That prickly-sunburn magic rolled over her again. She ignored it and kicked him in the ribs. "Back on your belly."

His eyes went wide. He stared at her in disbelief.

Shoot him. But she didn't. Couldn't put a bullet in his brain with him staring at her. She swung the muzzle to point at his shoulder, squeezed. That would keep the bastard from pointing at people, anyway.

She caught a flicker of movement out of the corner of her eye and spun.

The elf she'd missed had raced across the cavern while she dallied with Blue-hair. He bent smoothly as he ran, grabbed the sword from the ground, and spun as he brought it around.

"Gesundheit!" Cullen yelled.

The elf sneezed. And sneezed, and sneezed, and sneezed. Lily took aim, but in spite of the paroxysm of sneezes, he kept moving—not all that smoothly anymore, but he wouldn't

hold still. And he kept hold of the sword. He couldn't see
well because his eyes were red and streaming, but he moved
too fast for her to risk a shot, and then he was between her
and the cage where they'd locked up Rule and the others.
And then she couldn't shoot, dammit.

Behind her, Cullen cursed. She couldn't look over her
shoulder to see what was wrong, not with elf-boy twirling
that sword at her. Sunburn magic prickled over her again and
she knew one of the other elves was trying for her. Dammit,
weren't any of them staying up front to help Rethna with his
magic?

She backed up, wanting to get where she could see the
other end of the room, but sword-boy came after her, using
his blade to steer her. She caught a glimpse of Arjenie a few
feet away rising to her knees, clutching her shoulder, tears
streaming. Sword-boy kept himself between her and the cage
so she couldn't shoot. He'd figured out guns way too fast.

Behind him in the cage, Benedict crouched in a miser-
ably bent-over way to avoid the low, low roof—and landed
a perfect side-kick where the gate was joined to the bars.
Thud-rattle. She realized she'd been hearing that sound re-
peatedly as she ducked a sword stroke, danced back, and
watched Benedict do it again.

Something snapped. Rule and Paul and Lucas seized the
door then, grabbing it and twisting, and the metal shrieked—

"Lily!" Arjenie screamed.

She glanced quickly to her right. A yellow-haired elf
ran at her with a big knife. She snapped off a quick shot—
missed, dammit, but he'd swerved—swung her gun back
around to the sword-wielding elf—

Who collapsed beneath two hundred pounds of snarling
wolf, who seized his neck between his jaws and twisted.
Blood flew.

The cage's gate lay on the ground. Wolves poured out.
One—Rule!—it was Rule—launched himself at the yellow-
haired elf. The other three raced for the front of the room.

Cullen's voice came from behind a tumble of rock. "If
they point, get the hell out of the way!"

Lily stood there and panted, suddenly aware of how
winded she was, how much her arm hurt, and how shaky

and tired her left arm had grown. She let it fall to her side. Couldn't shoot now . . . and wouldn't have to. There was only one elf left, chanting silently in support of Rethna, who still stood with his back to the room. To the wolves racing for him.

Friar collapsed to the ground and lay motionless.

The chanting elf's eyes opened.

Rethna turned.

Two wolves leaped for him. He held out both hands as if his palms could halt them.

They did. The wolves halted in midair—hung there for a split second—then sailed backward several feet to land hard. He waved at the third wolf, a casual flick of his hand. That wolf—she thought it was Benedict—froze as if he'd been turned to a statue.

Rethna started toward her. He should have been swaying, exhausted from such major magical work. He looked dewy fresh.

Good news. *Now* she could shoot the bastard. Lily lifted her weapon.

Rethna smiled and twiddled his fingers. The metal turned instantly red-hot. Lily cursed and dropped the gun.

A ball of fire zipped out of a tumbled piled of rocks. *Dammit, Cullen, we agreed*—but before Lily could finish the thought, Rethna's upheld palm stopped the fireball in midair. Rethna kept walking. The fireball quivered—then started inching toward him again.

Rule and the wolf who'd killed Sword-guy streaked toward Rethna, zigzagging unpredictably.

Rethna continued to hold one palm up to the fireball. His other hand flicked the air in the general direction of Rule-wolf. He froze in midstride. The other wolf leaped.

Rethna's one remaining attendant shouted something, his hands flying through some spell. The wolf burst as if he's swallowed a grenade, blood and gobbets of flesh flying everywhere.

Rethna looked back at the other elf, frowning. The elf fell to his knees, babbling what had to be an apology. Blood and nasty bits stuck to Rethna's pretty clothes. Maybe he didn't like getting dirty. He spoke in that musical language, then glanced at the fireball still creeping closer. He snapped his fingers.

It vanished.

Lily's heart pounded so hard she felt sick. She started toward Rethna.

His eyebrows rose. "You must be the mate. A sensitive, I'm told." One of the wolves he'd sent tumbling stirred. *Flick.* The wolf froze. That left one wolf unfrozen, still lying motionless where he'd fallen. Just to be sure, Rethna aimed a flick at him, too. "Friar wants you. I've forgotten your name. What is it?"

"Call me Dirty Harry's best friend." Her SIG lay behind her on the ground. Her clutch piece, though, was in her sling—the snub nose Isen had loaned her. It wasn't accurate at a distance. *She* wasn't accurate at a distance, and the frozen Rule-wolf statue was too close to Rethna for her to take any chance of missing. So she'd get nice and close. She rubbed her right arm as if it hurt—it did—and slid her hand just inside the sling, still rubbing. Now if someone— anyone—was still able to move and distract him—

A reddish wolf raced out from the tumble of rocks, moving so fast the eye could scarcely track him.

Rethna glanced that way. *Flick.* Cullen froze.

Lily shot the elf lord.

The black stone on his chest glowed. He kept walking. "You've cost me quite a bit. Fortunately, you're worth quite a bit. Sensitives are—"

She squeezed the trigger again. Again. The black stone flashed with each shot, and Rethna kept coming. Then her gun flashed hot, crazy hot, and she had to drop it and he was only five feet away now, smiling faintly as if it amused him to be shot at.

"—extremely rare," he said, stopping. "Or I may keep you and sell your blood and breed you. Unless *she* requires you, in which case you will be very unhappy for a long time."

Lily glimpsed movement out of the corner of her eye. She kept looking straight ahead. "Do you know where sensitives come from?"

"No." His eyebrows lifted slightly. "Are you going to tell me?"

"Dragons." It was Arjenie she'd glimpsed—a grim and battered Arjenie who limped heavily, had one arm hanging down as if disabled, and held a nice, big rock in her other hand. "My grandfather won't like it if you take me away. I'm studying with him."

"You bluff poorly. There's no dragon who—"

Arjenie smashed that rock on his head.

He swayed. Staggered. Saw Arjenie—his eyes widened—and backhanded her. She fell next to a rock the size of a hassock, nearly hitting her head on the stone. And as he struck and Arjenie fell, a tiny woman with purple black skin sprang out from behind that rock and latched onto his leg. And bit him.

His eyes went big with fear or astonishment. "Dya," he said. Oh, yes, that was fear in his voice. He said a couple more words in that liquid tongue before his eyes rolled back in his head. His knees buckled. As he sank to the ground the tiny woman—no more than four feet high—clung tightly to his leg with her arms and mouth.

The last elf still standing shrieked and shrieked again. He started in with the gestures. As he did, reality split sharply into *other* behind him. Where a wolf had stood frozen, a man—naked and snarling as if he were still wolf—stood.

But only for a split second. Then Rule leaped at the lone elf and seized his head in a two-handed grip and snapped his neck.

Lily breathed. Just breathed for a moment, her heartbeat still hasty. A little tremor of nerves ran through her. She looked around and saw wolves starting to stir. With Rethna dead, the freeze thing was . . . no, that was an assumption. Better make sure.

She knelt beside him. The staring eyes and vacant face said dead, but she laid her fingers on his throat to be sure. No pulse. The little dark-skinned woman—she was naked—finally released his leg. She looked up and smiled at Lily . . . not a human smile, not in that face. Her eyes were huge and lovely, a soft violet, too widely spaced for human. But it was her short muzzle that really tipped her into otherness. And the fangs protruding from it. "You're Dya," Lily said.

Dya nodded—a very human gesture. "Now the Queens

will not have to send the hellhounds of the Hunt to kill him. You will be glad of that," she informed Lily, and turned to check on her sister.

Hellhounds? Lily shook off that question and looked at Rule. "Who was it he killed?"

"Paul." Rule's voice was harsh, his eyes still way too black, as if he needed to snap more than one neck. He raised his voice. "Change."

Here, here, and there, wolves slid into the Mobius-strip spin of Change. Suddenly Lily realized someone was missing. She shoved to her feet and looked at the gate. No white-robed man lay sprawled in front of it now. "Friar," she said urgently. "We've got to catch him."

"Shit," Rule said. "He's got a radio transmitter that will set off explosives at Clanhome. Benedict—"

"S'okay," Arjenie said fuzzily. She reached into her pocket and pulled out a small metal box. "I picked his pocket. After he told you that, I followed him and picked his pocket. Took out the batteries, too, to be safe."

Relief swamped Lily. She felt dizzy, giddy, exhausted. "Okay. Okay, that's good. Cynna was going to Find the explosives, but best if they don't get triggered. No telling how long it might be taking her and Cody to get them removed."

"Rule." That was Cullen's voice, strained. "We've got a problem."

"What?"

Cullen was crouched, magnificently naked, where he'd fallen as wolf, staring at the vague distortion that marked the gate. "The gate. Rethna tampered with it for his ritual. He didn't get it put back right. Almost, but not quite. It's . . . ah, shit." He sprang to his feet. "We've got to get out. We've got to get out *now*."

FORTY-SEVEN

"**LUCAS**," Rule snapped, "get Brian." He came for Lily.

Benedict ran to Arjenie. Dya ran away—to the other end of the cavern. Lucas raced back into the cell. Rule scooped up Lily. "Shut up," he said before she could protest. "I'm faster."

"Dya!" Arjenie called as Benedict lifted her into his arms. "Dya, we have to get out!"

"The tears!" The little woman's voice was high, childlike. "They're here, they're here!" She skidded to a halt by one of the chests and began trying frantically to open it. The lid didn't budge.

Benedict handed Arjenie to José and ran to the other end of the room. Cullen dashed up to Rethna's body, bent, and seized the black stone that had flashed every time Lily shot Rethna. He jerked it free, snapping the chain. Lucas emerged from the cell carrying a brown-haired man who seemed to be unconscious.

"Go!" Benedict shouted as he reached the frantic Dya. He pushed her small hands away. "Go, dammit!"

That's all Lily saw. Rule took off. Behind him streamed the rest—José carrying Arjenie, Lucas carrying Brian, Cullen and Sammy on their own.

"Light!" Rule snapped as they entered the dark maw of the tunnel, and Cullen obliged with a mage light, far brighter than he'd used on their way in. They ran.

The slope was steep. Even Rule must have felt the strain of racing up it carrying Lily. For her part, she held on with one arm and grimly ignored the jolts of pain in her bad arm and listened desperately for footsteps coming up from behind.

She could hear nothing but their own party. She couldn't force herself to ask if Rule heard him. But unless Benedict was much closer than she thought, he'd be coming up in the dark. "Cullen—can you set a mage light back there for—"

"I'll try. They follow the caster," Cullen said. "But I've set one behind me a couple hundred yards. He'll see it. He can't be too far behind."

Rule asked, "What exactly is it we're running from?"

"Gate energy's oscillating, out of sync." Unburdened and faster than the rest anyway, Cullen could have easily pulled ahead. He stayed beside Rule. "It's going to blow. That will release a hellish amount of energy. I don't know what will happen. Earthquake, maybe. Or suck half the mountain into the other realm, or shove matter from that realm here, or do some goddamn thing I've never heard of."

"Friar," Lily said suddenly. "I don't know if he had a gun."

"We should have seen him," Rule said, "if he came this way, but . . . Sammy. Take rear guard. Cullen, pull ahead and deal with him if you see him."

Cullen nodded and put on more speed. His mage light bobbled, but stayed with them even as Cullen vanished into the darkness ahead.

They ran. And ran.

The first part of the tunnel was either natural or had been dug much longer ago, and not by modern equipment. They reached the part Friar had added to join it to his house without seeing Friar, Friar's body, or Cullen. Without seeing or hearing Benedict, either.

Rule was breathing hard and streaming with sweat when they reached the end, where a simple wooden ladder led up to the trapdoor. He set Lily down. She swayed—no, it was the earth that swayed. Quake, tremor, call it what you like—

"Go!"

She didn't waste time arguing about who went first, but climbed as fast as she could. Cullen's face appeared in the square of light at the top. "No one here," he said. "Hurry."

She did. He hauled her up as she reached the top, set her on her feet outside the broom closet, and gave her a shove. "Keep going, dammit, you can't do a thing to help."

"He's not coming. He's sending the others up." She could feel Rule, motionless, at the bottom of the ladder.

The floor shuddered beneath her.

"Give him this one goddamn thing and get out of here!" Cullen snarled.

He was right. She forced herself to move. Pushed it into a run and pelted out of Friar's beautiful, empty house, stopping when she reached the car. No keys. She wanted to laugh. No goddamn keys, because they were in her purse, which was back in the house.

Lucas came running out carrying Brian. "How far," he gasped, "are we supposed to go?"

"I don't know." She wasn't going one step more without Rule.

Then José emerged with Arjenie. And Sammy and Cullen—and hard on his heels, Rule.

The earth groaned almost silently. Behind Friar's house, the mountain began to move—earth and rock shearing off, beginning to slide down.

"He's coming," Arjenie said frantically. "He's coming. I feel him."

Where were the militia guys? Calvin Brewster and his sergeant? Lily didn't see anyone.

The earth growled. And shook, and kept shaking. Lily fell. Lucas went to his knees, hastily setting Brian down. Cullen stumbled. José fell, Arjenie pitching out of his arms. Rule broadened his stance and stood, staring at the house . . .

Which twisted, groaning like a huge beast in pain. The lights winked out. Part of the second story collapsed. The earth rolled beneath Lily like it was liquid.

Benedict ran out the front door, weaving on the unsteady

stone of the veranda like a surfer riding a wave. He leaped—
and landed on grassy lawn just as the house shrieked and
groaned hugely. The rest of the second story and most of the
first collapsed in a horrendous crash. Dust billowed in the
moonlit night.

A few feet from the disaster, Benedict sank to his knees,
spent. Only then did Lily see Dya. She'd ridden his back like
a child, clinging to his neck with one arm. Her other arm
clutched a small satchel tightly.

Arjenie burst into tears and limped toward them.

The earth grew quiet.

Dya climbed off Benedict's back. "This is a brave man,"
she said solemnly to her sister as Arjenie reached them. "He
says he is yours."

"Yes," Arjenie said, sinking to the ground and holding out
one hand to Dya—her other arm still hung limp—and leaning in to kiss Benedict lightly. "Yes, he is."

He gathered her close.

For a moment there was only the groan and crash as the
debris that had been a house settled. Lily pushed to her feet,
needing Rule.

"Rule," Lucas said quietly. "We're losing him."

Lily moved the few steps to where Brian lay on the
ground. Rule got there first. As Lily sank down beside him
he was trying to take Bryan's pulse at the wrist. He abandoned that to lay his ear directly on Brian's chest . . . which
was rising and falling in quick jerks. Distressed breathing.
Not a good sign.

"He's bad," Rule said, straightening, "but he's not gone
yet."

"Dya," Arjenie said, "Dya, can you help him?"

The little woman shook her head sadly. "I changed back
to true venom to kill my lord. After you gave me the tears, I
hurried to change it. I knew his death was mine. It is not easy
to kill a lord of the sidhe, but the venom of a *dereet* of the
Binai will do so quickly." She sounded proud. "But now . . .
true venom is very different from what I use to make potions. Especially potions of healing. I can't change back so
quickly."

Lily unclipped her phone and turned it on. She'd had it

off for the op. "I can call Nettie. Maybe she could get here in . . ." Her breath sucked in. She'd forgotten. For a moment she'd forgotten where Nettie was, and who she was with.

"Isen's okay," Rule said, adding mind reading to his other abilities. "Or at least alive. What time is it?"

She glanced at the phone in her hand. "Twelve twenty."

"The Challenge must be over by now. He survived it."

Tears stung her eyes, making her feel foolish. Crying over good news? But Isen had made it. Most of them had made it. Most, but not all. "I'll call," she said. She touched Nettie's name in her contacts list.

Rule gripped Brian's hand. "He didn't want to die alone. I wonder if he knows . . ."

"Hearing's the last to go," Cullen said quietly as he joined them. "There's a good chance he knows we're here." He sat and reached for Brian's ankle, shook his head, then took his other hand and tried to find a pulse at the wrist.

Lily got Nettie's voice mail. She left a brief message. "An ambulance," she said. I'll call 9-1-1."

Rule looked at Cullen, who shrugged. "It can't hurt," Rule said.

Lily knew what they meant. They didn't think he'd last that long. Even if he did, EMTs, paramedics, doctors—none of them would have a clue what to do for a lupus whose magic wasn't able to fix whatever Rethna had done to him.

But they didn't *know*. They had to try. She punched in the numbers and gave the 9-1-1 operator their location and what little information she had about Brian's condition.

When she ended that call, Brian's breathing seemed worse. There was a rattling sound in his throat. Cullen was talking to him quietly, recounting aloud some escapade. Lily bit her lip and checked for messages. There was one from Jason, who'd accompanied Isen. That one came in thirty minutes ago. Another from Pete, Benedict's second, that was only fifteen minutes old. She touched the one for Jason first.

"Isen's okay," she said after listening. Rule and Cullen would have heard the message, but Benedict was probably too far away. "He took some damage, including a bullet that creased his skull. Nettie's keeping Isen in sleep. They're headed back to Clanhome. Ah . . . Javier's alive, too. Jason called the Challenge inconclusive."

"I'll talk to Javier," Lucas said, "when you're able to lend me your phone. He'll withdraw it when he knows the truth."

She nodded, then listened to the message from Pete. "Pete wants to talk to Benedict. The bomb squad's at Clanhome now." She looked at Arjenie, huddled against Benedict. "There's a good chance you saved a few hundred people when you picked Friar's pocket."

Arjenie's smile trembled at the edges. "Do you think he got out? Friar, I mean."

Lily looked at the dark, looming shape of the mountain behind the house. It hadn't collapsed entirely, but anyone underground when it rearranged itself . . . "I don't know. He didn't use the same tunnel we did, but there could have been a way up to the surface we don't know about. There were at least two militia guys here earlier. They seem to have vanished."

"José," Rule said, "the garage is around back. Friar has three vehicles—a red Ford Ranger, a black Porsche, and a '64 T-bird convertible. See if they're there. Sammy, patrol. Find out if we're really alone."

The two men rose and left.

Lily needed to call Croft. She needed to mobilize a manhunt for Friar, to find out the extent of the damage when the gate imploded and the earth shook. But at this moment none of that seemed important. She looked at the young man who lay dying in front of them. Rule held one of his hands. Lucas clasped the other.

Brian's eyes opened, but stared out blindly. "Rule."

"I'm here."

"Have to try." His voice was faint and hoarse. "You took . . . Leidolf. Take Wythe, too."

"I had a Leidolf great-grandmother. I don't have a blood tie to Wythe."

"But . . ." His eyes seemed to focus—but not on Rule or any of them. He looked . . . surprised. Then peaceful and happy. His lips moved, but Lily didn't hear anything except that rattle in his throat.

Lucas, though, stiffened and bent close. Rule leaned in, too.

A few seconds passed. Lucas straightened and looked at her. "Take his hand." He thrust that lax hand out to her.

"What?" Automatically she clasped it in hers. And jumped a little in surprise. The skin was cold, as if he were already dead—but his magic was so present. So strong and alive. Pine and fur seemed almost to press up into her own skin.

"The Lady wants you to take it," Lucas said urgently. "He sees her. Hears her. You're to take the mantle from him and hold it intact until it can be passed on."

She looked at him. "That's nuts."

"It's the Lady's mantle." He closed both of his hands over hers and the cold one she held and pressed firmly, as if he could squeeze the mantle out of Brian and into her. "You're the Lady's Chosen."

"I'm not—" But it was pushing at her. Magic didn't do that, but this was. "I can't do that. I'm not lupus."

"Consent is necessary," Rule said calmly. "If you could do it, would you?"

Would she?

It was a stupid question, like asking what she'd do if she won the lottery when she never even bought a ticket. She didn't know why she stopped to think about it, but she did. Would she allow a clan to die?

Wythe would be no more, but not all the clan members would die. Some—many? A handful? She didn't know— would eventually be adopted into other clans. Those who survived. Those who weren't sent wholly mad by the death shock. "Yes," she said slowly, "but it's a crazy question."

Put your hand on his chest.

She tugged her hand free from Brian's grip and put it on the chest of the dying man. She could feel the magic moving up him. How strange. It seemed to be moving up from his gut to his chest, heading for his throat . . . "Brian had a hallucination. If it gave him peace, that's good. But I don't know what your excuse is," she told Rule.

Bend close to him.

"Even if I could suck up his magic," she went on, bending low, "it wouldn't help. Once I absorbed it, it would turn into my magic."

Breathe his breath.

"It wouldn't be a mantle anymore." Lily finished with her face hovering over Brian's, his breath faint but perceptible, her own breath falling into his open mouth . . .

What the hell? What was she doing?

. . . as living magic poured out of the dying man with his last breath. And into her mouth.

Lily jerked upright. Her hands went numb. Tingles raced over her skin from the inside. She couldn't breathe. It was choking her, this huge ball of magic——*fur and pine and moonlight*—lodged in her throat, in her lungs—*blood and strength and moonlight*—no, it was settling in her belly. Large and living and *not her*. Not part of her, not any part of her.

"He's gone," Lucas said calmly.

"Son of a bitch," said Cullen. "Son of a bitch. She did it."

"Lily?" Rule took her hand, searching her face. "Are you all right?"

She looked down at her belly. "I feel like I need to burp."

FORTY-EIGHT

Two weeks later, in North Carolina

THE first time Lily had seen Leidolf Clanhome, it had been for a funeral. A young Leidolf clansman had died fighting a demon with her and Rule. That occasion had turned into an effort by the clan's crazy-mean Rho to kill Rule by forcing the heirs' portion of Leidolf's mantle into him. That hadn't worked out the way Victor wanted.

She was here for a funeral again. She and Rule were even in the same bedroom they'd been given that time. He refused to sleep in the former Rho's room.

"I can't believe she went into labor today," Lily said, sliding her arms into the sleeves of the silk tee she'd settled on for the ceremony, then lifting them carefully so it slid over her head.

She could do that now. Get dressed, wash her hair, even wear her shoulder holster. She still had to be careful, but she could do all the normal stuff again.

"I don't think she planned to," Rule said. He'd just finished brushing his teeth and was stepping into his jeans. Lupi dressed very casually for this sort of thing. "But I wish we were there."

"Not that she needs us." Lily slid her feet into her flats. Lupi might be informal, but she couldn't bring herself to wear athletic shoes to the *firnam*. "She's got Nettie and Cullen."

The full moon had come and gone without Lily feeling an urge to howl, much less discovering a knack for turning furry. First Cullen, then the Nokolai Rhej, had assured her she wouldn't. She hadn't told anyone how she felt about that, not even Rule. She barely admitted it to herself. Babysitting a mantle did not turn her into a lupus.

Turned out there was a precedent for what she'd done, though no one outside of Etorri and the Rhejes had known about it. Three thousand years ago it had been a Rhej, not a Chosen, who'd held the Etorri mantle within her for seventeen days before she found an Etorri lupus to carry it.

Lily might have to wait a lot longer than seventeen days. The only one who definitely carried enough of the Wythe founder's bloodline was too young to Change, much less assume the mantle and leadership of his clan. Soon, though, Lily would go to Wythe Clanhome and meet the entire clan and give the mantle a chance to go where it was supposed to be.

She rubbed her belly, frowning at the ball of otherness lodged there.

Rule slipped an arm around her. "Still bothering you?"

"It's like having a piece of spinach stuck between your teeth. Something's stuck inside me that doesn't belong." She had a strong feeling she wasn't supposed to poke at it the way she would a piece of spinach, however. She shrugged. "It doesn't hurt, and the bennies are good."

Like the healing. She didn't heal as fast as lupi—Isen's arm was fine now, as was his hard head—and they didn't know if she'd heal completely. There was a big dent in her biceps where muscle was just gone, and no one knew if her silent passenger would make it grow back. But the wound had closed up really fast, no skin graft needed, and the bone was well on its way to being healed. She hadn't even needed a cast—partly because of how fast it was healing, but also because of the way the surgeon had nailed things together.

Just the damn sling. Which she still used, at Nettie's very firm instructions, every time she left the bedroom. Well, almost every time. Any time it started hurting, certainly, and whenever Rule saw her. Or really, since they'd been staying at Clanhome, every time anyone saw her. Nearly healed did not mean healed.

Lily put that arm—her right arm—around Rule and snuggled close. Her body hummed in approval. It was so good to want him again. For a while after the shooting, touch had brought comfort . . . but nothing more.

Plenty more now. Rule stroked her hair. She closed her eyes and savored the feel of him, and the way her body responded. She stretched up, cupped his head, and pulled it down to sample his toothpaste secondhand.

She kissed him slowly but thoroughly, pressed close enough to feel it when his heartbeat picked up. And pulled away. "I hear the drums."

For a moment she thought he was going to tell her—as he had last night when they were supposed to go down to dinner with his Lu Nuncio—that he was Rho and could be late if he wanted. But this was nothing as trivial as a meal. He nodded and reached for her sling.

She let him help her into it. She gave her phone a regretful glance as they left. Cynna had called five hours ago, completely jazzed because she was having contractions. Rule had talked to Cullen about an hour ago. Nothing since.

Couldn't take a phone to the *firnam*, though. They headed down the stairs, and together they walked outside into dusk.

The air was warm silk. A few trees had begun turning color. A breeze whispered through boughs and leaves, the wind singing softly to accompany the drums.

The drummers, like the rest of those attending the *firnam*, were in a grassy field a short walk from the house. There were four of them. Like all the lupi, they were shirtless. Lily had seen their drums earlier. All were old, handmade, with hide drumheads. One had been made in Austria over two hundred years ago, though the drumhead had been replaced a couple of times.

LeBron's second son was one of the drummers. He took his father's place. In Leidolf, this was a hereditary position. Lily walked slowly beside Rule and thought about a bright smile, a shaved head, and a man who wasn't with them anymore.

They'd caught the bastard who shot him, though. Lily let that satisfaction ease the sting in her eyes. Sjorensen had kept the local homicide detective filled in on whatever the FBI had because the asshole in charge wouldn't. Between them, that detective and Sjorensen had tracked him down the old-fashioned way: lots of knocking on doors, lots of interviewing, and finally a break. Adrian Huffstead had lawyered up and wasn't talking. It wouldn't help. The friend who'd driven the truck—a truck with vanity plates, for God's sake—had flipped so fast, Sjorensen said, she never got to practice being the mean cop.

They had not caught the traitor who'd tried to kill Ruben. If Karonski even had a lead, she hadn't heard about it.

Ruben was doing okay. Not back at work, but okay.

They hadn't found Friar's body. Calvin Brewster and a couple of the militia guys were still missing, too.

Lily wanted to believe Friar was dead. There didn't seem to be any way he could have escaped the destruction of the cave system. But Cynna had tried to Find him—or his body—using hairs from his hairbrush. Her Gift was good up to about a hundred miles, but she got nothing.

Maybe his body was crushed beneath rock with a lot of quartz veining that blocked Cynna's Gift. Maybe.

Arjenie had put in for a transfer to San Diego. Some of the files she used were not accessible outside the FBI building, but much of her work could be done long-distance. She and Benedict had just finished a visit with her family in Virginia, and she was now able to speak her sister's name. Sam had removed the binding.

But her sister was gone. Dya had used Earth's only gate, the one in D.C. It opened in Edge, where she could take another gate to reach her home. The news she had to bring her people couldn't wait. Their lord was dead. He'd broken Queens' Law. The repercussions for the Binai could be huge.

The *firnam* was held in a field much like Nokolai's meeting field. Many people stood or sat in the grass—observers, not participants. Three dozen men formed a large circle around a generous pile of wood set on bare earth blackened by past fires. Lily and Rule moved to join them.

In front of that bonfire-to-be stood the Leidolf Rhej. She

was a tall woman, about forty, with a broad frame and skin a shade lighter than LeBron's had been. As soon as Rule and Lily took their places, she turned to the pile of wood. The Leidolf Rhej was a healer, not a Fire Gifted like Cullen; she couldn't call fire directly. But she'd set her spell for fire already, so it took only a word and the clap of her hands to set the wood alight.

The drums picked up their tempo as the Rhej left the circle. In the deepening dusk, the flames spread quickly over the wood. Lily's heart pounded along with the drums. She wasn't scared, she told herself. Kind of nervous, maybe, but not scared.

It turned out a *firnam* was nothing like the other death ceremonies she'd attended. There would be no spoken tribute to LeBron, no remembrances of his living.

A *firnam* was a dance. A warriors' dance.

For a moment, all was still except the drums. Then Rule threw his head back, gave a wild yell, took a few running steps and leaped over the bonfire.

Everyone shouted and began to move. First one, then another, jumped the fire, while those on the ground set the circle in motion—stamp, stamp, *step*—stamp, stamp, *step*—while others raced at the fire and leaped. This was a far simpler dance than the training dance she'd watched once—but with so many lupi, not all from the same clan, they needed to keep it simple. Lily moved with those on the ground— stamp, stamp, step!—until Rule landed beside her once more. He scooped her into his arms, backed up a few paces, tipped back his head, and let loose a yipping howl that could almost have come from his other form.

Then he ran with her in his arms—and leaped.

A shock of hot air blew her hair back. They landed. He passed her to José.

A *firnam* was a warriors' dance. Warriors are not always whole after a battle where one or more of their brethren have fallen. When one is injured, the others carry him . . . or, in this case, her. Rule had told her that if there were no injured, they would take turns hurling each other through the air. When one was, though . . .

Lily's feet didn't touch the ground again for a long time.

Every *reliquae* dancing the *firnam* had his turn to carry the wounded over the flames. Lily was passed from one pair of arms to the next. Sweat dripped down her face and itched between her breasts, and at some point she understood what the *firnam* meant. Understood in her blood and bones, not just her head.

For warriors, it was never just about the one. In battle some lived, some died, some were hurt. Those still whole carried on—carried the injured, mourned the dead—and kept leaping over the flames. Again and again. Together.

It was full-dark when she was passed to Rule once more. He set her gently on the ground in front of him and wrapped his arms around her. She leaned against him. His chest was wet with sweat. Her T-shirt clung to her.

The drums changed their beat, slowing, then letting the bass drum beat alone. A wolf—huge, tawny, his eyes black in the flickering light of the bonfire—stepped out of the shadows and walked up to the fire.

He was the elder of LeBron's sons.

The bass drum beat slowly five times . . . in place of the sixth beat they all shouted, "*LeBron!*" As they did, the wolf tipped back his head and howled.

Silence again. The drum resumed its beat as another wolf stepped out of the shadows. This one was gray, a little smaller than the first . . . Paul's brother. Paul had had a son, but the boy was three years old.

Again the drum signaled them with its pause. This time they all—Leidolf and Nokolai—shouted, "*Paul!*" as Paul's brother tipped his nose to the moon and howled.

Silence. The drums no longer beat. No one yipped or howled or spoke.

Then a tall, dark-skinned woman stepped through the circle and walked up to the bonfire.

Lily tipped her head, looking a question at Rule. Was the Rhej going to speak? He hadn't told her she was part of the *firnam*. Rule shook his head, looking puzzled.

"Leidolf!" she called. "I bring you word from the Lady."

That caused a stir. She waited until they were silent once more. "She has spoken to me, and to every Rhej. She tells each clan that we are to offer full and formal alliance with a human man—Ruben Brooks."

Lily's jaw dropped. There was a rising roar of questions, comments. Twice the Rhej tried to speak, but had to stop, unable to be heard.

Rule stepped away and bellowed, "Silence!" Silence fell, sudden and stark. "You will hear your Rhej."

The Rhej gave him a single nod of acknowledgment. "I don't know why she wants you to ally with Ruben Brooks. I have told you what she said. I must also tell you something she said three thousand years ago, something from the memories. You know most of this story well. You do not know the part of it I will tell you tonight."

Rule moved up behind Lily again, wrapping his arms around her, as the Rhej's voice fell into a storyteller's cadence. She spoke of the Etorri Rho who'd sacrificed his entire clan and who, in return, had been granted two boons: his Lady spoke to him directly, and she promised that his clan would never die out. "But they spoke of more than this. He asked many questions which she, from her love and pain for him, answered as clearly as she was able. Some of those questions were personal. I do not share them with you."

She paused and continued more softly. "Though this is an Etorri memory, I carry it, too. Every Rhej carries this memory, for it tells us when the war with our Lady's enemy will resume."

Utter silence now. No one moved. Lily's heart was beating hard. So, she realized, was Rule's.

"These are the words she spoke over three thousand years ago: When the two-mantled calls, you will come together. When a lupus daughter is born to one of you"—she had to raise her voice again, though this time no one grew loud enough for Rule to step in—"to one of you who carries more than moon-magic in his veins, war begins again. Tonight a daughter was born to Cullen Seabourne, sorcerer and lupus, and to Cynna Weaver, the apprentice to the Nokolai Rhej. She is lupus."

GLOSSARY

Historically, lupus clans in Europe and Britain used Latin to communicate with each other for much the same reason it was adopted by the Church—the need for a unifying tongue. Their version of the language evolved, as languages will, into a thoroughly bastardized tongue likely to make classical scholars wince. In addition, there are a few words in the lupus tongue that have no known derivation. Lupi claim these words come from an ancient language that predates Latin, but since Latin predates 1000 BCE, experts consider this unlikely.

The use of Latin to communicate between the clans is dying out now, since so many lupi speak English as a first or second language, though it's still considered essential for a Rho and his sons, who must negotiate with other clans. Several of the words and phrases remain useful, though, since they have no obvious English equivalent. Below are a few of the words and phrases any lupus would know.

amica: Uncommon, but still used. Means friend/girlfriend (fem); a lupus might call a male friend of the same clan *adun*, from *adiungo* (to join to, connect, associate).

ardor iunctio: Literally, fire of joining. Symbolic fire used at some ceremonies, most notably the *gens compleo*.

certa: A place of ice and clarity, where sensation is sharp enough to cut and action flows too swiftly for thought. It's a battle state; sensations heightened, thought clear but altered. Opposite of *furo*.

drei: Tithe or head tax; it's a percentage of income or wealth given to the clan.

du: Honor, face, history, reputation; has magical component. Predates Latin.

firnam: Derivation unknown; a memorial for one fallen in battle.

fratriodi: Brother-hate. A grave sin among the lupi.

furo: Also called "the fury." Battle fury or madness. Clanless lupi are especially subject to it, but it can happen to those within a clan, though it's rare.

gens amplexi: Literally, clan embrace; ceremony of adoption into clan. From *gens* (clan, tribe, people) and *amplexor* (embrace, welcome, love).

gens compleo: Literally, clan to fill up or complete; the ceremony in which a young lupus (at age twenty-four) is confirmed as an adult clan member.

gens subicio: Subicio means to put under or expose; to subject; to place near or present. When one Rho dies and a new one assumes the mantle, a gens subicio is held at which each member of a clan presents himself to his new Rho and ritually submits.

Lu Nuncio: Normally, a Rho's acknowledged heir; also acts as enforcer/prosecutor/second in command as needed. (Note: Leidolf has separated the heir from the Lu Nuncio.) *Nuncio* is from *nuncupo*—to name or pronounce solemnly. Derivation of *lu* unknown, but may be short form of lupi.

nadia: Mate (fem); from *nodus* -i m.—a knot; a girdle; any tie, bond, connection, obligation; also a knotty point or difficulty.

ospi: Out-clan friend or friend of the clan; from *hospes* (host, guest-friend, stranger).

Rhej: The title of a clan's bard/historian/priestess. Also predates Latin.

Rho: The ruler/leader of a lupus clan. Derivation unknown; legend says it predates Latin.

seco: Part of "to call *seco*"—to call the ceremony that removes a lupus from his clan.

surdo: An unflattering name for humans (m). From *surdus* (deaf, unwilling to hear, insensible).

T'eius ven: The intimate or informal form of *V'eius ven*.

terra tradis: The private area where a clan's male youngsters go before their First Change and live until they learn control. *Tradis* is a bastardized form of trado (to bequeath, to teach), so it means "the teaching ground."

thranga: A form of war in which the clans unite under a single battle leader against a common enemy; traditionally it requires the Lady's summons, but the nature of that summons may be disputed. Predates Latin.

V'eius ven: Probably derived from a phrase meaning "go in her [the Lady's] grace," though some sources suggest "ven" may be from *venor* (hunt) rather than *venia* (grace), or even from *vena* (blood vessel or penis). This form is largely ceremonial.

vesceris corpi: A major insult—translates literally as "eater of corpses" and implies taking a certain carnal pleasure in the act.

Unusual (non-Latin) words from *Blood Challenge*

Binai: The race of Arjenie's half sister, Dya. They live in one of the sidhe realms.

Divina'hueli: A sidhe kin name. Eledan is also related to this family, but is not considered a member.

Jidar: From the Binee language. It denotes kinship where there are no blood ties. In our world, for example, a mother-in-law or a stepsister would be considered *jidar* relatives. Dya's Binai family considers Arjenie—who is sister to their daughter— a *jidar* relation.

Sha'almuireli: A sidhe kin name, one of the Hundred. (The sidhe use only a hundred surnames.) Arjenie's father, Eledan, is a member of the Sha'almuireli.

Keep reading for a sneak peek of
the next Lupi novel by Eileen Wilks

DEATH MAGIC

Coming soon from Berkley Sensation!

LILY Yu was at the shooting range at FBI headquarters when she saw the ghost.

Her ears were warm beneath the headgear. Her bare arms were chilly, with her left arm out and steady; the right one ached and trembled. She'd fired a few clips right-handed before switching, which was dumb. Should have started with the left so her bad arm wouldn't be bitching so much. To bring her new Glock in line with her dominant eye while keeping her stance and grip neutral, she had to twist her right arm in a way that her damaged biceps objected to.

It objected to a lot of things. The humerus might be healed, the skin regrown nice and smooth over the entry wound, but the exit wound was bigger, bumpier, and dented. Lost muscle didn't regrow.

Except that Lily's was. Slowly, but it was returning.

A whiff of sulfur hung in the air. Sound slapped at her ears through the protective muffs as her neighbor to the right fired steadily on the other side of the divider. The fur-and-pine tickle in her gut—the reason her shattered bone had knit so quickly, the cause for her muscle's gradual, impossible regeneration—made her feel like she should burp. Fifty feet away, a drift of otherness obscured the paper target she'd been putting holes in.

It was white. Maybe that's why she immediately thought *ghost*. It drifted on a diagonal like three-dimensional rice paper—translucent, not transparent, its edges too clearly defined for smoke, its shape vaguely human but faceless. It floated on a steady, nonexistent air current, starting at the left-rear of the range . . . and coming straight at her.

The quick clamp of fear stiffened her spine as it widened her eyes.

As the thing floated closer it stretched out its hands—and yes, they were clearly hands. For all the vagueness of the rest of the form, those milky hands were painstakingly clear, from the mound at the base of the thumb to the lines crossing the palm to the band of a ring on the third finger of one hand.

The left hand, palm up. Beseeching.

A tremor went through the filmy shape. As if it had, after all, been smoke, it tattered, wisping away into nothing.

Eileen Wilks

USA Today **Bestselling Author of**
Mortal Danger **and** *Blood Lines*

NIGHT SEASON

Pregnancy has turned FBI Agent Cynna Weaver's whole life upside down. Lupus sorcerer Cullen Seabourne is thrilled to be the father, but what does Cynna know about kids? Her mother was a drunk. Her father abandoned them. Or so she's always believed.

As Cynna is trying to wrap her head around this problem, a new one pops up, in the form of a delegation from another realm. They want to take Cynna and Cullen back with them—to meet her long-lost father and find a mysterious medallion. But when these two born cynics land in a world where magic is commonplace and night never ends, their only way home lies in tracking down the missing medallion—one also sought by powerful beings who will do anything to claim it...

M110T0907

Discover Romance

berkleyjoveauthors.com

See what's coming up next from your favorite romance authors and explore all the latest Berkley, Jove, and Sensation selections.

See what's new

~

Find author appearances

~

Win fantastic prizes

~

Get reading recommendations

~

Chat with authors and other fans

~

Read interviews with authors you love